BLOOD OF THE
BELIEVERS

Also by Anne L. Simon

Blood in the Cane Field, 2014, Border Press
Blood in the Lake, 2015, Border Press

BLOOD OF THE BELIEVERS

Anne L. Simon

Border Press
PO Box 3124
Sewanee, TN 37375

Borderpress@gmail.com
www.borderpressbooks.com

Enjy!
Anne L. Simon

Library of Congress Control Number: 2017933874

ISBN: 978-0-9968737-6-5

Cover art by Nan M. Landry

Dedicated to everyone who works in the American system of justice—a flawed system, but the best as yet devised by man.

And to Dracos Burke, an inspiration.

Chief Characters

16th Judicial District
Judge Mari Johnson
St. Martin Parish
Det. Ted D'Aquin—Narrator
André—Ted's son
Charles Blanchet, Warden of the jail
Sheriff Louis Charles Chevalier
Sheriff Gabrielle Chevalier, Louis's daughter
Chief Dty. Sheriff Allan Roland
Det. Lorraine LaSalle
Det. Spike Badeaux
Det. and K-9 Officer Martin Castille
Dty. Kevin Collins
City of St. Martinville
City Police Chief Docelia Smart
City Police Sgt. Chad Boudreaux
Iberia Parish
Det. Deuce Washington
The 16th Judicial District Prosecutors
District Attorney Gerald Strait
Special Assistant District Attorney Dennis Byrne
Camille Byrne, Dennis's wife
St. Mary Parish
ADA Tony Blendera
Maria Blendera, Tony's wife
ADA Mandy Aguillard
Iberia Parish
ADA Tom Barnett, husband of Mandy Aguillard
The Defenders
Sarah Bernard

Ronald Dieudonné
Gerald Stone
John Clark

The Experts
Dr. Émile Pétain—Coroner
Richard Levy—Forensic Examiner
Ron Hubbard & Consuela Mavinata psychiatrists

Probation & Parole
Eugénie D'Aquin—missing wife of Det. Ted D'Aquin
Nicole Maraist

The Blessed Believers
Pastor Noah Norbert
Pastor Moses Allen—deceased
Former Assistant Pastor John Benjamin Gilbert
Sonja and Elena Trudeau

The Citizenry
Grampa (Armand) and Maman Boudreaux
    Parents of Eugénie D'Aquin
Robert Cane
Virtua Cane—deceased
Elizabeth Carter, Virtua's sister
Thomas Ernest
Patrick Ernest, his son
Charles "Jubilee" Joe—yardman
Deke Champagne, Manager of the Piggly-Wiggly
Roy Angelle, President of the Police Jury
Mark Gander, friend of Thomas Ernest

The Dogs
Tonnère—André's Lab
Hans—Det. Martin Castille's Search Dog
Plug—Det. Martin Castille's Cadaver Dog

PROLOGUE

Shaded by a canopy of drooping willow trees, a flat-bottomed bateau plied the shoreline of a narrow bayou leading from the south end of Catahoula Lake. The prow of the wooden boat poked in and out of stands of cypress knees protruding from dark sludge at the water's edge. Sitting on a plank in the stern of the bateau, an old man nudged the tiller to the port and starboard, his gnarled and sun-browned hand controlling their course. An outboard motor purred behind him.

A barefoot lad clad in a tattered t-shirt and faded cut-offs stood erect in the bow of the boat, his legs set wide for balance. His hand encircled the pole of a gaff. Beneath the brim of his battered straw hat, the boy's eyes scanned the water for little red floats he had set out earlier in the summer. Each float marked the location of a wire cage suspended beneath the surface.

No need for words to pass between the old man, Armand Boudreaux, and his grandson, André. These two had worked traps and fishing lines together since the boy grew tall and strong enough to handle a gaff and cast a line. When the boy sighted a float, he raised his hand to signal his pilot. The old man directed the bateau closer to shore. The boy dipped his gaff into the water and snagged the wire cage hanging below. He raised the cage to the gunwale, lifted a gate in its side, and spilled a few wriggling crabs into a Styrofoam ice chest behind him.

"You're right, Grampa. We got them special wigglers!"

The catch merited the boy's cry of delight. Catahoula Lake yields the delicacy of freshwater crabs for but a few precious weeks at the end of summer.

The trap now empty, the boy impaled a bloody hunk of

raw chicken onto a three-inch hook. He lowered the gate, fastened the clip closure, and heaved the cage back overboard. As the trap slipped down into the dark water, the old man gave his motor a little juice to reverse course. They backed away from the shore, took a ninety-degree turn to the starboard, and put-putted along to the next red float bobbing on the black-mirrored surface.

A third passenger, a coal black Lab, sat erect in the belly of the boat, just behind the ice chest. Tonnère they called him. His upturned head reached almost to the level of the shoulders of the seated old man. Tonnère kept close watch on the crabbing operation, the fetid smells of the swampy shore setting his slick black nose to twitching.

Two years ago, Armand Boudreaux found a pup at the animal shelter in St. Martinville and brought him home to be his grandson's companion. Since that day Tonnère has gone everywhere with the boy, always on guard to protect his young master from the perils of country life.

This late August afternoon, the trio—Armand, André, and Tonnère—had a heck of a time getting out of the house for their adventure. Maman, Armand's wife and André's grandmother, had put up a ruckus.

"No way, Armand." Hands on hips. The whole defiant stance. Maman had her hair all *ficeléed*. She had pressed her blue satin dress and laid her dancing shoes atop the quilted coverlet on their tall tester bed. Maman was ready for the weddin' dance scheduled right after Anticipated Mass at St. Rita's.

"Lordy, Lordy, Armand," Maman had fussed. "If you and that youngun' take off to the lake, no tellin' when you'll get home. It looks so bad to be showin' up at the church hall just in time for the fiddlin'! I can just hear Tante Lou's tongue clackin' on the roof of her mouth."

Maman wagged her finger and added a postscript. "And don't you two *dare* think about stayin' out late enough to gig frogs!"

The old man rolled his eyes but accepted his fate. He abandoned his plan to add enough time to their adventure to catch the makings of a tasty frog-leg dinner.

Around three that afternoon, when the high heat had not yet broken, the trio had pulled away from the weathered dock, reluctantly leaving behind the large froggin' torch and a gaff even longer than the one they would use to harvest the crab traps. Perhaps they could sneak away tomorrow. In the summer, except for being sure to make Mass at some time over the weekend, one day passed pretty much like another for an old fisherman and a young country boy.

Two hours later, when the bright sun had begun its descent, the bateau nosed into a stand of two-foot high cypress knees at the far end of the bayou. The prow bumped into something semi-solid. A low growl rumbled deep in Tonnère's throat—his thunder. The dog rose on all fours, his ears perked, his nose quivered faster. Abruptly, the thunder ceased. Five seconds of silence, then an explosion of insistent barking ripped through the quiet. Convulsions of the dog's body set the boat to rocking as if caught in a maelstrom.

"*Tais-toi,* Tonnère!" the old man scolded the dog. "*T'arrête!*"

In most of the Cajun parishes of south Louisiana mangled syntax and colorful expressions are all that remain of the native tongue of the French and the Creoles who settled the land behind the big swamp, but for the old folks, oral communication in the country is still in French.

Neither Armand nor the boy could hush Tonnère, and they respected his insistence. Many times, Tonnère tipped them off to danger. What did the big black Lab see or smell this time that set him to barking? Perhaps a fat cottonmouth water moccasin dangled from an overhanging branch or curled within the cypress knees at the water's edge. Perhaps a female alligator lay on her nest, alert for any disturbance. Perhaps a mischievous raccoon, or even a black bear, hid in the thicket of vegetation on the shore.

The eyes of both the boy and the old man followed Tonnère's point. Right off the bow, caught on a clump of reeds, a dark shape rocked gently in the wake. Instinctively, the boy raised his gaff to shove away the obstruction. A shout from the old man froze the boy's arm in mid-air.

"*T'arrête! T'arrête!*" Stop! Stop!

Armand cut the motor. Tonnère's barking receded deep into his throat. Ominous silence followed, then an unholy shriek from the boy shattered the quiet.

"*Momma! My momma!*" Three pairs of eyes—the old man's, the boy's, and Tonnère's—fell on a large rip at one end of what now revealed itself to be a burlap sack. All three occupants of the boat sucked air into rigid lungs.

"*Mon Dieu, mon Dieu,*" the old man whispered.

The object before them was not the usual threat from which Tonnère protected his masters. A human face protruded from a ragged opening in the sack, a display of tattered flesh providing an inviting dinner-spread for a half dozen skittering crabs. With a descending moan, André collapsed into the belly of the boat. He buried his face in Tonnère's fur and covered his head with his arms.

"*Non, non,* André," Armand called to his grandson. "*Ce n'est pas Eugénie. Ce n'est pas ta mère. Regarde les cheveux, les cheveux.*" No, no, André. That's not your Mama. Look at the hair.

Indeed, long dark locks floated out from the rip in the sack, entangling a half dozen crabs who were enjoying their dinner.

Did André hear the explanation from his Grampa? One couldn't know. André had curled into a rigid ball, tight against Tonnère side, hands covering his ears.

The old man recovered in less than a minute. He thrust the tiller forward, juiced the motor, and sent the bateau into a sharp turn. "*Tiens bien, mon petit!*" he called to André. Hold on tight!

Once free of the cypress knees and brush along the shoreline, the bow of the boat rose and the stern dug deep, gathering strength for a dash up the bayou and across the lake. Riding high on the open water of the lake, the trio sped toward home. Rushing wind dried the sweat popping out on the old man's chest. In the belly of the boat, André remained curled tight against his dog.

Armand pulled the boat to a weathered dock below the house. He delivered the boy into the embrace of his grandmother. He repeated to Maman his identification of the crabs' dinner. "*Ce n'etait pas* Eugénie, Maman. *Cheveux tres long. Noir, noir.*" It wasn't Eugénie, Maman. Long black hair. Black, black.

Within a half hour of a 911 emergency call, an armada of law enforcement vehicles assembled behind the headquarters of the Sheriff of St. Martin Parish. There were three black and white patrol cars, a jacked-up Jeep, and two water rescue trucks. One truck pulled a low-boy carrying a fast boat, the other an airboat on a trailer. Blue lights flashing, sirens blaring, the vehicles pulled out of the parking lot and headed north on Main Street. An ambulance and the coroner's Humvee tagged on to the end of the parade. The caravan turned right at St. Martin de Tours Catholic Church and crossed the bridge over the Bayou Teche. On the other side of the Bayou, they continued along the winding road leading to the village of Catahoula. The armada reassembled at Armand and Maman's house on the lake twenty minutes later.

Chief Roland strutted around the assemblage gathering information and preparing a plan. He chose the fast boat for the task ahead. With the old man riding shotgun as navigator, and Chief Roland in the seat behind the pilot, they raced back across the lake and down the bayou to retrieve a gruesome catch.

*   *   *

Dr. Emile Pétain had just settled down for the night in the doctors' lounge of Iberia General Hospital. A call from Chief Roland informed him of a request for his services. The doctor didn't need to change his attire for the job ahead—he wore hospital scrubs day and night. He downed a cup of day old coffee and descended the stairs to the hospital morgue. He topped his scrubs with a long white lab coat and a plastic apron, pulled on a pair of surgical gloves, and donned a brimless cap. A clear mask shielded his face.

Under the glare of overhead lights brighter than

noonday, Dr. Pétain reviewed the professional tools his assistant laid out in metal trays attached to the sides of a stainless-steel table in the center of the room: six sharp scalpels, three pairs of tongs, and a half-dozen pairs of tweezers ranging in size from three inches long to over a foot. Detailed examination of some of the specimens retrieved from the body would be carried out by Dr. Pétain himself. Other specimens would be sent to forensic specialists at the Acadiana Crime Lab or perhaps to a more specialized facility. Dr. Pétain's lab assistant, also clad in scrubs, mask, and gloves, observed the preparations.

A buzzer sounded. The lab assistant opened a side door of the morgue to admit two EMTs from Acadian Ambulance. The EMTs wheeled in the subject for the coroner's examination, a black bag containing a body. Two St. Martin Parish detectives, a man and a woman, tagged behind. Dr. Pétain smiled as the miasma of disinfectant in the air contorted their expressions. He handed each detective an apron and a white cloth mask to cover their noses.

Dr. Pétain plugged the cord of a small-toothed saw into an outlet on the side of the table. He signaled his assistant to roll forward the cart on which the EMTs had laid their cargo. Responding to further signals, the medical assistant and one of the detectives transferred the body bag from the cart to the metal table. Dr. Pétain switched on a microphone attached to the front of his plastic apron and rubbed his gloved hands together. He noted the time, the date, and the external condition of the bag.

Zzzippp. The unmistakable metallic buzz of the opening of a body bag bounced from the hard surfaces of the room. A putrid gray mass in a tattered shroud lay before them. The rising stench overwhelmed the odor of disinfectant. The detectives pulled in their necks like turtles. Impervious, Dr. Pétain bent his neck for a closer inspection. In life, thick black hair must have fallen to the woman's waist. Now, tangled strands were all that remained of what had been her crowning glory. Only an experienced coroner would know the display on the table had once been a lovely young woman.

Dr. Pétain chose a pair of tweezers from his collection. Apparently unaffected by the odor, and to the accompaniment of his own soft humming—was that really *Oh What a Beautiful Morning*? —the doctor bent to the task of picking off the few remaining critters still enjoying dinner on the woman's face.

His preliminary visual complete, Dr. Pétain tapped the microphone on his lapel to record the progress of his examination. He chose a scalpel from his collection and made the standard Y-shaped autopsy incision. He sliced open the chest and belly, cutting straight down past the navel. He reached for the saw, pressed the on button, and cut open her rib cage, the better to expose her heart and lungs. Shreds of skin alone enabled Dr. Pétain to distinguish the outside from the flesh inside the woman's body. The detectives turned their heads to find more salubrious air to breathe.

Dr. Pétain prodded and poked, selecting and then lifting specimens from the open cavity of the body. He placed them in the metal trays on the far side of the table. Throughout the process, in an emotionless monotone, he dictated a running commentary of his activity. As the doctor worked, Detective Ted D'Aquin, silently recorded his observations in a notebook. His partner, Detective Lorraine LaSalle, moved around the examining table snapping photographs of the doctor's procedures.

About an hour later, Dr. Pétain stepped back from the table and offered a thumbs-up. He had completed his harvest. Detective D'Aquin produced a package of evidence bags. Under the doctor's direction, with a pair of tweezers, the detective picked up the shreds of clothing, a piece of rope, and a lock of black hair the coroner had taken from the body. He bagged each item, recording the date, time, and the location on the body where the samples had been found. He and Dr. Pétain signed the label on each bag. Detective D'Aquin left the body parts to be dealt with by Dr. Pétain's assistant.

Satisfied with his work on the woman's body—

preliminary, of course, but sufficiently thorough to determine time and cause of death—Dr. Pétain turned his attention to a small object he had set out at the end of his examining table. There lay a perfect little form he had removed from the woman's womb—the body of a baby girl who had never taken a breath.

"Thirty-two weeks, I reckon. "

PART I

1

Good Friday is the most solemn day on the Christian calendar, but not in south Louisiana. Here, after attending a quiet meditation on the Stations of the Cross, the remainder of the day is observed as a High Holy Day of Indulgence.

Both pond and Atchafalaya Basin crawfish are large and plentiful in early spring. The price drops a tad; people convince themselves they're getting a bargain. There's a run on butane tanks. Pots are put on to boil in restaurants and backyard patios all over Acadiana. Sacks of wiggling crawfish, ears of corn and new potatoes, are dumped into red pepper-seasoned boiling water. Wherever you see a clump of cars on Good Friday, you can bet family and friends have gathered to enjoy beer and mudbugs.

This year, Louis Charles Chevalier, the Sheriff of St. Martin Parish, celebrated the occasion at Mulate's Crawfish Kitchen in Breaux Bridge. The Sheriff knew almost everyone in the dining room and enjoyed a rollicking evening of zydeco music and camaraderie—until a fiery hot crawfish tail took a wrong turn in the back of his throat. A reflexive intake of breath failed to dislodge the stubborn morsel. The sheriff gasped and made a vain attempt to speak. His normally florid complexion deepened to plum purple. With a futile lunge toward his bottle of Canebrake beer, his wife and children stunned to immobility across the table, and despite chest pounding, a Heimlich maneuver, and the exhortations to three different saints by a neighboring table of nuns, my boss, the Sheriff of St. Martin Parish, fell face first into a tin tray holding the remains of his double order of boiled crawfish. The massive coronary that ensued finished the job of delivering Sheriff Louis Charles Chevalier to his Maker.

He could not have wished for a better way to go. If there's a heavenly place where all our dreams come true, *The Man*, as the Sheriff was known throughout the parish to both those who loved and those who feared him, would forever be as he was that night, bellied up to a table laden with tin trays of succulent mudbugs.

An instant message brought the news to Chief Roland at his camp in the Atchafalaya Basin. After spraying the air with obscenities, he called his side-kick, Charles Blanchet, Warden of the jail.

"Charlie, get to the office immediately. Our asses are in serious shit. We gotta make a plan."

Warden Blanchet called me, Ted D'Aquin, the most experienced detective in the department.

It only took a moment for me to go from my initial shock to consideration of the ramifications sure to follow from the loss of our leader. *The Man* had been punching all the political buttons in St. Martin Parish for twenty years. He'd been my boss for ten. By God, my job was at stake! All our jobs.

Chief Deputy Roland entertained thoughts of a promotion, taking over the office of sheriff himself. So did the Warden. A call to the District Attorney for the three-parish area, the district's most powerful figure, quickly disabused them both of their ambitions.

"For twenty years, you've been doing the boss's dirty work," District Attorney Gerald Strait told them. "You two have too much baggage. We need a fresh face to present to the public in an election."

"Yeah, shit sticks. So, where we gonna find a man we can control?"

"Or a woman," Mr. Strait suggested. "How about *The Man's* daughter?"

After getting over the initial shock of hearing the DA's proposal, Chief Roland pronounced the idea "fuckin' brilliant." He expected an inexperienced woman to allow him even more license than he had enjoyed working for *The Man*. He envisioned maintaining the political power centered in the Sheriff's Office and preserving jobs for himself and over a hundred other deputies in the department. A double winner. I signed on to the idea as well. One of the jobs on the line was my own.

On Easter Monday, the Chief and I drove over to ULL, the University of Louisiana at Lafayette, to pay a call on Gabrielle Chevalier Bouton, head of the Department of Criminal Justice at the University, the former sheriff's daughter and his only child. Persuading Professor Bouton to sign on to our plan took several visits, but before the parish celebrated the day Our Lord ascended into heaven, we talked her into coming home to St. Martin Parish to serve as interim sheriff—a trial period to see if she liked the job. If she did, she could sign up for the election to succeed her father.

As it turned out, the professor liked being interim sheriff. She qualified for election to the office of Sheriff of St. Martin Parish—threw her hat into the ring, as they say. Evoking lineage to Captain Louis Chevalier, an early commandant of the Poste des Attakapas and a descendant of one of the first families to settle in what would become St. Martin Parish, Gabrielle resumed use of her maiden name. District Attorney Strait, the most powerful political figure in the three-parish judicial district, contacted all his people to spread word of his blessing.

The Chief and the Warden handled the campaign details, probably picking up a little more soil on their reputations in the process. At the end of a long, hot summer, Gabrielle Chevalier beat out four men for the job. She would be officially sworn into office in just a few days.

During the interregnum, the work of the sheriff's department had continued as usual. I did my job as detective without encountering a single bump in the road. Crimes were investigated. Files promptly made their way to the district attorneys. The testimony of the deputies supported successful prosecutions. I thought the District Attorney's plan to bless the election of the daughter of *The Man*, a complete success—until the Saturday afternoon when my son André, visiting his grandparents at Catahoula Lake, came upon the body of a pregnant young woman inside a burlap sack caught on a stand of cane reed.

When the 911 call, reporting the grisly find came into headquarters, I rushed out to Catahoula to assume my investigative duties and to support my boy. Later that night, when André had been safely tucked into his Grampa's bed, I picked up my assigned partner for this weekend duty, Detective Lorraine LaSalle. She had only been with us for a few months, following a couple years with the City of Lafayette. We began to work the case. We attended the autopsy on the body of the pregnant woman, put bulletins out on the wire, and wrote our reports. I didn't hit my own bed until two a.m.

My cell phone rang at six the following morning. Sheriff-elect Gabrielle Chevalier on the line. The hour of the call was the first thing she did to piss me off. I'd only slept four hours. Then came the second cut.

"Detective D'Aquin," she said. "I'm removing you and your partner Detective LaSalle from the investigation into the death of the woman found last night in Catahoula Lake."

I couldn't believe it. For four years as top detective, I'd been the one to decide who conducted investigations. I don't remember exactly what I said to her. Apparently, nothing.

"Are you there, Detective D'Aquin?"

I sputtered out my response. "Yes, ma'am. But why? Why are you taking us off this case?"

"As I understand it, your boy and your father-in-law discovered the body. We can discuss the matter at length sometime later. Short answer: there's a well-researched *best practice* for criminal investigations directing that investigators should not be involved in a case in which they have a personal connection. As for Detective LaSalle, she's one of our newest detectives. She needs to work under guidance."

I'd never heard of such a *best practice*. And there were other problems with the order of the Sheriff-Elect.

"Who've we got to do the job?" I asked. "This is a serious situation. A woman. A baby. Very unusual. At this point, everybody else in the department who's available is as green as grass."

"I'm aware of that. I've been talking with District Attorney Gerald Strait and we have a plan. I want you to go to New Iberia later this morning and join him at the home of his special assistant Dennis Byrne. Mr. Strait will be waiting for you at ten o'clock at the head of Mr. Byrne's driveway. Do you know where Mr. Byrne lives?" She answered her own question. "On the bayou side of Marie Street, a couple doors before City Park. Go there. Mr. Strait will clue you in on what we have in mind."

Again, I was speechless. It appeared the big DA, the most powerful figure in the three-parish district, would be pulling the strings.

"Are you there, Detective?" Sheriff Gabrielle asked me.

"I'm here, ma'am. Let me get this straight. You want me to go to Mr. Byrne's house on a Sunday morning? Maybe you don't know, but..." I hesitated to correct my boss.

"Yes, I know. We're not supposed to disturb Mr. Byrne's Sunday morning routine. But Mr. Strait made the call. He believes our situation justifies unusual procedure."

A bit of courage returned. "Why am I the one to go to Mr. Byrne's house? You've just told me I'm pulled from the investigation."

"Right. But you need to brief your successors on what's already been done. We'll talk about your reassignment duties later on. And by the way, I'd prefer you didn't address me as ma'am."

"Yes, Sheriff."

Hm-m. She liked being in charge.

A year and a half ago, after my wife Eugénie disappeared, I spent six straight months heading up the Sheriff's Office investigation into what might have happened to her. Did I have a personal connection on that investigation? You bet. My wife and the mother of my boy, André. No one, not anybody, ever suggested there was anything wrong with having me lead the missing person case. Only when *The Man* lost patience and said I had to give my fellow deputies a hand with the routine work of the department did I take a leave of absence. Eugénie had been a probation officer for ten years. Invited by her boss, I moved the headquarters of my investigation to Eugénie's former workstation in the office of Probation and Parole. P&P gave me my own space over there. I spent the next six months of the search doing nothing else, putting out more work on the case than anyone who didn't have my motivation.

Yeah. And what was the result? Zilch. Nothing. Nada. Every lead I pursued hit a dead end. I never found a trace of Eugénie after she called her office mid-afternoon on April 24, one year, six months, and eleven days ago. Eventually, I returned to my job at the Sheriff's Office even though a cold lump still sat in my gut just thinking about what might have happened to my wife.

The sheriff interrupted my effort to come to grips with her order.

"I've just talked with District Attorney Strait. He says the Sheriff's Office isn't the only under-staffed department in St. Martin Parish. He wants to send Mr. Byrne over there to head up his St. Martin District Attorney's office. And he's asked me to request the loan of an experienced detective from Iberia Parish as well."

Damn. Another detective coming in. I'm not just reassigned, I'm replaced.

* * *

I got to the head of Mr. and Mrs. Byrne's driveway ten minutes early. Of course, I did. Rule No. 1: never be late when you're meeting Mr. Strait. As I expected, the District Attorney arrived early also, parking his big Jeep right behind mine. I recognized the powerful build of Iberia Parish Detective Deuce Washington stepping out of the passenger seat, and then his broad smile. Just seeing him raised my spirits. Deuce and I had worked together a half dozen times in the past. If someone had to turn me out, I was glad it would be Deuce. I felt better. The investigation would be in good hands.

Mr. Strait and I exchanged a formal handshake. He

offered no preliminary explanation of our mission but immediately spun on his heels and took off up the 100-foot driveway to Mr. Byrne's house. Intensity powered his quick steps. Deuce gave me a fist bump and a wink, and we fell in behind Mr. Strait. Two six-footers, Deuce and I reduced our strides to accommodate those of the much shorter District Attorney. I'm as tall as Deuce but half as wide. Not that Deuce is overweight. He's just built. I have to face reality— I'm skinny. Note to self: Never arm wrestle with Deuce.

A light breeze shuffled the leaves of two giant *Magnolia grandiflora* in the front yard. Through tendrils of Spanish moss trailing from the limbs of three two-hundred-year-old live oaks, I could just make out Dennis Byrne and his wife Camille on the wide veranda of their gracious turn-of-the-century home high on the left bank of the Bayou Teche. I still couldn't believe Mr. Strait was going to disturb Mr. Byrne's legendary Sunday morning routine.

Through forty years of marriage, in military postings in five countries, and now in his retirement job as a special assistant district attorney, Col. Dennis Byrne and his wife Camille kept a tradition of spending a quiet time together after Sunday morning Mass. If anyone in the DA's offices or in law enforcement needed his expertise—which was considerable and offered freely to assistant DAs and deputies alike—we knew to wait until afternoon. Chores, pastimes, even visits with his family were on hold.

With Mr. Strait in the lead, we reached the steps to the veranda. The wide-eyed look on Mr. Byrne's face told me this visit had not been pre-cleared.

Camille Byrne raised her face to her husband for instructions. He nodded acceptance—closer to tolerance—of the interruption and walked down the steps to greet us. Camille pulled over extra chairs from the other side of the porch and slipped through the screen door into the house. As was her practice when they had company, she would soon reappear with a tray of coffee.

Mr. Strait made apologies for disturbing his special assistant, introduced his companions, and confessed his mission. He had come with what he labeled *a request*.

"Dennis, I want you to go over to our St. Martin Parish office for a while."

Abrupt, but not an extraordinary request. As a rule, Mr. Byrne only handled serious felonies in Iberia Parish, but I knew Mr. Strait had occasionally sent him to deal with a problem case in St. Mary or St. Martin, the other two parishes in our judicial district. But the DA usually delivered these assignments by stopping at Mr. Byrne's office, file in hand, to tell his special assistant about a trial in trouble or a confounding legal issue. Never political problems. Mr. Strait dealt with those himself. And never by disturbing Mr. Byrne's Sunday morning.

"So, what's the case you need me for?" Mr. Byrne asked.

I shook off the little shiver I felt down my spine. I had a premonition the *request* had something to do with my boy André's discovery at Catahoula Lake.

"Not just one case, Dennis. I need you to take over the whole shootin' match. The St. Martin Parish DA's office." He paused. "Until further notice."

"Sir?"

Mr. Byrne probably thought he'd become accustomed to surprise assignments. During his career in the Air Force, he'd had news of new postings by phone call, by an officer appearing at his door, by opening a letter with a government return address. And he knew a bit about handling unexpected developments. As a trial lawyer in JAG, and now as an assistant district attorney, he probably had witnesses go ballistic and turn inside out, had assistants wither under fire, had juries return inexplicable verdicts. And I knew he'd had the anxiety of his own sons sent to foreign wars. He probably thought he'd be immune to shock. No. There was something Mr. Byrne couldn't handle with equanimity: what he considered an unbelievably unreasonable assignment.

Mr. Byrne's eyebrows were twitching. "You're asking me to run the office over there?"

"Yes, I am."

Mr. Byrne took a deep breath to control his reaction. "Sir,

I can prepare witnesses and try a case anywhere, and I've done so all over the world, but managing the office personnel and screening cases to determine the appropriate charges to bring takes someone who knows the lay of the land. I know next to nothing about St. Martin Parish. Over there, whenever I get into a conversation deeper than pleasantries, I sense a level of communication taking place about which I haven't a clue. I have no idea what makes the people of St. Martin Parish tick."

Although twenty years his senior, Dennis Byrne addressed Gerald Strait as his superior officer. Similarly fit, energetic, and whip-smart, the difference between the two men showed most clearly to me in a social encounter. I'd rather go out for a beer with Mr. Byrne.

Mr. Strait slowly nodded his head. "Exactly, Dennis. Because you say you don't understand St. Martin Parish is the very reason I want you there. People who say they understand the parish are the ones who do not. Your experience has taught you that when you go to a foreign country you need to move carefully until you get to know the tribes."

The tribes? Ouch!

Journalists and novelists writing about our corner of south Louisiana often use the metaphor of a gumbo, a savory stew of disparate elements blended together for delicious effect. That figure of speech doesn't work for me. I've always found each ingredient in the St. Martin Parish stew a flavor bent on asserting itself. A tough assignment. Was Mr. Strait saying his special assistant needed to be punished?

Mr. Byrne had the same impression. Cautiously, he inquired. "Have I done something that displeases you, sir?"

Mr. Strait came close to smiling, but not quite. "My God, no. Not at all. Absolutely the opposite. The fact is I need your experience and your skill to get us through a bad patch. Wait. I think I see Camille behind the screen door holding a coffee tray. And I believe I catch the aroma of her wonderful biscuits." Mr. Strait turned to the Iberia Parish detective at his side. "Deuce, give Mrs. Byrne a hand with the door."

Deuce jumped up from his chair. "Let me take that tray, ma'am." The delicate souvenir from the Byrnes' years in Madrid looked ludicrous in Deuce's massive black hands. The little cups rattled in their saucers when he set the tray down on the table before us.

Deuce and I fell on the coffee and biscuits. Not a sound came from Mr. Byrne. Brow knit, he struggled to straighten out his thoughts. The plates picked clean, Mrs. Byrne took them away. Mr. Strait resumed his pitch.

"Circumstances have left our St. Martin Parish office in inexperienced hands."

I knew mobilization of the National Guard had sent St. Martin Parish's First Assistant District Attorney to Afghanistan, but I thought Mr. Strait had that covered. Mr. Byrne had the same impression.

"Didn't you call Tony Blendera up from the St. Mary Parish office to ride in to the rescue?" he asked.

"Ah, yes. And he's been helping out when he's able. He'll try a case now and then, for example. But Tony lives in Morgan City, and…" Mr. Byrne paused. "Tony has a tricky situation at home. He can't take on full responsibility for the St. Martin Parish office day to day, from sixty miles away."

"And Assistant District Attorney Mandy Aguillard? How about her."

"Mandy has promise, but she's been handling felonies for only a couple years. And she and Tom are expecting twins. She isn't sure what they will mean for her career with us. The rest of the assistants? Let's just say they'd best stick to misdemeanors, juvenile, and public body counsel. Events last night tell me we need experienced felony trial boots on the ground. That's where you come in Dennis."

"I'm afraid I'm not up to date, Mr. Strait. What events last night are you talking about?"

"I guess you wouldn't know, enjoying your sanctuary here on the banks of the Bayou Teche." Mr. Strait nodded in my direction. "Yesterday, Ted's son André and the boy's grandfather, Armand Boudreaux, spent the afternoon crabbing in a canal leading out of Catahoula Lake. Late in the afternoon, they came upon the body of a woman in a burlap sack. Grisly sight for Ted's boy, I'm afraid. The autopsy conducted later in the evening revealed the woman to have been eight months pregnant. The Sheriff's Office cranked up an investigation, but Tony was nowhere to be found to give them advice and counsel."

I wondered if Mr. Strait had been called at home in the middle of the night. He wouldn't have liked that.

"The added problem is with our investigation teams. I'm proud that our K-9 officer Detective Martin Castille is scheduled to take his dog Plug to New York City to help out at the World Trade Center, but his absence, plus our new sheriff's ideas about *best practice*, leave the department seriously short-handed."

"*Best practice*?" Mr. Byrne tipped his head at an angle and a deep furrow creased his forehead.

"Oh, I see you haven't heard that one," Mr. Strait continued. "Sheriff Gabrielle comes from the ivory tower of academia, you know. She has the idea that *best practice* dictates detectives should not be assigned to cases in which they have a personal interest. The most experienced detective of St. Martin Parish—Ted here—got called off the investigation because his boy found the body."

Mr. Byrne's wrinkled forehead told me the so-called *best practice* was a new one for him also. "So, who's in charge of investigating the Catahoula death?" he asked.

"Right now, City Police Chief Docelia Smart and Detective Spike Badeaux are on the job. They have a tentative ID—a missing person reported last week—but not much else. I'm on my way to ask the Iberia Parish Sheriff to send Detective Deuce Washington to St. Martin Parish to pitch in."

"Deuce?" Mr. Byrne asked. "Doesn't Chief Deputy Allan Roland run law enforcement in St. Martin Parish?"

Mr. Strait tented his hands on his lap. A smile teased his lips. "That was Allan's plan, but he's finding out we've hand-picked a successor to *The Man* who has a mind of her own. I believe Camille has the swearing-in of Sheriff-Elect Chevalier on your calendar for tomorrow morning. You'll need to be there, Dennis."

Mr. Strait continued his pitch to persuade Mr. Byrne to take on the new assignment. Both men were very careful with words. "Dennis, you've spent a career in the exercise of the bedrock principle of equality before the law. Well, right now St. Martin Parish needs a steady hand in pursuit of that very principle. The death of the old Sheriff, Ted pulled from the investigations, the limited commitment from Tony Blendera, a new Sheriff in town, all of that leaves a vacuum. We need your skill, your experience, and your steady hand on the tiller."

Tiller? The choice of that word pricked. Did the DA want Mr. Byrne to steer the boat in a particular direction? Did his flattery to Mr. Byrne mask a purpose? No. I was getting paranoid in my pique. I swallowed my suspicions and snapped to attention to hear Mr. Byrne ask Mr. Strait a question.

"Tell me more about the discovery of the body of the pregnant woman, sir. I assume you don't think she died of natural causes."

"Hardly. Bound, stuffed into a burlap sack, found caught up on cypress knees or some piece of vegetation on the edge of a bayou leading from Catahoula Lake to the levee. Dr. Pétain—he did the preliminary autopsy—believes she'd been in the water for three or four days. And pregnant."

"Pregnant? Are we talking about the death of 'more than one person?' First-degree murder?" Mr. Byrne asked.

Oh, my God. Mr. Byrne was thinking ten steps ahead of me. I hadn't considered having a capital case on our hands. You definitely cannot leave a death penalty investigation in the hands of newbies. I was beginning to understand what had triggered Mr. Strait's concerns about the St. Martin staff.

I watched Mr. Byrne. His eyes widened, he straightened his back, his hands folded and unfolded on his lap. "You say they have an ID for the woman?" he asked.

Mr. Strait's expression flirted with a smile. He had a fish on his line. His special assistant DA couldn't resist wanting to know more about a homicide.

"Tentative ID," Mr. Strait said and stood up. He looked at his phone. "The Iberia Parish Sheriff is expecting me downtown in his office in five minutes, Dennis. I need to talk to him about lending us Deuce for a patch. Why don't you talk over the St. Martin assignment with Camille? I don't need an answer today. The ceremony to swear in the new Sheriff of St. Martin Parish is at eleven o'clock tomorrow. Meet me at the DA's office over there at one-thirty." Mr. Strait turned to me. "Ted, you stay and brief Mr. Byrne about what we know so far. You'll be invaluable to him as he learns his way around the Parish of St. Martin." Another hint of a smile. "*If* he takes the assignment, of course."

Wink, wink, I thought.

Mr. Strait stepped down from the veranda. He beckoned Deuce to join him.

I don't need an answer today. Meet me at the office over there at one-thirty.

Mr. Strait had given Mr. Byrne a deadline of tomorrow to talk over the assignment with his wife and come to a decision! Why ask me to brief him now? I knew the answer to my question; Mr. Strait was confident his special assistant would take the job.

Mr. Strait, Deuce at his side, walked briskly down the driveway to the street. Next to me, Mr. Byrne let out a monster sigh. "I think we need another cup of coffee. Apparently, Ted, you've been designated to be my native guide to the mysteries of the Parish of St. Martin."

Camille Byrne reappeared with her tray. She smiled when Mr. Byrne told her of Mr. Strait's so-called request.

"Orders in civilian life may be delivered more smoothly than in the service, Dennis, but they're orders nevertheless. I think you have little choice in the matter. Fine. You love a challenge, and St. Martin Parish is a pretty interesting place." She tipped her head and gave her husband a mischievous smile. "Here's a plus. I won't have to pack us up and call the mover for your assignment to this foreign country. I'll be able to stay right here on the Bayou Teche where I belong."

2

Mr. Strait and Deuce vanished around the trees. I sat back, swung my feet up onto the porch railing, and took a deep breath. Oops!

"I'm sorry, sir." I dropped my boots to the floor. Mr. Byrne's Irish eyes were twinkling.

"Go ahead, Ted. Make yourself comfortable. When Mr. Strait enters a space, he sucks in all the air. When he leaves, the air seems to go out with him."

Mr. Byrne settled beside me. "I'm kicking myself for not congratulating Deuce on being honored as Louisiana Peace Officer of the Year. That's big. He deserves all the praise for his heroic effort to try to save that guy from jumping off the Whiskey Bay Bridge."

"He'll be glad you didn't mention it. The fame embarrasses him. He says he doesn't deserve an award because he failed to stop the guy. I think the publicity might get him into a Smoky-the-Bear hat sooner. That's his goal, you know. To be a Louisiana State Trooper like his father before him."

"I'd hate to lose Deuce, but that man should get what he wants." Mr. Byrne picked up a legal pad from the end table and sat back in his chair. That's one of his legendary habits— always a legal pad at hand. "Your assignment is to brief me on the body found at Catahoula Lake, Ted. We'll get to that in a minute. First, if you would, I'd like to hear about your wife. I understand she hasn't been found. I'm truly sorry about that."

"Thank you for asking, sir."

That's what I always say: thank you for asking. How many times? I couldn't guess. Unlike most people, Mr. Byrne didn't take my standard response as permission to move on. He persisted. "You look 100% better than when last I saw you. I believe if Hollywood came looking for a Cajun to play the part of Ron Guidry, the New York Yankees ace strike out champion from Lafayette they called 'Louisiana Lightening', you'd get the casting call. Curly black hair, sparkling black eyes, unusually long arms…"

"No, Mr. Byrne. Guidry was a lefty. Now if my son André keeps looking like me, he'd get the part. He's already a pretty fair left handed pitcher."

"Where are you on the investigation? I'd like to know."

"Nowhere, sir. Eugénie's been missing a year and a half now. I still don't know what could have happened to her. After this length of time…"

"Do you still have your search operation set up over at Probation & Parole?"

"Yes, I do. Eugénie's boss has been terrific. I didn't go over there as much this summer, with André out of school, but I haven't given up."

I didn't tell him the other reason I'd been keeping my distance from Eugénie's old office. I'd been dodging her former partner Nicole. Another story.

"So, tell me about your investigation, Ted. From the beginning." Mr. Byrne folded over the top sheet of the legal pad to give himself a clean page. He picked up a pen. He leaned toward me, eyes alert, an invitation for me to tell him more. OK. If he wanted to help, I should take advantage. Maybe someone with many decades of experience would have an idea of something else I could try.

"Eugénie went missing on Thursday, the 24th of April." Mr. Byrne wrote down the date. "She'd scheduled field appointments with her probationers on this end of the parish. I'd gotten off early, so I picked up André after school to take him to Lafayette to look for new baseball shoes. Summer Little League coming up; he'd outgrown everything. We got back home around six. Eugénie wasn't there, which was unusual. After an hour or so I called the possible places she might have gone—to visit her parents, my sister, a couple close friends. No one had seen her. I called in to the Sheriff's

Office and asked patrol to be on the lookout for her car."

Mr. Byrne's eyes hooked on mine, his eyebrows raised in anticipation of important information he might hear.

"Around seven, patrol spotted her green Corolla at the Evangeline Pepper plant, the location of her last appointment for the day. Do you know the plant? Bridge Street, across the bayou, then left to the big smoke stack?"

"I've seen the smoke stack."

"The probationer she'd visited, one Roland 'Digger' Jeanbaptiste, worked there. Digger once had a second job cleaning up the cemetery, which explains the nickname. At 4:15, Eugénie called in to her office and said she would be back soon. She never came.

"I've talked to Digger, and so did everyone else. I'm satisfied he had no idea where she went after their meeting. He was probably the last person to see Eugénie…"

I still can't say *alive* without cracking.

"With the car found, but not the driver, Chief Roland approved a full-scale investigation. We activated the missing person protocol, scoured the area, of course, and questioned everyone around the plant. Nothing. So, we went wide. We notified law enforcement everywhere. Eventually, we distributed pictures, put info out on social media, put together a kitty for the reward, the whole bit. I'm still keeping all the notifications active."

"Dogs? I suppose you put them on the scent."

"Right. Do you know Detective Martin Castille? He doubles as our K-9 officer. He had Hans and another search dog then. They sniffed the sweater Eugénie left in her car and worked the area. Later, when Martin got Plug and trained him as a cadaver dog, we searched again. Plug didn't have any better results than Hans."

I shuddered, remembering how even hearing the words *cadaver dog* scared the hell out of me. Watching Martin work the dog was even worse. Every time Plug's quivering nose lowered to the ground, my stomach dropped. I was terrified he'd alert.

I paused to see if Mr. Byrne had enough. No. With a

compliment for Eugénie, he encouraged me to keep going. "I met Eugénie when she worked in Iberia Parish for a while. I liked her work and her lovely manner. I'm really sorry."

"Thank you, sir."

"I suppose you questioned the other probationers she saw that day?"

"You bet. They got a good going over. We found nothing out of the ordinary. Then we moved on to look at the rest of Eugénie's caseload."

"I bet that was a good number."

"One hundred and twelve, as I remember. Probation keeps records of both the office visits and the field."

I ran through the reporting procedure Probation & Parole put in several years ago. Each probationer reported in person to the office only once a month. For the other bi-monthly contact, the officer visited the probationer at home or at work. You always learn more on the field visits, but they take time. And the field can be dangerous. Probation officers are armed and trained. Eugénie carried a 9mm Glock.

"I suppose you put out a description of her weapon."

"We got the serial number on the wire the following day."

"Did you pick up anything from the examination of her car?"

"The Acadiana Crime Lab scoured the car without finding a trace of anything that shouldn't have been there. The glove box was undisturbed. Fingerprints and fibers were all those of family, friends, and repairmen. No DNA because no medium. No blood, semen, or urine. The car had no damage."

Mr. Byrne's eyes asked, 'and what next?'

"Near the end of the year, we were done with her active docket and preparing to take a look at every person Eugénie ever supervised—into the thousands. My boss lost patience with me. I can't fault him for that. I wasn't doing any of the regular work of the department and I took a lot of time off. My fellow detectives had been covering for me and never complained. My buddies in law enforcement all over the state would call me whenever they had a woman's body they couldn't identify. I'd jump in my car and head to wherever."

I didn't go into what that did to me. I woke up each morning thinking of a regular day ahead, but before my feet touched the floor, a pall fell. No Eugénie. That reality cut me like a knife in the gut, which I'd actually suffered once. My whole life had changed. The only way I could cope was to plunge into the search. I was obsessed. Looking back, I realize I'd been living exhausted and emotionally yanked up and down. Mostly down. Sometimes I came to work without having been to bed. I was in real danger of running off the road somewhere.

"I'd papered the walls of the squad room with mug shots of the probationers, put up tables to lay out the files, and hooked up an extra computer just for the investigation. People tell me I got kind of crazy." My voice cracked. "The Sheriff was right to think I was a pretty worthless employee."

Mr. Byrne nodded. "Understandable."

"*The Man* needed his squad room back. Then Maman, my mother-in-law, came to the Sheriff's Office with her paraphernalia. Her visit was the last straw. The Sheriff had enough."

Mr. Byrne raised his eyebrows, which sent a horizontal wrinkle across his forehead. "Her paraphernalia?"

"Oh, yes. My mother-in-law is a *traiteur*. I don't believe in all that, but she does."

Mr. Byrne's eyebrows rose even higher. Now he had *two* horizontal forehead wrinkles.

I continued. "Maman stormed right into *The Man's* office and told him what she'd been telling me for months. The deputies looking for Eugénie would have success if she could work with them—and if they'd truly believe. The Sheriff blew up. He said he couldn't have voodoo and superstition going on in government space."

"I can picture the scene." Twinkling eyes again.

"I moved my search effort out of the Sheriff's Office. I couldn't bring it all home; I was trying to provide a reasonably normal life for André. Eugénie's boss at Probation & Parole saved the day. He offered me an office, a computer, manpower—womanpower really—and said I could base out of there as long as necessary. I'd learned one lesson, for sure. I didn't let Maman come anywhere near the place."

Mr. Byrne liked that.

"I continued to monitor the routine inquiries I put out there and moved onto investigating every probationer Eugénie ever had. A huge job. Time and again I'd run across someone who might have had reason to be mad about his probation, follow the lead, and come up with nothing. After six more months of working the list, I had no more pertinent information than the whole department had uncovered in the first six. My shrink—the department sent me to a shrink —said I should go back to doing what I was trained to do. The guys were damn glad to get me back. I've been on the job there since April, but I still check into Probation every chance I get."

"I suppose you looked at whether Eugénie might have had something personal going on in her life. Maybe a family problem?"

"We sure did. Right at the beginning. In any missing person case, like any suspicious death, we look for someone who might have a motive or reason, and we always look first at the spouse. For objectivity, the department did that part of the investigation—and gave me a good going over in the process. They came up with nothing."

I remember the grilling the detectives gave me. I was resentful. Actually, I was mad as hell to be questioned like a suspect. I vowed to remember the feeling when I'd be the one on the investigators' side of the table.

"How about Eugénie's family?" Mr. Byrne asked.

"That's her parents, Maman and Armand Boudreaux in Catahoula. Great people. There's one sister, Marie. She lives in Lafayette. Marie organized prayer vigils, a fundraising walk, and flooded social media. You name it. She's supported me in every way she could. There're no problems in that family."

"And you haven't given up?"

"Hell no. Just last week I cut out some time to go to Jeff Davis Parish to talk to them about their situation. Over the past five years, they've found the bodies of ten women and been unable to solve the crimes. But Jeff Davis has positive ID on every body they've found. Nothing about their situation gave me any ideas."

"Their victims were all in *the life*, right? Eugénie doesn't fit the profile."

"I know, but I'll follow any lead. People have really been great. There's a rosary at St. Rita's in Catahoula every Thursday morning; Eugénie's name heads the list of people they pray for. And I know Maman has never stopped with her 'white' magic, even though Eugénie used to fuss at her mother for having faith in that stuff."

I didn't give Mr. Byrne word for word what my Mom had to say about my mother-in-law's doings. *Idolatry. Conjure from Africa by way of the Caribbean. Hocus pocus no good Catholic should have anything to do with.* My Mom is usually pretty tolerant, but this subject got her goat. I know it all stems from when I first told her I was quitting college to go into law enforcement, and that Eugénie and I were going to get married. Mom was disappointed. She had to be mad at someone, I guess, so she blamed Eugénie.

"I did get my mother-in-law to take off that piece of root she'd put on André's wrist, and she promised not to 'treat' her patients, clients, customers—whatever she calls them—when André visits."

Each time I talked about treating, Mr. Byrne's pulled on his earlobe. I didn't admit to him I'd made a *cordon* of sassafras root myself, dipped it in a running stream—for us that's the Bayou Teche—and put it on my wrist. Maman had told me to wear that thing and I'd find what was lost, if I'd believe. Dammit, I believed like hell for four months. Zilch.

Mr. Byrne sat back again. "Ted, sometimes when you least expect…"

"That's the hope I cling to."

Mr. Byrne made an offer. "If you still have all your material over at Probation, I'd like to go there with you sometime and have a look at your files. Maybe a fresh set of eyes will turn up a new angle."

I told him the files were mostly online now. We could bring them up on the computers.

"I'd like you to come, sir, and I hope you'll be frank with your opinion of my investigation. Sheriff Gabrielle thinks an investigator can be too close to a case. What do you think about that?"

"I don't want to get crosswise with your boss. I suppose an investigator who gets angry could lose perspective. But I promise you, I won't pull any punches about your work."

"Thank you, sir."

Maybe Mr. Byrne would see something else I could do. I stayed quiet for a few moments. Mr. Byrne was watching me.

He asked how things were going at home with my boy.

"As well as can be expected, I suppose. André's always been a quiet kid. Baseball, poking around Catahoula Lake with his dog, that's what he likes to do."

I didn't get into the dozens of times André had picked up something of Eugénie's—a coat on the hook by the back door, her favorite coffee mug, the box of cereal she liked but he didn't—and froze. What should I do about all Eugénie's things? One day when I felt emotionally strong, I moved all my clothes to a closet in the hall. When I ran into something of hers around the house, I picked it up and stashed it in the bedroom closet. I'm trained to be objective, but I didn't let myself think about the slim chance of getting good news after all this time.

"I think it was Winston Churchill who said, 'You can get used to anything but hanging.' I'm waiting for that acceptance. I'm not there yet. Back to the present. My assignment from Mr. Strait is to bring you up to date on what Lorraine and I did last night. The new floater case, he calls it. Shall we get to that?"

Mr. Byrne flipped to a clean page of his legal pad. "OK. Right. Go ahead."

"I was on duty this past weekend. I dropped André off at his Grampa's house early Saturday morning. He's always spent a lot of time at the lake, but since... since his mother's been missing, he wants to go out there every chance he gets.

He loves the outdoors, and I think he cares as much for the dog Tonnère as he does for his grandparents. My father-in-law got the dog to help André handle the loss, and maybe dull the ache in his own heart. When André visits, poor Tonnère doesn't know which of them to follow. Fortunately, André and his grandfather are rarely apart.

"Late Saturday afternoon, when they'd been working the traps around the lake for a good while, André sighted their last little red float. Armand brought the boat close so André could pull up the trap beneath. The prow bumped into something soft. André raised his gaff to push it out of the way. Armand called out to stop him. Through a torn place in the lump—a burlap sack it turns out—they saw a woman's face, covered with crabs. André lost it. He thought he'd seen his mother."

Mr. Byrne rubbed a hand across his forehead. "God, I'm really sorry your boy had that experience."

"Tough. They beat it back to Grampa's. As soon as the pair got back to the dock, Armand called 911. And they called the Sheriff's Office. I called my current partner Lorraine to meet me there. The guys were willing to cover weekend duty for me, but when I asked André to come on home, he said no. He wanted to stay. He was worried someone might be around who could hurt his grandparents —or his dog. That seemed to be his main concern, that they'd be safe."

"He sounds like a good kid, Ted."

"Yes, he is. You know the irony? André has this big interest in the Attakapas Indians who used to live out there. He and Tonnère spend hours in a pirogue poking around the shore of that lake, digging for Indian bones. *On dit*, an expression you hear around here, people say the Attakapas were a bloodthirsty tribe. The name in Choctaw is supposed to mean man-eater; Catahoula means Lake of Sacrifice. The lore is the Choctaw killed their enemies and threw them into the lake. André has found arrowheads and bits of pottery, but never any bones—never human bones, that is."

"I'm glad for that."

"I am too. His Grampa tells him he never will find human bones. Grampa doesn't say the sacrifice stories aren't true, mind you, just that a mysterious stream down deep at the bottom of the lake goes under the levee and flows into the Atchafalaya Basin on the other side. Any Indian bones have long ago been swept away to lie deep under the silt of the river or washed out into the Gulf. Crazy, huh?"

But maybe not. Grampa says old timers tell him everything used to be different out there before the "High Water" of 1927. The Atchafalaya River periodically fed the Lake and the area all around. When the Corps of Engineers built the big levee to keep the flood waters in the Atchafalaya so there'd never be another flood of '27, Catahoula Lake got shut off. It's possible there could be an underground stream still open under the levee.

"The Attakapas have completely died out, right?" Mr. Byrne asked.

"Some live around Opelousas, I'm told. And in Catahoula, there are a few Creoles who say they have Indian blood. My in-laws live on a road called Stranger's Tree, which sounds Indian to me. No one seems to know the origin of the name."

Crinkles appeared around Mr. Byrne's eyes. "Ted, if just a couple of Catahoula people could prove they had Native American heritage, they'd have money jingling in their pockets! We'd have another casino right there at the Lake."

I needed a laugh.

"So, you started your investigation right away, Saturday night?"

"Yes, we did. SO—the Sheriff's Office—beeped me about five-thirty. I got out to the lake around six fifteen, at the same time our fast boat returned to my father-in-law's dock with the body of the woman. Lorraine and I began to work the case. I took statements from Armand and from the deputies who brought in the body. I even questioned André. I wrote up what he said and could make it into a sworn statement, but I don't plan to get him to sign unless you think it's necessary."

"No. No need for that unless he said something different from his grandfather."

"He tells the same story. Lorraine and I went to the morgue at Iberia General in New Iberia to observe the autopsy. Mr. Byrne, I'll never forget seeing the little body on the end of the table. Perfect. I felt sick."

Mr. Byrne wrote something on his pad.

I told him Lorraine had photographed the coroner at work. We picked up the physical evidence—shreds of cloth, a piece of rope, bits of the burlap sack, a lock of hair—and went back to the station to secure the bags in our evidence locker. I ran the missing persons' database looking for a match. No luck.

"Lorraine and I were working by ourselves at first, but when Docelia—Chief of the City Police, Docelia Smart— heard the news on the wire, she came over. She had important information for us. Do you know Docelia?"

He didn't.

"You will. She's as good as her name, Smart. The city of St. Martinville had the first contact with the case. Last Thursday two women came into the police station. Do you know about that?"

"No. Tell me."

"Sisters-in-law, Sonja and Elena Trudeau. They were worried about their friend Virtua Cane who hadn't shown up for church duties for two days. The friend was eight months pregnant. The guy who was on the desk when the sisters came in, a fairly new hire named Chad something or other, called the woman's husband."

Mr. Byrne interrupted, with a smile on his face. "Chad? A month ago, a city policeman named Chad gave my granddaughter a ticket for going six miles over the speed limit in the St. Martinville city limits. Do you recall the last line on a traffic ticket that asks for *Disposition*? I suppose that's for how the citation eventually gets resolved. This Chad guy had written in *Good*. Now my granddaughter has a certificate testifying to her good humor!"

"I like it! Chad doesn't have a fancy education, but he

handled this case by the book. He called the woman's house. The husband answered and said his wife had gone to North Louisiana to visit her family. Then Saturday morning the husband called in to say he found out his wife hadn't gone to her family. She was missing. Chad passed the information to Chief Smart.

"Saturday night, Chief Smart picked up on the wire the discovery of the body of a pregnant woman in Catahoula Lake. She came right over to the Sheriff's Office and we put the woman's name and description on the wire. We started thinking about questioning the husband, maybe even getting a search warrant, but unfortunately, we couldn't reach Tony Blendera, the ADA who's supposed to be in charge of the St. Martin office."

Mr. Byrne frowned. "That's the problem Mr. Strait is addressing by shipping me over here."

"Mr. Strait is right, as usual. We need a full-time DA here. At any rate, shortly before two a.m., I decided to call it a day and crank up the investigation again this morning. I went home to bed. This morning Lorraine and I got called off the case. End of story. You'll have to get the next chapter from someone else."

Camille Byrne appeared in the doorway, a questioning look on her face. Mr. Byrne told her we were fine. We didn't need anything else. She disappeared in the house.

Mr. Byrne had a question for me about the new sheriff.

"Tell me, detective, how did Gabrielle Chevalier do as Sheriff-Elect? She's been on the job as interim for over four months now. You must have a pretty good idea what she'll be like."

"With me, other than this recent situation, she's doing just fine. But then I'm used to her. I took some of her classes years ago when I went to UL. Actually, I met Eugénie in her class."

I didn't pass on that the deputies did a good bit of eye rolling and talk behind her back. Some of them came right out and said a woman can't do the top job. And on occasion Chief Deputy Roland had been known to refer to her as *our egg-head b--*. The word he didn't say was not boss.

"Is it true our Sheriff-Elect comes to us with no practical law enforcement experience?" Mr. Byrne asked.

"Zero, except maybe what comes with her genes. She has lots of theories she's read in books. Thinking I can't be professional in a case involving my son is one theory I can't understand. What do you think about that?"

"I'm not going to start off on the wrong foot by second guessing your boss, Ted. You'll just have to watch this investigation and not be directly involved. If we get Deuce on the job…"

"That would help a hell of a lot, Mr. Byrne. I'm glad Detective Martin Castille can take Plug to help out in New York City after nine-eleven, but he's left a hole in our ranks. If Deuce comes on over… For that matter, if you come give us a hand…"

Half a smile. "I haven't given Mr. Strait the final OK, but I think you'll have me in St. Martin for a while."

I felt better already. He and Deuce would be welcome additions to our ranks.

"Tell me about Detective Castille and his dogs, Ted. I've had him testifying on my cases in Iberia Parish many times, but they were all drug cases. They don't need a drug dog at Ground Zero."

"You haven't met Plug? He's trained as a *cadaver dog*. Martin got him as a pup eight, nine months ago. You should hear Martin talk about how Plug can detect human smell, dead or alive, hidden anywhere, even under water."

"I'd like to see him do that."

"We didn't have Plug when Eugénie first disappeared. Or when that homeless guy walked into the Police Station with the skull of the newborn baby." Mr. Byrne tilted his head and lowered one eyebrow. "You missed that one?" I asked.

"I must have. Tell me."

"One bright morning last summer, a homeless man appeared at the City Police Station. You know where that is? Behind the church, next to the museum? He carried a bundle. They all do, you know, carry their earthly possessions with them everywhere. He unties his bundle and pulls out something wrapped up tight in an old T-shirt. He lays the shirt package on the counter. He loosens the shirt and lifts something out. A little skull."

"I'll be damned!"

"The cops wouldn't let him have his T-shirt back. Might be evidence, they told him. Poor guy. For doing his civic duty he's short one item of his wardrobe. And you can bet he didn't have much to start with."

"Did the guy say where he found the skull?"

"Evangeline Park. Where he spent the night. Everybody in the police station freaked out. Docelia got the skull to the coroner who pronounced it a newborn baby, probably full term. They never found the rest of the body or the woman who gave birth."

"And I guess they had no idea how long the skull had been there in the park."

"Nope." I checked my watch. "I've been out of touch all morning, Mr. Byrne. I need to get back."

"I'm sorry for taking up so much of your time. Give me your beeper number. I'll contact you tomorrow after the ceremony."

I laughed at that request. "Oh, no! You haven't heard my assignment? The Sheriff and Mr. Strait want me to be your tour guide to St. Martin Parish—starting tomorrow for the swearing-in of Sheriff Chevalier. Mr. Strait told me to firm up details with your wife."

That made Mr. Byrne laugh with me. "Mr. Strait has the picture. I go where I'm told. Call Camille tonight, Ted. When she left us a while ago she no doubt put a smock over her Sunday clothes and picked up her brushes and her palette. She's probably now down by the Bayou getting a head start on her Sunday afternoon painting.

3

The Byrnes parked on the street behind St. Martin de Tours Catholic Church and walked through the old cemetery. I met them by the statue of Evangeline. As instructed, I had settled the time and place for our meeting with Mrs. Byrne. She shook her head and mumbled in exasperation.

"We almost didn't make it, Ted. Dennis had eleven stuck in his head. I caught him at the back door ready to walk to his office at the Iberia Parish Courthouse to get in an hour of work before the ceremony." Mrs. Byrne pulled the printed invitation from her purse and read aloud. "Installation of Gabrielle Chevalier, Sheriff of the Parish of St. Martin, 11 a.m., St. Martin Parish Courthouse." Then she read the line below. "Preceded by Mass, St. Martin de Tours Catholic Church, 10 a.m. Procession will form on the lawn at 9:45. Can you believe it? Dennis never read what had been staring at him from the refrigerator door for over a week."

The rebuke just rolled off Mr. Byrne. "As ever, my dear, I thank you for keeping me socially correct. And you're looking particularly lovely this morning. I don't think I've seen that smart suit since the General's farewell reception for us in Madrid."

"Pshaw. Flattery, flattery." Clearly, the exchange between these two was nothing new. And the flattery worked. Mrs. Byrne didn't mention her pique again.

Mrs. Byrne moved over to look more closely at the grave of Emmeline LaBiche, the legendary Evangeline. "There she is, sitting here waiting for her lover, Gabriel, to come floating by on the bayou. So sad!"

That's what people were starting to say to me. So sad.

"Do you know how that statue came to be here?" I asked

Mrs. Byrne.

"No, I don't."

"Delores del Rio starred in a movie made from Longfellow's poem. They filmed it right here in St. Martin Parish. When they finished filming, she gave the statue as a gift to the town. But let's go on inside. We should be in our places before the arrival of dignitaries."

St. Martin de Tours Catholic Church sits in the center of downtown St. Martinville—the heart of the town in more ways than one. It's one of the oldest churches in America. The lovely Romanesque exterior is as unpretentious as the Acadians who first worshiped on the spot. We entered through the center door. *Established 1765* read the inscription set in a marble disk in the floor at the head of the center aisle.

Mr. Byrne noticed the date. "1765! That's before we were an independent country."

Softly tinted plaster statues adorn the pale walls of the interior of the church. Knee-high half-doors enclose red cypress pews. At one time the church levied an assessment on the communicants; as long as the payments came in on time, the family name could be inscribed on the end of a pew. This morning, white ribbons reserved the first two dozen rows for visiting dignitaries.

We turned away from the center aisle and found seats in the left transept, facing a twenty-foot high reproduction of the Grotto of Lourdes. Although all three of us made the sign of the cross to acknowledge the lovely replica statue of Bernadette—the young woman who heard the Virgin Mary say *I am the Immaculate Conception*—I overheard Mr. Byrne mumbling to his wife.

"That pock-marked wall behind Bernadette bears little resemblance to the stone grotto I remember from our travels in France. Do you suppose someone threw a bushel of peanut shells up on a surface covered with Gorilla glue?"

Mrs. Byrne poked her husband in the ribs with her elbow.

To the strains of Purcell's Trumpet Voluntary, the robed

judges, a dozen sheriffs from throughout the state, the St. Martin Parish Sheriff's deputies in their dress uniforms, the soon-to-be Sheriff of St. Martin Parish, and then the cross and clergy, made their way up the center aisle. The Mass began. Mr. Strait read one lesson; the president of the St. Martin Parish Police Jury read the other. From the high pulpit, Monsignor Richard from St. John's Cathedral in Lafayette read the Gospel and delivered the homily. He assured all souls present that Sheriff Gabrielle Chevalier, descendant of a Commandant assigned to the Poste des Attakapas who brought the faith to the heathen Attakapas Indians, would uphold the fine Catholic qualities exemplified during the tenure of her late father.

Catholic Acadiana has its own concept of the appropriate relationship between church and state.

During the recessional hymn, Mrs. Byrne whispered a request. "Ted, if we have a moment before going to the swearing-in, could we take a closer look at the painting over the altar? It really is stunning."

We walked forward. Mrs. Byrne studied the canvas, then stepped back and gave her review. "Nice, don't you think? Very European. Not many churches in the new world have paintings over the altar. The Roman soldier Martinus holds his sword aloft, ready to rend his crimson cloak to give half to the beggar shivering at his side. A circular composition. The figures of the soldier, his snow-white steed, and the beggar curve against a dark background. The canvas appears to be lit by the shimmer of the brass vessels and candlesticks on the altar below. Beautiful."

I don't have an artist's eye and never really noticed anything more than the soldier on horseback who, they tell me, would become St. Martin of Tours.

Outside the church, we joined Mr. Strait—alone because he was at the moment between wives—and walked the few blocks to the parish courthouse. The State of Louisiana has four courthouses built before the War Between the States. I don't know which one is the oldest, but this one must be the loveliest. Unfortunately, in dire need of modernization. I'd heard a long overdue renovation was in the offing. Mrs. Byrne stopped to admire the tall Ionic columns. No time, I told her, and urged my charges inside.

Judge Mari Johnson presided over the ceremony. She called Mr. Strait and Gabrielle Chevalier forward. She wore a sheriff's uniform for the first time. District Attorney Gerald Strait stood at her left. On her right, her husband and her teenage daughter held a large, well-worn Bible. She raised her right hand. Following the prompts from Mr. Strait, Gabrielle Chevalier swore to uphold the Constitution and laws of the United States and the Constitution and laws of the State of Louisiana. Judge Johnson made appropriate congratulatory remarks and the new sheriff thanked everyone for coming. Mrs. Byrne beamed, no doubt nostalgic for the countless ceremonies she had attended during their military years.

Mr. Byrne raised his chin and gave his wife a leprechaun's smile.

"My dear, I'm certainly glad you got me to the church for the Mass before the swearing-in. Otherwise, you'd have dressed to the nines for a ten-minute event."

At the bottom of the front steps, on the sidewalk, Mr. Strait and Roy Angelle, President of the Police Jury, stood gazing at the facade of the courthouse. Each held the corner of a blue paper roll of an architect's building plans. President Angelle spoke.

"When we're done, other than a new coat of paint, the building will look almost unchanged. I promise you'll not be able to tell we've added another courtroom, doubled the size of the offices of the District Attorney and moved them downstairs to the area now occupied by the Clerk of Court. The Clerk gets a brand new building in the rear."

"And may I assume the courthouse will still be white?" Mr. Strait inquired with mischief in his eyes.

"Damn right it'll be white. You think I'm a slow learner? Now I know better than to agree to change the color of the exterior of this building."

I knew the story. Ten years ago, the parish received a generous grant of federal restoration dollars to renovate the courthouse offices, weatherproof the exterior, and rewire the building for computers. Badly needed improvements. The *quid pro quo*? They were obligated to paint the building the so-called 'original color.' A Washington preservationist who examined a chip from an exterior wall said the original color had been beige. President Angelle said taking the money with an obligation to paint the building beige was the worst mistake he'd ever made in his political career. For three years, protesters showed up at every meeting of the Parish Council loudly demanding white paint to cover the dirty brown.

"How can people care so much about the outside color of a building?" the Police Jury President asked.

"How about the outside color of humans?" Mr. Strait added. "But the complainers got their way, right? You repainted the building?"

"Eventually. We had to wait a decent interval. We just couldn't afford to give back a million bucks."

Mrs. Byrne wanted to stay for lemonade and sandwiches after the swearing-in, but her husband told her they didn't have time. He needed to take his wife home and get back to meet Mr. Strait at one-thirty. Dennis Byrne paid attention to time when an appointment concerned his work.

*   *   *

Mr. Byrne and I walked into the library in the St. Martin DA's office at one-thirty sharp. Detective Deuce Washington was already there, which must have meant his boss had approved his transfer to St. Martin Parish. Good. Deuce introduced Mr. Byrne to the City of St. Martinville law enforcement pair in the room—Chief of Police Docelia Smart and Sgt. Chad Broussard.

I flipped the pages of the notebook I carried and handed it to Deuce. "Here's what Lorraine and I stayed up half of Saturday night putting together. Statements, reports, a list of the physical evidence I signed into the locker. I'll be glad to answer any questions you may have. Who's going to be your partner for the Catahoula investigation?"

Deuce's broad brown face opened in a great smile. "I

think our new sheriff is a diplomat. So as not to cause a family fight by choosing someone from your office, she got Chief Smart away from the City. Looks like we'll have three loaners on the investigation—me and Mr. Byrne from Iberia Parish and Chief Smart from the City of St. Martinville."

Sheriff Gabrielle and Mr. Strait came through the door. Mr. Strait cast his first smile of greeting in the direction of Mr. Byrne and got right to the point.

"Are you on for this, Dennis?" he asked.

"Yes, sir."

Of course, he was. Mr. Byrne couldn't resist handling a serious felony. Maybe even a first-degree murder.

Mr. Strait took a seat at the head of the table. This room might now be Mr. Byrne's office, and Deuce Washington might be the lead investigator on the case in question, but with District Attorney Gerald Strait in a room, he took over.

"As you all now know, Mr. Byrne will be running this office for the foreseeable future. If you need a District Attorney, he's your man." He turned to the new sheriff. "Sheriff Chevalier, Detective Deuce Washington is in charge of the investigation into the Catahoula Lake floater, correct?"

"Yes, sir. And I thank you for working everything out with the Iberia Sheriff."

"Happy to do so. Deuce will be working with Chief Smart as his partner. Are you OK with that, Sheriff?" Mr. Strait asked.

"Yes, I am," said the Sheriff. "I look forward to being able to return the favor. We're recruiting more officers even as we speak."

Mr. Strait turned to me. "Ted, since we're all together here, and you had first contact with the case, perhaps you would give us your report."

I repeated what I had told Mr. Byrne Sunday morning. The call from the sheriff pulling us off the case came at six a.m. *Finis*.

Mr. Strait next called on Chief of Police Docelia Smart. Short cropped graying hair, biceps bulging under her shirt-sleeves, brogans on her feet, someone not to be toyed with.

And that husky voice! She gave her report.

"Last Thursday we received a call at the station from one Sonja Trudeau. She said her friend, name Virtua Cane, had gone missing. Ms. Trudeau had expected Virtua at their church to help with an upcoming rummage sale. When Virtua didn't show, Sonja went by her house. Nobody home. She gave a nod to the young patrolman at her side. "Chad Broussard, just a few months on the job at the City, took the call. He wrote up Sonja Trudeau's description of the missing person, took down something of the circumstances, but went into delay mode. Even from his scant experience, Chad knows it's wise to drag your feet a bit before setting a search in motion. Most 'missing persons' turn up within a few hours."

Sgt. Broussard puffed up hearing the *attaboy* from his boss.

"Chad suggested Sonja go by the house again in a few hours to see if her friend had returned. Sonja didn't want to do that on her own. On Friday, she and her sister-in-law Elena Trudeau came into the station again. Describe the women for us, Chad."

Sgt. Broussard swallowed hard before speaking, his Adam's apple traveling a good two inches up and then down. To me, he looked barely out of his teens. Funny the way we males mature, one part of the body before the other. Sgt. Broussard had yet to grow up to his neck.

"I looked through the glass and saw them there, a matched pair. Longish dresses, same printed material, same heavy black shoes set one against the other, hands folded on their laps. They both had long hair wrapped into a loose ball at the back of the neck. Not the usual persons who come in to report a crime."

Sgt. Broussard looked around to see if he still had the floor. All eyes were on him. He flushed.

"When Virtua hadn't shown up at the church on Friday morning, the pair checked her house. No Virtua and no kids. Sonja told me Virtua's husband is the Assistant Manager at the Piggly-Wiggly Market. You know where that is, Mr.

Strait? West Main Street, just inside the city limits. I offered to go there with the sisters-in-law, but they begged me to go by myself. They appeared to be kind of afraid of their friend's husband.

"I found Virtua's husband, Robert Cane—that's his name, Robert Cane—in the produce department. No problem, Cane said. His wife had gone to North Louisiana to visit her family. The children stayed in St. Martinville with his sister. I went back to the station and told the Trudeaus that everything seemed OK. They went on their way. Then Saturday morning Mr. Cane himself called in. He was worried now. His wife was not with her family and she had not come home. I issued the BOLO: *Be on the Lookout for White Female, twenty-five years of age, eight months pregnant.* Saturday night Armand Boudreaux and his grandson ran their bateau into the body of the woman now tentatively identified as the same Virtua Cane." Sgt. Broussard handed his report to Mr. Byrne.

"Your thoughts, Chief?" Mr. Strait asked Docelia.

"Unexplained death of anyone, look first at the spouse. I say we bring Mr. Cane in for questioning and get a search warrant for their house."

Mr. Strait frowned. "And your *p.c.*, probable cause, for a warrant?"

"Well…"

"I think we need a bit more, Chief Smart. You could go talk to Cane. He just might give you permission to search his house. It's amazing how often people say yes." Mr. Strait stood up. "But look to Mr. Byrne for guidance from now on. I'm on my way."

The intercom buzzed. Mr. Byrne looked around before realizing he controlled the turf. He picked up the phone. "Byrne here." After a moment, he said, "Send Mr. Blendera on in."

My God! So, now the District Attorney who's supposed to come from St. Mary Parish shows up to help us? Not acceptable. You can't put together a probable homicide case with a part-time DA.

"I'm on my way," Mr. Strait said, throwing a line to Mr.

Byrne as he left the room. "You're in charge here, Dennis." Sheriff Chevalier followed Mr. Strait out the door, passing Tony Blendera on his way in. With a wave of her hand, Docelia dismissed Sgt. Broussard as well.

Deuce, Docelia and Tony started to dig into the papers on the table. I should have left at that point, but until someone told me to leave, I'd sit still and try not to be noticed.

"I'm reading your report, Chief Smart," Mr. Byrne said. "It was Sunday, after the body had been discovered, that you went back to the Piggly-Wiggly to talk to Robert Cane. Right? Fill us in on that visit, if you would."

"Sure. Chad and I found Deke Champagne, the manager of the Piggly-Wiggly, standing on an observation platform at the front of the store. The pulpit he called it. Shiny black pants a couple inches too short, knit shirt with a silly looking pig dancing on the front."

Mr. Byrne enjoyed Docelia's fashion critique.

"We asked him if Robert Cane had come to work. He said yes, his eyes all the while focusing on something over our shoulders. I thought him rude until I realized he listened to our questions and at the same time kept watch on a wide-bodied lady who strolled the aisle in "Meat and Fish." Her commodious dress offered a handy hiding place for packages of Savoie's smoked sausage she appeared to be examining with unusual care.

"Robert Cane clocked in a little late, Deke said. Deke was really surprised he'd come in at all, his wife found dead and everything. Deke said we would find Cane over in Produce.

"We found him there, a medium height, pleasant-faced white man, late twenties at the most, demonstrating to a stock boy the fine art of stacking bananas on a rotary bin. He meticulously arrayed bunches around a center disk, arching the fruit outward like the petals of a flower. A chrysanthemum, I guess. Pretty cool."

"So, he wasn't too upset, you'd say?" Mr. Byrne asked.

"Not at all. And Deke had told us that the week before, when his wife was missing, Cane came in for all his shifts. We asked Cane a few questions. He gave the same version of events he told Sonja Trudeau and her sister-in-law. He said his two children were spending the night with his sister. Thursday morning, he left his wife sleeping when he went to work. He came home Thursday night to an empty house. He said he hadn't been worried because he assumed his wife had made a long-planned visit to her family. But on Saturday, when she hadn't returned, he checked with her family and they had not seen her. Cane claimed to have no idea what could have caused her to end up in Catahoula Lake."

Docelia turned to me. "What do you think, Ted? You picked up the piece of dress material and the burlap sack from the autopsy. Do you think we have enough to ask for a search warrant to look for similar stuff at his house?"

Damn. I wish she hadn't said my name and called attention to my presence. Mr. Byrne raised his eyebrows, and the now familiar lines appeared across his forehead.

"Not my call, guys," I said. "I'll see y'all later."

4

Two stacks of incident reports lay on the surface of my desk. A post-it note on each stack had Chief Roland's initials and the words *Ask Me*. Leafing through the reports, I saw that every one detailed a burglary. Crap! Burglary cases bore the gizzard out of me. But as instructed, I picked up a stack and went down the hall to Chief's office.

"I know, I know. You hate to work burglaries. But burglary affects more of the citizens we serve than the handful of homicides we deal with each year. Probably twenty-five times as many. Our clearance rate is hovering around ten percent, and we're taking heat."

"Victims just don't understand, Chief. They expect us to find fingerprints at a crime scene and pick up a perp before sunrise. Doesn't happen. Unlike on TV, we rarely get good prints from the field. Anybody can buy a pair of garden gloves at the Dollar Store for a couple of bucks. Even barehanded, few burglars touch a surface that preserves a print. The textured covers on most electronics give them a pass. And if we do get some evidence we can turn over to the prosecution, I know the fate that awaits. No convictions. Good defense attorneys let a jury know the interpretation of fingerprint and hair follicle evidence has never been tested to the rigorous standards now routine for DNA. We just make a show with our kits of talcum powder and a brush."

Which made me think about the cloud of powder the techs left behind when they processed Eugénie's car. My fellow detectives worked extra hard because of me and because Eugénie was a probation officer. They only picked up twenty-four readable prints. They identified every print as Eugénie's, André's, mine, or those of Nicole, her partner. Like any victim, I couldn't accept their conclusion. I spent a good three days, on my own, trying unsuccessfully to bring up at least one partial print of a stranger to run through the records. No success.

Chief scratched his chin. "I've got a thought, Ted. Sheriff Gabrielle has to make the rounds the civic clubs to introduce herself. She asked me to think of a topic for her to talk about. Maybe she could give them a heads up on the problem? You could go with her in case she needs to supply credible details."

"Sure. I can do that."

"But in the meanwhile…"

"OK, OK. In the meanwhile, I should get with it."

From beyond the grave, I heard my first-grade teacher Sister Hélène tapping her ruler on my desk. *Teddy D'Aquin, where is it written you're so special? Sit down and do your work.* OK, Sister. Will do. My work right now is to process these burglaries.

I returned to my office and dug in. Whatever personal problems I might have—like a good dose of feeling sorry for myself for having been removed from the Catahoula homicide—the victims whose reports sat on my desk deserved my best effort. Pique about the assignment I'd been given paled before the real pain in my life.

I walked a high wire in the first months after Eugénie disappeared, balancing management of the frantic search with an attempt to keep some semblance of a normal home for André. Nightmares about what could have happened to my wife haunted my sleep, and André's as well. During the day, I would think I had myself under control only to get an unexpected memory blast like a barrage of gunfire from around the corner.

As time wore on, I had to consider that Eugénie might never again be here in this life with me. The sharp stings of loss gave way to a dull ache of depression. And loneliness. My stupid indiscretion with Eugénie's former partner Nicole happened about the same time I passed from one stage of grief to another. Cause? Effect? Mere coincidence? I couldn't say. Definitely stupid, for sure. No, worse than stupid. Selfish and cruel.

To stop beating myself up about what happened, I pulled my chair closer to the desk, took a deep breath, and dug into the first stack of incident reports.

Chief Deputy Sheriff Allan Roland is good for a lot more than politics. I quickly realized he'd picked up two common themes and separated the reports accordingly.

The first stack detailed larcenous activities around Pinaud Street, the area across the Bayou Teche inexplicably known to the natives as the American Side. As Mr. Byrne's guide to the idiosyncrasies of St. Martin Parish, I'd have to tell him about that designation—inexplicable because the City of St. Martinville has no rigid ethnic divisions. Descendants of Africa—whether of slave ancestry or Free People of Color, as they were once referred to—live on many of the same streets as those who trace their heritage to England or to France. And although the French descendants have been known to harbor prideful distinctions if their forefathers (not usually foremothers) came here with the original Commandants des Attakapas or with the high-born refugees from Napoleon's time rather than with the country folk of the Acadian diaspora, in St. Martin Parish they intermarry and live side-by-side. Then there's a sprinkling of the descendants of Italian and German immigrants and oil business Texans in our mix as well.

Over the past months, people on the left bank of the Bayou Teche had awakened to find their small lawn mowers, weed-eaters, hand tools—anything portable and able to be fenced—missing from carports and unlocked garages. If I went out and canvased the pawnshops, I'd find an assortment of similar goods, but no pawnshop keeps reliable records of the provenance of the small stuff. And what household could prove ownership anyway? No one writes down the serial number of a weed-eater.

How could I crack these cases? Perhaps an operating surveillance camera on the funeral home or the adjacent mausoleum across the bayou had captured the burglars at work. I made a few calls—without success. Shutting the barn door after the proverbial horses had fled would be better than nothing. I called Henri Bienvenu at *The Teche News* and asked him to run a public service announcement in the weekly paper. He obliged. The next issue would carry a two-column notice in a bold box on the front page. *Citizens Take Note. Secure your outdoor equipment. Remember to lock your cars and trucks.*

I tackled the second pile of reports. The common element in these cases was the target—unoccupied camps on the levee. These cases had a fair chance of being solved. Maybe as high as a fifty percent chance. I could forget about tracing the missing food and beer—the miscreants would have digested the edibles days ago—but three of the camp owners had recorded the serial numbers of their TV sets and guns. I put the numbers out on the wire. But most of the perps would probably be juveniles who fenced the product of their nightly raids the following day. If we caught them, they wouldn't return the items because they couldn't. The haul would have passed through a half-dozen hands. They probably wouldn't even serve a day in juvie.

A better bet for cracking both stacks of burglaries would be an informant. The draconian penalties facing a poor schmuck found with a few baggies of weed had a way of making a handcuffed bird sing like a canary. I gave our narcs a call for help. I gave them descriptions and serial numbers of the missing guns and TV sets, and told them I might be able to arrange favorable treatment for someone who could, and would, give us some 'help.'

"When you suit up for work tonight, guys, keep your eyes and ears open for someone who might have information we could use."

Which made me remember the time a state trooper stopped Willie Nelson's tour bus for erratic driving on I-10 in north St. Martin Parish. The Trooper found five pounds of weed stashed under Willie's guitar. Five pounds is a hell of a lot of grass. After getting Willie's autograph, the star-struck state trooper chose to accept Willie's story: the stash was all for his *personal use*. The resulting charge? A misdemeanor citation for simple possession. Two months later, a high-priced lawyer flew in from California to arrange a plea—six months in the parish jail, suspended, to be expunged if Willie didn't bring drugs into the parish during the next two years. I guess Willie had to detour around St. Martin Parish for a while, or maybe just be sure he had a driver who didn't sample the cargo.

My mind kept slipping back to something I really cared about—how Deuce and Docelia were going to get Robert Cane to give them permission to search his house. Now if I were in charge of that homicide investigation… In my head, I ran the narrative of my well-practiced good-cop/bad cop routine. I'd be the good cop, of course. After some harsh words from one of my buddies, my practiced amiability would lull Robert Cane into talking too much. He'd tell me to go right ahead and make myself at home.

Damn my new boss' notions of best practice! I want to go back to investigating homicides.

And then I saw a couple of papers by themselves under a calendar on a back corner of my desk. A note on these papers read: *Give me your thoughts ASAP.* Three complaint forms asked the District Attorney to do something about vote buying and public intimidation of election officials in the recent sheriff's election.

I made another trip down the hall to Chief Roland's office.

"What's this all about, Chief? We can't be impartial investigators of the complaints about the sheriff's election? No way. We're deputies in the same department. That's a kind of conflict of interest I do understand."

The political campaign to elect Sheriff Gabrielle had been brutal. Several men previously deterred from running against *The Man* by his tentacles of power had seen opportunity. Only by pulling out all the political tricks honed in the land of Huey Long and Edwin Edwards were Chief Roland and the Warden successful in getting Gabrielle Chevalier elected on the first ballot—saving their jobs and mine. Was I supposed to investigate them?

Chief Roland tipped his chair back and folded his hands over his belly.

"A few years ago, the US Justice Department came to town to monitor a statewide election for alleged violations of the voting rights of minorities. Those earnest, wet-behind-the-ears, East Coast types were no match for us. Federal election monitors sat at the polls all day long and never had a clue about what was really going on.

"First problem: the monitors only came for Election Day. Half of any 'encouragement' to vote is past history by then. Wily candidates lease any number of vans for the days of absentee or early voting held two weeks prior. Hired drivers pick up passengers around the parish—so-say a necessity because country people lack transportation although every one of them manages to get to Walmart at least once a week. The drivers pass out the ballot numbers of favored candidates and deliver the voters to the courthouse. The play runs again on Election Day. When the drivers complete the deliveries, they report to a certain spot for their reward: barbequed chicken, beer, and a little more money as *lagniappe*. You can drive around the parish on election night and see the cookout fires burning. Truth be told, few African-American or poor white voters were being deprived of their votes. Some were well compensated for marking their ballots as instructed."

"I did hear tell someone pulled a new trick for this election. One of our supporters infiltrated the enemy camp, hosted an all-day *boucherie* with an ample supply of the usual liquid fare, and invited a bunch of the opposition's drivers. They got so sloshed they couldn't take their routes."

"Tsk, tsk. Isn't disgraceful! I say we turn these complaints over to the Feds and let them try to figure out how to charge anyone with a voting rights violation for that!"

"Right, Chief. They'd send another newbie fresh out of the Ivy League to do an investigation. He'd never figure us out.

Enough already. I left the office a half hour before the usual quitting time so I could pick up André in Catahoula and get him back to town for the end-of-the-summer season All-Star baseball game at six o'clock.

I pulled into my in-laws' shell drive shortly after five and parked behind a mid-size truck I didn't recognize.

Down by the lakeshore, André and his grandfather were just docking the bateau. Smiling from ear to ear beneath his straw hat, looking like Huck Finn himself, my boy held up a string of catfish for me to admire. He motioned to a table next to a water hose leading out from under the porch. André and his Grampa were about to clean their catch. Not anxious to have a hand in that operation—and smell fishy all during the ball game—I gave them a wave and climbed the concrete steps to say hi to André's grandmother, Maman.

A wide screened porch stretches around three sides of my in-laws' house. Deep on the side away from the lake, I saw the back of someone I didn't recognize—a woman facing Maman across a little wooden table. I first thought she was a friend come to pass the afternoon. No. A printed scarf wrapped Maman's head and the table display between the two of them told me otherwise. Damn. Maman was up to her old tricks.

Blood rushed to my cheeks. Maman had spread out the paraphernalia of her trade: a couple dozen bottles of assorted sizes, each partially filled with murky water; a blue carton of table salt labeled When It Rains It Pours; several bunches of leafy stalks; a pile of bare roots. A hand-lettered placard faced her guest—and my eyes. *Home Remedies Are No Replacement for Competent Medical Care.* A legal disclaimer, no less. Crap! Maman was treating again. She had promised me she wouldn't treat when André visited.

I felt my blood pressure rise, but then I looked past the porch to see André and his Grampa bent over the fish-cleaning table. Wide smiles lit up their faces as they went about what to most people is a nasty job. My initial anger faded into resignation. There was no place on earth my boy would rather be than here at Catahoula Lake with his Grampa. I'd take up the topic of Maman's foolishness with my father-in-law Armand on another day.

Should I tell André not to mention Maman's activities to his other grandmother, my mother? If she got wind of it, she'd have a fit. What do you expect from country Cajuns, she'd say? If André hadn't seen Maman's customer, I'd just be calling attention. André and I were halfway back to town before one-half of my head stopped arguing with the other half, and my pulse slowed to normal.

André is a natural ball-player. He'd started to toss around Styrofoam balls before he could walk. That night, in the All-Star game, he made a key play in the sixth—and last—inning. He caught a line drive, moved the ball to his bare hand—he's a lefty—and nailed it to the first baseman for a game-winning double play. André may have smelled like fish, but the coach wouldn't say a word about the pungent odor of his best utility infielder.

One day after I had returned to my regular detective duty at the sheriff's office, I had time off. André begged me to drop him at his Grampa's for the day. I agreed. With school around the corner, he'd soon have fewer afternoons for fishing. Special Assistant District Attorney Dennis Byrne seemed to be serious about his offer to help the investigation for my missing wife. A clear morning meant I could get back to the probation office and put together material to show him. I told André I'd try to get off early and join him at the Lake when the day's heat had cooled.

But… If I went to the probation office, I might run into Nicole. Oh, God. For the umpteenth time, I reviewed what had happened between us. It didn't get any better for the repetition. I'd been stupid, weak, foolish—lots more. Nicole, Eugénie's former partner, had been a terrific help in my search, and I'd blown it. I was an idiot. Since that night, we hadn't seen each other—even to say hello. Three weeks tomorrow.

That day, the day I was so stupid and selfish, I'd had a long, rainy trip back from north Louisiana. I'd looked at one more unidentified body I knew at first glance was not my Eugénie. I had a headache, yes, but the real ailment was smothering exhaustion. I came to a decision. No more physically running down every report that came my way. When some jurisdiction had an unidentified body of a woman, I'd give their investigation time to run its course.

Nicole worked late that day also. I poured out my frustration to her, and my decision to give the field trips a rest. I suggested we go to my house for a beer. The evening started with a beer and a hug for comfort. It didn't end that way. Not at all. I can't explain how the situation got out of hand. I'd been an animal. I hit my all-time low the following morning when I saw blood on the sheets. A spasm of nausea cut off my breath. Nicole, ten years younger, her first job, I had no business taking advantage. I absolutely had to apologize.

Several times I'd gone to the Probation office with firm resolution to do so, only to be relieved when I didn't find her at her desk. I told myself I'd run her down when André would be back in school. And maybe, just maybe, she'd forgive me and we could work together again.

If I didn't feel bad enough about taking Nicole to bed, Eugénie's and my bed at that, the reality of Eugénie herself had begun to dim. I no longer saw her in every corner of the house, sitting next to me in my car, hiking with me through the Kisatchie woods. Unlike in the beginning, Eugénie wasn't the vision that flashed across my consciousness every time a barking dog woke me in the night. Sometimes I even had the thought that I wasn't searching to find her but to reach certainty so I could go on with my life—and hated myself for having such thoughts. Damn.

I parked behind the probation office building and used the card they'd given me to enter the back door. The card was a real favor. The high security at the front is a hassle—and ludicrous since probation officers are required to meet their probationers—criminals every one—out in the field.

The office Eugénie's boss provided for me lay immediately inside the back entrance. I didn't settle in at my desk right away. I took a deep breath and walked toward the front. *Just getting a cup of coffee*, I planned to say if anyone should ask. I passed Eugénie's old station—still empty—and

looked farther into the room to what had been her first desk.
Nicole sat there. I know Nicole saw me but she dropped her
head and glued her eyes to her papers. She didn't look up at
all when I passed her door again on the way back to my
office. That was my excuse for walking on by. Maybe I'd have
an opportunity to apologize later... Or on another day.

You Goddamned coward!

I was rapidly approaching the end of the list of
probationers Eugénie had ever supervised, way back to when
she first went to work at Probation. What would I do when I
finished investigating those last few names? Would I do what
so many urged me to do? Put the investigation on the back
burner, continue monitoring the reports coming over the
wire for possible connections, and wait for a break?

I punched the on button of my computer with enough
force to knock the keyboard onto my lap. Damn! The record
of Devon Washington, one of Eugénie's very first cases, pre-
dated our computer records. I would have to go back up to
the file room to try to locate the paper file. Nicole had the
phone at her ear. She didn't acknowledge my passing.

Devon Washington had been convicted of unauthorized
use of a motor vehicle. He'd stolen his grandmother's car and
wrecked it. Three years suspended, three years probation. The
address of the victim rang a bell. Catahoula Highway, close to
the pepper plant Eugénie visited on her last day at work.
Hope ticked up my pulse rate. Maybe at last? I flipped the
pages looking for disposition of the probation.

And found it. *Closed sat /June 12, 2007.* But wait? Why
the closure so early in probation? And sat—satisfactorily?
More pages and I had the answer. Devon had died. Crap. So
much for that guy. On to the next. And so it went, one name
after another.

I'd never detected any reason for someone to have a
serious grudge against my wife. Most of her probationers had
eventually finished probation satisfactorily. Two went on to
more crime and were guests of the state, but a surprising
number stayed in the area and passed successfully through
those dangerous years for poor young men—poor black

young men, that is. Most hadn't picked up any serious charges after her supervision. I tipped back my chair. Dead end. Good God, I'd be happy if Mr. Byrne had an idea of some other way to find some answers.

And I'd be happy if I could figure out how to talk to Nicole.

Almost six o'clock, I looked up to see Nicole in the doorway of my office, not leaning against one side but standing smack in middle. Stiff. Chewing the inside of her cheek. She spoke, tapping out her words as if she'd memorized a speech.

"I ran the names we worked on a few weeks ago, Ted. Nothing stood out. I made notes in the files for you. Eugénie had very simple cases her first few years."

No greeting. No "How've you been?"

"Kind of like the docket you had when you first came to work here?"

"Right."

Whew! Maybe we were just going to pretend nothing had happened between us. I couldn't ask for anything better than that.

No. Not so lucky. Nicole had more to say. But first she pushed the backs of her hands against the sides of the doorway, bracing herself. Her eyes fixed on a spot beyond my head. Her voice squeezed out of her tight throat. Tears threatened. Her voice wobbled.

"I'm totally ashamed of the way I acted the last time I saw you. I just threw myself at you. I want to apologize and tell you I won't be like that again."

My head spun. I couldn't tell at first where the pitcher had hit me with the fastball.

"What? Wait a minute, Nicole." I stood up, knocking some papers to the floor, and for a second took my eyes off the doorway. "Wait a bloody minute. *You're* apologizing? I'm the one who lost it. I want to apologize for *my* behavior."

When I looked at the doorway, Nicole had turned away. I was talking to an empty space.

And she didn't return to her office. She had disappeared.

Coward that I am, I didn't try to follow. Maybe tomorrow I'd find her and explain myself.

As I started to pack it in for the day, my cell phone buzzed. The Sheriff's Office on the line.

"Detective D'Aquin here."

"It's Chief Roland, Ted. A citizen just called in a shooting at 205 Evangeline Street. Possible 10-7. He says some yardman shot his wife and he shot the yardman. We had patrol in the area—Deputy Kevin Collins. He's fresh out of the Academy but seems to be doing everything right. Fuckin' mess in there, he says. Backup will be on the scene in less than five minutes. Be there."

My pulse quickened. A homicide! Double.

"Yes, sir. Evangeline *Street* you say? The one off Hwy 31, on the north end of St. Martinville?" There must be a half dozen streets in the parish carrying some variation of the Evangeline name: Evangeline Street, Evangeline Place, Evangeline Acres Subdivision, Rue Evangeline.

"Right. On the Gold Coast. Swing by the office and pick up Detective Badeaux on your way out there. He'll be waiting outside. You'll be case agent for this one, Ted, with Detective LaSalle as your partner. I've told her to meet you at the scene."

Real work. Thank God.

PART II

5

The call from my boss, Chief Roland, gave me a jolt. Just in time. I'd been sinking into a doze. With my cell phone between my right ear and my shoulder, I grabbed my jacket off the clothes tree in the corner. I wasn't in uniform. The big white letters on the back of the black jacket—SMPSO—St. Martin Parish Sheriff's Office—would give me cred in the field.

"Any ID on the vics?" I asked Chief.

He answered my question as I reached the door. "Probables. I'll prep you when we both get out there."

As Chief promised, Detective Spike Badeaux waited for me in the covered loading area of our new headquarters across the side street from the courthouse, cherry cheeks, bright-eyed, all five foot two of him aquiver. Detectives salivate over the initial look at a crime scene before the required paperwork smothers our zeal for pursuing the bad guys. Dead victims mean forensics teams will follow behind us with the proper supplies to document, film, and preserve the evidence. First responders have only two standing orders: secure the area and don't fuck up the scene.

"Any more details come in since I talked to Chief?" I asked Spike.

"If so, Chief didn't pass 'em on to me. My assignment is to wait for you and take orders. He told me you're the case agent on this one and Lorraine will be your partner."

Chief Roland is always clear about who's in charge of a case. Detectives tend to be prima donnas. He doesn't want to have to arbitrate issues of control.

"OK, Spike. Let's go see what we can see."

The house at 205 Evangeline Street sits fifty feet back

from the curb, at the rear of the U-shaped street curving off the highway that leads out of St. Martinville toward Parks and Breaux Bridge. The lot is at least 150 feet wide. The Bayou Teche is particularly lovely there, flowing slowly past woods on the other bank. Fifteen years ago, a local real estate developer shut down an old dairy farm on the site and created a subdivision where the milk cows used to roam. The lots sold quickly. Pleasant two story brick homes now nestle beneath the shade of hundred-year-old oaks, each house displaying well-tended shrubs and seasonal flowers. The good soil is the product of rich Mississippi River sediment overflow rather than Red River clay prevalent farther north in the parish. We don't get many calls from this area.

I passed up the concrete driveway of number 205. A black and white patrol car sat behind an eleven-year-old blue Mercury in the carport. I pulled over to the curb in front of the house of the neighbor. The rookie patrolman who had first responded here had a lesson to learn. When you're not sure what you're getting into, you place your vehicle in a get-away position. He should've parked on the street or backed into the driveway. I hoped he wouldn't learn the lesson that day, the hard way. I'd tell him, but not right now.

As I turned off the motor, two wide eyeballs in a dark face appeared at my window. I read the nametag on the chest of the uniform: *Deputy Kevin Collins*. His words sputtered out of his mouth, but he gave me precisely the information I needed to get started.

"Two dead inside there, sir. One African-American male and one white woman. As soon as I got here the homeowner walked out the door, calm as you please. White male, age 53. Name: Thomas Ernest. He says it's his w-w-wife Kitty and 'the yardman' in there. He only knows the yardman as Jubilee Joe. Ernest says Joe shot his wife and he shot Joe."

"OK. And where is this Thomas Ernest right now?"

"In the back seat of my patrol car. I read him his Miranda rights from the card and told him to sit tight. I have my eye on him, sir."

"Very good. Have you been inside the house?"

"Yes, sir. I went in just to verify what he was saying. Two bodies, all right. White woman, black man. I didn't get real close to either one. I called in the information and came out here to wait for backup."

I looked over to the house. "Which door did he come out of? The one on the side, from the carport? Or did he come out of the front door beyond?"

"Beyond. He came from the door in the center of the front porch, sir."

"Good work, Collins. I want you to take me in there to have a look."

I gave Spike an assignment I knew he wouldn't like. "Go to the car and stay with the man." His chin dropped. "Someone has to ice the witness, Spike, and I need Deputy Collins to be my guide inside." Spike followed my order. Not for nothing he had the moniker of a faithful dog.

Our new Sheriff equipped her patrol deputies with the ordinance necessary for country warfare: tear gas, bug repellant, first aid kit, radio, micro-recorder, pad and pencil, assorted small tools. Other than the pistol holstered on his right hip, Deputy Collins had attached everything he might need to the wide belt he wore bandolier-style across his chest. Deputy Collins looked like a Boy Scout and apparently believed in being prepared.

The miracle of Velcro. He pulled off a flashlight and held it in his left hand, his pistol in his right.

"Are you telling me we need a flashlight in there?" I asked.

"It'll be dark pretty soon, sir, and we shouldn't be touching any switches."

Collins led the way. Guns drawn, we walked past his black and white patrol car and into the end of the open garage. We turned left at the back fender of the Mercury and passed through the doorway into the house. The first victim lay on his right side, right at our feet.

Deputy Collins stepped carefully over a pair of dirty tennis shoes on the feet of a black man lying on his right side. I did the same. The man's one visible eyeball, not yet cloudy with death, stared up at the wall. A splotch of red jelly trailed from a hole in his head. I pulled on a pair of surgical gloves and bent down to feel for a pulse. The rising odor of stale sweat closed my throat. The poor guy had no pulse on either side of his neck.

"He's gone," I said.

Deputy Collins and I picked a path around a rifle lying parallel to the body, carefully avoiding spent shells and spots of blood spattered on the tile floor. Collins whispered the answer to my next question before I had a chance to ask it.

"I was very careful, sir. I didn't disturb anything."

Normal people whisper in the presence of death. I'd give Collins a year on the job for him to lose the awe. Maybe six months since he'd already faced a double homicide.

A right turn and then another left turn put us in a hallway running the length of the house, parallel to the street in front and the bayou behind. The sound of a TV blared from somewhere down the hall. Collins guided me in that direction, past the doorway to the kitchen on our right. A large den lay next, also on our right.

"The other one's in here, sir," he said.

At the rear of the den, two large picture windows looked out to the bayou. Between the windows, a hearth of brown roman brick displayed the body of a woman, her head flopped back into the grate in the fireplace. A purple satin mule dangled from her right big toe. Her toenail polish matched her slipper. Getting closer, I made out a dark spot bulls-eyed on her white neck. Blood oozed onto the bricks from another hole, this one in her forehead. Her open eyes gazed into eternity.

No need to feel for a pulse on this body.

"Let's make a check around the rest of the house. You lead the way, Deputy Collins."

Our guns still drawn, Collins took me on a quick tour, upstairs and down. No people, but in every room dolls—big dolls, little dolls, beribboned dolls, plain dolls, some solo and some assembled in scenes.

"What's with all the dolls, sir?" Collins asked.

"Beats me. I guess it takes all kinds."

After our quick tour, we left the house through the front door and walked out onto the porch.

"Have you got yellow crime scene tape in your unit?" I asked the deputy.

"Oh yes, sir."

"We'll be attracting a crowd. Get it out and secure the area in an arc at least thirty feet from the house. I think you can string the tape from one tree trunk to the next, about chest high. Do you know how to do that?"

"Yes, sir. We had training on that at the Academy."

An armada of law enforcement vehicles had begun to assemble on the street directly in front of the house. Sirens shrieking, blue lights flashing, a fire engine and two ambulances pulled in first. I beckoned to the EMTs who stepped out of the ambulance and asked them to follow me into the house to make my grim assessments official.

"Step where I step, guys, and be damn careful about it. We're gonna film the scene as soon as the cameras get here, then gather evidence. After that, you can remove the bodies —provided you agree with me they're both 10-7."

They verified my initial conclusions. Two dead.

A Jeep pulled up, Chief Roland at the wheel. Sheriff Chevalier stepped out of the passenger side. Chief said the videographer and the crime lab van were right behind him and that Deuce was on his way to give us a hand. I'm always glad when Deuce Washington is on my crime scenes. I appreciate that Chief gets me whatever support I need, but then lets me run the show.

"We'll put Deuce in charge of the yard. Chief, keep an eye on the spectators until he arrives. I'm going over to talk to this Ernest fellow, the homeowner. When the crew is all here, we'll go in with the video." Chief is so persuaded of the need for clear lines of case authority that he lets the detective in charge of a case give orders to him as well.

Thomas Ernest sat in the back seat of Deputy Collins' patrol car, on the driver's side. I invited him to step out. A scuffed, pointed, upturned toe of a light-colored ostrich boot emerged first. Expensive. Then the rest of him unfolded. Middle-aged, six foot two, 175 pounds, slight stoop, a long, craggy face.

"I'm sorry about all that in your house, Mr. Ernest. Must be quite something to have that happen."

"You bet it is. Quite somethin'. I'm in shock." Ernest had a voice as deep as Old Man River.

"I'm sure you are. You don't need to talk to me at all right now if you don't want."

"I'm in shock, all right, but I want to talk to you. What did you say your name was?"

I hadn't said. "Ted D'Aquin. Detective D'Aquin."

"Glad to know you, Detective." He put out his hand. A tad ingratiating.

Ernest had dressed with care today: starched white shirt neatly tucked into creased brown slacks, bolo tie, a whiff of Old Spice.

"Mr. Ernest, I'd like to tape our conversation so there's no mistake about what we say. There's a tape recorder right there on the dashboard. Is it OK with you if I run it?"

"Oh yes, sir. I want to talk. I want to tell you everythin'."

I turned on the recorder and introduced the scene: the time, the people on hand, what we were there to do, and Ernest's agreement to have me record our conversation.

"As I say, Mr. Ernest, you're not required to talk to me now, but if you do, I want to tell you that anything you say can and may be used against you. Do you understand?"

"Oh yes, sir."

I launched into the rest of the Miranda warning. Deputy Collins had said he'd already given it, but I wasn't taking any chances. My deferential tone masked my mission—to gauge his emotional state. I read him his rights, one after the other, and gave him time to respond, all while the tape ran. Ernest's voice was clear and strong, with a twang. Not as far north as Shreveport or Monroe. Probably central Louisiana.

"We have the right to go into your house to verify fatalities, Mr. Ernest, but we'd like your permission to look around. We could do that right now if that's OK with you."

"Oh, yes. You have my permission. I want to know everythin' about this. I'm in shock, you know."

I looked hard at his face. An impassive mask. Not a twitch. In shock? Doubtful. Deputy Collins' briefcase lay on the front seat of the unit. I pulled out two forms—the Acknowledgement of Rights and the Permission to Search—and handed Ernest a pen. After I read the contents of the forms to him and made a short explanation of the legalese, Ernest rested the papers on the hood of the patrol car and signed his name on each form, with a steady hand, in the appropriate places.

"Mr. Ernest, I'll be asking you to give a detailed statement later—that's routine when we have fatalities—but for now I'd like you to tell me briefly what went on in there."

"Oh, yes. Of course, I want to cooperate in every way I can. I was in the bathroom in the back, cleanin' up after doing a little yard work. I'd picked up the guy to help me with that. Kitty, that's my wife, has some friends, her doll friends, comin' over tomorrow mornin' and she wanted the yard to look nice. She likes everythin' real nice, you know. I was in the bathroom, pulling up my pants when I thought I heard gunshots. I came through the bedroom and out to the hall. There was that yardman, Jubilee Joe, standin' in the door to the den with my rifle in his hands. I looked over and saw Kitty there on the fireplace. Lyin' there. I could see what had happened. He'd shot her. Jubilee had shot her. At the sight of me, he took off down the hallway to the back door."

"What's Jubilee Joe's last name, Mr. Ernest."

"I think it's Joe. I think Jubilee's his front name."

"Really? Where's he live?"

"Somewhere off South Main Street, I think. He'd come around a few days ago to ask if anybody needed yard work done. I didn't need anyone then, but today I did. I remembered his name and where he said I could find him—the carwash on Ledoux and South Main. There's an empty lot behind there where guys hang out. They have kind of an all-the-time poker game goin' on."

"So, he took off down the hallway. What did you do?"

"Well, I came after him. He kept runnin' down the hall toward the back door. I wrestled the rifle away from him."

"And then?" I prodded. I had lots of questions, but at this point, I wanted just the short version of his story.

"I shot him. I couldn't tell you how many times I shot him, I was so furious. But I know I killed him."

"And what did you do then?"

"I went into the kitchen and called 911. 'Y'all come quick,' I said."

In the yard, I could see people gathering, both inside the yellow tape and out. We needed to get organized to film the crime scene. I could take a formal statement from Ernest later.

"Do you have family close by, Mr. Ernest? Someone you can call to be with you?"

"Yes. I have a son and a daughter. I called them after I called 911. I think I see my daughter's car over there. Outside the tape."

"Good. Why don't you go be with her? Stay close by, if you don't mind. We're going in to film the scene, and I'll want to talk to you again after that."

Ernest thanked me politely and turned to walk away. I gave Deputy Collins a high sign. I had instructions for him.

"Deputy Collins, let Mr. Ernest's daughter inside the tape. Her car, too. Mr. Ernest needs some place to sit. He's going to talk to me again after we go inside." I clasped my hands together behind Ernest's back, signaling to Collins I wanted him to keep Ernest in tight. Collins settled Ernest in his black and white.

Daylight had begun to fade. The curious, and those who had nothing better to do than follow sirens, formed clumps under the canopy of trees. One attentive observer stood apart from the others. Dennis Byrne, our recently assigned DA. I beckoned him over and raised the tape to let him inside.

"Mr. Byrne, come in here with us."

Detective Lorraine LaSalle pulled up and walked over to us. "Chief Roland assigned me to be your partner on this one, Ted. I hope you can put up with me."

Chief Roland drew a circle in the air to tell me he had the first response team assembled and ready to go into the house.

6

The video of the crime scene at 205 Evangeline Street is over thirty minutes long. I probably watched all or a good part of it a dozen times during the next three days. And each time I got the shivers. A frisson, my mother-in-law Maman would say. That beautiful home. So much blood. Everywhere those freakin' dolls.

My face on the video gave me away; I was damn excited to be back doing real work, not sitting at a desk pushing papers.

The first few minutes of the video show the preparations for entering the crime scene. I gave out the assignments. We would go in through what Thomas Ernest called his back door, the side door off the garage, not the one on the front of the house where Deputy Collins said he first saw Ernest. Although the bedroom and the kitchen opened onto a deck across the rear of the house, no stairway led down to the back yard from there.

I led the party. Detective LaSalle and Spike followed, handing out surgical gloves for everyone to wear. Spike carried a packet of tented evidence markers to place next to each item we wanted to film in place, *in situ*, as they say. Lennis Trahan, the deputy who doubled as the department videographer, followed close behind us, then the still photographer we had on call, and the two 'squints' from the Acadiana Crime Lab: Richard Levy, my favorite geek, and his assistant. They were to pick up the evidence after the rest of the group—including Chief Roland, the Sheriff, and Mr. Byrne—had a chance to see the items where they lay. Only then would the EMTs be given the OK to come in and remove the bodies.

From the back door, I turned left to the beginning of the hall running the length of the house. A man's body lay there, on his right side, next to a small pump rifle. A garish painting of two white camellias in an elaborate—might I say tacky? — frame stared down at the body. I narrated for the running audio. *Catch that, Lennis. Each flower is a face with wide eyes and a cupid mouth, the better to smile upon the bloody mess below.*

I picked my way carefully around the body. Spike, right behind me, began to place numbered evidence markers next to each spent shell and spot of blood. Lennis pointed his camera at each item. I gave instructions. *Catch each splatter of blood. The edge of the doorframe to the utility room, right there on the floor, the wall, the ceiling. Good. Now catch each of the shell casings. That one, that one. Good. Now zero in on the body. Catch the soles of the black man's sneakers, catch his hands, the wounds in his chest and his head. Come around the body, carefully, to catch the rifle from a distance so we can see how it lies.*

Chief inserted a comment into my narration. *What a frickin' mess.* The rest of our group silently watched the photographers do their work and then followed behind.

I continued the narration as we made our way down the center hallway, in the direction of the aggravating blare of a TV. On our right, the bayou side of the house, we passed the kitchen. I pointed out a purse lying open on the counter.

"Catch that, Lennis."

On our left, the street side of the central hall, lay two rooms probably intended by the builder for formal living and dining. No longer. They had been transformed to accommodate what must have been the hobby of the owners: the creation and display of dolls.

A large oval table commanded the center of the first doll room. Dolls in varying stages of construction covered the surface. Cloth bodies, china heads, and bins of sewing supplies—material, ribbons, and buttons—spilled from the shelves of china cabinets along the walls. The second doll room showed off the finished products: groupings of the most elaborately dressed examples of the collection. Probably fifty little ladies in satin dresses had at hand their imagined needs: miniature tables, chairs, utensils, carriages for their babies.

A wisecrack from my new partner Lorraine interrupted my narration and startled me. *Apparently, not one of these ladies has the need of a mate.*

The master bedroom lay at the end of the hall. The video picked up Chief Roland's voice. *Ah, that's where the damn noise is coming from. Spike, snuff the freakin' racket.* The sound of the TV ceased. Stairs to the second floor rose from the foyer between the two doll rooms. We continued our way down the hall to seek out the second body, leaving the upstairs for later.

I continued my narration. *We're now entering a large den on our right, on the bayou side of the house. At the back of this room, a fireplace of brown roman brick is flanked by picture windows looking out over the wooden deck and the Bayou Teche beyond. Charlie, catch the doll decor everywhere: dolls on the windowsills, on every table and on whatnot shelves on the walls. Catch the decorated tree there in the corner.* A hundred eyes peered at us from ornaments attached to the tree by tiny bows in autumn colors: identical cupie-doll faces, each one surrounded by a halo of lace. I'd seen that practice before: a tree that stays up all year, changing accent colors with ornaments according to the season.

I continued my narration. *The body of a white female, tentative ID Kitty Ernest, lies on the hearth, her left hand rests on her chest. Point your camera directly in there, Lennis. Catch the bullet wounds: a clean hole in the center of her tipped-back neck, blood oozing onto the hearth from a hole in her forehead, a third hole in her chest under her left thumb. Looks like powder burns around that one. I gave instructions to my entourage: Back off now, Lennis, to catch the full scene. If anyone goes in close, be careful not to disturb the spread of newspapers in front of the hearth and the paint cans supporting that little fence she was painting.*

I remember the scene well. The woman appeared to have

been creating another doll display. A small paintbrush, still wet, balanced on the top of an open can of white paint. A little fence surrounded three satin-gowned Victorian ladies sitting before her at a miniature table set with teacups and spoons. In the audio of the film, you can hear Mr. Byrne's editorializing. *Mrs. Gulliver sits in Lilliputia, serving tea to her guests when she is rudely interrupted by being shot dead.*

I resumed the narration. *Now catch each shell casing. There, there, there. Look closely at the face of Mrs. Ernest. Wow! I believe I'm looking at the same face as her dolls.*

Damn. She created herself! How many times? As the tally of doll faces in the house continued to rise, I figured close to a thousand.

While the crew worked at marking, photographing, then saving evidence to be examined in the lab, I poked my head into the bedroom at the end of the hall. A peach satin stuffed heart, encircled by a halo of lace, decorated the headboard of the large bed—bigger than king size—on the far wall. A dress, a slip, and a sweater had been carelessly thrown on top of rumpled pink sheets and pillows. I asked the photographers to take some shots in the bedroom when they had finished with the second body.

After recording the scene, we moved into the large adjoining bathroom. A scent of gardenias wafted from a basket of potpourri on the back of the commode. A little doll smiled at us from her perch on the petals, another from the crocheted cover on a spare roll of toilet tissue. Lotions and potions littered the counter.

Toiletries, toiletries, Mr. Byrne mumbled. A movie buff, Mr. Byrne probably recalled the aluminum siding salesman in *The Tin Men* pitching into the trash all signs of his departed wife. *Do you think a man ever set foot in this place?* Mr. Byrne asked of no one in particular. The video camera played on Mr. Byrne's alert expression.

I pointed out for Mr. Byrne what I thought was the one masculine item in the bathroom: a six-inch square plastic tray on the counter holding a toothbrush, a razor, and a small container of shaving soap. *Ha,* Mr. Byrne said. *I found another item of the masculine persuasion.* He pointed out for the videographer a tattered copy of a *Playboy Magazine* under a pair of shoes in the bottom of the closet.

I'm getting to enjoy Mr. Byrne's sense of humor.

Halfway back down the hall in the center of the house, we reached the foyer. I led about half the entourage up the stairs to the second floor. We shot video of three more bedrooms and two baths. More poofy curtains, frilly pillows, and dolls sitting about on every surface. Showroom neat. No room had any sign that people lived there.

Downstairs, heading back to the door we had come in, I saw Spike on his belly peering into the first of the doll construction rooms.

Playing alligator, Spike? Someone asked.

I thought I saw something under this display case. Yes, here it is, Spike called to the videographer. After describing the location of the find, Spike picked up the object with a gloved hand. *A piece of metal.*

Deputy Collins called from the kitchen to report something else we hadn't seen at first: what looked like the butt plate of a pistol in the otherwise empty kitchen trash can. The videographer filmed the object in place and the crime lab guys gave it a home in their collection of evidence bags.

The filming and evidence gathering complete, we reassembled on the lawn outside the house. Daylight had retired for the night. Within the crime scene tape, tree trunks cast eerie fingers of shadow on the lawn. Beyond the yellow tape, the cars winked their headlights as people walked by. The wind had picked up. The branches of the magnificent live oaks rubbed together, sounding like a crying baby. A stage set for tragedy.

I gave the EMTs the OK to go back into the house to retrieve the bodies. I went in with them to supervise their operation, unfortunately too late to prevent them from walking on the newspapers spread before the body of Kitty Ernest.

Ernest's daughter, and son if he had come, hadn't asked to

see their mother. I kept quiet. I wasn't about to invite what would surely be an emotional scene.

The EMTs placed a body bag on a litter next to the black man. They carefully worked a sheet under the body. One EMT at the head and one at the feet slid the sheet over onto the litter. Blood sopped through the sheet at the head. They pulled up the sides of the package. ZZZip. After carrying the body to one of the ambulances, the EMTs came back to the house and, in the den, walked to the fireplace. They moved aside a doll's chair, positioned a second litter next to the woman, and slid her off the hearth onto another body bag. The maneuver disturbed her hand and exposed a second bullet hole in the woman's chest. The medics gently crossed her arms on her chest in a casket-like display. Blood also marked the head, but not enough to drip through the sheet. Another ZZZip.

Outside again, I addressed my crew. "OK. We're done here for tonight. Detective LaSalle and I are going to follow the EMTs to the morgue, observe the autopsies, and pick up what evidence we can. Clothing and any slugs in the bodies, for sure. We'll get them out to the lab in the morning. Deuce, as soon as we pull out of here, how about you doorstep the neighborhood? Go door to door and ask if anyone saw or heard anything interesting this afternoon. Chief, do we have any word on the identity of the second victim?"

Chief shook his head in the negative. He said he didn't recognize the name as one of our regular customers, but he had a preliminary assessment of the situation. "This looks to me like a standard burglary gone bad. We've got the weapon and the open purse on the counter in the kitchen. I think Ernest saved us a shitload of work by taking care of the perp."

I heard an exhale beside me. Mr. Byrne held a large evidence bag, the rifle inside, turning it this way and that. Those deep wrinkles ran across his forehead again. He handed the bag to Richard Levy of the Crime Lab, with a question.

"There seems to be some damage here on the magazine, Richard. Did you see this?"

"I did. And I tested the spot before I sealed the bag. Positive for lead."

Deputy Collins spoke up. A few hours on a homicide scene had turned Collins into a veteran. Calm, no longer stumbling over his words. "I got some information on the man, Chief Roland."

"Go ahead, Kevin. Tell us."

"Mr. Ernest calls the dead guy Jubilee Joe and says the guy came around the subdivision last week looking for work. A neighbor confirms. Mr. Ernest didn't need anyone to do yard work that day, but today he did. He remembered the name and how the man could be reached—through his brother's car wash in Ledoux. I know the place. I called the owner. He told me Jubilee's last name is Joe—I'd first thought Jubilee Joe was all his front name. He lives in a trailer behind the car wash. I called in the name. They're running the databases now."

"Good work, Kevin." The Chief was pleased with his new deputy. Collins had earned the first name familiarity of those on the inside of things.

Deputy Collins continued. "I have some more information on Mr. Ernest, Chief Roland. He owns and runs Ernest's Quality Cleaners on Main Street, one block past the big church. He has an attached office on the side. People think he sleeps there sometimes."

I complimented the new deputy to the Sheriff.

"Another one of my former students," she said. "And I'm not going to let a good black deputy slip through our hands."

"It's dark now. We can make a much better search of the scene tomorrow in the daylight, but we can't leave the house unattended overnight. We need someone to babysit." I looked around for a volunteer. Everyone seemed to drop eyes to the feet. Except Spike.

"I'm on it, sir."

Mr. Byrne spoke up. "While you're in there, Spike, take a look around. It's possible another gun figures in this picture."

It is Basic Investigations 101 to account for every gun and every bullet you find at a crime scene. Mr. Byrne must have seen something I hadn't. Nor had Spike.

I added more instructions for Spike. "So far, we haven't found any papers—insurance policies, money, a will, all the *tra-ca* the man of the house has to take care of. Strange. Maybe he keeps his personal records at his office."

Spike had one request. "I'll stay the night but could you ask patrol to stop in now and then to see that one of those dolls hasn't come alive and done me in?"

Richard Levy gathered the evidence bags into a large cardboard box, a separate bag for each item, large and small. I overheard him mumble.

"What did I hear you say, Richard?" I asked him. "Odd man out?"

"Right. Not all we picked up comes from the same weapon. The scraps of metal Spike found in the first doll room could be pieces of a different gun. I'll have a full report when I finish my examination and run some tests."

Chief brushed imaginary dirt off his hands. "All this looks pretty straightforward to me."

The horizontal wrinkles across Mr. Byrne's forehead told me he was not so sure of Chief's conclusion. I took the cue. "Let's hold off any opinions until we hear from the lab. Lorraine and I are off to the hospital for the autopsy. We'll need one working day to put some thoughts together. Could we gather in your office Tuesday morning, Sheriff Gabrielle? We won't have the labs yet, but we can at least keep each other abreast of what we're doing."

"I have a meeting with the Catahoula team at eight Tuesday morning. Let's make our meeting at ten."

"OK. Now let's see if we can get the crowd to go home. I see the press out there. Do you want to make some kind of statement, Sheriff?" I asked her.

Chief Roland spoke up for his boss. "Let me do that. We need to say very little."

Chief walked down the front walk and addressed the young reporters who were waiting, notebooks in hand, in front of the crowd. The Sheriff started back to the Jeep, which gave me an opportunity for a quick sidebar with Deuce.

"Catahoula case going OK, Deuce?"

"We're close, Ted. We're putting together the evidence for an arrest. We're pretty sure it's what we all thought from the beginning."

Which must have meant they believed the husband to be the perp.

Chief Roland addressed the crowd. "I know you've been waiting a while everybody, but here's all I'm gonna say right now. This afternoon at 3:26 we received a 911 call about a shooting at 205 Evangeline Street. We responded and found two bodies in the house. One body is that of Mrs. Thomas Ernest, Kitty, identified by her husband. The other body is that of an as yet unidentified black male. We have made no arrests."

A volley of questions peppered back.

"Do you have a suspect?"

"No comment."

"Have you determined a motive? Robbery?"

"No comment."

"Is it true that the unidentified man had an accomplice who got away?"

"No comment."

"That's the rumor to that effect out here, and the neighbors are scared. Can you reassure them?"

"No comment."

"But, Chief Roland, people want to know if they should be concerned. Should they take precautions?"

"There will be no further details released until we have identified the second body and notified his next of kin."

And then we will still try to say as little as possible. A fine example of why law enforcement is plagued by bad press. We don't give the reporters what they want.

7

If I hadn't known where the new sheriff was supposed to be sitting, I might have missed her entirely, buried in a massive burgundy leather chair behind the eight-foot wide desk. Once spotted, she looked like a little girl in a sheriff costume come to visit her Daddy in his office. As the necessary parties for the meeting came in, making small talk so as not to leak any information about the case to someone who might be passing by, our new sheriff extended a welcome. We all called her Sheriff Gabrielle, the name she preferred. She rejected in no uncertain terms the moniker of The Lady so often suggested by people who thought they were the first to think The Lady should succeed The Man.

"Chief Roland, would you be so kind as to put some chairs in a semi-circle in front of my desk? We all need to hear what each person has to say."

Chief looked a bit startled to be assigned a lowly task, especially since he'd already given us his opinion that our investigation would confirm his view that Thomas Ernest had taken care of justice by himself. But he complied. I gave him a hand.

Sheriff Gabrielle hadn't changed the decor of the office during her interim service. Of course not. She played the succession card for the campaign. I bet in a month we'd see some signs of redecoration. Unless I'd judged her totally wrong, Gabrielle Chevalier Bouton hadn't inherited her father's pretensions along with the office of Sheriff of St. Martin Parish.

The left wall of the dark paneled room still displayed photographs of *The Man's* triumphs: a photograph of his hand on the muddy collar of a murderer flushed from hiding in the Atchafalaya swamp; another of his booted foot resting on one of six bales of marijuana found tucked inside rolls of hay on an eighteen-wheeler his deputies had stopped on I-10 for crossing the center line; a third of his proud face framed in the door of an airplane, an extradited molester handcuffed to Chief Roland who was barely visible over his shoulder.

Politics determined who made the cut for the display of photographs on the opposite wall, to the sheriff's right. Generous donations to election campaigns yield a photo op with a public official of some prestige. The Man stood with President Ronald Reagan in one signed photograph and with the Chief Justice of the Louisiana Supreme Court in another. Behind us, at the rear of the room, framed prints of the past five years of duck stamps and a shelf holding a dozen mounted birds attested to the bona fides of the old sheriff. Got to show empathy with the second amendment crowd. A shiny shovel stood upright in the corner, a memento of the groundbreaking for the office and jail building we now occupied.

My prediction? Sheriff Gabrielle would keep the duck stamps, the wildlife, and the shiny shovel. The photographs of her father's triumphs and the certifications of his political contributions would soon be gone.

What about the well-worn Bible and the picture of *The Man's* wife—Gabrielle's mother, dead now some twenty years —on the right corner of the desk? Would they be displayed in the new regime? I didn't know. Gabrielle's own choice of decor would tell us what she truly cared about, but we'd have to wait a decent interval for the revelation.

Following Sheriff Gabrielle's gestures, her secretary, appropriately called an administrative assistant, sat at her left. Chief Roland, Mr. Byrne and all the detectives on the case occupied the chairs in the semi-circle. My partner for this assignment, Detective Lorraine LaSalle, sat at my side. She looked more like a detective's girlfriend than the real article. Slight build and red-blond curls. She'd been with us for a year but I'd never worked with her before, probably because I'd been on leave. I'd heard from my fellow detectives that you make the mistake of thinking she's a softie at your peril.

The semi-circle in front of the Sheriff put everyone on equal footing. I don't believe Chief Roland liked that, but it's good technique. I guess you learn stuff like that in criminal justice grad school.

The Sheriff called the meeting to order.

"Detective D'Aquin, you're case agent on this investigation. Why don't you begin with a summary of where we are so far?"

"Yes ma'am—Sheriff Gabrielle. I'll start with Mr. Thomas Ernest, the only eyewitness to the circumstances that resulted in two deaths—his wife Kitty and Jubilee Joe, the man he'd picked up to help him in the yard. Ernest has a story to tell. He tells it calmly, with little detail. He says he left Jubilee Joe in the carport and went to the bedroom to change clothes. He was in the bathroom, which is connected to the bedroom at the end of the hall when he heard shots. He pulled up his pants—why he had to tell us that I don't know—and rushed into the hall. Jubilee Joe stood there holding his—Ernest's— rifle. Ernest glanced into the den and saw that his wife had been shot.

"Ernest says Jubilee took off down the hall toward the back door. Ernest followed in pursuit. He says he caught up with Jubilee at the end of the hall, near the door to the garage. He took possession of the rifle and fired at Jubilee point blank. Ernest says he doesn't know how many times he fired. He then went into the kitchen and called 911. End of his story."

"Do you buy it?" the Sheriff asked. I rubbed the end of my nose. The Sheriff smiled at my signal. "Are you telling me his story doesn't pass the smell test?"

"I'm not comfortable, Sheriff. Ernest is quite consistent in the two statements he gave at the scene, and even in the longer video statement we did yesterday morning in the interrogation room at HQ, but…"

"But what, Ted? What gives you reason to doubt his story?"

"Timing, for one thing. I asked Ernest what time he picked up Jubilee. He said around two in the afternoon. As you know, the call to 911 came in at 3:26. I asked Ernest what he did for an hour and a half. He said he talked to his wife to get instructions on what she wanted done in the yard. So, I asked, 'And you left Jubilee outside in the carport for all that time?' Silence. No answer. The recordings and the videotape are ready for anyone to hear and see. I made two copies. Watch his face as *he doesn't* answer my questions."

"But you didn't really cross-examine him."

"Professor, you taught me better than that! I wasn't going to raise his suspicions and have him lawyer up on us. We'll get a lot more out of him in the next few days if he thinks we've swallowed his story."

"I give you an A for that."

"Here's another red flag, Sheriff Gabrielle. I told Ernest we found the butt plate of a pistol in his kitchen trash can and asked if he had another gun. I can't say he was surprised at my question or feared we were onto something. He just looked puzzled. He said he once had an *ol'* pistol but that was a while back. He didn't know what happened to it. As I say, I didn't want to spook him by pushing the issue."

I overheard Mr. Byrne's mumble. "Not much for me to use so far."

Sheriff Gabrielle turned to my partner, Lorraine. "I understand you gave him a lie detector test."

All eyes turned in her direction. Lorraine looked down at her hands. I came to her rescue.

"AMA, as they say. Against medical advice. I don't believe in lie detector or stress analysis tests, but Lorraine asked me to humor her. Ernest jumped at the opportunity. Lorraine hooked him up to the machine; he passed with flying colors, which raises even more questions in my mind. If your wife is murdered and you shoot the murderer, don't you think your stress level would rise just a little bit? Ernest showed nothing."

Mr. Byrne rubbed a hand over his head. "There are good reasons why those tests are not admissible in court."

I was just about to go into my conjecture that Ernest could have been on something, maybe a tranquilizer, but the Sheriff had moved on.

"Detective LaSalle, I understand you may have some prior acquaintance with Mr. Ernest."

"I recognized him as soon as I saw the videotape. We are in the same aerobics program at the City Park in New Iberia. I go twice a week. He's there every time I am, so he probably goes even more often. He always stays in the back of the class and doesn't socialize with anyone. I have the idea he's embarrassed, being older and a man, but he works real hard. I admire him for that. He always goes up to Ashlie, the instructor, after class and thanks her. He's very polite."

"Have you had any conversations with him?" The sheriff asked.

"No. Just hi and bye."

"OK." Sheriff Gabrielle continued. "We may have a source of information about Mr. and Mrs. Ernest. Mark Gander called me several times yesterday, and he called again this morning. Do y'all know him? The Prudential agent?"

"I know him like that," Chief responded.

I like the expression. If Mr. Byrne asked me to translate, I'd tell him it means you recognize the man's face, perhaps pass a greeting, but never engaged in any extended conversation.

The Sheriff kept going. "Mark Gander and Thomas Ernest were apparently pretty close. You may have noticed the stocky man—that's being kind—in shorts and a tank top holding up the Ernest children in the yard Saturday night. Mark Gander is a pest, but he may be a source of information for us. I'll take his call and see what I can learn. Unless you want to deal with this, Ted."

"He's all yours, Sheriff Gabrielle. Of course, you could always have Chief take his statement."

That put a twinkle in the Sheriff's eye. "F---, Hell, no. Gander's skittish. I'll see what he has to say."

Well, what do you know! An F-bomb. Before long our Sheriff will be talking like her father. That's what happens when you spend time with cops.

I called on Deputy Collins. "Kevin, I believe you have a few things to tell us about Jubilee Joe."

Like a schoolboy called on in class, Collins sat up straighter to give his answer. "Yes, sir. I've done some digging."

"Go ahead. Tell us what you've found out."

"First of all, Joe is his last name. His front name is Charles. Charles Joe, but people call him Jubilee. I talked to some guys who hang out at the car wash on the south end of Main Street. They seem to know him well. They say he is— was—forty years old and lived with his sister and her four kids. That's in Ledoux Subdivision. He pays regular child support for two kids of his own. I ran his rap sheet and found a juvenile record—petty thefts mostly. In his early twenties, he got into adult trouble—an aggravated battery pled down to simple, a felony theft, then a conviction for aggravated burglary of a pharmacy. Yep, he was into drugs and he had a gun. He went to prison. Inside, he trained as a mechanic, but once out on parole, he had trouble getting work. The usual story."

A bell went off in my head. Could Charles Joe be in the probation records as someone Eugénie had supervised? I could call Eugénie's former partner Nicole at Probation and Parole to ask her the question. Should I do that? Or would she refuse to take my call? As soon as this meeting ended...

I snapped back to listening to Deputy Collins. Articulate and proven to be competent under stress, he was totally professional. His connection to his own community could prove quite valuable to us in this and in many other cases. We get a lot of business from that end of town.

Collins continued. "I hope you don't think I'm just sticking up for another person of color, but what we're dealing with here, double homicide in the course of a robbery, is out of character for Jubilee at the age he is now. The people I talked to think he's straight, and if he'd suddenly relapsed, they think they'd have seen the signs."

The dispatch deputy who'd been on duty when the 911

call came in spoke up next. "I ran the records on Jubilee also, and I don't disagree with your impression. The weakness is there, I suppose. And the temptation. Jobs are hard to come by for a black man with a felony record, but Jubilee hasn't had any problems for a long time. I've also done some background on Mr. and Mrs. Ernest, Thomas and Kitty. You want to hear that?"

"Yes," said the Sheriff. "Let's have it."

"Thomas Ernest owns and runs Ernest's Quality Cleaners on Main Street, across and down a block from the church. He's not your Rotary type but certainly a solid citizen. Pays his bills on time and has never been in our system. He's quiet, kind of a loner, people say. He grew up on a farm in the Alexandria area. He met Kitty at some church function, they married and moved here to where she grew up."

The deputy looked around to see if he still had the floor. He did.

"Mrs. Ernest now, she's the gregarious one. She has—had —a big circle of friends: mostly fellow doll enthusiasts and members of their church. The Ernests and Gander, incidentally, belong to the Church of the Blessed Believers. I've never been there, but it's apparently across the Bayou, off the Catahoula Highway. One of those metal-building churches, I suppose. That's all I know about it."

Chief Roland spoke up. "The Believers? A few years ago… Never mind. We don't need to get into that now."

"OK, everybody. Any more information to share about our cast of characters?"

My turn. "After the filming at the scene, I came back here and asked Lorraine—Detective LaSalle—to find the tape of Ernest's emergency call. Have y'all heard it?"

No one had.

"Listen to this. Sheriff, would you open the drawer there and press the button on the tape recorder inside? I have it set to go. The dispatch deputy takes the call."

I recognized the voice, the nerve center of the external department. A burly, middle-aged black man, he'd worked for *The Man* forever. On duty, he spoke with the precision required by his position, but I'd met him a couple times on the outside and learned he had a whole other way of talkin' in the 'hood.

St. Martin Parish Sheriff's Office, Dispatch Officer speaking.

Get someone to my house. Some guy shot my wife.

OK, sir. Stay calm. What is your address?

205 Evangeline Street.

That's the Evangeline Street on the north end of St. Martinville?

Yes, sir. Get someone here.

Have you called an ambulance?

No, I haven't.

Do you want me to call an ambulance?

Yes. Send two. I killed him too. A pause. Uh-h-h. I believe I killed him.

"Hear that guys? Dispatch asks him if he called an ambulance. He says no. Then he says 'Send two. I killed him too. T-O-O?'"

Chief Roland stood up. "All this conjecture is worthless. As Mr. Byrne says, we need to get started gathering real evidence he can take to court. And anyway, I can't believe anyone would be so stupid as to think we'd fall for a scheme to pick up some N..., some dude and frame him for the murder of his wife. Ernest can't be that dumb."

Mr. Byrne tipped back in his chair and raised one eyebrow. That meant he had only half a forehead wrinkle. "No? When did our clientele get smart? Criminals are stupid. Actually, we could call our whole show 'CSI-Jackass.'"

After we stopped laughing, Mr. Byrne got serious. "Whatever our suspicions, Chief Roland is right. I need solid evidence to put before a jury. Where's Ernest right now, Ted?"

"At his son Patrick's house, out in the country. I've had a tail on him since he left the crime scene Saturday night. The tail lets me know every time he moves. So far, all he's done is go to his office and back to his son's house."

That topic interested the Sheriff. "Tell me, what do we know about his son Patrick?"

I'd never heard of him, but Chief had information. Chief's an invaluable resource for our new sheriff.

"I know *of* him. He lives north of Breaux Bridge. Big house. Apparently, lots of money. We don't know where it comes from but we have our suspicions. He's on a few boards, does civic work, makes contributions for the betterment of society. No one asks questions about his sources."

Mr. Byrne delivered another one of his gems. "I've noticed that money purifies by volume."

Spike raised his head to say something but didn't. After a minute, when he did speak, he was on a different subject. "OK. What's the plan for the day? I know what I want to do. While we still have possession of the house, I want to get out there to look for some concrete evidence we can give Mr. Byrne. We've got the butt plate from a pistol but no pistol. The night this came down—God, it was only two days ago—I looked everywhere but couldn't find any weapon to marry to that plate. Finding a pistol would be nice. And I realize we haven't checked out Ernest's car. But unless I find something, I want to call in the divers. The Bayou is right there in the back yard."

I spoke up now. As case agent, I should be calling the shots.

"Good, Spike. You do that. By the way, you get combat pay for your night with the dolls."

"At least I had no trouble staying awake, with all those glass eyes lookin' at me."

I turned to the DA. "Mr. Byrne, do you have anything you want to add or any suggestions about next steps?"

Mr. Byrne tilted his head and ran his hands through his thinning hair. "It appears to me two good sources of hard evidence have yet to come in—the autopsy report of Dr. Pétain and the ballistics reports from the Acadiana Crime Lab. We need both reports before we start advancing theories about what happened out there. Unless Dr. Pétain finds something beyond his expertise—and not much is beyond him—we'll have the autopsy report in a few days. Ballistics is going to take longer. In the meanwhile, I suggest we keep gathering information but not form any conclusions." His eyes visited those of each person in the room. "We make no statements to the press or anyone else until the investigation is complete. No conjecture, no 'unidentified source' leaks. Just this: 'We are engaged in a full-scale investigation of the circumstances.'"

Sheriff Gabrielle had a contribution. "I'll give Richard Levy a call, Mr. Byrne. Just to make sure he understands how important it is for us to have his ballistics reports PDQ. No, I have a better idea. I'll ask him to come by as soon as possible. Meet with just you, Ted, and Lorraine. Lorraine knows a hell of a lot about firearms."

Really? I didn't know much about my new partner. Maybe Sheriff Gabrielle knew her from her past life.

The Sheriff again, and this statement caught my attention. "Now that Deuce has turned over the investigation files in the Catahoula Lake case to the District Attorney, I'll be calling on the entire department for assistance on this case."

Did I hear that right? The Catahoula case was wrapped up? I was chomping at the bit to call Deuce and get the story. Maybe the Sheriff would take off my handcuffs.

"Anything else anybody?" she asked.

Chief spoke up. "Rest assured everybody, my boys will be keeping a very close watch on Mr. Ernest."

8

My cell phone went off at six thirty a.m. Chief Deputy Sheriff Allan Roland on the line. "Two divers will be at 205 Evangeline with their search equipment one hour from now. Be there."

Damn. I may have been case agent in the Ernest case, but Chief kept his finger in every pie. He gets us what we need all right, sometimes more quickly than we expect. And earlier in the morning.

My plan for the day had been to track down the Sheriff to ask her to let me back into the Catahoula case. With the investigation files turned over for prosecution, surely I could be brought into the loop. Chief's call reset the clock.

"Yes, sir."

I rolled out of bed, woke André, and laid out his cereal and milk. I dumped grounds into the coffee pot and put water on the stove to boil. The school bus would pick André up before I had to leave to meet the divers. Good. My Mom and my sister were right next door and never turned me down, but I'd called on them way too often over the summer. Thank God, André seemed as comfortable over there as in his own house.

Top priority: learning the origin of the butt plate we found in the kitchen trash can and the scraps of metal we had picked up in the hall on the night of the double killing. Spike had been over every inch of the house for the second time without finding another weapon. But Thomas Ernest's explanation—that he'd once owned a .380 pistol but junked it way back—didn't wash. Maybe those metal pieces could have been under the cabinet in the doll room for a good while without anyone noticing, but no way any length of time passes without someone emptying a kitchen garbage can in a house where two people ate and slept. Especially when the homeowner seemed to be a neat freak. The more I chewed on Ernest's story, the bigger it got. I didn't know exactly how two people ended up dead at 205 Evangeline, but finding the missing weapon might be the Rosetta stone.

We needed to take full advantage of our access to the house while we had Ernest's sworn permission to search. As soon as some friend or a family member with legal smarts got wind of all this, he'd tell Ernest to pull the plug. After that, we'd need probable cause to get a search warrant to go back in.

Finding anything in the Bayou Teche is a challenge. Using just mask and fins would be pointless. Even at high noon, suspended particles of dirt extinguish all light just a few inches below the surface. I remember when my parents took us on a vacation trip to North Carolina and we stopped to wade in a mountain stream. I never knew water could be clear like that.

Chief Roland had a plan and the connections to get the job done. The owner of Downhole Specialists, an oilfield service company, and a long-time political supporter of *The Man,* was quite willing to 'resolve' his collection of speeding tickets and get in good with the new sheriff. He'd loan us a day's use of a piece of sophisticated underwater detection equipment—a black box the size of a Yeti cooler that emitted a ping when within a couple yards of metal. As I say, Chief gets us what we need for our investigations, one way or another.

The neighbors, and certainly the press, were sure to get curious when a wet-suited crew wearing air tanks, face masks, and snorkels set up their equipment on the bayou bank behind a house so recently in the news. I needed a cover story for public consumption. Ladling boiling water over the coffee grounds, dark roast, of course, I thought through how we could spin the search operation for inquiring minds. *There's nothing unusual going on with this search. When people haven't died in their beds, we always check adjacent bodies of water as part of the investigation. One fact we know for sure, I could say, the two people we found in the house did not die of natural causes.*

The press beat me out to the site. When I arrived, I gave them the spin. They listened but continued to set up their cameras. I didn't know if they bought my story or not. Probably not. They know we have to play the game.

I sympathize with those guys. In a small town, photographers from the local newspaper have little chance of taking a prize-winning photograph on their routine assignments. No Pulitzer committee gives recognition to a shot of a meeting of the School Board or the City Council, nor of properly dressed ladies installing a mini-billboard to celebrate the Garden of the Month. I couldn't fault them for monitoring our effort to dredge the bayou after a double homicide. Something newsworthy just might occur.

Spike beat me to the site. "This operation will go faster with a third pair of eyes under there, but I can't swim a lick. I had the divers bring a spare wetsuit and tank. Will you join them?"

"I could, Spike. But why don't you call Lorraine? I've heard she loves this stuff."

I was afraid the dive would be all over before Spike could run down my partner, but as it turned out, we cooled our heels a couple hours waiting for delivery of the fancy search device. As I predicted, Lorraine jumped at the chance to go under.

Time on my hands, I got to thinking about Jubilee Joe. Something about the name seemed familiar. Had I run across him in my investigation into Eugénie's probationers? If I caught Nicole in the Probation office, and she took my call, she could run the name through our database. But she might see the caller ID and not pick up. I took a deep breath, blew out my fear, and dialed. Nicole answered.

"Would you have a few minutes to do me a favor, Nicole?"

"Yes, I do."

Other than a slight hesitation before speaking, which I

may have imagined, she sounded OK. I had to make an apology to her as soon as I had a chance, but not over the phone. Coward! I always had some reason to put off pain.

"Does the name Charles Joe, aka Jubilee Joe, mean anything to you?" I asked.

"Not right off. Who's he?"

"I guess you've read about the 'two-dead' situation at 205 Evangeline Street. *The Teche News* carried an article about it last night."

"I saw the article. Your investigation?"

"Yes. One of the victims is Jubilee Joe, real name Charles Joe, and he lived in Ledoux subdivision on South Main. I'm thinking the name is familiar. Certainly, the location is. Does the name ring any bells with you?"

"Hm-m. I don't think so, but I could run it."

"Would you do that for me?"

"I'm out in the field today, but I'll be in the office tomorrow. Would that be soon enough? I could make a quick pass over there between appointments if it's urgent."

"Tomorrow's soon enough. I'd appreciate the help. This case is hoppin'. I don't know exactly where I'll be at any given time tomorrow so just call my cell. It may be important."

Nicole sounded perfectly normal. Did I?

Just before noon, two roughnecks from Downhole arrived at the Ernest house. With the help of the divers, they offloaded onto the bayou bank a heavy black box bound in foot-wide canvas straps as thick as a fire hose. Lorraine pulled on a wetsuit, and the trio dragged the box into the water. Pulling it along the bottom, they began their search. In the deeper areas of the Bayou, they submerged and continued the quest out of our sight. Spike and I followed their route by watching the bubbles.

The search area covered the distance anyone could have thrown a gun from Thomas and Kitty Ernest's back porch: forty feet upstream, forty feet below the property line, and across to the other bank. As they worked, the divers brought their treasures to the surface and turned them over to us. We examined each item they unearthed: cans, plastic bottles, coat hangers, hubcaps, tire irons, unidentifiable springs and pulleys—enough hardware to create some prize-winning yard-art. They did not find a .380 pistol or any pieces of one.

With no reason to go farther, thoroughly saturated in mud, the trio shut down the operation mid-afternoon. When they pulled off their masks, only Lorraine wore a smile.

"Not the Caribbean, for sure. But I always love to go down. Oops. Don't take that wrong."

I didn't know her well enough to quip in response.

I called Chief, gave the report, and he arranged for return of the equipment. Lorraine went home to take a shower. Spike and I walked slowly across the back of the garage and on around to the front. Where could we search next?

"You gave Ernest's car a going over, I suppose?"

"Sure did. A pair of exercise shoes and a dozen pecans in a crumpled paper bag on the back seat. That's all."

Rounding the front corner of the garage, Spike let out a yelp. I thought he'd encountered one of the deadly critters we have around here, at least a water moccasin. Not at all.

"Holy crap! I just thought of someplace I skipped. The night of the shootings I tore my hand searching in the back of the garage. I gave up to go find a Band-Aid, expecting to go back when I had a stronger pair of gloves. I clean forgot."

"Where is it you want to search?" I asked.

"There's a bin of oily rags and broken tool parts in the back of the carport. I need to get all the way down to the bottom—with better gloves. These I have on are all cut up from assembling our undersea scrap metal collection."

"I've got a pair of garden gloves in the trunk of my car. You could try them. I'm going to take one last look inside the house."

A half hour later, I heard Spike yowling again. "Bingo, Ted. I've spotted it! Bring the camera and an evidence bag. ASAP," he shouted.

I found Spike standing in the back of the garage—his face one big smile. He greeted me with a high five, and we did the most elaborate hand sashay Deuce had been able to teach us.

"There it is, Ted. Just sittin' at the bottom of the pile of rags."

I looked in. A pistol.

Spike sputtered with excitement. "I just had my snout down in that bin full of rat poop and dug out pieces of wire, scraps of cloth, broken tools, a good four feet of trash. I'd better check up on my tetanus shots, Ted, and maybe malaria and rabies while I'm at it."

The gun didn't just happen to fall back in there. It was buried. A .380 pistol, with a missing plate and clip. I recorded the location of the find with my camera. We sealed our treasure in an evidence bag and made the proper notations. Spike was ecstatic. He thought he'd found the mother lode. Maybe he had.

As usual, I looked for possible problems. "After Ernest did the deed, that is if he did it, do you think he had time to hide this pistol before calling 911?"

"Let's do a test," Spike suggested.

"Good plan. I'll walk through his possible route. You see how long I take."

I entered through the front door of the house, walked quickly down the hall and around the corner to the kitchen, then stepped high over the location of Jubilee Joe's body to go outside again. I entered the carport and headed for the bin. I pantomimed throwing the pistol in and collecting a supply of junk for cover. Then I scurried back into the house, again through the front door, walked quickly down the hall to the kitchen, and picked up the phone.

"How long did it take, Spike?"

My re-creation took four minutes. Ernest had time. There was a good possibility that's the way it happened.

Maybe. We've lost a case or two because juries expect scientific evidence like they see on TV.

"Spike, you know Mr. Byrne is going to want more than this one pistol to take the case to court. Let's take another look inside the house. Even if the crime lab ties those pieces of metal and the butt plate to our pistol, we still have only circumstantial evidence that Ernest committed double murder. Remember what Mr. Byrne has to do—support a scenario that negates *every reasonable hypothesis of innocence.* If this pistol was fired during the mess last Saturday afternoon, there's got to be a spent casing somewhere. All we've found so far are casings from the .22."

We looked. Nothing. We could demonstrate how Ernest covered his tracks, but not how he actually committed murder.

I could just hear a defense lawyer drawing out a reasonable explanation from Ernest. 'It's just an old gun I forgot about. Kitty was a demon cleaner, you know. We don't know when she found that butt plate, maybe just that morning.' Why do I always have to see problems?"

Spike looked crestfallen. I had to give our loyal dog an *attaboy.* "You did great, Spike. And we're a damn sight better off than we were this morning. For now, we've done everything we can do. Let's wait until we hear from forensics."

We dropped off our treasure at the Acadiana Crime Lab and headed back to town, calling Mr. Byrne on the way. He congratulated Spike, making lots of nice noises, then he said exactly what I expected him to say.

"I still need to figure out exactly *what* came down in that house. Could you come by the office on your way home? I know you've had a long day, but I have something I want to show you."

I called Lorraine to meet me there. We found Mr. Byrne at his desk, holding a remote control.

"Watch this with me guys," he said. The video of the crime scene rolled in front of us one more time. Mr. Byrne fast-forwarded through the preparations to enter the house, through the discovery of the body of Jubilee Joe, and on through to the pictures of the body of Kitty Ernest spread on the hearth in the den. The camera moved on to the master bedroom. Mr. Byrne froze the video on a frame showing the oversized bed.

"Look carefully as Charlie lowers the camera, guys. What do you see under the bed?"

My eyes popped open. "Wires. Can you run it again, Mr. Byrne?"

"Sure. I found another shot, but it doesn't shed any more light than the first one."

Lorraine sat forward in her chair. "I remember seeing wires under there, Mr. Byrne, but the bedside table was jammed with electrical devices. There was a telephone, a lamp, an alarm clock, a radio, and I saw a vibrator—which caught my attention. They were all plugged into an extension cord on the floor. Do you want me to go take another look at the stuff? And maybe pick it all up as evidence?"

"I do. We're racing the red hand on the life of our permission to search. Can you go out to the house right now? I'd like to go with you. We'll take some pictures to record the wires in place. We'll bring in as evidence anything that can be moved without being damaged. I think a *picture* of the vibrator will be sufficient. Poor dead lady deserves a little privacy."

We had to light up the area under the bed with a powerful flashlight to get a decent picture. In a tangle of wires, one of which had been attached to the telephone cord, sat a mini-recorder with one micro-cassette on the spool. Guided by advice from Mr. Byrne, we left the wires and the instrument in place but snapped out the cassette.

Back in his office, Mr. Byrne went in search of a cassette player. He found one. We pressed rewind and heard the deep voice of Thomas Ernest.

Friday, September twenty-ninth.

That would be the day before the shootings.

Silence, except for the whirring of the tape. Mr. Byrne let it run. After three minutes, we heard the ring of a telephone, and another voice. A woman's voice.

Hello-o.

Hello, my honey. How you doin'. A man's voice. Heavy drawl. Not Thomas Ernest. Way east of central Louisiana. Probably Alabama.

The woman again. *I have some wonderful memories. But no, I'm not doing too well. I miss you.*

And I miss you. I just have a minute because I'm leaving to visit a customer, honey. I can call you tomorrow. OK?

Oh, OK.

Bye, honey.

Mr. Byrne let the tape run to the end. Nothing further.

Well, I'll be damned. We may have found a motive. Kitty had a sweetie.

9

Once again, Chief surprised me by knowing more about my case than I did. He called to tell me the funeral for Kitty Ernest would be tomorrow morning at The Church of the Blessed Believers. I hit the internet for directions and called my partner.

"Lorraine, we have a funeral to go to tomorrow morning. OK?"

"Has to be OK, Ted. That's the way it works around here. The case agent is the officer, and the privates follow orders. Whose final celebration will we be going to?"

"Kitty Ernest's."

"Oh boy! That should be interesting. Thomas will surely attend services for his wife. Where and when?"

"*The Church of the Blessed Believers*, tomorrow morning at 11:00."

"Church of the Blessed Believers? What on earth is that? I've never heard of such a church."

"Me neither. Not until Chief gave me the name. Then I did some digging."

The funeral home website told me there'd be a sign on the right five miles up the Catahoula Highway. I supposed I'd be able to find it, but I must have driven the road out to Eugénie's parents at Catahoula Lake hundreds of times and never seen a church or a sign for one.

"I'll pick you up at the office at ten. Bring a Bible, if you have one. Preferably well used. My guess is they're deep into The Word." I hesitated. "Street clothes, of course. No uniform."

"Duh-h. You think I don't know that?"

"Sorry. Just making sure. We don't want to attract

attention."

"I'll be as modest as a Seventh Day Adventist. Hey, what's the denomination of the Believers?"

"I don't know. But I know a detective named Lorraine who'll surely be able to figure that out for me."

I drove Lorraine's white truck. A white truck is the most common vehicle on the road in these parts. I thought my electric blue Ford 350, even four years old, would be conspicuous.

Five miles past the bridge over the Bayou Teche, the Catahoula Highway takes a sharp curve to the left. Vigilance is required. When you have your attention focused on maneuvering the turn you can't be looking around for signage on the other side of the road, which is why I'd never noticed the hand-painted board tucked into the underbrush. *The Church of the Blessed Believers.* An arrow on the board pointed up to a battered street sign—*Oak and Pine Alley*—pockmarked with bullet holes. Shooting up street signs seemed to be a rite of passage for teenage boys in St. Martin Parish. The funeral home website hadn't given a street address for the church, probably because no public body maintained the access. I slowed to a crawl to maneuver a right turn into the narrow alley.

"Do you know the story of this road?" I asked Lorraine.

"Nope. I'm a northerner, you know."

"Yeah, yeah, yeah. From all of thirty miles north of here."

"You've got to admit there's a different culture north of I-10. We don't claim roots to the original French royalty, and we think the pretensions in St. Martinville are a joke. But no, I don't know the story of the road. Tell me."

"Shortly after the Louisiana Purchase, I think sometime around 1820, a high-born and wealthy Frenchman named Charles Durand came to St. Martin Parish…"

"Sorry to interrupt, Ted, but you've just made my point. We aren't favored with the 'wealthy' and 'high-born' where I come from."

"Anyway, he had his slaves build a mansion back toward the Atchafalaya River. They hadn't built levees and made the spillway back then. He planted—well probably slaves planted —these oak and pine trees. Alternately, an oak, then a pine, then an oak, and so forth on either side of the lane leading to his house. I can just imagine what traveling the road was like in those days. Elaborately gowned ladies and swashbuckling gentlemen coming to call by horse and carriage. Must have been magnificent."

"For some. I'm always amused when people yearn for the good old days. A lot went into supporting magnificence. I bet you picture yourself as a gentleman riding in the carriage and not the one cleaning horse shit out of the barn."

"OK. Point well taken. As the story goes, for the wedding of his daughters some years later, Charles Durand gilded the lily. He had hundreds of spiders brought from Catahoula Lake to spin a canopy of spider webs through the treetops and across the road. Then he had the canopy blown with gold dust. Now there's an idea for you, Lorraine. I think I heard you telling someone you have a wedding in your family next year."

"Oh my God! Promise me you won't tell my sister that story. She's already signed up enough ridiculous pageantry to break the bank!"

Oak and Pine Alley is but a shadow of its former glory. Hurricanes and winter storms dealt cruel blows, toppling some trees and leaving others as wounded warriors bandaged with hairy poison ivy vines as thick as a fire hose. The vines provided better protection for the trees than a suit of armor. Anyone attempting to groom the path would end up in the hospital with a killer case of poison ivy, begging the docs to administer a shot of cortisone.

And the potholes! In Texas, you can just squirt a trail of blacktop and have a road. In south Louisiana, we're just one good rainstorm above the swamp. When the rains come, relentless attention to maintenance is required to keep a passage in repair. This road did not have the benefit of any attention at all.

Without warning, I hit a tree root. We bounced, and Lorraine smacked her head on the roof of the car.

"Sh-sh...! I don't believe the years have favored the fortunes of Monsieur Durand's descendants. Are they still around?"

"Maybe somewhere, but I don't think back here."

"So, how much farther do we have to go?"

"The online directions to the church said to follow the alley for about a mile, then turn left into the parking area of the church. I haven't seen any sign of it yet."

In another quarter mile, I did. A shell driveway sliced a passageway between two tree trunks, exposing a clearing dominated by a large metal building with a white clapboard façade and a steeple on top. A wooden sign out front read *Church of the Blessed Believers, Noah Norbert, Pastor.*

A half dozen structures clustered around the church, one a screened pavilion the size of a basketball court, another a frame building with a sign reading *Church Office.* An elaborate climbing wall rose from a playground well equipped with swings, seesaws, and a jungle gym. Trimmed paths between the buildings and beds of seasonal flowers demonstrated one principal tenet of the Believers' creed: careful attention to the care of their compound. A startling contrast to the neglected access road. I checked my rearview mirror. A repainted school bus and a handful of cars followed us.

We were early for the service, but a couple dozen cars and a number of vans had already parked in the lot.

Lorraine was dazed and amazed. "Kind of like a summer camp. Who could know about all this back here?"

The people walking toward the church building looked friendly enough, greeting each other with a *howdy* and a wide smile. The women all wore modest dresses, heavy shoes, and gathered their long hair into tight buns at the back of their necks. Many carried Bibles—I called that one right—and what appeared to be trays of food and pitchers of a strawberry-colored drink. I couldn't help but think of Jim Jones and cyanide-laced Kool-Aid. Lorraine must have been on the same wavelength.

"I don't plan to partake of any refreshments."

"Neither me. Are you packin'?" I asked her.

"I sure am. And I'm counting on you to slap down anyone who goes feeling around for where I've stashed my piece. Are you?"

"Yes, but I'm locking my Glock in the glove box. Too bulky to conceal."

We stayed in the truck and watched a dozen more cars come in. Fifteen minutes before eleven, a black hearse with white pleated curtains pulled up to a side door of the church. Eight men with flowers in the lapels of identical—so probably rented—shiny black suits unloaded a white casket. They carried their burden inside.

"Let's go, Lo. I'll look for two inconspicuous spots for us in the rear."

About thirty people were already seated in the church. Another thirty came trailing in. We sat in the last row of chairs set up behind the permanent pews.

At the front of the room, a tall white man wearing an electric blue robe with a white cross emblazoned on the front stood on an elevated platform behind a podium. Like the statue of Christ above Rio, he held his arms spread wide in silent greeting to the gathering crowd. A great smile. He looked out over the white casket, now covered with flowers, on the floor before the podium. Stage right, a dozen men and women with a range of skin tones swayed in a syncopated rhythm as they hummed a dirge. Stage left, a gray-haired woman perched on the front edge of a bench before an upright organ. She nodded her head to direct the choir. A ten-foot-square banner on the wall behind the podium proclaimed *Let the Believers Testify to His Glory.*

Lorraine whispered in my direction. "Not much like one of those big Baptist cathedrals in Iberia Parish. More like my grandmother's Pentecostal church in Drippin' Springs, Alabama. I still don't know what flavor of church we've got here."

I could see the back of Thomas Ernest's bowed head in the front row. The woman and the man who flanked him appeared to be his daughter and son.

Lorraine gave me a poke and jerked her head to the right. "Look," she whispered. "There's Deuce." She had spotted Detective Deuce Washington slumped low in his seat. "What the hell is he doing here?"

When Deuce saw us he cut his eyes away. I gave Lorraine a negative head-shake. Deuce had signaled he did *not* want to be recognized.

Deuce didn't stand out because of the color of his skin—I estimated the crowd at a quarter African-American with a few Asians mixed in—but was noticeable because he's so damn big. He didn't carry a Bible.

With a few chords, the organist slipped into playing *Rock of Ages*. The choir and the congregation stood and sang. No hymnals. Everyone knew the words, even to the third verse.

When I take my dying breath
And my eyelids close in death
When I rise to worlds unknown
And behold thee on thy throne
Rock of Ages, cleft for me
Let me hide myself in thee.
Amen. Amen. Amen.

With the last Amen, the choir took their seats. The organist left her bench for a chair behind. Everyone hushed. All eyes fixed on the man behind the podium.

"Good morning, my Brothers and Sisters, Believers in the Lord."

"Good morning, Brother Noah."

"Today we bless the Lord."

The congregation responded, "We bless the Lord."

"Today marks six months that I have been your pastor."

In the center of the crowd, a woman stood and raised her arms in imitation of the Pastor. "We are so blessed that you came to us, Brother Noah. Indeed, we bless the Lord."

After asking the Lord to return the favor by blessing the Believers and reciting a couple verses from Isaiah and a few extraneous platitudes, Pastor Noah Norbert launched into the occasion for this gathering.

"Today we are here to thank the Lord for the life of our

beautiful Believer, Sister Kitty Ernest."

"Yes, Lord. Our beautiful Believer, Sister Kitty Ernest," the crowd responded.

"Oh, yes. Our Sister Kitty has left us for the heavenly kingdom, to see the Lord on his throne. Her beautiful crafts, including the banner that hangs behind us, testify to her faith and service to her church."

"Yes, Lord."

"We know from her worthy life that she will see the Lord on his throne."

"She will see the Lord on his throne."

Yada, yada, yada. The rhythm of the call and response lulled me to the point of dozing until I was startled to hear the pastor speak directly to Thomas Ernest.

"Brother Thomas, you truly know what it is to believe. You were in darkness. You had no sight. But you believed, truly believed. By your faith and the power of prayer, your sight was restored. Isn't that right, Brother Thomas?"

"Yes, Brother Noah."

"You were blind and now you see!"

"Yes, Brother Noah."

Lorraine gave me another poke, tilted her head, and mouthed a question— "really? He regained lost sight?" I shrugged my shoulders in response. I knew nothing about that.

The Pastor continued. "Brothers and Sisters, the family of Sister Kitty is here today to receive your support. Uphold them up in their loss, my Brothers and Sisters. Uphold them in their loss. We rejoice for Sister Kitty because she is with the Lord, but her family will surely miss her."

"They will surely miss her."

Brother Norbert spoke more and more softly, but he kept the cadence. When almost down to a whisper, he broke the rhythm. He raised his arms and shouted at the top of his lungs. "Believers! Praise the Lord!"

A good dozen Brothers and Sisters jumped out of their seats. Their response came back three times, just as loud. "Praise the Lord. Praise the Lord. Praise the Lord." The Pastor bowed his head and folded his gowned arms across his chest, like a great egret settling to roost for the night. Everyone sat down. The Pastor sat behind the podium. The gray-haired lady returned to her organ. Everyone stood again as the choir and the congregation sang *Amazing Grace*—at half speed.

One good thing, all that up and down kept the people from dozing off during the slow times.

I once was blind but now I see...

There was more from The Pastor. And more and more. Approaching the second hour, I wondered when this performance would come to an end. After a string of additional prayers—for the elimination of sin and our ultimate reunion with God—we were in for a real sermon.

"Open your Bibles, brothers and sisters. Hear the Word of God. Open your Bibles and turn to Ephesians, near the end of the Good Book. St. Paul's Epistle to the Church at Ephesus. Chapter 4. Are y'all with me?"

"Yes, Brother Noah."

"Good. Let us begin at verse 17.

Now this I affirm and testify in the Lord, that you must no longer live as the Gentiles do, in the futility of their minds, they are darkened in their understanding, alienated from the life of God because of the ignorance that is in them, due to their hardness of heart; they have become callous and given themselves up to licentiousness, given to practice every kind of uncleanness, recklessly abandoned themselves to sensuality, with a lust for the business of impurity...

"Oh, I see it everywhere, Brothers and Sisters. Everywhere sensuality and lust. Men and women abandoning their lives to sensuality. To a life of sin, in every form."

"Yes, Lord."

"My people, we see drinking and dirty dancing. We see gambling and drugs. We see infidelity. We know because the Bible tells us, that when a nation and a people turn from God's ways, evil fills the void. I give you the word of God, my Brothers and Sisters. The only path to our salvation is to root out evil and redirect our lives to the Lord. The old way of life must go. It is rotten through and through. Get rid of it! Take on an entirely new way of life.

"Sister Kitty knew the word of the Lord. Now, after her life of purity, she is with the Lord at his throne. Repent, repent, my brothers and sisters so you may be with Sister Kitty in Paradise. Praise the Lord."

The response came again. "Praise the Lord."

"Continuing in Ephesians, my good brothers and sisters, St. Paul tells us how to turn from evil.

Avoid the company of such men. For while once upon a time you were in darkness, now in the Lord, you are in the light: lead the life of those who are the children of light (for the fruit of the light consists in all that is good and right and true), verifying what pleases the Lord.

"Eliminate the sinners, my brothers and sisters. Eliminate the sinners from your life. When sin is eliminated, the Lord will take away darkness. You know that, Brother Thomas. Right? You were in darkness; you had no light. You could not see. The Lord gave you the power and now you see."

Pastor Norbert beckoned to Thomas Ernest, and cried out in a loud voice. "Testify, Brother Ernest, Testify!"

Ernest stood and called out, "Right, Brother Noah. God gave me the power and now I can see. I testify to a miracle of the Lord."

"Right, Brother Thomas," came the Pastor's response. "I say to all of you. Let the Lord take away your darkness. Eradicate sin and the sinful from your lives. Cast away sinners."

Ernest stood again and opened his arms, palms and chin upturned. "Right, Brother Noah. Root out the sin. Right, right, Brother Noah. Root it out."

As the Pastor and Thomas Ernest engaged in this call and response, a woman about halfway back in the crowd rose from her seat. She spread out her arms. Swaying to the rhythm of their words, she began to mumble. The mumble grew louder. Unintelligible gibberish! *Yodo lologrib, donafile.* I couldn't make out a word of it. I was squirming, embarrassed by the display, but the congregation kept up the

'Amen, Brother,' and 'Right, Brother' responses, with a good sprinkling of 'Praise the Lord' for good measure. A half-dozen people stood also, raised their hands, and responded with gibberish of their own.

I whispered to a wide-eyed Lorraine. "Speaking in tongues, by God."

The Pastor interrupted his sermon to accommodate the demonstration, and then resumed.

"The Lord tells us to give up the life of sin, brothers and sister. Darkness and sin. That is his call to all of us. Eliminate sin from our lives." He was shouting now. "Will you do that, my Brothers and Sisters? Will you eliminate sin and sinners from your lives? Will you live in the light of the Lord, Brothers and Sisters? With our sister Kitty to lead the way for us, we will find holy peace in the light of the Lord. Now and forever. Amen."

The people responded, "Amen. Amen." He had 'em rockin'.

The Pastor finally wore down. The organist slipped back onto her bench. She played softly. The choir stood and resumed their swaying and slow hum. The crowd hushed. Brother Noah delivered a final blessing and a dismissal prayer. The service had come to an end.

For that I praised God.

10

"Let's scram," I whispered to Lorraine. We slipped through the back door of the church—and came damn close to colliding with Deuce doing the same. We showed no sign of recognizing each other, but each headed straight to our cars. Deuce pulled away first. I maneuvered Lorraine's truck out of the lot and turned into the alley.

Speed was impossible, but I kept trying anyway, which meant we bumped all the way to the Catahoula Highway. I've been on roller coaster rides that were smoother. My cell phone vibrated in my pocket. Deuce on the line. I handed the phone to Lorraine. She punched talk, and I heard her ask: Really? Then say: yes, yes.

"Deuce wants us to meet him at Sheriff Gabrielle's office ASAP," she said.

"Tell him we're already on our way. The conversation was longer than that, Lorraine. What else did Deuce have to say?"

"He said Mr. Strait *suggested* he go to the Church of the Believers this morning. It seems the folks in the Catahoula case went to the same church as the Ernests. You know, that Catahoula case you're not supposed to be involved in?"

"The same church?"

"Yeah. Deuce says Mr. Strait wanted the benefit of his opinion of the Believers before he left the parish."

"And what was his opinion?" I asked Lorraine.

"All he said was that he was stunned to see us there. He had no idea his victim and the victim in our case went to the same church."

I couldn't imagine any connection between these couples either. Mark Gander brought Kitty and Thomas Ernest to this church, but I doubted he did the same for Virtua and Robert

Cane. A produce manager at the Piggly-Wiggly wouldn't have money for investments. Just a coincidence? I've heard Mr. Strait say it many times: *most coincidences aren't.*

I drove as fast as I dared through a big curve in the highway. My cell phone rang again. Lorraine still had it on her lap.

"It's Nicole, Ted."

Damn. I wanted to hear from her about Jubilee Joe, but not at this moment.

"Punch in the *Can't talk right now* message for me, Lorraine. I'll call her later."

The phone rang again. Lorraine took this call also and said it was Deputy Collins. Oh, yeah. The patrol deputy who found Kitty Ernest's body. I gave Lorraine the same message to deliver: *Can't talk right now.*

Deuce's car was already parked in the lot at headquarters when we pulled up. We sprinted up the staircase, passed up Chief's office, and barged right in on Sheriff Gabrielle. Now her uniform fit her to a tee, but the color brown did her no favors. This time no one gave a thought to the placement of chairs. Deuce stood before her desk. His words tumbled out.

"Sheriff, Mr. Strait wanted me to go check out the Church of the Believers before I left St. Martin. I assumed his request was because my victim, Virtua Cane, went to that church. I went to the website and saw this morning they'd scheduled the funeral service for the victim in the other case. It's incredible the way Mr. Strait seems to know everything that moves in the district."

My head and Lorraine's nodded our agreement with that opinion.

Deuce continued. "Well, who should be there at the service but Ted and Lorraine. Bottom line, Sheriff, there's some kind of connection between your two cases. You need to release Ted to follow his nose. He needs to be able to look at the whole picture."

"Easy there, Deuce. Why don't you guys sit down and tell me about what went on this morning."

We did, but we'd hardly gotten started with our report

when the Sheriff asked us to hold up while she summoned Chief Roland. The Sheriff and her chief deputy listened to our story in silence, and then Chief carried the ball with our boss.

"Turn Ted loose, Sheriff. Deuce has given Tony his investigation file. He's going home. If anything else is needed on the Cane investigation, which I doubt, Chief Smart can run it down until Martin Castille gets back from New York. We have to let Ted follow his nose."

The sheriff nodded agreement. "You're right, Chief. Ted, you have my blessing. Have at it."

Satisfied to have my restrictions lifted, and not wanting to say anything indiscreet like *I told you so*, I started to get up. Deuce was doing the same. The sheriff waved us back into our seats.

"Wait, guys. This is as good a time as any to say thanks to Deuce. A great job Detective Washington. You got hard evidence and a confession. We're giving Mr. Byrne—or rather giving Tony Blendera who'll be the DA handling the Cane trial—a damn good package. The Grand Jury will have no trouble bringing in a True Bill on this one. Congratulations."

"Thank you, Sheriff. I was glad I could pitch in."

"You should know that Mr. Byrne is already researching the ramifications of a capital prosecution for a pregnant victim. Get used to it everybody. As usual, Dennis Byrne is thinking a few steps ahead of everybody else."

Deuce again got up to leave. The Sheriff again waved him back into his seat.

"I have more to say, Detective Washington. I watched the tape of Robert Cane's confession. A masterful job. You led Cane down the primrose path by reciting the evidence you had against him as a hypothesis. The alphabet technique. *Mr. Cane, what would you say if A, B, and C?* Cane stuttered out an explanation for A), the piece of rope you found in his yard that matches the rope around the burlap sack. Cane said he borrowed the rope from his Dad to use to tie up his dog. For B), the scraps of cloth buried in the trash that match the shreds of cloth on the body, he said Virtua had made the dress herself. But when you got to C), the copy of the sales receipt from the neighborhood hardware store for a container of rat poison Cane purchased that's consistent with the poison in the coroner's tox report, he broke. He couldn't come up with any alternative explanation, and the confession came tumbling out. If I were still teaching, I'd figure out some way to redact the identifying references and use your tape in the classroom as an example of interrogation. Kids today think rough technique is necessary. It isn't—not if law enforcement does its job."

My thought: Criminals are by and large fuckin' stupid. If Cane had half a brain he wouldn't leave a trail like that. I could make use of the tape also, but as material for a TV program Mr. Byrne might write one day—CSI-Jackass. Deuce was thinking along the same lines.

"I appreciate the compliment, Sheriff Gabrielle, but you know, Cane isn't the sharpest knife in the drawer." Deuce's words were intended to end the conversation and he stood again to leave. For some reason, the sheriff wanted to talk some more.

"Detective Washington, I owe you serious thanks. You know you're making me look good. A month on the job and a murder solved. Robert Cane will be a resident in our jail before the sun goes down. I have my doubts Cane will even go through the charade of pleading not guilty."

Deuce opened his mouth to speak—but stopped. Sheriff Gabrielle would learn soon enough what happens when a defense lawyer enters the picture. Of course, everything depended on the charge the Grand Jury returned. Or more accurately, the charge the DA set them up to return. I joined the conversation on that subject.

"Sheriff, do you know what charge Tony plans to bring against Robert Cane?"

Chief answered for her. "I hear there's a hot debate going on in the DA's office on that very subject. At Tony's suggestion, Deuce prepared the arrest warrant for first-degree murder. Question: Do we have one victim or two when the victim is pregnant? We don't know what the Grand Jury will say, but the DA usually gets what he wants out of them."

Lorraine entered the conversation. "If Mr. Byrne goes with a charge of first-degree murder for Cane—a capital offense because we have two victims—we can look forward to imported talent, demonstrators on the courthouse lawn, complaints from the Police Jury about the high cost of experts, and a long ordeal before we get to the end of the road. And if he doesn't ask for the ultimate penalty, if he ignores the death of the baby, the political fallout will be brutal."

Good insight. My new partner must have experience with serious cases. I'll have to find out where she's been the past few years. She's right. Capital murder cases are hard enough to try, even without whipping up public involvement.

I stopped for a cup of coffee on the way out of the office. Deuce joined me, wanting to talk.

"Did you listen to that preacher this morning, Ted?"

"Listen? I couldn't help it. He shouted at the top of his lungs."

"I thought about Cane's confession as I listened to Pastor Nobert. Sheriff Gabrielle says she watched the video of Cane's confession, but I don't think she picked up on some of his rants. What did you think when Cane said Virtua finally had what she wanted most, to be in heaven with her Lord? Do you suppose Robert could have thought he was doing 'the right thing?' Something honorable?"

"Wow! I think you may be onto something. You'd make a good defense lawyer, Deuce."

"Defense lawyer? You sure know how to hurt a guy!"

I recalled Pastor Norbert's telling the congregation to be instruments of the Lord. *Will you do that, my brothers and sisters? Will you eliminate sin and sinners from your lives?* Preacher-man was damn close to telling his people to take the law into their own hands. Most defense lawyers—and Sarah Bernard for sure—would jump on that as indicating Cane had been influenced to kill.

I've seen it over and over. Even when defendants admit to guilt to start with, by the time a few months go by, they spin a whole new scenario in their minds to justify what they did.

Soon they actually believe they aren't guilty! Happens all the time. I never cease to be amazed.

I tried to return the call from Nicole. She wasn't in. I left word and resolved to apologize when she called back. Apologies are better in person, but an apology on the phone is better than no apology at all, which was the way I seemed to be headed.

I had a headache. Thinking about the Church of the Believers did a good job of tanking my mood.

In the hands of good defense lawyers, the religious influences on both Robert Cane and Thomas Ernest would be fertile ground for a juror's sympathy. Especially for a death penalty defense team with access to public money for psychiatrists. Speaking of money, I'd lay mine against Chief's view that Cane wouldn't even put up a defense. No way we'd get a plea of guilty on this one. And now, dammit, we'd probably have to put up with a sideshow from Right to Life. I didn't usually get down like this about my investigations, but ever since Eugénie disappeared, I'd found it harder to see the bright side of things.

Did I hope the DA would wimp out and settle for prosecuting Cane for second-degree murder? No. The sight of that perfect little body—dead—on the end of the autopsy table had taken up residence behind my eyes, right next to my headache.

PART III

11

Detective Martin Castille and his cadaver dog Plug made a triumphal return from Ground Zero. Homeland Security gave Detective Castille a plaque of recognition to add to the Sheriff Department shrine of trophies. Plug's collar displayed a genuine New York City Fire Department badge at his throat. Chief Roland pronounced the pair's exemplary service worthy of one of the department's suppers. Cooks who found themselves incarcerated in the St. Martin Parish jail prepared barbeque chicken and warming trays of spicy hot jambalaya. The Chief himself fixed a mess of cracklins.

As the crowd of sheriff's deputies, judges, district attorneys, public defenders and invited public officials drained their first beers at Cochon's camp on the levee, Martin took Plug on a promenade between the tables. The pair moved quickly. Just over five foot two, swarthy skin, black eyes and hair, Detective Martin Castille could have been taken for one of those wiry Cajun jockeys who make themselves rich and famous at the prestigious horse tracks all over the country. Next to his dog Plug, a magnificent brindle —part German Shepherd, part bull-mastiff—and nattily clad as short men like to be, Martin presented the same incongruity as a jockey in colorful silks leading a twitchy thoroughbred to the winners' circle at Churchill Downs.

The tour of the tables completed, Martin secured Plug in a kennel in the bed of his pick-up; Plug's training did not include turning him into a party animal. Martin moved his truck so he could keep an eye on Plug while he enjoyed the food and the adulation.

Good cadaver dogs are rare and valuable. In Plug, Martin had a genuine, *bona fide*, certified, number one exemplar.

Plug enjoyed a reputation all over south Louisiana as the dog who liked nothing better than to take a romp, on dry land or swamp, sniffing for the odor of a person gone missing too long.

From the time Plug had been a puppy, Martin nurtured the dog's natural instinct to seek out gamey odors. For no other behavior did Plug receive comparable rewards: not for parlor trick obedience, not for cooperation with other animals, and certainly not for being a twitchy watchdog. Just a super sniffer. The presence of rotting flesh caused Plug to freeze on his tip-claws, coal black nose aquiver, tail out straight like a banner in a stiff north wind.

I remember Plug's predecessor. He couldn't hang around the office or live at home with Martin. Pacing, snorting, sniffing, he drove us all crazy. Now Plug, he passed most of his days curled on a blanket in a corner of the squad room or on Martin's back porch. He only went to work when instructed to do so and willingly knocked off at quitting time.

When Martin returned from his truck, he headed for our table. Chief waylaid him and asked him to say a few words to the crowd about the experience.

"Dogs trained to find survivors arrived at Ground Zero while the smoke still swirled. I didn't see the need to go then. Law enforcement up there had plenty of dog-power for initial search duty. Cadaver dogs followed when hope of finding the living had faded. We arrived in New York ten days after September 11th.

"We worked the disaster site for two weeks, dawn to dark. When Plug sniffed out human remains, we pulled back and called in the recovery teams. Dangerous, dirty, and depressing duty. We welcomed the order to move our skills to a tract across the Hudson River where, once the fires had cooled, trucks brought load after load of rubble for careful sifting. Over there we were in less danger of coating our lungs with carbon or being buried alive. We worked in the New Jersey Meadowlands for another three weeks.

"Praise for our work came mostly from the firemen at Ground Zero, and from the coroners and forensic scientists who processed the debris in New Jersey. Not from the victims' families. They wanted the certainty that discovery of the body parts of their loved ones would provide, but they didn't care to hear or see details."

Would I, if or when we found Eugénie?

"I want to thank Sheriff Gabrielle and everybody else too for letting me go. Not all a good experience, but one of those times in life when you see much to admire about how selfless and giving people can be. Like when we have hurricanes. Maybe Plug has already forgotten everything up there, but I never will.

"Now I need to catch up on work around here, and I have a bunch of invitations from other departments and civic clubs all over Acadiana who want to hear about what Plug did at Ground Zero. Guys, I promise I'll do those appearances on my own time. You've been more than patient with me."

I'd been with Martin and Plug on one of those appearances. He'd describe the devastation and the accomplishments of his wonder-dog. When anticipation to see Plug do his thing built up in the audience, Martin took Plug out of his kennel and put him through his paces. Without fail, Plug alerted on one box of the three Martin had set out—the one hiding a piece of week old boudin. Plug savored blood sausage, of course.

Ongoing training to keep Plug's nose sharp required Martin to take Plug out into the country at least once a month. André and I loved these adventures. We preceded the dog and his handler to set up the double-blind, locations unknown to either one of them. We hid special treats—road kill, pieces of chicken long past expiration date, or Plug's favorite quarry, the contents of the garbage cans of a St. Martinville fireman who moonlighted as a taxidermist. His cans yielded pungent remains from dressing ducks, squirrel, or deer—whatever the hunters brought him after a weekend hunt. When the bait had been set out, Martin released Plug from the lead and gave the command to *fetch*. Dogs don't understand a string of words nearly as well as one sharp sound. Plug didn't get to keep the treasures he found. Martin rewarded his dog by giving lots of praise and tossing him a pull toy stuffed with liver treats.

One afternoon Plug alerted on an extracted wisdom tooth André had wrapped in a Kleenex and put in his pocket. André pronounced him much more reliable than the tooth fairy.

Sometimes Plug had a real assignment. The Iberia Parish Sheriff asked for his services to locate what might remain of a favorite hunting dog who had not returned to his master's duck blind at Lake Fausse Point. After a walk along the shoreline yielded nothing of interest, Martin borrowed a pirogue and took Plug out on the water. Plug rode up in the bow of the boat, relaxed, enjoying the breeze on his face, but each time they passed near a certain area the dog tensed, his tail stiffened, his nose began to quiver. He alerted on what remained of the lost dog's body under five feet of water. André had not come with us on that trip, thank God. He might have had flashbacks to the mess of crabs dining on the face of Virtua Cane in Catahoula Lake.

I wish we had Plug around a couple of years ago when a homeless man walked into the City Police Station in St. Martinville carrying a little skull he said he'd come across in Evangeline Park.

What if Plug found traces of what I wanted to find and, at the same time, didn't—my wife Eugénie? I shook my head to toss off the thought.

Nicole had once expressed interest in seeing Plug at work. I talked myself into inviting her to come along on a Saturday's adventure, also planning to use the occasion for my long overdue apology. I was damn tired of losing sleep about what to say to her; I would just say what I felt—agony about being so selfish, thoughtless, and just plain stupid. I called Probation & Parole and asked for Nicole's extension. The receptionist switched the call up front to Nicole's boss.

"No, Ted. Nicole doesn't work for us anymore."

"She doesn't? How come?"

"She asked to be transferred to Lafayette. I don't know

why. She just said personal reasons. I hated to see her go."

I couldn't wrap my mind around the report. I'd have to think about what to do next. Should I try to find her? Or had she made the move for a reason—to sever all connection to St. Martin Parish and to me? Once more I decided against action. I'd think about what to do tomorrow. I invited Lorraine to come along to Plug's training.

Saturday brought us one of those knock-your-eyes-out beautiful late winter days, the best time in Louisiana to be outdoors. Martin drove his truck; Lorraine and I squeezed into the cab with him. Plug's kennel filled the truck bed. Martin gave us ongoing commentary about a dog's senses. Lorraine ate it up.

"You know, a dog's nose is way better than yours. The surfaces in there accommodate hundreds of times the number of smell receptors. Plug's breed isn't even the best. Bloodhounds have twice as many receptors as he does. The complicated architecture of a dog's nose contributes to the efficiency. It's not just two simple passages—nostrils—like we have. Humans either sniff in or blow out. Canines do both at the same time."

Lorraine took a few intakes of breath. "What? How can anybody do that?"

"Crazy, right? When dogs pull air in, the air already inside the nostrils blows out of the side slits. Tiny wind currents created by the maneuver draw more air in."

"Go on! How can anybody know they do that? Does somebody look into that architecture, as you call it, and watch invisible air?"

"Fancy photography, I'm told. They blow up pictures of a dog's nose at work."

I liked that Lorraine didn't just accept what she was told. She had to understand. The mark of a good detective.

Martin rewarded her fascination with more information.

"Dogs can't distinguish the meaning of one word or another—they react more to the sharpness of tone, or lack of it, in voice commands—but they have a huge smell vocabulary. Properly trained, they can differentiate up to fifty distinct animal and vegetable scents. Damned if I don't think Plug could distinguish minerals as well!"

Late in the afternoon, when we had been tromping through fields for hours, we returned to Martin's truck. Plug settled into his kennel, sighed, and curled up on his blanket. The sun had warmed the cab. At the end of a clear fall day, the sky sparkled with stars. I almost broke the silence to point out the waning moon, a sliver sitting like a gondola on the Grand Canal—not that I'd ever seen Venice except in a picture. Lorraine's eyes had closed. She leaned against me. I'd forgotten the feeling of contentment from the closeness of a sleeping woman.

*　　*　　*

Before he left the parish to return to Iberia, Deuce obtained a warrant for the arrest of Robert Cane on the charge of first-degree murder. He served the warrant and Cane went to jail. At his First Appearance, Sarah Bernard, the public defender, took the appointment to represent Cane.

Tony Blendera wanted to take the case of State v. Robert Cane to the next Grand Jury. He was usually one to explore every way to resolve a serious case without going to trial, but not this time. He told Mr. Byrne he had good hard evidence and a confession. In his view, there was no doubt that Robert Cane murdered two persons. Tony saw no reason to delay.

Mr. Byrne didn't openly disagree with Tony. He just scratched his chin and steered the conversation in another direction. No victim hounded the prosecutor's office with demands for "justice," but that alone wouldn't explain Mr. Byrne's inertia. Two weeks went by.

"Clearly first-degree murder," Tony argued to anyone who'd listen. "You know the definition… *(W)hen the offender has a specific intent to kill or to inflict great bodily harm on more than one person.* The legislature worked during a long hot summer session refining the definition of *person* to be… *a human being from the moment of fertilization and implantation…* Intent? You can't tell me Robert Cane didn't know his wife was pregnant."

Mr. Byrne delayed the Grand Jury call and assigned his newbie Mandy Aguillard to search Louisiana cases for a similar prosecution. She found none. He had the DA's Association dig around for any other jurisdiction that even thought about bringing a homicide charge when the second person killed was a fetus. None. When Tony brought up the charge on another occasion, Mr. Byrne asked him the rhetorical question: why do you suppose no one prosecutes for first-degree under these circumstances? Maybe because experienced prosecutors know the legal issues would be the occasion for endless motions for post-conviction relief.

Mr. Byrne delayed and Tony fumed.

Lorraine thought she knew what was driving Tony to get to trial. His wife, Maria. Maria wanted her own baby more than anything in the world but suffered one miscarriage after another. She had spent days in Baton Rouge lobbying for an amended definition of *person—a human being from the moment of fertilization and implantation.* One night KLFY late news showed footage of a demonstration on the Capital steps. Lorraine spotted Maria in the middle of a group carrying a banner reading *Save the Unborn.* If Tony didn't prosecute Robert Cane for first-degree murder, he might go home to an empty house.

I almost put in my two-cents worth with the suggestion they ask Mr. Strait to settle the dispute. No. I should stay out of it. Not my call, and I was damn glad of that. If they took a plea to life in this case, I'd be OK with it, except... I couldn't get out of my head the image of the little body on the end of Dr. Pétain's autopsy table. If we don't remember the unborn, who will? Mr. Byrne promised to keep me posted on the difference of opinion. I turned my attention to seeking justice for the two victims whose fate was my call: Kitty Ernest and Jubilee Joe.

We didn't need a cadaver dog to detect odor rising from Thomas Ernest's account of what happened on the afternoon his wife received fatal shots in her house on Evangeline Street. Who goes to town to look for a yardman with only a couple hours of light left in the day? What neat-freak has no explanation for leaving around parts of a gun he claims he last used 'long ago?' What man wouldn't be driven to extremes by uncovering his wife's infidelity? But I had to accept Mr. Byrne's opinion that we did not yet have enough to meet the requirements for a conviction based upon circumstantial evidence—evidence sufficient to rebut every reasonable hypothesis of innocence.

Additional tapes of Kitty Ernest's conversations with her lover must exist, and surely, they would confirm and flesh out our theory about motive—a jealous spouse who lost it. Motive is not one of the elements of the crime of homicide, but every prosecutor I've dealt with wants that arrow in his quiver. If I could find additional tapes, Mr. Byrne might approve Thomas Ernest's arrest. Where would Ernest have stored mini-cassettes? Ah! A logical place would be his office. I prepared a search warrant for Mr. Ernest's Quality Cleaners. Mr. Byrne approved.

Blank trip. We found a tape recorder but no cassette tapes.

Mr. Byrne had a suggestion. "You know, when Ernest inherited and then sold the family farm in central Louisiana, our busybody Mark Gander put him into a substantial annuity—payments to Ernest and a nice service fee for the agent every month. Gander kept Ernest close, protecting his cash cow. In fact, he brought Kitty and Thomas into his church. See what you can get out of Gander."

Lorraine called Mark Gander and asked if we could come by for a visit and talk to him about his friend, Thomas Ernest.

"Oh, I don't know about that. Thomas Ernest is my friend and..." Yada, yada, yada. He went on with his waffling. Lorraine put me on the line. I usually played the bad cop when I worked with Lorraine.

"See here, Mr. Gander. It looks to me like you're getting your jollies being in the know with this investigation, following us on your scanner, saying you want to help. But you tell us nothing at all. I know you want to keep your paying account happy, but at this point, you have no choice in the matter. Unless you give us some help, I'm going to charge you with interfering with a criminal investigation."

His response came sputtering out. "OK, OK. What is it you want to know?"

"I want you to come in to the station, or if you prefer, we'll come to your house. Then we're going to talk. You're going to tell me everything you know about the relationship between Thomas Ernest and his wife Kitty."

After an audible sigh, Gander agreed to an appointment for the following day, at his house, by myself, no uniform, unmarked car.

I left my car two houses away from Gander's and walked up the road to his back yard. I found him pumping his short, fat legs around in a fenced area containing yard equipment, a couple of chain-link dog kennels, and three yellow Labs off lead. Gander wore gray sweat pants cut off above the knees, a muscle shirt of the same limp gray material, dirty athletic shoes, no socks. Although the dogs howled like hyenas as I walked up, once inside the yard, they loved me up. Martin's lecture had given me greater respect for a dog's olfactory skill, but I could do without a demonstration on my crotch. I may not have enough receptors to sniff out rotting flesh under water, but mine are good enough to know the kennels could have used a good hosing down.

I asked Gander to put the Labs in the kennel. He did so. After a few preliminaries, I went to work on an interrogation.

"Mr. Gander, did you ever know of Thomas Ernest taping anybody's telephone conversations?"

The snap turn of his head told me the correct answer was *yes*, but he stumbled to say he wasn't sure. I spotted a sawhorse next to a lawn tractor and sat on it. I leveled my eyes on his.

"I'll ask the question again, Mr. Gander, and this time you *will* answer."

"Well, yes, yes," Gander sputtered. "I remember one time I walked into the office at the cleaners and saw him sitting at his desk with his fingers on the buttons of a tape recorder. He was flustered to see me and quickly proffered an explanation. He said he'd been trying to tape an employee he suspected of stealing cash. He hadn't succeeded."

"Did you see any more tapes around there, other than the one in the machine? A stack or a box he could have used to tuck them away? Anything like that?" I asked.

"No, I didn't. What are you saying?" Gander pumped around the dog yard again, staying close to the kennel. Sweat had popped out on his fat forehead and darkened the underarms of his gray shirt. The temperature that day wasn't above sixty.

"Just suppose Thomas Ernest had some cassette tapes he needed to put away somewhere, not in his house or his office. Somewhere else. Where do you suppose he'd take them?"

"Well, I don't know."

And why do you think I might know something like that? his tone implied.

"I'll help you think, Mr. Gander. Do you suppose he might hide tapes in his son's house? You know, Patrick's house up the line, in the country?" I asked.

Gander answered, and I remember his exact words. "That's a good guess. Your guess is as good as mine. Patrick calls the place his *farm*. There's a big barn out there guarded by a couple of Dobermans. That would be as good a place as any, I guess. Those animals are *serious* watchdogs. Sure. That's it."

Later, Gander's lawyers would claim I lied to get a search warrant for the son's house. Gander had sworn to his lawyers he never told me the tapes were there. Maybe not in words of one syllable, but that's how I interpreted his equivocations.

After that revelation, I thought I had Gander on the defensive, in a mood to spill more.

"Mr. Gander, we have reason to believe Thomas Ernest bugged the telephone in his bedroom in order to tape his wife's conversations with someone—a man. Do you have any information to lead you to believe he might have thought his wife was having an affair?"

"Wowee!" Let me think about that a minute." Gander made another circuit of the dog yard. He stopped. He perched one butt-cheek on the Workmate, the loose material of his shorts expanding to accommodate the swell. "Let me tell you this. About three weeks ago I had Tom's annuity check to deliver. You know, I put him in a very nice plan when he sold the family farm. I called his office, but he was just leaving to go home. He asked me to come out to his house. I'd never been invited there before. His house is just up the road a bit. Well, I guess you know that." Gander laughed at his own stating of the obvious. "Let me say this: that day Kitty Ernest looked entirely different from any time I'd ever seen her before."

"Explain that to me, Mr. Gander. How did she look different?"

"Well, in Church, Kitty'd always be all proper, like Queen Elizabeth, I'd say. You know, flowery dress swelling over her big buzooms." He moved his arms around an imaginary beach ball on his chest. "She'd carry her pocketbook before her in the fig leaf position." Gander stood up and crooked his left wrist to hold the straps of an imaginary object in front of his crotch. He took a few mincing steps. He demonstrated the royal beckoning wave with his right hand, adjusting his puffy lips into a saccharine smile. His little dance step broke me up.

Gander continued. "Kitty was the vamp at the house that day. She was dressed to flirt—and flirting—a mini skirt, heavy make-up, false eyelashes. I was shocked." Gander smirked. "She couldn't have dressed like that to come on to me; she wouldn't have had time."

Damn! I snorted. He was serious! Kitty Ernest hadn't had time to prepare herself for Gander's visit, but she woulda if she coulda! Maybe there were a few other reasons to think Kitty Ernest hadn't dressed to snare Mr. Gander. Gander would never make the cover of *True Romance*. He had, as my father-in-law would say, been hit by an ugly stick.

Mark Gander was now wound up to tell his story. "I had this premonition. I looked at Kitty dressed like that. I looked at Tom's face looking at Kitty dressed like that. I looked at his boot where I knew he packed a pistol. I came home and said to the wife, 'I think Tom Ernest is going to kill her.' I really said that. You can ask my wife."

Gander stood up and paced around a bit more. "Yes, he might hide something at his son's house."

It was a stretch, but I used this information to justify asking Mr. Byrne to approve a search warrant for Patrick's house.

I knew again why I wanted to be a detective. I'd been a good student all through school. My mom always thought I'd be a lawyer. But we had no money when my father died, and I had to drop out of college. Mom said she could go to work and I could take some temporary job to save up to return. I had another plan.

I told Mom I didn't want to go back to school. I signed on with the Sheriff and went to the Police Academy. I fell in love with Eugénie Boudreaux; six months later we married. André was on the way.

Mom was crushed. 'I just don't understand. Why do you want to pour through someone's old garbage?' she asked me. 'You need to look at what's to come, make some contribution to the future, not the past?'

Because, I told her, figuring out what actually happened races my motor. I don't spend every weekend going out to the swamp to kill something—ducks, turkeys, squirrels, whatever is in season. This is my hunt, and I love it.

All of which is probably why my Mom had been cool to her daughter-in-law Eugénie. That and the fact that Eugénie's mother was a *traiteur*.

Gander and I talked a little bit more about the Ernests, but I was antsy to go looking for tapes. A few nice noises and I was out of there, on my way to see Mr. Byrne for help preparing a search warrant for Patrick Ernest's house in the country. Mr. Byrne approved the application easily enough, but he had other concerns.

"Are you going with Lorraine?"

"Well, yes. Of course. She's my partner on this case."

"I'm going to ask Chief Deputy Roland to send a unit to cover you two out there. There's a bit of suspicion about that guy."

"Suspicion of what?"

"We don't really know, but Chief Roland implies something shady. He has a huge house and no visible means of support. Not his wife's money because he has no wife. Chief Deputy Roland will probably be happy we have a way to get a look in there. But be careful."

12

Patrick Ernest lived in north St. Martin, in the fragment of the parish split from the more populous south by the Interstate Highway. In ages past, the Red River coming out of the west cut deep fissures in the terrain as it roared through on its way to join the Atchafalaya River, a path now blocked by the levee the Corps of Engineers built after the High Water of 1927. Beautiful country, but not suitable for cultivation. Stands of forest remain uncleared, preserving an impenetrable thicket rather than the fields and individual specimen trees of the south. The topography holds at bay encroachment by cotton farms on the north and sugarcane fields to the south. Here nobody borrows a cup of sugar from a neighbor. Like the Attakapas Indians who once roamed the area, inhabitants treasure the natural contribution to their isolation.

In the affidavit attached to my application for the search warrant for Patrick Ernest's house and barn, I swore that Mark Gander 'said' Thomas Ernest would hide a treasure on his son's property, admittedly a stretch. Lorraine and I headed for the address 911 had provided—405 Coulee Rouge, Breaux Bridge. I caught sight of a black and white unit in my rearview mirror. Comforting. I didn't mind a bit Mr. Byrne's arrangement for the department to keep us covered.

After we passed under the Interstate, we found a sign in English—Red Coulee Road—and turned in. At first, we saw no numbers on the weather-beaten houses set back from the road. We had been told Patrick had a beautiful big house. Nothing measured up to that description. We hadn't even seen a blade of tended yard—only untrimmed trees and scrubby weeds.

Rounding a curve, we confronted a faux French Provincial, one and a half stories tall, on a spread of lawn. Had to be Patrick's house. A shell drive curved around the front and disappeared into trees and underbrush in the rear. Not really a mansion, but what passed for one in present company. A hip roof and wide double doors indicated the barn, Mark Gander's candidate for the most likely place to conceal a treasure. A dark green BMW sports car sat in the drive that connected the house to the barn.

I had called ahead to say Lorraine and I were coming out to talk. I hadn't mentioned the search warrant. We introduced ourselves to the man who answered our ring at the front door. He had the long face, angular features, and tall, lean frame of his father. Not the deep voice, however. Patrick got the squeaky sing-song from his mother's genes.

Patrick was not alone. The twitching, snorting muzzles of two black and chestnut-brown Doberman Pinchers flanked his hips. Four unblinking eyes fixed onto ours. From deep in their throats, a feral rumble rolled as background for our introductions.

I handed Patrick a copy of the search warrant and asked him to tie up the dogs so we could go to the barn to look for micro-cassette tapes belonging to his father—unless he wanted to cooperate and turn the tapes over to us on his own. He claimed to have no idea what we were talking about.

Lorraine and I reached into our pockets for surgical gloves. What little hospitable expression Patrick had, fell away. Poker-faced, he pointed to the outbuilding. "Have at it," he said.

With a parting command to the dogs to sit and stay, Patrick closed the animals inside the house. He sat down on the front step and stretched out his legs. His gray boots made a directional signpost for our path to the barn. When we were out of range for him to hear us, Lorraine mumbled. "Ostrich like his father's. I'd price that footwear at $450 minimum."

Searching the so-called barn didn't take long. There was next to nothing inside. A clean, zero-turn riding lawn mower, a gas can, and fewer tools than I had in my outside shed to cut the grass at my 50-foot lot in town. No farm equipment. No tapes. No storage containers that could have held them. We returned to the house.

Patrick stood up as we approached. "I told you guys I don't have any tapes. Hell, I don't even know what they are. See you around sometime."

Lorraine picked up her chin to level her eyes in a challenge. I nodded a signal to cue her to lead the confrontation.

"We're not leaving quite yet, Mr. Ernest. We're going inside your house. You can tell us where the tapes are or we can tear your house apart. Your call."

Patrick repeated his denial. He scowled. His eyes stripped her naked, which pissed me off. Lorraine must have sensed my ire because she mouthed 'chill.'

Undeterred by what she knew was a menace on the other side of the front door, Lorraine mounted the steps. She passed around Patrick, turned the knob, and stepped inside. The two dogs stiffened their backs and held their ground, uncut tails curled in an S down their backsides. Their ears rotated to pick up their master's command. Patrick repeated his order for the dogs to 'sit' and 'stay.' They obeyed. Lorraine walked around them and I followed.

Under cathedral ceilings, we passed through a formal entry, formal dining room, and stopped in a formal living room. Straight out of a furniture store. No one did much *living* in these cold rooms. Lorraine crossed to one of two leather sectional sofas, picked up a bottom cushion with her left hand, and held it aloft. She reached into her pocket with her right hand and drew out a folded knife. She snapped it open. A switchblade, no less. She held the knife a few inches from the cushion.

"The easy part is over, Mr. Ernest. We aren't leaving here until we find those tapes. Do you want to tell us where they are? We might make things messy."

I enjoyed watching Lorraine's routine but kept poised to intervene should Patrick call her bluff. He stared her down for a few moments, then turned those fancy boots to a doorway on the right.

"OK, OK. Wait here with the dogs."

We didn't wait but followed to see where he'd go. He strode into a kitchen worthy of the pages of *Dwell Magazine*. He walked past a good spread of dark granite counter and stopped at a closet on the far side of the room. He opened the door, reached up, and snapped open a breaker box. He threw a switch. Was the house wired for an alarm? A booby-trap? Lorraine exhibited not a twitch of fear. Cool. We returned to the living room.

With a sweep of a very long arm, Patrick indicated the hall on the other side of the kitchen, directing Lorraine to lead the way. I brought up the rear. Behind us, the Dobermans settled in the doorway, blocking our retreat.

A few steps into the hall, Lorraine reached toward a doorway on her right, and with the same motion, turned the knob and pushed inside. The dogs came to attention, scraping their toenails on the wood floor and chugging like a pair of locomotives. Four ears pointed straight up. The feral rumble we'd heard on the front step resumed.

Quickly reacting to Lorraine's movement, and the cue from his dogs, Patrick rushed to Lo's side. He grabbed her arm and dragged her back into the hall.

"No! Not that way. Over here," he said. Being man-handled, Lorraine probably didn't see very far into the room. I did.

A long counter stretched along the far wall and turned the corner around to the left. In the semi-darkness—the window shades were lowered—I saw a score of computer screens spaced along the surface of the counters. Terminals of some kind rested at each. Stacks of light blue paper lay beside them. A battery of buttons in a rectangular box hung above the counter on the left wall. A switchboard?

Patrick snatched my arm and pulled me behind Lorraine. He prodded the two of us farther down the hall and into another bedroom, one conventionally furnished in masculine brown tones. Lazy-boy, wide screen TV, table of snacks, refrigerator on the far side. Here Patrick did his *living*. He shoved the door closed behind us and turned the key in the lock, thankfully shutting out the dogs but raising my internal temperature. He pocketed the key; we were locked in. The three of us stood in a silent, triangular face-off.

My body went into the ready position: shoulders dropped, abs pulled in, fingers and knees flexed. Patrick had me by four inches and at least forty pounds, Lorraine by double that. Her arms moved almost imperceptibly away from her body, her right arm poised for the next move— either to reach for her weapon or to stiffen her hand and deliver a chop.

Without a word, Patrick bounded onto the king-sized bed in the center of the room. He spread his legs for balance and reached over his head to pull down the light fixture in the ceiling. He let it swing on the springs that had held it in place. He thrust his hand deep into the exposed hole and pulled out a small briefcase. He let the briefcase fall onto the bed below. He stepped down to the floor, leaned over the bed, and snapped open the clasp.

At first, I thought the case was empty. Bingo! I saw two stacks of micro-cassettes, each secured with a rubber band, and a few scraps of paper. Patrick stood back and said nothing.

I've done hundreds of searches in my time but never looked behind a light fixture in the ceiling. I will from now on.

With gloved fingers, I snapped the briefcase closed, leaving the contents inside. Lorraine filled out the Warrant Return and gave Patrick a copy, receipting for one small briefcase containing two packages of micro-cassette tapes and three doctor's prescriptions I couldn't decipher. Patrick unlocked the bedroom door and commanded the dogs to the side. Without revealing either our satisfaction at having found the tapes or anxiety about the creepy setup, we walked out the front door and got into our car.

Lorraine and I did not speak until the house had vanished from our rear-view mirror. I caught a glimpse of the sheriff's unit perched behind a fortuitously located stand of trees.

"Holy Mary, Mother of God! Those dogs!" Lorraine sank back into the car seat and closed her eyes. Being turned on by an aggressive woman was a first for me.

"You were terrific, Lo. If you were afraid of those beasts, I sure couldn't tell. You've got your 'I can handle anything' face down pat. I thought any minute I was going to see you go into a Crouching Tiger, Hidden Dragon routine."

"Right now, I could throw up."

"Really? You want me to stop?"

"Shit no. I want you to beat it out of here just as fast as you can."

Lorraine pressed the button to lower her window. The sound of deep breathing swished toward me from my right. Almost back to headquarters, I dared talk about our search.

"You OK?" I asked.

"Just about."

"Did you get a look into that first room?"

"Not really. I thought I saw some sort of table across the way, but Patrick jerked hard. I thought I'd fall down. He sure didn't want me to see any more. Did you?"

"The light was pretty dim, and I only had a few seconds before he pulled me out. A counter stretched all across the far wall, beneath windows with the shades pulled down. The counter made a curve to the left and continued past where I could see. Looked like computers and messy stacks of blue paper were spaced along the surface. Between the windows, a rectangular frame with buttons of some sort hung on the wall above the counter. Maybe a switchboard?"

Lorraine sighed. "A farm with no farm animals, a barn with no equipment, a huge house with one guy living in it, serious watchdogs, a room with a battery of computers."

"Yeah, and no visible means of support says Mr. Byrne."

"What the hell has Patrick got there?" Lorraine asked.

"Actually, I don't give a fuck. I just want to hear the tapes we cadged."

Back at the office, Lorraine set up the cassette player, put the first tape on the spindle, and pressed *Play*. We listened to our prize. On the first tape, and on every one thereafter, we heard the deep voice of Thomas Ernest. The master of ceremonies announced a date. For a good stretch, we heard nothing but the whir of the tape, then the ringing of a telephone, and another pause. A voice we soon learned was Kitty Ernest oozed a melodious *hello-o*. A third voice identified itself as Reggie. On the first tape we listened to, and on most of those that followed, the billing and cooing of two lovers, an exchange of moans followed by sharp cries, both female and male, left little doubt about what was up between these two.

"Well, whaddya know," said Lorraine.

I rewound the first tape, again pressed play to listen and fix the words in my mind. Thomas Ernest's voice announced a date:

Wednesday, September 7. A telephone rang.

Hello-o.

Hello, my dahlin'. A Mississippi drawl.

Oh, Reggie. It's you!

Whatcha doin' my dahlin', Kitty, my Kitten?

Just catchin' a few extra minutes of sleep. I stayed up so-o late last night, working on my dolls. I made some really cute ones, Reggie—little round faces with itty-bitty lace halos.

I bet they're beautiful because they look just like you, Kitten.

Giggles. This morning I just couldn't wake up. You know what? Thomas came to wake me. He stood by the bed and asked me if he looked any different. I kept my eyes shut. 'I shaved my mustache,' he said. 'That's what you wanted, right?'

So, I guess you looked at him, my honey. Did he look better?

Not to me, he didn't. Looked like the same old mule face to me. He wanted to know if now he got a little kiss. Ugh! One of those wet, fish-mouth kisses? No way. I quick gave him a little peck.

Nothin' else?

Nothin' else. He left. You know what, Reggie? I don't think he can do anythin' else. That's what my friends tell me. They say they have the same problem. Men just wear out faster. But I know better. Some men his age have plenty to give. Right, Reggie? More giggles.

Right honey. I have plenty for you. A long pause and Kitty Ernest spoke again. *By the way Reggie, I'm not going to be able to go to Mobile weekend after next.*

Oh, dahlin'. You won't? The male voice said, *whoa-went. Is anythin' wrong? I'm so disappointed.* The male voice cracked.

My phone bill comes on the 18th so I need to be here. Kitty giggled some more.

You do?

To get the bill before he does. I don't want him to see the charge. Giggles again. Deliberate torture. *Oh, Reggie. I was thinking of coming this weekend instead!*

Oh, oh, you naughty, naughty kitten! You had me really scared. This weekend is even sooner.

Reggie, my darlin'. I'll be waiting for you know what!

A conversation to make a cuckold lose his self-control.

Lorraine and I made tracks to the sheriff's office. A message from Nicole waited for me at the front desk. 'No mention of subject in P&P files.' It was a long shot at best. I asked the desk to call Nicole and tell her thanks. I'd get back to her as soon as I could.

Lorraine carried the ball reporting to Sheriff Gabrielle and Chief Roland. The barn was clean; we found a bunch of tapes in a back bedroom ceiling fixture. Chief was impressed.

"By God, you've got it now. Let's go see Mr. Byrne."

Mr. Byrne listened to a few samples and agreed. He had no doubt about the activities taking place at both ends of the conversation. We had a green light to prepare an arrest warrant for first-degree murder, twice. I saved our report on the computer room at Patrick Ernest's house for last. Chief Roland took over on this topic.

"Mr. Byrne, we believe our man Patrick has a dirty little secret. A few months ago, the phone company told me there were seventeen phone lines going into that house. All unlisted numbers. We notified the State Police, and they're planning to bring in the Feds. They suspect Patrick is part of a gambling operation—not something for us to fool with on the local level." He turned to me. "Ted, Patrick may have dangerous connections, which is why I had a unit tailing you, just in case."

Mr. Byrne scowled. He didn't want to hear this. "A complication. My priority right now is a double murder. I'm going to need Patrick Ernest on the stand to get those tapes in evidence. I'll see if I can get the FBI to hold off. And guys," he glanced at each one of us but stopped at Chief as he completed his instruction. "Lips zipped on this one."

Mr. Byrne continued. "I have more news. I just received Dr. Pétain's report on his autopsy of Kitty Ernest. Why don't you and Lorraine come by tomorrow morning, and we'll go over what our coroner has to say. Maybe soon we'll have enough evidence to make a move."

"We'll be here first thing."

"Good. Get these packets of cassette tapes signed in to the evidence locker. By the way, Ted, Patrolman Collins is looking for you."

"Damn it. I know, and I just haven't gotten to him. We can't seem to be in the same place at the same time. I'll give him a call."

But I didn't. I was distracted.

We already thought Patrick and his sister had a puzzling reaction to the discovery of their mother's body. Now, this. A son more interested in his shady livelihood than in the tragedy of his father knocking off his unfaithful mother. I needed a break to get my brain straight. I asked Lorraine to come with me to take André out to Possums for one of those meals he loves. Everything deep-fried.

After we'd finished our dinners, Lorraine pulled a baseball out of her purse and asked André to show her how to hold her fingers on the lacing to throw a curve ball. Pretty obvious strategy to get him into the conversation, I know, but it worked. I'd had to leave him on his own a lot lately so I appreciated her attention. Satisfied with the day's adventure and the evening's pleasure, I looked forward to a good sleep.

Not to be. I awoke around midnight, disturbed by car headlights playing on the wall of my bedroom. After a third round of the light show, I got up and stepped out onto the front porch. A BMW parked under a streetlight flashed SOS with its headlights. A green BMW convertible.

What kind of a creep was Patrick Ernest anyway? His father's troubles were not his main concern. We'd just seen him give up the tapes rather than let us uncover his business operation, but he must have realized I had a look-see into that room full of computers. Did he think I wouldn't know what was going on? No, he knew I would. He thought he could scare me into silence.

I wasn't afraid, but I wanted to get word to him that I didn't give a crap about how he made his living. I couldn't, not without having him realize I had his father in my sights for a charge of capital murder. Although Patrick had shown no sign of caring for anyone but himself, I had to believe he'd think twice before helping his father get sent to Death Row.

13

Lorraine and I didn't go into Mr. Byrne's office for our meeting. When we checked in, the District Attorney's receptionist Marlene showed us into an unoccupied office. Mr. Byrne had commandeered the room for the Ernest case. There's an advantage to being understaffed—extra space.

Mr. Byrne stood military at ease behind a large rectangular folding table in the center of the room—not in a military uniform, of course, but in the coat and tie he always wore to work. He had pushed a desk and chairs against one wall. On another wall, he had taped poster paper on which he'd drawn two figures, one male and one female, as large as life. No body parts. Only long dark locks marked one figure as feminine.

"Come in, detectives. A good afternoon to you both, and welcome to my workshop. May I introduce you to Kitty Ernest and Jubilee Joe."

Gentlemanly words but he didn't take his eyes off the posters. Lorraine picked up the game. "Good morning to you, Mrs. Ernest and Mr. Joe." I like that she is quick.

Consulting the pages of the ballistics report from the Acadiana Crime Lab he had spread on the folding table, Mr. Byrne decorated the figures by drawing bullet holes in the referenced places. He used a red marker, of course. Blood. He scratched his chin and mumbled something, but I didn't catch it.

"I couldn't hear what you said there, Mr. Byrne."

"I was thinking out loud. *Curiouser and curiouser, said Alice.* Have you ever heard of two persons who have no connection to one another each shooting two different victims in the same pattern, within minutes?"

A rhetorical question. Of course, we hadn't. Mr. Byrne pointed first to one figure and then to the other.

"The coroner's report tells us each of these victims first received a shot here in the left upper chest, where, incidentally, a lay person believes the heart to be. It isn't. More like in the center of the chest, tilted to the left. In both instances, the initial shot was not fatal. The woman, who had been seated, then took a shot to the forehead. The man, who had been standing, took a second shot in the forehead as well."

Lorraine spoke up with a question. "Are you saying we can conclude from the wound patterns that the shots were fired by the same person? Ernest admits he shot Jubilee, therefore—"

"At this point, we're a long way from making conclusions. I'm just finding the patterns curious. That's all."

Again, consulting the Acadiana Crime Lab report on the table, Mr. Byrne read an excerpt from the study of the clothing of Kitty Ernest.

Microscopic examination of gunpowder particles taken from Exhibit G-7, the blouse removed from the body of Kitty Ernest during the autopsy, indicates the barrel of the weapon was between three and five inches away from her chest. Note: The coroner's report, attached, states that the shot to the chest was the first shot fired.

"So, Mr. Levy concludes Kitty Ernest was shot at close range?" I asked.

"Yes. And more. Remember where Mrs. Ernest was sitting—on the hearth on the far side of the room, the side of the hearth closest to the bedroom. According to Ernest, he heard shots, came out of the bedroom into the hall and saw that his wife had been shot. And Jubilee was running down the hall." Mr. Byrne dug out a floor plan of the house and pointed out the area at the end of the hall. "If Jubilee was the one who had just shot Kitty Ernest, he would have had to enter the den from the hall. He would have had to cross the room and walk right up to her without her being alarmed. Impossible."

This impossible scenario had me excited. "Would Kitty Ernest, a middle-aged, southern, white woman, just sit there playing with her dolls, as an African-American yardman, whom she'd never in her life seen before, carrying a rifle, walked right up and blew a hole in her chest? No way. Couldn't have happened. Only for someone well known to her would she have sat still. Thomas Ernest is a murderer, and he's walking around free as a bird. I say we get an arrest warrant and slap his ass in jail."

"No, not yet, Ted. At this point, I can give a pretty fair hypothesis of guilt, but that won't do the job. Remember my burden. To succeed with solely circumstantial evidence, I must rule out *any other reasonable hypothesis of innocence.* I'm afraid we're going to have to keep working until we have the evidence to explain what *did* happen, not just that Thomas Ernest's version is baloney."

I knew he was right.

"And Ted, we have a lot better chance of finding physical evidence persuasive to jurors, conditioned as they are from watching CSI, if Ernest is walking free, without a lawyer, than we do if he's in jail. I'm waiting for the analysis of dust prints taken from the newspapers spread in front of Kitty Ernest. From what I saw the night of the homicides, there was only one shoe print on the papers, and that print did not match the very distinctive sole of Jubilee's sneakers."

I pictured the hearth corner where Kitty Ernest sat. Someone coming from the bedroom could reach her from the left, her right side, where there were no newspapers. In order for someone coming in from the hall to avoid the newspapers, he would have had to go around in front of her first. If the dust print lifter analysis did not show Jubilee's sneaker tread, did that rule him out? I was working through the scenarios in my head when Mr. Byrne dismissed the whole inquiry about dust prints.

"I'm not going to count on shoe prints or the absence of them to save the day. If we go for the penalty of death, the case will be on the capital track, and we don't know yet which judge will be the lucky loser. A couple of the judges don't take kindly to new forensic methods. *Not generally accepted* is probably what we'd hear. How do you get a new procedure generally accepted if you can't get it out on the table?"

Marlene stuck her head in the door. "Richard Levy from the Acadiana Crime Lab is downstairs right now, Mr. Byrne. About to check through security. He says he'll be upstairs in five minutes."

He wasn't. After an additional fifteen minutes, Marlene came back with an explanation. "The reserve deputy they brought in to man the security screener freaked out at the sight of what Mr. Levy is carrying—a rifle and a pistol. They're all nervous down there because of the demonstration going on out on the front lawn."

"Demonstration? What's that about?" Mr. Byrne asked.

"I can help with that," I told him. "I saw a bunch of people marching around the front lawn carrying signs and shouting something about a baby killer. I suspect news of the Catahoula case has hit the airwaves."

A weary sigh came from Mr. Byrne's direction. "How have people found out about that? Tony hasn't even been to the Grand Jury to get an indictment. I guess I'm being naïve, the way things are today. the Teche telegraph, I think it's called."

I suspected the leak came through Maria Blendera by way of her husband Tony.

Mr. Byrne asked Marlene to send Mandy downstairs to vouch for Richard Levy's good intentions.

"Is Mandy going to be second chair on this case?" I asked Mr. Byrne after she left.

"We're a long way from even thinking about who'll handle the trial. This is the period of investigation. We have to keep open minds. Who knows? Too many investigators— and too many DAs for that matter—get hold of a theory and look for evidence to support it rather than letting the evidence lead."

I felt chastened. Had I been too quick to judgment? Maybe Jubilee shot Kitty Ernest and Thomas, the outraged spouse, killed the culprit?

No. No way. Lorraine was on the same wavelength. "Yeah. And maybe it was a bushy-haired stranger."

I'm learning to count on Lorraine to get off a sassy comment and hope our superiors aren't offended. But her behavior at Patrick Ernest's house was no joke. She handled the situation like a 20-year veteran detective. I wanted to know a lot more about her.

Mr. Byrne said something that made me understand his caution.

"There's interesting psychological research that says we're more likely to find a specific result if we test for that specific finding—like autism or PTSD, for example. The number of positive results is higher than if all the pertinent questions are buried in a general study and we analyze that data. I don't know if the hypothesis has ever been applied to guilt or innocence." He paused. "Enough of the theorizing. I do know I want more evidence for the trial than I have right now, and I'm more likely to get more if Thomas Ernest is a free man. Right?"

"Right."

"OK. And if we leave him free while we look for more evidence, we aren't exposing the public to a repeat crime. Thomas couldn't commit the crime a second time—bump off his unfaithful wife! Already been done." That from Lorraine of course.

Before long, Richard made it through the downstairs security scanner and up to Mr. Byrne's workroom. He unloaded three evidence bags onto the table. Mr. Byrne, Lorraine and I drew up chairs. Richard had made extra copies of his report so we could follow his lesson in forensic science.

Mr. Levy started with the evidence bag containing the larger weapon, holding it aloft for our inspection. "Gentlemen, we have an interesting situation on our hands. We have here a .22 caliber slide action pump Rossi rifle with a tubular magazine. In all four of his statements, Ernest tells us he kept such a rifle handy for security, 'propped just inside the utility room by his back door,' he said." Richard Levy handed the evidence bag to Mr. Byrne, who had those wrinkles of concentration across his forehead. "Exact same words in each statement, by the way."

"Thomas Ernest was no big game hunter. This is the kind of gun you might be given at a street fair to take a shot at winning a teddy bear for your girl."

Mr. Byrne smiled at the disparagement.

"Ernest says he chased Jubilee down the hall and wrestled the rifle out of his grasp. He then turned the weapon on Jubilee and shot him, he did not know how many times. We picked up the rifle lying on the floor at the end of the hall, next to Jubilee's body. A plausible story, but..."

Mr. Byrne's raised eyebrows sent another deep furrow across his forehead. I'm getting good at reading his face. My interpretation of his expression? Don't give me theories, Mr. Levy. Just describe what you have. Richard read him as I did and turned to his evidence bags.

"OK. What I have for you today can be lumped into three categories. First, I have the rifle we've just talked about." He held up the largest evidence bag. "Second, I have a pistol." He held up the smaller bag, "And then I have a large bag containing a good number of smaller bags. In these small bags are the cartridge cases, bullets, and other items we gathered in the hallway, plus the items the detectives brought me from the autopsy. Follow me?"

"I follow you."

"I'm not prepared to give you my final report on the third bag—the one containing the cartridge cases and bullets—but my report on the two guns may get you started on analysis. I didn't want to sit on it any longer. Shall I proceed?"

Mr. Byrne circled his hand in the air. *Get on with it, Richard.* "I'll keep in mind there's more to come. Tell us what you have."

"Let's take a look at the rifle." Mr. Levy raised the gun—still in its protective bag—with his left hand and began to describe the appearance and operation of the weapon. His right hand indicated the part of the gun he described. "We see here the brown wooden handle or stock, as it's called. In front of the stock," he pointed to the area between the stock and the barrel, "separating it from the tubular barrel, is the chamber. On the underside of the chamber is the trigger. Then here, at the front, we have the long barrel. On the underside of the barrel, we have the tubular magazine. Are you with me?"

"We're with you, Richard." Mr. Byrne responded for us. I think I was with him.

"OK. Now here's how one loads the bullets into a .22 Rossi. You plop each bullet, nose first, into the front end of the magazine. When you're ready to fire, you pull back the slide. The maneuver loads the bullets into the chamber. You fire the weapon by pulling the trigger. The trigger action expels the bullet. The copper jacket that had been around the lead core of the bullet falls to the floor."

"Keep going, Richard."

"As you know, when we were called to the scene on the evening of the crime, we picked up the rifle, unloaded it, and secured it in an evidence bog. At the time, I made two observations. First, I noted one live round in the magazine and no cartridges in the chamber. Second, look here at the magazine. The magazine shows damage. See this spot?" Richard indicated an irregular indentation on the magazine. "The damaged area of the magazine blocks the passage of bullets making their way to the chamber."

"We noticed the damage on the magazine as soon as we picked up the rifle," said Mr. Byrne. "We asked you about it. You tested the indentation and told us the spot was positive for lead. Right?"

"Right. Later, my test in the lab confirmed the presence of lead on the damaged spot—and also the presence of copper."

"Meaning?"

"Lead and copper would be compatible with a bullet from a .380 pistol. And as you know, the weapon Spike brought to us was a .380 pistol."

"Meaning?"

"Meaning, in all probability, another bullet was fired at

the rifle. That bullet probably came from the .380 pistol."

Mr. Byrne rubbed his head. "OK. When? When did that happen? The damage could have been there for some time."

"No. Think about the scenario. We know from the coroner's report that both victims were shot within a short period of time, four bullets at Kitty Ernest, a larger number at Jubilee. I can't time the damage to the rifle, exactly, but it must have occurred after the rifle had fired some bullets. If it had occurred before the afternoon of the crime, only the bullets already in the chamber could have been shot. We picked up casings for more shots than could have been in the chamber."

"So the rifle had been fired *shortly* before Jubilee was shot," I suggested.

Mr. Byrne drew the same conclusion. "Fired at Kitty Ernest. The coroner dug matching shotgun bullets out of her body and out of Jubilee."

"Right you are. After the shots were fired at Kitty Ernest, the rifle sustained damage from another weapon. We have that weapon in my second evidence bag. The .380."

I wish Spike could have been here for this report. The faithful bulldog's perseverance got us the second weapon. He had learned well a basic principle of investigation technique —before reaching any conclusion about a crime scene, account for every shot fired by locating the guns and bullets.

I still had questions.

"Do you know the exact sequence? How many shots at Kitty before the damage and how many after? Same question for Jubilee?"

"I can't be certain. We don't know the number of bullets in the Rossi to start with and we don't know whether it was reloaded."

Richard Levy held up the second evidence bag, the one containing the pistol. "Here we have our candidate for the other weapon in the scenario. A .380 caliber semi-automatic pistol with missing parts."

Richard dug into the third bag he had brought and pulled out a smaller, clear bag. "And here, guys, we have the butt plate you detectives picked up in the hallway, opposite the entry to the kitchen."

"The butt plate matches the pistol?" asked Mr. Byrne.

"How did you guess? Yes. After examining the pistol and the butt plate, I conclude that together they comprise a whole. In my professional opinion, that is." Richard smiled. He enjoyed speaking as if he were answering a question in court.

He frowned. "Unfortunately, I did not identify any trace of ammo from the .380."

"There should be an empty shell casing if this is the gun that damaged the rifle, correct?"

"Yes. And we don't have it."

Again, Mr. Byrne had those deep creases running horizontally across his forehead. He passed his hand over his scalp. His bald spot appeared to have grown a bit since the last time I saw him. I could figure what he was turning over in his mind. How the hell do I get all this through to a jury? Diagrams? Models? A simulation by video? Straight testimony from nerdy Richard would have no impact. The three of us had professionals' understanding of how guns work, but a jury would not.

Richard continued. "The pistol was most probably fired in the hallway, where we found the butt plate. The butt plate must have been in place at the time. After the butt plate came off, the pistol would not have been able to fire." He paused. "Something else that's curious. Except for the missing butt plate, the pistol is in firing condition; there's a live round in the chamber."

"I can't understand," said Mr. Byrne.

"Nor can I. We know Mr. Ernest's version of the shootings doesn't hold water, but we can't say exactly what did occur. I'm just giving you a description of these weapons. We have a way to go."

Mr. Byrne had a question for me. "Ted, this is going to be damn hard for a jury to follow from testimony. When we're sure we know what happened—and I'm not yet at that point —we're going to have to explain it to the jury. I want to see some kind of demonstrative evidence, maybe a model of the hallway."

At this point, Mr. Byrne's secretary came into the room carrying two pink telephone messages. She handed me a please call message from Deputy Collins—damn, I hadn't done that yet— and she placed another one on the desk in front of Mr. Byrne, with an apology. "I told Mr. Strait you were in a meeting. He said you had to be disturbed."

The message distracted Mr. Byrne. Richard paused to regain his attention but didn't get it. Mr. Byrne stood up.

"Richard, I'm going to have to ask you to leave us what you have to report so far and come back to finish another day. Mr. Strait wants Ted and me to meet him in Sheriff Gabrielle's office. Right now."

"No problem. As I said when I came in, I want to locate each of the casings on a map of the hallway. I came today to give you a head start on the guns. I'll be back whenever you say."

"Wait. Do you have a list of all the items you picked up at the scene?"

"Yes. Of course."

"Perfect. That's exactly what I need."

Damn. I had hoped the end result of this afternoon would be a warrant for the arrest of Thomas Ernest. There was one murdering husband behind bars. I wanted the other one there also.

The *urgent* meeting that took place in Sheriff Gabrielle's office threw a monkey wrench into my Saturday plans. I had in mind taking Lorraine to an afternoon on Catahoula Lake. I couldn't count on many more perfect-fall-weather Saturdays before winter.

We learned Mr. Strait wanted to send me on a mission to north Louisiana. There was a plus to the plan. Lorraine would be with me. My having to work would be no problem for André. He'd be just as happy to go to his grandparents without us.

PART IV

14

Buttoned up in my Christmas and Easter suit, and wearing an appropriately somber tie, I sat on my front porch waiting for Lorraine to pick me up. She pulled to the curb five minutes late. "Sorry, Ted. You know, in the morning I don't pop up like toast."

Being a bit late was OK, but the vehicle Lorraine drove was not. A black and white unit with the seal of the St. Martin Parish Sheriff's Office on the doors. Lorraine read the disapproval on my face.

"I know, I know, Ted. We don't need to telegraph cop when we're trying to win friends and influence people. But my truck is in the shop. I planned to pick up something nondescript from the narcs' motor pool, but they're still out working on a raid they did last night. The only plain wheels I found in the lot behind the Sheriff's Office might not make a two hundred fifty-mile round trip to Forest Hill. Can we use your truck?"

"Sure. Take that billboard back to the lot. I'd rather drive anyway. I'll be right on your tail."

Lorraine raised an eyebrow. I felt myself flush—and saw that she looked rosier than usual. Looking back, I see our mutual embarrassment indicated a developing charge in the atmosphere between us.

Lorraine had dressed for a funeral. A sophisticated black suit, her tangle of reddish-blond curls gathered into a sleek knot at the back of her neck. And make-up. I must have stared.

"Do I look OK?"

"You look excellent." She did. Stunning, actually. I didn't know enough about feminine enhancement to know what she'd done to herself. She read my expression perfectly.

"So you want to know the secret of my transformation? Just for the day, I ditched the hideous brown polyester uniform *The Man* had decreed his female staff must wear. I'm waiting a decent interval before I ask for an upgrade. Even our boss looks sick in her uniform. You'll notice she rarely wears one."

Lorraine puts a smile on my face. I looked forward to a day in her company.

Shortly, we were on our way to the north on Interstate Highway 49, I-49 as we call it. Lorraine wanted an explanation of our mission. I told her what I knew.

"Mr. Byrne says Mr. Strait has had The Church of the Blessed Believers on his radar screen for some time. Something happened out there a year or so ago and no one will talk to him about it. He says when he tries, faces go rigid. Now we have two cases with membership in the Church of the Blessed Believers in common."

"What about that Gander guy? Did Mr. Strait question him? You had good luck getting him to tip you off about the tapes of Kitty Ernest's phone sex."

"Hey, there. How can you call my success with Gander *luck*? I conducted a masterful interrogation. Mr. Byrne sent me to try to talk to him about the church. Gander wants to talk all right, but not about his church. Mr. Strait thinks the congregation of the Blessed Believers has been given instructions not to have anything to do with us."

"What makes Mr. Strait think Virtua Cane's family would know anything about a church in St. Martin Parish?"

"They've got to be unsympathetic to the place, at the very least. Their daughter came to a tragic end down here after she became a passionate convert. Anyway, I've learned you can't go wrong trusting Mr. Strait's intuition."

I'd been fascinated with the idea of how Mr. Strait found out about the service we were on our way to attend. For over two weeks the coroner had been antsy to move Virtua Cane's body out of the morgue. He couldn't get her family to respond. They swooped down here the day after her body was discovered, picked up the two kids, and went back north. Now they weren't even answering phone calls from this area code.

"The hospital that had Virtua's body appealed to Mr. Strait for help. He gave them the name of Sonja Trudeau. I'm getting to really like the Trudeau sisters-in-law. They step up to the plate. They drove up to Forest Hill, found the family, and got them to have the hospital send the body to the funeral home in Alexandria. Mr. Strait made a routine call to the place to ask about 'the arrangements.' Off we go."

I'd done some background work on the church and come up with little information. "The Believers may be heavily into Pentecostal or fundamentalist practice, but they aren't noticed by any Pentecostal churches I know anything about. Mr. Strait says the Believers don't belong to any superior body or larger organization for their mutual benefit. They're apparently totally on their own. Strait says he sensed some hostility about their independence. Anyway, he persuaded the sheriff we needed to go investigate for ourselves. We take orders. You sure have a lot of questions this morning. But then, you usually do. They can put this on your tombstone: *Lorraine LaSalle. Born Curious.*"

"Not soon, I hope." Rat-a-tat—a-tat of the bumps along the shoulder of the road warned me I'd strayed from my lane. I heard a quick intake of breath from my passenger. "But if you run us off the road at least I'm already dressed for my 'arrangements.' By the way, what are 'the arrangements' for Virtua Cane?" Lorraine asked.

"Everything will be at the Sacred Heart Chapel in Forest Hill. Visiting begins at nine, Rosary at eleven, Mass at one, burial to follow in the cemetery right there. And now you and I have a date for the day."

I meant to be light-hearted, but when Lorraine snapped her head on its axis and put those wide eyes on me, I regretted being flip. I didn't know much about my partner. Apparently, she could deliver smart remarks but didn't enjoy being on the receiving end. She grew up in the uppermost corner of our parish, north of Breaux Bridge, and was competent and confident. And looked great in a suit for a funeral. That's all I knew. Why was I reluctant to ask personal questions? The Nicole experience told me I'd forgotten how to play. Stick to business. It's safer. I steered the conversation to talking about how different Louisiana and Louisianans are in the north and the south.

"Have you ever been up here?" I asked Lorraine.

"No, I haven't. Not much to see."

"Interesting topography, just because it's different from ours. When the ice melted across the land that would one day be Louisiana, the changing paths of three fresh-water rivers brought different types of soil within close proximity to each other. A gently sloping arc across the ankle of our boot-shaped state marks the dividing line between the mostly Red River silt that proved to be best for cotton and pine trees in the north and the rich black soil best suited for growing sugar cane, rice, and magnificent oaks. This area had once been fed by the Atchafalaya and Mississippi Rivers in the south. And people are a bit different also."

"How's that?"

"White Protestant settlers found the north to their liking; the south attracted French Catholics. The populations in both north and south Louisiana were augmented by immigrants and by slaves who were imported to do the hardest kinds of work. The two populations retain distinctions. An oversimplification, perhaps, but the southerners let the good times roll; the northerners are more apt to stick to business."

"I'm glad I'm a southerner."

I turned off the highway at Lecompte, north of Turkey Creek, and rode a two-lane blacktop westward on that imaginary dividing line. The road occasionally veered into piney woods on the north and at other times dipped south to pass through wet, open fields. But whether we were north or south of the line, the country was uniformly low rent. Small frame houses and trailers, chickens running in yards, a lot of dogs off leash. Almost every dwelling had a 'yard car' up on blocks. Lorraine pointed at a yellow, plastic-sided trailer.

"Lots of the dwellings around here move, but the cars do

not. Could not!"

An occasional Stars and Bars fluttered in the breeze. The only business establishments we saw were a clapboard grocery store, a cluttered shelter for a shade tree mechanic, and a butcher who advertised his prowess with dressing deer. The oil and gas commerce that brought improvements to much of Louisiana had not reached here. A dreary landscape, until we came to our destination—the neat little town of Forest Hill.

In the center of town, opposite a much larger, red brick Baptist Church, I pulled into a shell parking lot next to a sparkling white frame building with a simple wood sign— *Sacred Heart of Jesus, Masses Saturday at 5:30 p.m. and Sundays at 8 a.m.* Apparently, Sacred Heart did not have a full-time priest. Only five cars sat in the lot. Lorraine and I decided to take a look around town to wait for more people to arrive.

We were pleasantly surprised by what we found. We walked on real sidewalks. We passed a dozen large homes with elaborate gardens and numerous smaller homes with neat, well-tended lawns. Even the most modest of them displayed their owner's pride. The five-block-long Main Street showed signs of historic preservation, always an indication of private as well as public money at work.

"Now I realize where we are, Lorraine, just south of the Kisatchie National Forest. For a couple of centuries, leaf litter has washed down here from what remains of the Louisiana Eden. The folks who live here probably own or work in plant nurseries—a profitable and pleasant occupation that takes good advantage and good care of the rich earth." I walked over to a vacant strip of land and dug the toe of my shoe into soft ground. "Look at this rich, crumbly soil! It's lovely here in Forest Hill. I wonder why Virtua ever left."

Lorraine shook her head. "Did you get a good look at the downtown? King Brothers Old Tyme Drug Store and Soda Fountain. Richardson's Country Store. Where's the action? If I were under twenty-one, I wouldn't stay in this burg one second longer than I had to."

When we got back to the church, cars and trucks filled most of the parking lot. Lorraine and I walked in the front door and tagged onto a line forming up the center aisle. First, however, Lorraine dipped her fingers into a stone bowl of holy water and made the sign of the cross: forehead, chest, each shoulder. I haven't done that for years. The only sound in the building was the soft shuffle of shoes on the wooden floor as the mourners moved slowly forward to a sad little group standing between the front pews. The family. Behind them, flanked by tall candles, two coffins rested before the altar rail—one regular sized brown coffin and one very small white box on a stand. Both were closed.

"See that, Lorraine. Two coffins."

"Of course," she whispered.

Each mourner extended handshakes, hugs, and words of sympathy to the family. Some knelt on a prie dieu for a few moments before moving on.

I whispered to Lorraine. "Here's my plan. I'll head for the old couple in the center. They're probably Virtua's Mom and Dad although they look like grandparents. I'll identify us as the deputies investigating the tragedy of their daughter's death and extend our condolences. If they have no interest in conversation, which I expect will be the case, I'll move on and target one of the people standing on the left side. You take the right. You may have more experience with this than I have. Any thoughts?"

"As good a plan as any. There's no script. We'll just have to feel our way and look for a friendly face before pressing in. If I see one, I usually say something like 'I'd appreciate it if you would talk with me a few minutes.' Try that."

When I spoke with the older couple, their eyes fixed on empty space in the middle distance. They didn't even take my hand. But I found a friendly pair of eyes in the group on their left. Elizabeth Carter, a middle-aged woman who gave us her name and identified herself as Virtua's sister. She allowed herself to be drawn over to the side aisle. I gave Lorraine a quick glance and she joined us.

"I know this isn't the place for a long conversation, Ms.

Carter. I'm willing to come back any time to talk with the family—if you'll allow me. I'd really like to know more about your sister, Virtua."

"Sir, please don't bother my parents right now. Actually, please don't bother them at all. They're very fragile. They aren't well, and this death has been devastating. What is it you need to know?"

I had practiced my pitch. One day, at a trial of the person who did this, the prosecutor would have to tell a jury about her. I asked what I hoped would be an open-end question to lead Mrs. Carter to talk. "You're a big family, apparently. Is that right?"

"Yes, sir. Five siblings. I'm the oldest daughter and Virtua was the youngest. Our three brothers are in between."

"How did Virtua come to live down in south Louisiana?"

She pressed her lips together. "I had something to do with that, sir. My husband and I were living down there, working in the nursery at Jefferson Island. When Virtua graduated from high school she came down to stay with us. She met Robert Cane. Before we knew what happened, they were married."

"Do you live in Iberia Parish now?"

Wouldn't that be a break? We'd be able to talk to her anytime.

"No, sir. When my Dad got sick we came back home to take over the family nursery. Maybe you've heard of Stephenson's? We specialize in ground covers and bedding plants." Elizabeth cut a glance back to the family. "But this is not a good time to talk."

She wasn't saying there wouldn't be another time, so I pressed. "Yes, of course. I'll give you my card, and please let me have your phone number." I handed her a little notebook I carried in my pocket and a pen to write with. "I'll call you in a week or so and come back up to talk some more another time."

Elizabeth looked me square in the eye. "That boy Robert… That church of his. Yes. Anything I can do to help my sister."

Bingo. She said that church of his? Her tone was definitely unfriendly to the church and friendly to us.

Lorraine spoke up. "Is there any other member of the family we might meet with while we're here?"

Shut up, Lorraine. We had what passed for an invitation to come back. We couldn't expect anything better.

"My brother would talk to you, but not right now. He's the one holding up Dad and Mom."

Lorraine pressed on, but for this question I was grateful.

"Mrs. Carter, how are the children doing?"

Her face softened. "Thank you for asking. Little Robbie doesn't understand what happened to his mother, but Rebecca does. They're with my kids right now. I don't know if I'll bring them over for the service. We're watching Becca real close."

"You know, we have a fund that pays for counseling for victims. Perhaps we can make arrangements for that if you think having her see someone to talk to would help."

"Maybe so. I'll think about that."

I said our parting words and urged Lorraine down the side aisle. She stopped after a few steps.

"I know this isn't your cup of tea, Ted, but would you mind if we stayed a bit? I'd like to say the rosary for Virtua."

I usually made a point of skipping out before a rosary, but I could see Virtua's sister had her eyes on us. "I'll make a deal with you. I'll sit through the rosary, but afterward, we take a little detour up the road to check out the nurseries. Maybe we could find Stephenson's. My mother's birthday is tomorrow, and I haven't had a single idea."

We took seats in a pew close to the front. As the *Hail Mary* began, Elizabeth Carter sent us a warm smile. We'd made a good contact. My guess? Elizabeth Carter felt some guilt about having played a part in her sister's tragedy. Perhaps she introduced the couple, or maybe she just felt bad that love—or pregnancy—happened on her watch.

We found Stephenson's. A black wreath hung on the office door. The two greenhouses on the side were locked up tight, but we spent a good half hour checking out the three acres of open rows in the rear. A neat tag with the Latin name introduced each row. Familiarity with Stephenson's Nursery would be an icebreaker for future conversations with sister Elizabeth. We crossed over to the nursery next door to pick up a Purple Dawn Camellia for my Mom's birthday. It was the perfect time of year for gardening. Thank you, Eugénie, for what you tried to teach me about plants.

On the drive home, I gathered the courage to ask Lorraine to tell me about herself—how she came to be a cop.

"I was married to one. In Lafayette. We'd been married less than a year when Richard went into the service. He was killed in Afghanistan."

"I'm sorry about that. I didn't know."

"That's OK. Five—no six years ago now. I stayed on the base for a while but decided to come back home and do the job he had hoped to do. I like St. Martin Parish better than Lafayette P.D. where I started."

"You're very good at your job and seem to like it. That's important."

She smiled at the compliment.

"People tell me I can be pushy."

I dropped Lorraine off at the office. A long day. When I got home, André wasn't there. I found him next door. One look at the boy and I knew he had something to tell me. His shifting eyes said he didn't want to talk in front of Mom.

Back home, André went straight to the pile of mail on our coffee table. He picked up a brochure entitled *How to Train your Doberman* and handed it to me. "Stuck in the screen door, not in the box with the regular mail."

The picture on the front of the brochure—a close-up of the open mouth of a Doberman—thin lips pulled back tight, teeth bared—sent a stab of anger into my gut. There was worse inside. The first few chapters of the brochure detailed how to select a good dog. A reliable breeder—not a puppy mill or a pet store. Then came a chapter on what shots to give, the best dog food, a proper training routine. Menace oozed from the illustrations. The photographer's style was close-up, and God gave these animals a long narrow muzzle and prominent incisors. The last two chapters of the pamphlet popped my eyes out. *Loyalty to the Master* and *Attack and Kill*.

With half-page illustrations, the text on loyalty gave the steps to teach your Doberman to chase, grab, and secure anything, animate or inanimate, including a stranger with an unfamiliar scent. The final text presented a list of trainers who would sharpen a dog's incisors and teach him to grip a jugular on command. Thank God, no trainer listed in the brochure lived in our district.

If André had gone through the entire pamphlet, he had good reason to be wide-eyed. And he hadn't even seen Patrick Ernest's dogs.

I stumbled out reassurances. I asked Chief Roland to approve a patrol drive-by of my neighborhood on every shift. And I didn't turn down any opportunity for André to spend nights out at Catahoula Lake with his Grampa.

15

I turned over the Thomas Ernest investigation file to Mr. Byrne in mid-November. Lorraine and I had finished our work. Two weeks later, a long two weeks later, Mr. Byrne called and asked us to come to his office first thing in the morning to look at some expert reports. Praise be. Maybe now he'd approve a warrant for Ernest's arrest. It just galled me to have that guy on the street when we were certain he killed his wife, framed a poor black guy for the murder, and then killed him also. Louisiana law doesn't make a big deal about premeditation—we have a more complex definition of criminal intent—but there's no doubt Ernest qualified for a blue ribbon in any contest for the maximum penalty. I was convinced Thomas Ernest had planned every detail to accomplish the death of two people. When his plan to shoot Jubilee with the pistol hit a snag, he quickly took a different tack to reach the same goal. No one could ever say there was anything spur-of-the-moment about his motivation.

Unfortunately, Thomas Ernest in jail wouldn't have any effect on the shenanigans I had to endure from Thomas' son Patrick. André wasn't favored with any more brochures about training Dobermans, thank God, but we still had an occasional nighttime show from the headlights of a green Mercedes convertible. I was more annoyed than frightened. My rational mind told me he'd have done something by now if he really intended us harm, but I didn't let down my guard. Nor did patrol; they passed by my house many times each night. And I kept close watch on André.

I ached to tell Patrick Ernest I wasn't going to expose his gambling business, that I couldn't care less. But Mr. Byrne asked me to have no contact with him. He needed Patrick to testify about hiding his father's tapes and wanted the trial subpoena to come as a surprise. In the meanwhile, all my boss could offer me was a bit of extra surveillance from patrol.

Sheriff Gabrielle assured me she wouldn't go out of her way to inform the FBI about what Lorraine and I saw, but I couldn't be entirely sure about Chief Deputy Allan Roland. He said he wouldn't make an official report, and I could believe that, but whatever his intentions, I had my doubts he could keep hold of inside knowledge. A scoop made him feel important. If the FBI guys came around, I was afraid he wouldn't be able to resist telling what he'd *heard*. Only the passage of time would assure Patrick that I either saw nothing, not even the display of computers, or I was too scared to talk.

The first expert report Mr. Byrne had to share with us was the dust-print analysis of the newspapers spread on the floor in front of Kitty Ernest's body. Negative for a print of Jubilee Joe's sneakers. Every shoeprint on the papers matched the shoes of the EMTs who took away Kitty Ernest's body. With that report, Mr. Byrne felt safe concluding Jubilee Joe did not come close enough to Kitty Ernest for his shot to have left powder burns on her chest. To the best of our knowledge, and consistent with every statement from Thomas Ernest, only one other person was in the house that afternoon—Thomas Ernest. He alone had access to Kitty Ernest from the side without newspapers. The shooter had to have been Thomas Ernest. Good stuff.

The second report Mr. Byrne received was from a blood spatter expert from Dallas, Texas. I'd never heard of the specialty. The expert, David Spence, studied the video and the still photos of the crime scene. Ernest had said in three statements that he kept his rifle by the back entrance, outside the closed door of the utility room. The expert found a splatter pattern on the wall above Jubilee Joe's body that continued to the inside of the utility room doorframe. He also found blood of Ernest's type on the open purse in the kitchen.

I couldn't get excited about the blood-spatter expert, but Mr. Byrne thought he would make two persuasive points. He would testify that someone cleaned up a bit after the shootings; tidiness fits with what we knew of Ernest's personality. And the expert's testimony contradicted Ernest about the position of the door to the utility room.

Mr. Byrne told me the more he and Richard Levy studied the guns and bullets, the surer they were Ernest did it. But they still couldn't be certain of every detail. And the evidence was still circumstantial, even conjecture, but an accumulation of circumstantial evidence gives a defense attorney many different items to explain away. We had a pretty good accumulation.

Mr. Byrne approved a warrant for the arrest of Thomas Ernest for first-degree murder of his wife Kitty, and he approved another warrant for first-degree murder of Jubilee Joe, each murder committed in the course of the other. I had the green light to serve both warrants. Lorraine came with me to enjoy the payoff from our labor. She was as anxious as I was to get his ass in jail.

We found Thomas at his business, Ernest's Quality Cleaners on Main Street. I asked him to step into his adjoining office; we had something to give him. He obliged. I handed him the arrest warrants and read him his rights one more time. He called his son Patrick with the news. They weren't surprised. The two of them talked about calling a lawyer they'd already consulted.

Thomas Ernest came to jail meek as a lamb—ever the people pleaser, even to the people who locked him up.

Whatever counsel Ernest hired, the result for our investigation would be the same—the end of law enforcement getting any further information from father or son. The first bit of advice from anyone with a law degree is always the same—don't talk to anyone without getting clearance from an attorney.

A large part of a detective's job is tedious. Some parts are dangerous. But danger and tedium are worth it for the satisfaction of putting the collar on someone who's done something really bad. Ernest would stay locked up. Probable cause for a charge of first-degree murder, which we surely had, would mean no judge would set bail.

Booking took a couple of hours. Mr. Byrne had asked me to come back and give him a report on the arrest. It was past noon when Lorraine and I returned to the office of the District Attorney. Mr. Byrne waited for us. Today none of us would have lunch.

Mr. Byrne's secretary Marlene stood up when she buzzed us in.

"Go right in to Mr. Byrne's office, Ted. He's waiting for you."

"But I think I hear someone in there already. We can wait."

I could hear a low hum of words from Mr. Byrne; the other voice was that of ADA Tony Blendera, loud, clear, and angry.

Goddammit, Mr. Byrne! Are you telling me my case against Robert Cane is bumped from the next Grand Jury? I'm ready, and I've been ready for a couple weeks.

Marlene urged me to open Mr. Byrne's door and walk in. "Those are my clear instructions, Detective. He wants you in there."

I took a deep breath and pushed open the door. Tony was dancing around the room, face flushed, sweat on his forehead. Mr. Byrne sat behind his desk, fingers tented, perfectly composed.

"I've *been* waiting for you two. You've done the deed? You have Thomas Ernest booked into the jail?" he asked.

"Yes, sir. Piece of cake."

"Fine. I've been explaining to Tony here that Thomas Ernest would be our guest before the sun went down, and we'd be going to the Grand Jury with the Ernest case in three weeks."

Tony interrupted. "And I want to know why you won't let me take the Cane case to the same Grand Jury? I've been ready—for over a month. Cane is in jail, without bond, and the Public Defender Board has named Sarah Bernard to represent him. I can't believe you want me to put my case off.

"I have a couple of reasons, Tony. First, I don't want to take our two serious felonies to the same Grand Jury session, and… Well, in Cane, we still have a few details to work through."

"What the hell do you mean by that? A few details to work through? We've got the good hard evidence we found in his house—the rope, the dress material, all of the circumstances. We have the manager of the hardware store where he got the rat poison. And we have a gold seal confession."

Mr. Byrne spoke at half speed. The madder the person across his desk, the slower Mr. Byrne talked.

"First, Tony, we have some decisions to make about who might have been Cane's accomplices. You've said it yourself. Someone helped Robert Cane take his wife's body out to Catahoula Lake. Who was it? If we could ID the helper, there's a possibility we could turn him into a cooperating witness. Prosecution gets a hell of a lot easier."

"Sometimes." Tony looked way more upset than warranted by a month delay in his case. I didn't understand either the rush or the delay. The more Mr. Byrne sat cool as can be, the more Tony fumed. Finally, Mr. Byrne gave Tony the real reason for putting off his case.

"You need to be talking to Mr. Strait, Tony. He has some reservations about the charge of first-degree murder."

With this statement, Tony flushed two shades deeper. He spat out his words. "What? The charge? What the hell do you mean? It's always been Mr. Strait's policy to let his prosecutors decide on the charge for the cases they are assigned. I've decided. First-degree. Twice. And a recommendation of death. That guy killed his wife and his baby. You're not going to tell me he didn't know his wife was pregnant?"

"No, Tony. That's not the problem. We've just never had a first-degree charge for killing two persons where the second person was a fetus. Not in Louisiana or anywhere else we've been able to find."

"But the legislature changed the definition of person—a fetus from the moment of conception. So, we have the killing of two persons."

"The legislature tried to accomplish that result, I'll admit, but they didn't finish the job. Killing one person is second-degree murder unless that one person is also a law enforcement officer, someone over 65, etc. They did not add 'pregnant female' to the list of single victims whose killing constitutes first-degree murder, and thus the possibility of the penalty of death."

Tony's face flared red. His breath came out in puffs.

Mr. Byrne continued. "The prosecution instructs the Grand Jury on the law, Tony. We need to consider the charge very carefully before we present."

"'We 'need to consider' you say? I consider on my case. At one time, you could have said the law was unclear. No longer. Clear as a bell, dammit! We've got half the committee that went to the legislature last summer out on the courthouse lawn reminding us of the new definition of *person*. A human being *from the moment of fertilization and implementation.*"

Now I got it. Tony's wife had the pressure on. One night on the TV late news I saw a clip of a crowd in Baton Rouge marching around the capital building with banners that said *Save the Unborn.* There was Maria Blendera, front and center. Every night now, Tony probably went home to the third degree about the lack of progress in the case against Robert Cane.

Mr. Byrne still tried to soothe his prosecutor.

"That's a reason right there, Tony. Mr. Strait wants demonstrators to get tired of demonstrating and tempers to cool down before we make a final decision on the charge. All it takes is one juror who believes in *Roe v. Wade* and we don't have the unanimity needed for the conviction of first-degree and for a verdict of death. If we can keep everybody satisfied without having a death penalty trial, we do so."

Tony wouldn't be soothed. "Mr. Byrne, you're going to prosecute Thomas for the murder of his wife and poor hapless Jubilee Joe. Fine. Have at it. You get to decide what to do in that one because you're the prosecutor. I prosecute Robert Cane. I get to make the decisions about him—unless Mr. Strait goes back on his word."

Mr. Byrne stood up. Very cool, but quite firm. His tight upper lip told me he'd lost patience.

"Speak to Mr. Strait, Tony. That's all I have to say."

Tony's mouth dropped open. He turned and gave us his back. Mr. Byrne sat down and waved us into the chairs on the other side of the desk. We sat. A good two minutes of silence. I knew he'd just been taken to the edge.

"I want to go over a few things with you, Ted." Mr. Byrne sat still for another patch. I proffered help.

"Maybe you don't have all the background on Tony Blendera, sir. Do you know about the heartache in his marriage?" I asked.

"No, Ted. What's that?"

I turned to Lorraine for help. She knew the story better than I did.

"Tony and Maria have no children, Mr. Byrne. One miscarriage after another. And Maria's had a hard time accepting the losses. Six weeks ago, the last time Maria lost her baby, she was far along in the pregnancy—and she'd undergone some fancy and expensive interventions to get pregnant in the first place. She had to get special dispensations from the Church to have some of the procedures done. I hear she goes to Mass seven days a week. She's put little angels suspended on string flying all around the house. She's flipped."

The wrinkles across Mr. Byrne's forehead appeared again. Not straight lines now. The pain he felt for Tony contorted his forehead.

"God, I probably made it worse. I shouldn't have come on so strong."

I spoke up. "Strong? No way. You were as measured as a monk. A capital trial is an ordeal for everyone involved. Just one wrong word can be reversible error. For the defense, failure to cover one aspect of the client's story could cost him his life. Given the confession, Cane might take a plea to life in order to escape a possible capital verdict. In my view, that's always worth considering."

I was feeling guilty. I was supposed to be Mr. Byrne's guide to the natives and I hadn't told him Tony's story. Tony was a pinch hitter from down the Bayou Teche, not a native of St. Martin, but I wasn't going to make an excuse. Mr. Byrne sets an example. He never blames something he feels he has to do on Mr. Strait or 'just following orders.' That's the honor code he lives by.

"Does Mr. Strait know about Tony's personal situation?" I asked Mr. Byrne. "If not, we'd better tip him off he has an angry ADA coming to see him."

"I'll see to it he knows."

I would have put money on Mr. Strait knowing already.

I stood up to leave. Lorraine stood also. Mr. Byrne stopped us.

"Wait, guys. I had another reason for asking you to come in today—other than approving an arrest warrant for Thomas Ernest, that is. Let's go get a cup of coffee. There's something I want to show you in what has become my office annex."

16

Mr. Byrne poured us each a few inches of coffee. I would have preferred lunch. We downed the bitter brew and tossed our empty paper cups into the trash.

"Come follow me," Mr. Byrne instructed. He bounced down the hall with the step of someone half his age. Any regret he may have had over causing pain to Tony Blendera evaporated faster than a Louisiana summer shower. His eyes sparkled in anticipation of something I didn't yet know.

With a flourish, Mr. Byrne pulled a set of keys out of his pocket. He unlocked the door to the spare office we'd visited before. Pitch dark in there. I saw nothing until he reached around to the right and clicked on an overhead light. Lorraine and I followed him through the doorway. Once inside, he put a key in the inner keyhole and threw the bolt, locking us in.

Political posters—RE-ELECT GERALD STRAIT DISTRICT ATTORNEY—had been taped over the windows. If anyone other than Mr. Byrne had locked us in a dark room I would have been spooked. Even so, reflexes trained during years of answering calls in sketchy places caused me to spread my legs a tad wider and touch the weapon on my hip.

The folding table previously in the center of the room had been moved to one end. A hodgepodge of pieces of mailing cartons sat in its place. What on earth was that? Apparently, top secret, but something made of old Fed Ex and USPS cardboard couldn't be dangerous. Not with Mr. Byrne's eyes sparkling with mischief.

"Can you guess what we've got here?" he asked. He was on the verge of laughter.

"Not yet. All I see are pieces of cardboard set every which

way."

Mr. Byrne walked to the far end of the construction. He dropped to the floor—he's pretty supple for a guy more than twenty years older than I am—and lay down. He lifted a cardboard flap on the end of his construction, closed one eye, and pantomimed looking through a spyglass. He had taken a horizontal sighting through the construction, parallel to the floor. He raised up like a cobra and made a pronouncement.

"Ladies and Gentlemen. I am now in the doorway of the master bedroom in the home of Kitty and Thomas Ernest at 205 Evangeline Street, St. Martinville. I am looking down the hall that runs parallel to the Bayou Teche. I see ahead of me, on my left, the doorways to the den, to the kitchen, and to the utility room. All of these rooms overlook the Bayou, although the utility room lacks windows. Now I'm looking down the right side of the hall, parallel to Evangeline Street. I see the doorway to the doll display room, the foyer, and the room dedicated to the fabrication of dolls."

"I get it. You've built a model of Thomas Ernest's house!"

"Yes, my good man. Now I believe I see at the dead end of the hall a body, a dead body if you will pardon my pun."

Mr. Byrne played some kind of game. Lorraine could play too.

"Well, I'll be damned." She walked closer to the construction and looked down. "From up here, we have a God's eye view. You've raised the roof!"

"Not bad, Ted. There's hope for your partner."

Mr. Byrne clearly had fun with his project, but why did he build this display in the first place? Was he trying to make a model to use as demonstrative evidence at the trial? No way he could get this junky looking construction into a courtroom. And taking a jury to this room would never qualify as a trip to the scene of the crime.

He anticipated my question.

"You're wondering why I built this model? I think Richard Levy would enjoy using it to give his weapon testimony to the jury. He could get down on the floor like I'm doing and pretend to shoot the guns. He could show every odd piece fall in the place we found it." Mr. Byrne spoke in imitation of Richard's New York accent. Brooklyn, I'd say.

"What?"

Lorraine was a step ahead of me. "He's kidding, Ted."

"Right you are. I built this construction to test various gun hypotheses. You know, who shot whom, how and where. Richard can also use the model for his study also, but I thought I'd tell him he had to testify from a prone position just to make our scientist loosen up a bit. I'd tell him I would do the same in closing arguments."

Again Mr. Byrne made a pantomime of looking through a scope.

"Ladies and Gentlemen of the jury, Thomas Ernest is having a busy afternoon. After lunch, he goes downtown to Ledoux at the south end of town to find a patsy for the deadly scheme he has in mind—to locate someone he can set up for the murder of his wife. He finds Jubilee Joe picking up pecans on the side of the road. Do you remember that crumpled little paper bag of pecans on the back seat of Ernest's car?"

I did remember Spike telling me about the bag of pecans but hadn't seen any connection.

"You know, Ernest would not have invited Jubilee to sit in the front. That bag is a pitiful indication of where he rode on the way to get shot to death. Detectives," he continued, "we are absolutely certain of very little about what happened next. We do know Ernest's version of what happened is not possible. We have good evidence the same person shot both victims, but that's about it."

Mr. Byrne paused to get out of his uncomfortable position on the floor. He took Lorraine's God's eye view.

"Detectives, here is my working theory. Ernest asks Jubilee Joe to come out to his house to rake a few leaves. Are you with me?"

Lorraine and I nodded assent.

"Ernest tells Jubilee to wait in the carport while the boss man changes into yard clothes. Ernest goes into the house. He goes back to the bedroom. Somewhere along the way, he gets a hold of his rifle.

"Ernest comes out of the bedroom and takes a left turn to a position from which he can see into the den. Ernest says he saw Kitty already dead. I'm thinking what he saw was his wife busy creating a scene for one of her doll displays. He goes right up to her. Pow! Shots. He then goes from the den into the hallway and down the hall to what he calls the 'back' door. That's the door into the carport. He opens the door and tells Jubilee Joe to come in. He backs up a bit in the hallway.

"When Jubilee comes inside, Ernest gives Jubilee the rifle. Maybe he calls out, 'Here Jubilee,' and tosses the rifle to him. Ernest pulls his pistol off the top of that cabinet in the doll workroom on the right side of the hallway. Remember the empty holster? He fires a shot straight at Joe. Pow! Dead on."

Lorraine and I were both aghast. Mr. Byrne got to his feet.

"That's my working hypothesis. What I have to do next is place Kitty Ernest, Thomas Ernest, and Jubilee into the drama and work every piece of our evidence into the scenario to see if it fits. Every shell casing, bullet, and piece of the pistol. Every spatter of blood. I want Richard Levy to do the same. He will give the evidence to the jury so he has to be certain my theory works. When I tell the jury the evidence proves the case, beyond a reasonable doubt, that no other hypothesis is reasonable, not even possible, I've got to be sure those are true statements."

Lorraine's blue eyes were shining. "Wow!"

Mr. Byrne rubbed his balding spot. "I need some props for my studies—some actors to put on this stage so I can run through dramatizations of possible versions of the events."

"Actors?"

"Yes. I need three figures, each about ten inches tall. I'm hoping you can help me. Any ideas?"

I had the spirit now. "Maybe a Barbie Doll for Kitty Ernest and two Ken Dolls for Thomas Ernest and Jubilee Joe?"

Mr. Byrne slapped his thigh. "Perfect. Can you find some Barbies for me?"

I told him I thought I could. I'd just ask around the squad

room to see who had girls the right age to have those dolls. Or I'd go to Walmart. "But you've got to promise me I can be a spectator when you tell Richard Levy to get down on the floor."

I studied the construction, walking around to see it from different angles. I had another idea.

"Do you think we need an accident reconstructionist?"

"Like for an automobile accident? Maybe. We have to think of sight lines, but that's about the only common element. I thought about working with a video simulation. Videos for court cost thousands of dollars to produce. I suspect a jury of simple country folk—which is the jury I hope to choose because they know the innocence of types like Jubilee—would be turned off by an expensive exhibit. A model might be a good middle way—halfway between a flat floor plan and a TV show."

"Construction will take some time."

"I don't really need the model for the Grand Jury. A floor plan will be sufficient there. Who do I get to make a model?"

"An architect?"

"I'll start with the Judge's brother. If he can't do it, he'll know someone who can."

Mr. Byrne led us back to his office, locking up his construction. He invited us to sit more comfortably and talk about the case he was putting together for the Grand Jury. I'd be his first witness and walk through the investigation. All I needed in the way of preparation would be a read-through of my investigative report. Then Richard Levy would come second to testify about how the deed was done. Mr. Byrne had a few other witnesses in the wings: a woman who thought she saw Ernest's red Mercury—a behemoth of a car —cruising around Ledoux in the morning and again after lunch. Funny how white people believe they're invisible to people they think don't matter. Then he thought he'd put on Lorraine to testify about the incriminating tapes. He wouldn't subpoena Patrick Ernest or Reggie for the Grand Jury; he didn't need Kitty's lover and he wanted the trial subpoenas to him and to Patrick Ernest to come as a surprise.

Sarah Bernard rarely had her clients testify before the Grand Jury. Mr. Byrne didn't need an investigation into Thomas Ernest's background. Come trial, however, he'd face another situation entirely. For this defendant with no criminal history, Mr. Byrne would have to be prepared for Sarah to put her client on the stand. From the moment I'd talked to him at his house, Thomas Ernest had said he wanted to tell all. His lawyers probably wouldn't be able to hold him down.

"If/When you get one or both of the first-degree murder verdicts, are you really going to ask for the penalty of death?" I asked Mr. Byrne.

"The State's track record on prosecution of white on black crime is dismal. You don't see many white guys on death row for blowing away a poor black man. Nor do you see people of means on the Row. That's not right. When the shoe fits, we should wear it."

I agreed.

Mr. Byrne continued. "The jury may give Ernest a pass for killing his unfaithful wife and a black man. It could happen. But I can't in good conscience discount the death of either victim—the woman or the black man. I know the State is going to have years of post-conviction relief to process and pay for, and for no good end. Louisiana hasn't put anyone to death in years. But I can't control that outcome."

"So you aren't working on a plea to some lesser offense?"

"Not at the moment. My call and I've made it. We go for two capital charges. We have a pretty good chance." He paused. "Now in our other murdering husband case, State v. Robert Cane, the motivation appears to be different. Mr. Strait will have to deal with Tony on that one."

The decision behind him, Mr. Byrne sat back and changed the subject. He asked me when he could come to see the investigative work on my wife's disappearance. He hadn't forgotten. He said he could come Saturday. I readily agreed. Lorraine surprised me by saying she wanted to see my work also.

As our meeting broke up, Mr. Byrne's secretary came in

and handed me another message from Deputy Collins, the rookie patrolman who was first on the scene at Thomas Ernest's house. I had dispatch run him down so I could apologize for taking so long to connect. Kevin was not on patrol so he came right over. He looked quite different in his backyard barbeque clothes. He had an interesting issue on his mind.

"Detective D'Aquin, I want to tell you something that's going on in my old neighborhood, Ledoux, in the south end of town."

I remembered Collins's familiarity with the area had been helpful in getting information about Jubilee Joe. Something about a car wash and an all-day poker game had been important.

"Sure, Kevin. And call me Ted."

"I don't know if I could do that."

"Just try. It'll come to you."

"I'll try, sir. I told you I grew up in Ledoux and still have friends and family there. I moved out when I had kids of my own. It's not the same place it used to be, but I still go back. Lately, I'm getting the feeling I'm not welcome—because I'm a cop."

What could I do about that? A shame, but...

Kevin guessed what I was thinking.

"There is something going on in other jurisdictions to address the disconnect. I have a suggestion, Detective, ur... Ted, about what we could do to help if you're willing. You could work with me on some outreach in Ledoux. I don't know much about that sort of program, but I think our boss, Sheriff Gabrielle, would be interested."

"You were her student also, right? You know she'd be interested. That outreach has a name but I've forgotten what they call it. What happens is a few cops, patrolmen, and officers, black and white, male and female, show up at baseball games, family reunions, any excuse to seem human and comfortable in the crowd. Let's see if we can catch our boss."

Community policing is what Sheriff Gabrielle called it,

and she jumped at the opportunity. I left the two of them making a plan for a focus group of Ledoux residents to look into the whole idea. Rule One, she said, is to have the community design their own program.

*   *   *

Mr. Byrne made good on his offer to review my investigation into the disappearance of my wife Eugénie. He and Lorraine met me at Probation & Parole. I showed them the cabinet containing my investigation files. I had five cartons of physical evidence, expert reports, and the narrative accounts by the officers who led the search. I taught Mr. Byrne how to use the computerized records of probationers, the older paper files, and to decipher my copious entries. My notes don't indicate any connection between Eugénie's disappearance and our records, but he wanted to read them to be sure.

Nicole would have been a big help with all this. I pushed down any thought of calling and asking her to come over to give us a hand. She wanted to shut the door. She'd made it clear in two different ways—from her attitude and from her move to Lafayette. My thought of a formal apology was for my own benefit entirely—to assuage my guilt. Nevertheless, I couldn't put out of my mind the prerequisite for being forgiven—an apology.

I pulled a sheet of paper out of the printer and wrote a three-line apology. I found an envelope and a stamp, addressed the envelope to Nicole Maraist at Lafayette Probation and Parole, and put it in outgoing mail. Done. Page turned. From time to time I still beat myself up about my stupidity, but the instances became less frequent and less intense.

Mr. Byrne and Lorraine worked on the probation files separately sometimes and together at others. I went out for pizza and kept them plied with coffee and cokes. At five o'clock Mr. Byrne had to admit he hadn't thought of another thing we could do.

I offered to take them both to Crawfish Kitchen as my

thank you. Mr. Byrne declined.

"Camille will have dinner for me. And I have to recognize that having a long day requires a man of seventy to get to his easy chair."

Lorraine had an alternate plan. She asked me to pick up André and come to her house. She had supper for both of us.

17

I'd never seen Mr. Strait quite like he was the afternoon Elizabeth Carter came to tell us what she knew about the Blessed Believers. Ordinarily, when he wanted information, he assigned his assistants to the task. They would conduct the interviews and make a report. But when I told him Elizabeth Carter planned to come to our district to visit some friends she'd made when she worked at the Jefferson Island Nursery, he asked me to schedule her whenever I could. He would clear his calendar and talk to her with us.

Of course, with us would mean he'd be in charge.

At first, Mr. Strait wanted only me at the meeting. I persuaded him to include Lorraine. I'd watched Lorraine establish rapport with Elizabeth when we went to Forest Hill. She had sympathetic words, yes, but her manner scored. The slight dip of her chin, the soft voice, the fix of her blue eyes on Elizabeth's darker ones. I offered to give up my place to Lorraine if Mr. Strait thought four people would be too many for easy conversation. Mr. Strait agreed to have us both but cautioned he might send me away. Clearly, he was on a mission.

Elizabeth gave me a day and time she could come to the Iberia courthouse, Mr. Strait's central office. He had his staff pick up all the books and papers from the library table, put on fresh coffee, and send out for cookies. He showed no irritation when Elizabeth came fifteen minutes late.

Elizabeth had been dressed in her Sunday best at the service for her sister, with a formal manner to match what she wore. She appeared at this meeting in comfortable work clothes: plaid flannel shirt, jeans, all-weather boots and a red bandanna to hold her hair in check. Her happy face gave me two bits of information: Elizabeth felt most comfortable in gardening clothes. The morning at the nursery had gone well. Come spring, she told us, Jefferson Island Nursery would be sending north a truckload of tropical plants they had grown. Stephenson's in Forest Hill would return the truck filled with flats of *Liriope*, ajuga, English ivy, and confederate jasmine— their specialty ground covers.

Mr. Strait had the gardening vocabulary for this meeting. He could talk about the best season for planting, which plants tolerated our heat and tropical rainstorms, and which required spraying with insecticide. Lorraine came next with expressions of sympathy for the family's loss. She asked specifically how Becca (she remembered the nickname) and little Robbie were coming along. Better every day, Elizabeth said. I didn't contribute to either topic. I felt I had only limited permission to be on the playing field and no leave to carry the ball.

Social niceties complete, Mr. Strait jumped rather abruptly into the topic of interest to him.

"I understand your sister Virtua was a member of the Church of the Blessed Believers on Oak and Pine Alley on the road to Catahoula. Is that right?"

"A member? I guess you could say that. Of course, our family never recognized she was anything other than Catholic. She was baptized Catholic and made her first Communion. She faithfully attended our little church in Forest Hill before she came to New Iberia. When she lived with us here, she went with my family to Mass at St. Peters every Sunday. Correction: we usually went to Anticipated Mass on Saturday evening. She was buried Catholic too. Are you Catholic, Mr. Strait?"

"Yes, I am." His eyes touched each one of us. "All three of us here are Catholics."

"Then you can understand how the family felt about Virtua being so gung-ho about the Blessed Believers. Our parents wouldn't even talk about it."

"Her husband Robert introduced her to the Believers, I understand."

"Yes. He brought her in."

"Was Blessed Believers always Robert's church?"

"Oh, no. He was a convert."

"How did that happen? Do you know?"

"Virtua told me someone at Robert's work—at the grocery store, not offshore where he worked before they were married—turned him on to the Believers. But once they got there, both Robert and Virtua took to the church in a big way. They were baptized in the Holy Spirit, Virtua said, although of course she was baptized already. For Virtua, the Believers were not just a Sunday morning activity. She was out there many times a week, at everything from prayer services to rummage sales. She went all the way."

"I have the impression from the way you're telling us about this you didn't much care for the idea of your sister going to the Believers," Mr. Strait asked.

Elizabeth answered Mr. Strait's questions, but her eyes found Lorraine's.

"No. That's not quite accurate. In the beginning, I thought it was a good thing. Robert was wild before he went there. When he got off work, he'd head straight for the bars. Our parents didn't know about that, but I did. Once Robert became a Blessed Believer, he turned a corner. He stopped drinking; he helped out at home; he was transformed. For the first couple of years or so that Robert was in that church, Virtua's life was much better. And they provided a lot for Becca and Robbie. That church takes care of its own. Virtua was helped and she helped others: after-school care, weekly suppers, the rummage sales, you name it. When anything went on out there, she was in it."

"Apparently, Robert didn't stay reformed."

"No. He turned totally against the church."

"And why was that? Do you know the reason for the change in Robert?"

"Well, I think I do. Two reasons. Speaking in tongues was kind of a sore subject between them."

"Glossolalia?" Mr. Strait asked. I could tell from his wide eyes this was the first he'd heard about that.

"Yes. Robert was upset he never could do it. I don't understand the beliefs of the group, but Virtua told me Robert thought he had to be able to speak in tongues or he'd go to hell. And then there was the business about Pastor Allen's death."

Mr. Strait sat straighter in his chair and opened his eyes wider. I knew getting information about the pastors of the church was the whole reason for the interview, not that I understood why.

"I believe Moses Allen was the pastor before Noah Norbert, right?"

"Yes, sir. And they all loved him."

"That was his real name? Moses Allen?"

"Only name I ever heard."

"Did you know him?"

"I guess you could say I did. He was the pastor a few times when I went there with Virtua."

"Tell me about his death, if you will."

"Pastor Allen got real sick. He had cancer, I think. That was about a year and a half or two years ago. He told the congregation to pray for him. In fact, Pastor Allen told them if they prayed hard enough, he wouldn't die. Virtua and Robert were on their knees for hours. But Pastor Allen got sicker and sicker and then he did die. When that happened, Robert flipped out."

"Flipped out? How was that?"

"He turned totally against the church. He didn't attend services with Virtua and the children, and he went back to his old habits of drinking and staying out late in the bars. He gave Virtua no help at home. It was bad. I felt really sorry for Virtua. She was pregnant again, and Robert was awful. You know, Virtua was the youngest child in our family and our parents were older."

My guess? When Virtua was growing up, Elizabeth ended up taking care of her little sister. Virtua met Robert here, on Elizabeth's watch, you could say. Given what happened, Elizabeth probably had a shitload of guilt about it.

But Mr. Strait had little interest in Virtua's family

dynamics. At each opportunity, he pressed Elizabeth to tell us everything she could about the church pastors.

"Do you know if there was an assistant pastor when Pastor Allen was there?"

Mr. Strait had reached the point of his interview.

"Yes, there once was an assistant. He was the youth minister, I think. I didn't have much contact with him because Virtua's children were so young."

Mr. Strait leaned forward. His expression didn't change, at least not to someone who didn't know him well. No muscle moved, like a dog on scent.

"Do you remember the name of the assistant pastor?"

"No. I don't. Wait. Gilbert. Brother Gilbert."

"Was Gilbert his first or last name?"

"I don't know. Probably first. That seems to be the custom."

"Can you tell me anything about him—anything at all." Elizabeth was shaking her head. "Maybe you could tell me what he looked like?"

"He was in his early twenties, I'd say. Average height, dark hair. Oh, he was a white man. Did I say that?" She asked Lorraine that question. Lorraine just smiled.

"Do you know where he lived?"

"I think he lived at the church. He kept up the place, as I remember, so he was there most of the time."

"Do you know if the assistant took over after Pastor Allen died?" Mr. Strait asked.

"No. He didn't take over. In fact, he left a few months before that. Virtua didn't talk about what became of him. Some scandal, I think. I wasn't here then. I'd moved back to Forest Hill. I hated to leave Virtua. She was pregnant with the third child and life was hard for her, but our parents were sick. My husband and I had to pitch in at Stephenson's, the family business…"

"Some scandal, you say? Can you tell me anything about that?" Mr. Strait may have thought he asked a casual question but he gave equal emphasis to each word. Anyone who knew him would know he had reached what he hoped would be the motherlode.

"I can't really. I don't know what happened."

"What did you hear?" Mr. Strait probed, quietly but with tell-tale emphasis.

"Really nothing. It was more the way Virtua just closed down when anyone mentioned the assistant that gave me a funny feeling. I think it had something to do with the church children because he left right after the summer camp. He'd been in charge of the camp."

"And you say you don't know the assistant's last name?"

"Wait. Now that I concentrate I think I'm pretty sure Gilbert was his first name. I remember some people calling him Gil. I never heard the last name."

Mr. Strait sat back in his chair. Lorraine had been squirming. She had questions of her own but had been reluctant to interrupt. With what seemed to be a stopping place in the interrogation, she put a toe into the water.

"Ms. Carter…"

Immediately Elizabeth's expression softened. She welcomed the change of questioners like a cool drink on a blazing hot day. "Please call me Elizabeth," she said.

"I will. Elizabeth, you say Virtua *spoke in tongues*. That practice is pretty foreign to me and, apparently, foreign to the way Virtua was raised. Did you see her—I guess I should say *hear* her—doing that?"

"I sure did. Well, really only once. I was there one year on Pentecost."

"Tell me about that."

"I'll never forget it. I'm used to a bit of to-do about Pentecost, and I guess you are too. After Christmas and Easter, Pentecost is supposed to be the next most important day in the church year. Only *inside* our churches, however. Father wears carmine vestments and red carnations fill the vases on the altar and on the sills under the windows. We have special prayers. Retailers have yet to convert Pentecost into a festival of commercial consumption or an occasion for dancing and libations."

For just a moment, Mr. Strait smiled and allowed the

conversation to veer away from his mission. Mr. Strait said he was a lector and on Pentecost often read the second lesson from Acts. He knew it by heart and gave us a recitation, with theatrical flourish.

"When the day of Pentecost had come, they were all together in one place. And suddenly a sound came from heaven like a rush of a mighty wind and it filled all the house where they were sitting. And there appeared to them tongues as of fire, distributed and resting on each one of them. And they were all filled with the Holy Spirit, and began to speak in other tongues, as the spirit gave them utterance."

Elizabeth enjoyed the performance. "Of course we believe in the Holy Spirit, but I always thought the wind and those tongues of fire came on one occasion a couple thousand years ago. We commemorate that occasion as a call for a community of passion, to feed the hungry, clothe the poor, love those who have no one else to love them. But Virtua told me that for the Pentecostals, the Holy Spirit descends with the signs of their belief every time the faithful gather. They believe all the faithful have the powers of healing, prophesying, and speaking in tongues. Anyway, Robert was upset that he couldn't do it. He thought he didn't have the Holy Spirit. Then Pastor Allen died in spite of their prayers. The last straw, I suppose."

Mr. Strait wanted to get the conversation back to the pastors of the Church of the Blessed Believers.

"Elizabeth—may I call you Elizabeth—do you know anything about the governance of Pentecostal churches? I don't believe they have Bishops running the show, the way we do, but is there some other governing body with supervisory authority?"

Elizabeth said she didn't know anything about that. Nor did I. But I thought Pentecostals weren't a separate denomination. Many protestant denominations had Pentecostal practice. If Mr. Strait thought he'd get an investigative report from some governing body he'd be disappointed.

Lorraine ventured into the conversation again.

"So you were there when your sister Virtua did that speaking in tongues?"

"I was."

"Can you tell me about that?"

"The behavior of my little sister freaked me out. As Pastor Allen preached, she was moaning and groaning in some kind of spell. Then she drew herself up to standing—she was very pregnant with Robbie at the time—and began her gibberish. At the end of the billowing sleeves of her tunic, her open palms swayed toward the rafters. Eyes closed, face in rapture, she called aloud something like *Kalumbara doper ganmado, hrander, fimulatum.* Made no sense to me. On her right, Rebecca sat straight and proud, rocking in rhythm to the unintelligible words, beaming a heartbreakingly beautiful smile at her mother."

"And where was Robert when all that was going on?" Lorraine asked.

"Sitting on Virtua's left, clutching his hands in his lap, his eyes fixed on the base of the pew in front of him. His stiff back made it clear he wasn't into the emotion in the room. As soon as Virtua finished speaking, he made a beeline out the door. Come to think of it, I don't know how he got home that day."

I could picture the scene. I was damn glad Lorraine and I hadn't witnessed that business of speaking in tongues. I would have lost it.

Elizabeth had more to say about her sister's Pentecostal behavior.

"When Virtua was done, she convulsed in an orgasmic shudder, if you'll excuse the expression. She crumpled to her seat. In response, an Amen, two more, and then a chorus of Amens swelled from the congregation. Pastor Allen raised his arms. *Thank you, thank you, Sister Virtua, for sharing your gift with us today. You are truly baptized in the Holy Spirit. May the Lord's name be praised, in many tongues. Forever.* He repeated it several times. He was given to repetition, which I guess you know. About five rows behind Virtua, and across the aisle, another woman rose to her feet. She launched into the same mumbo-jumbo. She was a generation older than Virtua, pudgy face, chalk-white complexion with bright red-rouged cheeks. Pastor Allen gave a kind of benediction. *Blessed Believers, we have seen and heard today evidence of the Holy Ghost. You are saved by your faith and heaven awaits you."*

Elizabeth said she needed to get on the road back to Forest Hill before dark. Mr. Strait was gracious with his thanks. Lorraine also, hers with assurances they would stay in touch. Lorraine walked Elizabeth out to the reception area. She stopped at Marlene's desk and asked Marlene to take her to her car. "Check on her, Marlene. See that she has anything she may need. Water, enough gas, whatever."

Lorraine returned to the library so we could post-mortem the visit.

"Do you suppose the other speaker could have been Kitty Ernest?" Lorraine asked.

"If so, I'd say good fortune doesn't come to those who speak in tongues."

I waited to hear what Mr. Strait thought of the meeting. Did he get the information he wanted? No.

"I've tried to get someone in the Believers to open up about their pastors. Without success. I've contacted various organizations that include Pentecostal churches. Not one has ever heard of the Blessed Believers. I think they're some kind of renegade church. Flying without a net."

We got more information from Elizabeth than from anyone else, but what Mr. Strait really needed was the name of that assistant pastor so I could run him down. I had a suggestion. A good one, as it turns out. I asked Mr. Strait if he had spoken to the two women who started the ball rolling in the Robert Cane case—Sonja and Elena Trudeau.

If at that moment I needed something from the most powerful official in our three-parish district, I could have gotten it. I've never seen him react the way he did. He leaped up from his chair and gave me a bear hug. Whadda you know? That man actually has joy. But briefly. He sat down and stared at his hands.

After about a minute, I deigned to interrupt. Mr. Strait halted my effort with a raised hand. After a good five minutes more of contemplation, he reached for the phone. He dialed Mr. Byrne's office in St. Martin.

"Dennis, is Tony in today?"

"Yes. He's here. Do you want to talk with him?"

"Yes, but with you and the detectives. Detective D'Aquin and Detective LaSalle will be coming over there with me to meet with you and Tony right now. Will that work for you?"

"Yes, sir. I'll let Tony know. I'm sure he'll make that possible. Should I have anything ready for you?"

"Just yourselves. I'm going to push the reset button on our prosecution schedule."

PART V

18

District Attorney Gerald Strait didn't tell Mr. Byrne and Tony why they'd been summoned to receive us at the DA's office in St. Martinville. Mr. Byrne could handle uncertainty, but Tony probably stewed in confusion for the twenty-five minutes we took driving over. Sometimes I think Mr. Strait keeps his assistants a bit uneasy to enhance his control. He spoke directly to Tony as he walked into Mr. Byrne's office.

"Tony, I'm about to make you a happy man. I've changed my mind about the priority case for the next St. Martin criminal jury term." Tony blinked. A slight smile played on Mr. Strait's face. As usual, he wasn't exactly forthcoming. I studied his expression to see if I could figure out what he was thinking.

Mr. Strait continued. "If all goes as expected when you present the Robert Cane case to the Grand Jury, and they return a true bill for first-degree murder, Cane can be arraigned the following week. Then you can put State v. Robert Cane at the top of the priority list." He waited a moment for Tony to absorb the news. "Will you be ready?"

Tony couldn't believe the turn in his favor. "Sir? Of course, I can be ready. Totally ready. But what about State v. Thomas Ernest?"

"Dennis will be behind you."

"Call me a cockeyed optimist, but I was hoping I could persuade you to change your mind. I didn't cancel any of the witness prep appointments I had scheduled."

"Very good. I believe you are expecting Sonja Trudeau to come in tomorrow morning?"

How does Mr. Strait know that? Because he knows every damn thing that happens in his offices in all three parishes—

and probably in the offices of the three sheriffs as well. Tony was sputtering.

"Yes, sir. I am, sir," Tony sputtered. "She's coming in at nine. My plan is to present the investigation chronologically, as it unfolded, and it all began with Sonja Trudeau's visit to the St. Martinville City Police Department to report her friend Virtua Cane had gone missing."

"Perfect. As soon as you finish with Sonja Trudeau, I want you to send her over here to Dennis' office. I have some business with her that doesn't involve Robert Cane."

Flushed and grinning, Tony looked like a cherub in an old Italian painting. He spilled out the rest of his scheduled appointments.

"In the afternoon I'll see the coroner and some important fact witnesses like the clerk at the hardware store where Robert bought the rope and the rat poison. That guy also gave him the burlap sack that ended up being Virtua's shroud. Deuce is coming the following morning. He may take all day, so I don't have firm times for the appointments past that point, but I do have the others ready—"

Mr. Strait cut him off. "Fine, Tony. Fine. Whoever you want. How about the public defenders? Are they ready to move forward?"

"Sarah says they're ready for arraignment whenever we are."

"Good." Mr. Strait turned to Mr. Byrne. "Dennis, you may also go before the same Grand Jury session with the Thomas Ernest case—or not. It's up to you."

"I may want to think about it overnight, but—," Mr. Byrne stopped himself. "No, It's a go. Yes, sir. I'll be ready."

What else could Mr. Byrne say except *yes, sir*? Col. Dennis Byrne, Retired, knew how to respond when the wishes of his commanding officer were clear. In fact, Mr. Byrne was well ready. I'd be his lead witness. He had pored over my investigation report and worked with me on how he wanted me to tell the story. Not about to put himself in the crossfire, Mr. Byrne didn't say another word.

Mr. Strait hadn't finished with Tony. His right hand

burrowed under the papers on Mr. Byrne's desk until he'd found a No. 2 pencil. He picked it up with his right hand and passed it to his left.

"I would like to know, Tony, how you plan to explain the pertinent law to the jurors?"

"As I usually do, sir. I read the statutes. In this case, I'll read R.S. 14:30, paragraph 3, the definition of homicide applicable to our case. *First-degree homicide is the killing of a human being ... when the offender has specific intent to kill or to inflict bodily harm upon more than one person.* Then I'll read the definition of Person found at R.S. 14:2 –Definitions *"[P]erson" includes a human being from the moment of fertilization and implantation…"*

Mr. Strait moved the pencil back to his right hand. "And will you tell them the possible penalties for violation of these statutes?"

"Of course. Yes, sir. And I'll have to explain *beyond reasonable doubt* and *probable cause*, and tell each jury the standard applicable to their role in this process."

"In straightforward language, you plan to make it possible for the Grand Jury, and ultimately the trial court jury, to return a finding of first-degree homicide, punishable by death?"

"Yes, sir."

As Mr. Strait delivered his questions to Tony, Mr. Byrne's eyes appeared twice their normal size.

Mr. Strait passed the pencil again, drilling down on his prosecutor.

"Tony, am I correct in the assumption that you have not even explored with Sarah—I assume Sarah will be the Public Defender for Robert Cane—the possibility of a plea to a lesser offense?"

Tony didn't give an inch. "You are correct, sir." Firm, equal emphasis on each word.

"First-degree with capital recommendation." The pencil took another trip. "You are taking on the burden of producing a perfect trial record? You are committing the parish government to enhanced trial costs for jury sequestration, expert fees, and the cost of responding to years of post-conviction proceedings, particularly lengthy when the matter is one of first impression?"

"Yes, sir. I know that."

"Also, you know the present reality. The chance of a capital sentence being carried out in the State of Louisiana is slim to none. You will be committing our office to a pointless dance."

"Yes, sir."

"The other side of the reality is that a life sentence means life. If Robert Cane should plead to a sentence of life in prison, it is true that the public would pay for his keep for the rest of his natural life, but not as much as the cost involved in capital prosecution and his incarceration on death row during the never-ending post-conviction process."

"Yes, sir."

Mr. Strait again passed the pencil from hand to hand. "Please favor me with an explanation of why you are doing so, in spite of the realities."

I felt my temperature rise, and I wasn't even the person under Mr. Strait's scalpel. If Tony had any doubt about his decision, I couldn't see it. He hadn't a quiver in his voice.

"Mr. Strait, it is my firm belief that a prosecutor should bring the charge that fits the facts. If the Grand Jury in the preliminary stage, and the trial court jury in the guilt/innocent and penalty phases to follow, fail to bring in a capital verdict, so be it. The prosecutor will have done his job." Tony had drawn a line in the sand, and he knew it. "I also know, sir, that I serve at your pleasure."

Mr. Strait sat perfectly still. Seconds ticked by. Would Mr. Strait hold the pencil in both hands, snap it in two, and fire Tony on the spot?

I'll be damned. Mr. Strait blinked. He took a deep breath.

"OK, Tony." He had turned the page. "Let me know when you're finished with Sonja Trudeau tomorrow morning. I'll be waiting with Dennis."

Damn. Tony had won the day, but he opened his mouth to speak again. Would he blow it?

"Wait a minute, sir. Are you saying you want to present Sonja Trudeau to the Grand Jury? I don't see why you should do that when..."

"Get that stick out of your butt. Hell, no. I said nothing to do with Robert Cane. Sorry for my language, Lorraine."

Lorraine brushed off some imaginary dust in the air. Mr. Strait looked at his watch. "I'm due at a political meeting at Cochon's on the Levee, but I have something I need to discuss with Dennis, Ted, and Lorraine."

In other words, get out of my sight, Tony. Mr. Strait hadn't fired Tony, but by dismissing him from this meeting he signaled Tony no longer had full access to information in the office. Tony stood up and left the room, briefly nodding to each of us as he left.

Assistant District Attorney Tony Blendera had won the battle, but he'd lose the war. I wouldn't bet much on him having his job this time next year.

Mr. Strait motioned to us to stay. He leaned back in his chair, coming as close to exhaling as you can get without actually doing so. Then we heard why he had summoned us to this meeting.

"Detectives, I have a special assignment I want the two of you to undertake. I've cleared this with Sheriff Gabrielle, without telling her more than I needed to. She didn't ask to know any more, agreeing on the wisdom of discretion."

Was Mr. Strait telling me to leave Chief Deputy Roland out of a loop? I think so. Maybe Mr. Strait felt as I did. Chief Roland blabs.

"I need an investigation concerning the Church of the Blessed Believers." He let that statement sit a minute. "More precisely, I need to know all there is to know about the former assistant pastor. Where did he come from? Why was he dismissed? Where did he go?"

"Yes, sir."

"Good. Now I will share with you why I'm making this request. Two years ago, I heard rumors about a scandal out there. I made discrete inquiries. No one would talk. I had to put my interest on a shelf. Last month the principal of St.

Martin Middle School came over to my New Iberia office to talk to me. The school system is, as you know, a mandatory reporter of information they come across about possible sexual offenses. One of his teachers had concerns about an essay a student—a male student—had written for her class. He described an activity at a summer camp run by the assistant pastor of the Believers."

Well, what do you know? Not the first time we've had monkey business behind church doors.

"The student wrote about a game of musical chairs with a twist. When the music stopped, the boy without a chair had to take off a piece of clothing. The first boy to be completely naked had to run to the assistant pastor's cabin. What happened after that the boy's English paper did not say."

Lorraine and I both raised our eyebrows but did not speak. Maybe we'd hear more.

"I want to renew our investigation into the matter— starting with what I hope to learn from Sonja Trudeau tomorrow morning. Be there."

                              *   *   *

At nine o'clock Lorraine and I sat on a bench inside the locked door of the District Attorney's office, not completely into the *sanctum sanctorum,* but a more favored status than the crowd of supplicants waiting on the hallway benches to see an assistant about traffic tickets or whatever. I assumed we would get an investigation assignment should Mr. Strait happen to learn anything from his meeting with Sonja Trudeau.

Mr. Strait's receptionist called us in close to ten. Then she went to Tony's office to fetch Sonja Trudeau; they had finished, she told us. With a stranger present, Mr. Strait favored us with a few minutes of social exchange before he got to the purpose of the meeting.

"Mrs. Trudeau, I have been very impressed with your willingness to come forward to help us with the business of prosecuting those who seek to disrupt the peace and tranquility of our parish. Not everyone is such a good citizen."

"Thank you, sir. Virtua was my friend and fellow churchwoman. I will do anything I can to help."

That's a relief. I had thought we were going to be dealing with a church like the Jehovah's Witnesses. They decline to participate in the institutions of government.

He continued, "I hope you had a satisfactory meeting with Mr. Blendera?"

"Yes, sir. He went over the questions he plans to ask me when I talk to the Grand Jury. He will have me tell of my friendship with Virtua, how worried my sister-in-law Elena and I were when Virtua didn't come to help us prepare for the rummage sale, and how we reported her absence to the St. Martinville Police Station."

"Very good. As I suppose Mr. Blendera told you, Robert Cane's lawyer will not be at the Grand Jury. The Grand Jury is like a dress rehearsal before curtain time. His lawyer *will* be there at the trial."

"That's exactly what he said, sir."

"Good. I have something totally different on my mind. I'm hoping you can help me with a bit of information."

"I will if I can, sir. I love my church, and I'm happy to share the Word."

Unlike our experiences questioning Thomas Ernest's friend and investment advisor Mark Gander, and unlike what had apparently been Mr. Strait's efforts to talk with other members of the Church, Mrs. Trudeau didn't shut us out. She didn't even hesitate.

"Thank you. How long have you been a member of the Church of the Believers?"

"I was baptized in the Holy Spirit four years ago. By Pastor Allen," she said proudly.

"The former pastor. Right?"

"Yes, sir."

"And your sister-in-law Elena?"

"The same. She received the Holy Spirit at the same time I did. She was also baptized by Pastor Allen."

"There was an assistant pastor at the Believers around

that time, correct?"

"Yes, sir."

"Do you remember his name?"

"Hm-m. Gilbert. We called him Brother Gilbert."

"Was Gilbert his first or last name?"

"Last, I believe. Ben Gilbert."

Virtua's sister Elizabeth probably had it wrong. A member of the congregation would know best. Now we had a first name.

"He's not there any longer. Can you tell me anything about him?"

Maybe a hesitation here. "Like what did he look like?"

"Yes, that's a good way to start."

Sonja gave the same information as Virtua's sister Elizabeth. A white man, under thirty, medium build and weight. He lived on the grounds and took care of the place. He also ran the children's activities and the summer camp. He left town before Pastor Allen died. Asked to leave, apparently.

"Do you know what Brother Gilbert might have done to cause him to be asked to leave?"

"No. I know nothing of my own knowledge. Only rumor, and it's against our religion to spread rumors."

Here we go again. There was that taboo. The Believers seem to have just one. They won't spread rumors. I had a fleeting thought; maybe I could get them to explain hearsay to our over-zealous detectives! Right now, we had yet another Believer who might know something important but wouldn't talk.

Lorraine leaned forward and, with a lift of an eyebrow, asked permission of Mr. Strait to try some of her own questions. He nodded his acquiescence.

"We have a serious matter on our plate, Mrs. Trudeau. It concerns the safety of children. Perhaps you could give us the name of someone who does have first-hand knowledge of Brother Ben Gilbert's activities, and maybe what he might have done to displease Pastor Allen. Do you know of anyone with first-hand knowledge?"

Sonja didn't hesitate. "Elena Trudeau, my sister-in-law.

She knows what went on. Her older boy was at the summer camp when they had the problem."

Mr. Strait didn't really smile, but all the muscles in his face eased. His narrow eyes widened.

"Do you know where we might find Elena Trudeau today?" Mr. Strait asked.

"Oh yes, sir. She's right downstairs. She drove me here, and she's waiting to take me home."

Blind hog found an acorn, as the expression goes. Mr. Strait buzzed Marlene and asked her to invite Elena Trudeau upstairs to meet with us. Mr. Strait nodded to Lorraine, a signal for her to take the lead in the questioning. Lorraine had shown what I'd come to recognize as her gift for setting people at ease. After preliminaries, Lorraine asked Mrs. Trudeau if she remembered the assistant pastor that used to be at the church.

"Yes. I remember him."

"We've heard that there was some kind of problem at the summer camp, and the assistant was asked to leave. Do you know what the problem might have been?"

"You know, at the Believers we do not repeat rumors, and I won't do that either. I really know very little."

Lorraine knew how to play. In just a few sentences she suggested a way for Elena to tell us what we needed to know.

"Did you or one of your children have a personal experience involving the summer camp? That wouldn't be a rumor."

"I can tell you this. My son was very uncomfortable there. He quit the camp halfway through the summer and wouldn't go back."

"Did he give you any reason for his discomfort?"

"He said Brother Gilbert was a creep."

Lorraine jollied her along a bit. "We're not familiar with the vocabulary of eleven-year-olds, Elena. Maybe you could translate for us? What did he mean by saying Brother Gilbert was a creep?"

Right then there was a knock on the office door. Without waiting for an invitation to enter, Marlene pushed through.

"My apologies, Mr. Strait—and Mr. Byrne. We have an emergency. Patrick Ernest's house on Coulee Rouge, north of I-10, is on fire. Chief Roland wants Detective D'Aquin and Detective LaSalle to go there immediately."

Damn. We were at a critical point with Elena.

Marlene continued. "They don't even want you to stop to call. Radio in from the road. The firemen don't know the inside of the house. It's an unusual building, they say."

Lorraine and I both scrambled to our feet. Mr. Strait stood up also. "Of course, of course. Do what you need to do and be careful. We'll ask Mrs. Trudeau to talk with us one day soon."

"Does the Sheriff know if Patrick is in the house?" I asked Marlene as I passed her desk on the way out.

"They don't know. That's why they want you."

19

Highway 31 borders the meandering course of the Bayou Teche north through the Parish of St. Martin. The State Office of Tourism calls it a scenic byway, but this evening we were not taking a pleasure trip. We verified by phone that Chief Roland wanted us to get to Coulee Rouge ASAP. That required lights, siren, and pedal to the floorboard. A matter of life or death, he said. Sirens may make emergency speed relatively safe on a straight road, but if I went much over the limit on Highway 31, I'd have a pretty good chance of landing us in a deep ditch by the side of the road, or maybe even in the Bayou Teche itself. As it was, Lorraine kept a white-knuckle grip on the handle of her door most of the way. Chief Roland gave us the briefing he'd promised.

"Patrol in the north part of the Parish radioed a fine home ablaze at 405 Coulee Rouge. I figure it had to be Patrick Ernest's. There isn't another "fine" home in those parts. The fire departments are just getting there now. Our units are en route."

"You don't know if anyone's inside?"

"No one answered the telephone number in the phone book, but we know he has a lot of other lines. A bunch of cars would tell us something, I suppose. In any case, you and Ted are the only people we know of who've been in. Give the firemen your help with the lay of the land."

Chief had on his serious voice. Lorraine resisted saying aloud what she mouthed to me over her hand. They could get Patrick's Dad out of jail to give them a tour.

We turned off Highway 31 onto Coulee Rouge. Blinded by the glare of the late afternoon sun, I flipped down the visor. A half-mile before we reached number 405, two of our own units blocked the road. One of the deputies directed us around the roadblock, but not before giving firm instructions to check in with the Fire Chief as soon as we got to the site.

"He'll be in the fire engine red Silverado," the deputy said.

I knew the protocol for fires. Report immediately to command. In addition to maximizing the effectiveness of his equipment, the one in charge at a fire scene has to keep close check on the rescue forces.

Lorraine and I heard the fire before we saw it. Anyone who has ever been close to a building on fire remembers the sounds. At the start, there is no sound. The fire silently stalks his prey like a lion beginning a hunt, putting his eyes on what he has chosen for dinner. Then come crashes and crackles as the lion heads through the bush. A fire in full control of a building roars like *Samba* devouring his kill.

We arrived for the "kill." Gusts of black smoke swirled up from the site, obscuring the setting sun. A building on fire has a smell you'll never forget. Choking and sour.

Three fire engines—two pumpers and one hook and ladder—had pulled up on the lawn. An ambulance with a clear path for exit sat on the circular drive. Three of our patrol cars and the Fire Chief's Silverado had parked on the shoulder of Coulee Rouge. Shouting over the roar, the Fire Chief acknowledged our arrival.

Two firefighters in full bunker gear unrolled thick hoses from one of the pumpers. They directed arcs of water into the right side of the house, what they perceived to be the heart of the fire. Water hitting the flames hissed like a copperhead snake being dive-bombed by a blue jay trying to protect her nest. A second pair of firefighters, fearing the fire might claim another structure, soaked the ground close to the blaze and out about twenty feet. In truth, only Patrick's "barn" on the far left of the property sat near enough to feel the heat.

Lorraine described the floor plan to the Fire Chief. Patrick's bedroom in the left rear, where he'd hidden the tapes in the light fixture over a king size bed, appeared to be the most heavily used room in the house. Lorraine remembered a well-worn Easy-Boy facing a giant screen TV and a small refrigerator in easy reach. The windows of the room overlooked a pasture in the rear.

"He may not be at home," she shouted. "I don't see the green BMW."

"The left rear is the least involved part of the house at the moment," the Fire Chief said. "I'll direct a crew to see if they can get inside through there."

"If he were home, surely he'd have stepped out to say hello. I'll see if his car is in the barn. Or any other vehicles." Lorraine turned away from the blaze and jogged quickly in that direction.

The Fire Chief led the pair of firefighters around the left side to check out the rear bedroom picture window. I followed but stopped dead as a thunderous crash took down the second story over the kitchen on the right side. Scared the dickens out of me. For the moment, the high part in the center of the house that accommodated the fourteen-foot cathedral ceilings remained intact.

"It's all gonna go, guys. We have only a brief window of time," the Chief told his crew. "When the fire reaches the center there, and we'll know when we hear it fall, no one should attempt to enter anywhere until the flames die down."

I stayed a dozen feet behind the firefighters as they took axes to the back windows, watered their path, and took a few steps inside. A blast of heat and smoke drove them back. I stepped back also—and actually bumped right into Mr. Byrne who had come up behind me.

"I hope you're not thinking of going in a burning building with no protective gear." Mr. Byrne shouted at me. "Neither one of us has any business near there. I'm an amateur in expert territory, and I'm not sure you're much better."

Mr. Byrne took my arm and backed us up behind Chief Roland. The firefighters exchanged some hand signals and vanished into the smoke. In less than three minutes they reappeared, shaking their heads.

"The entire internal wall collapsed in front of us. Maybe someone's in there but we couldn't see crap."

Mr. Byrne again urged caution. "I want my witness alive, guys, but not at the price of your lives."

The Fire Chief returned to the front of the house to resume his supervision of the operation. The pair of firefighters on our side of the house continued their effort to find a way in. Mr. Byrne and I circled behind the house and around to the right. The pair with the hose over there was also still outside, helpless. We were all watching a building burn to the ground.

Only when the flames and noise abated did I realize I hadn't seen Lorraine since she went to check the barn. I glanced at my watch; she'd been gone an hour.

"Damn it, Mr. Byrne. I haven't seen Lorraine."

"She's got to be around somewhere. She isn't like some people I know, foolish enough to think about going into a burning building."

"No, but…" I started to run in the direction of the barn, shouting over my shoulder. "She went to check for Patrick's car!"

Mr. Byrne heard the concern in my voice. "I'm right behind you Ted."

I started to tell him to stay where he was, but remembered he was military. He probably had better emergency training than I did. But I had almost thirty years on him and more recent practice.

Would the entry to the barn be locked? I tried to remember if Patrick had given us a key on the day we came to search. I didn't think so. The only image I could resurrect was Patrick on his front steps with the dogs.

Dogs! Dammit! Where were they? Burnt to a crisp inside the house? Maybe they were in the barn?

"Where the hell are the Dobermans?" I shouted my rhetorical question to Mr. Byrne. I found the barn door unlocked and pushed in.

Pitch black. Silence, then low growls from somewhere deep in the darkness. I curled my hand around back to the right, blindly groping for a light switch. I found one and snapped it on. Across the room, I saw the two Dobermans, legs splayed wide and stiff, noses pointed to the far corner. Growls rumbled even deeper in their throats. One of them twisted his head around to check us but snapped back to keep a point on his quarry.

Lorraine sat slumped against the far wall. The two dogs held her at bay. I choked on the fear she could be hurt.

At the sight of us, Lorraine screamed. "Ted! Get these damn dogs off me!"

Her voice made me feel better. She had her spirit. "Hang in there, Lo."

Her face looked OK, but I saw blood on her hands, her arms and her legs. She'd taken off that brown polyester uniform shirt and torn it into pieces. She'd wrapped one long piece—an arm of the shirt, I guessed—around one of her legs. She held another piece to her left temple.

It didn't take me but a second to make up my mind about what to do. I pulled my pistol off my hip and plugged both dogs. They fell over, twitched, and lay still.

I shoved one of them out of the way with my boot so I could reach Lorraine. I knelt beside her. I can't remember what I said. Probably nothing. I just held her. She cried with relief.

Mr. Byrne poked around the bodies of the two dogs.

"Leave the fuckin' dogs. They won't be giving any more trouble."

"I'm checking the rabies tags. They're current."

God, I hadn't thought of that. I called out my thanks and asked him to go get the EMTs from the ambulance. He was already at the door.

"It's not as bad as it looks," Lorraine whispered. Her call for help had exhausted what little strength she had left. "They only went for me when I tried to get up. They got me pretty good here, though." She moved the cloth on her left temple. "I think I'm going to need some stitches."

An understatement. Blood pooled to her side, and I could see a six-inch gash through a rip in one leg of her pants. She might need blood.

"I took it from those chiseled teeth, but the bleeding has

about stopped." She started to get up and wobbled. I held her down.

"Just sit still, Lo. Help is on the way. And a blanket. I don't think you want to go out there dressed for Michael's Men's Club."

The EMTs came in with a litter, covered her, transferred her, and carried her to the ambulance. Lifting her started another spurt of bleeding. Lorraine was mumbling something I couldn't catch.

"Don't try to talk, Lo."

"Tell the firemen the car's not in the barn. Patrick's probably not in the house. Just let the fucker burn."

I called over my shoulder to Mr. Byrne, but didn't break my pace. "If anyone's looking for us, we'll be at Lafayette General." No ER nurse would be stitching Lorraine's face.

I followed the ambulance to the hospital, lights and siren blazing. I radioed Chief Roland with a report. I prayed.

I felt I should be calling somebody for her. All I really knew about my partner was that her husband died in Afghanistan. I didn't know if she had parents, siblings, anybody. Which gave me one more thing to beat myself up about. We'd been riding together for more than a month. I was so focused on avoiding the temptation of entanglement I hadn't even asked about her emergency contact.

But I was in charge now. Where would she go after they patched her up? I couldn't take her to my house without some time to prepare André, but I didn't plan to let her out of my sight.

When they had Lorraine settled on the table in the emergency room, a nurse at her side, and an ER doctor on the job with his sewing kit, I asked her if I could call someone for her.

"I'll call my sister in a little while. I need to tell her where I am, but I'll see how I feel when the doc is through with me. Maybe they'll keep me overnight."

Her voice was slurred but she was thinking more clearly than I was. They kept her. I spent the night on a chair in her room.

I took Lorraine back to her house in St. Martinville in the morning. Two blocks from mine, as it turned out. She immediately went to sleep.

I checked in at headquarters. Chief said Patrick Ernest's house had burned to the ground, and they'd found no one inside. The firefighters thought the blaze started in a downstairs room, far from the usual first sites of an accidental fire. Chief Roland suspected arson and made a report to the State Fire Marshall in Baton Rouge.

I went looking for Mr. Byrne to thank him for giving us a hand at Patrick's house. I found him in the DA's library scratching his head. Mandy Aguillard sat by his side, taking notes.

"Come on in," he said. After asking about Lorraine, he explained their project. "I have Mandy deep into cases dealing with getting evidence from a missing witness. I fear Patrick won't be willing to help us out, now that he's lost his livelihood."

"I'm sorry about that."

"I hadn't planned on offering the tapes at the Grand Jury anyway. Without opposing counsel, I think the demonstration of the guns and bullets will carry the day. But I'll need the tapes for the trial. Laymen want to know about motive."

"What about getting the sweetie himself? Reggie something or other? He could vouch for the tapes. Could we get him?"

Mr. Byrne slapped the table. "I had just come to the same thought. Running him down is a job for a detective! We only know Reggie's first name, but I suppose you could find the phone number he made the calls from. Maybe a search warrant for the motel records?"

Here's an idea with possibilities. Maybe Lorraine would be up for an out of town trip to interview a witness? No, man. Be patient. Lo was absolutely wonderful to spend time with. We were definitely on the same page. But I damn sure didn't want to do anything I'd be sorry for in the morning, as the expression goes.

With the help of Ernest's phone records and the internet, I located a Reggie Throckmorton in Mobile, Alabama, and drove over to pay him a visit. A balding, overweight, really ordinary looking guy. He said he'd be quite willing to come testify to the affair—actually, he was rather proud of it. His little swagger and satisfied look would make him a perfect witness for our side.

*   *   *

Judge Mari Johnson empaneled the St. Martin Parish Grand Jury the following Monday. I testified on State v. Thomas Ernest. When Deuce came to testify on State v. Robert Cane, he and I had lunch together at St. John Plantation. The rest of the week, waiting for the results of the Grand Jury, I made sure Lorraine didn't overdo while we both caught up on paperwork.

We were both off duty Saturday. I needed to get outside. Lorraine, André and I joined Martin to take Plug to a training for law enforcement dogs in Baton Rouge. We picked up a copy of *The Teche News* before we left town. We found the following article on the front page:

GRAND JURY RETURNS
TWO INDICTMENTS
FOR FIRST-DEGREE MURDER

At seven P.M. Friday night, the St. Martin Parish Grand Jury returned two True Bills for first-degree murder. Robert Cane is accused of the homicide of his wife Virtua Cane and their unborn child on September 18, 2001. Thomas Ernest is accused of the homicide of his wife Kitty Ernest and of the homicide of Charles Joe on September 28, 2001. Both defendants are residents of St. Martinville.

If found guilty of the charges, both Thomas Ernest and Robert Cane could receive the penalty of death by lethal injection.

The indictment of Robert Cane for first-degree murder is believed to be the first brought in this state for the killing of a pregnant female. Last summer the Legislature passed legislation providing that life begins at conception.

On September 21, 2001, two fishermen found the body of Virtua Cane in Catahoula Lake. The coroner reported that she was eight months pregnant. The following day her husband Robert was arrested for her murder. He remains in the parish jail under a $1,000,000 bond.

On September 30, 2001, St. Martin Parish Sheriff's Office deputies arrested Thomas Ernest for the murder of his wife and Charles Joe, the man Ernest claimed had entered his house and murdered his wife. Ernest remains in the parish jail, without bond.

"The Grand Jury has spoken. The State will vigorously prosecute the charges brought," stated Assistant District Attorney Dennis Byrne. Sarah Bernard, the court appointed attorney for Robert Cane did not return a call placed to her office. The attorney for Thomas Ernest is presently unknown.

20

While I prepared to testify to the Grand Jury about the Thomas Ernest investigation, and Lorraine's wounds were healing, Sheriff Gabrielle redecorated her office. I called it right about the pictures on the wall. The gallery of her father's triumphs had disappeared. A five-foot wide Greg Girouard photograph of a rosy sunset at Lake Fausse Pointe held down one wall. An eight-foot tall piece of cypress driftwood replaced the commemorative shovel. Another wall had been painted light green. I don't know much about color, but the whole room seemed brighter.

A low coffee table and four upholstered chairs sat on an oriental style rug just inside the door. We found Mr. Strait and Sheriff Gabrielle sitting there. They invited us to join them. No coffee on the table, just a couple of yellow legal pads, a pen, and a No. 2 pencil. The Sheriff had picked up on Mr. Strait's idiosyncrasy.

Two minutes for chit-chat. Lorraine complimented the Sheriff on the new decor. Mr. Strait asked Lorraine about her recovery. Then Mr. Strait turned to the issue that brought us together.

"I asked Sheriff Gabrielle if I could borrow your services for a special investigation, and she gave me the OK. Your summons to the fire at Patrick Ernest's house interrupted the conversation we were having. Do you recall what we'd been talking about?"

I answered. "Yes, sir. The principal of St. Martin Middle School reported to Sheriff Gabrielle about a troubling student paper. Something about a game at the summer camp at the Church of the Blessed Believers that involved boys taking off their clothes. We spoke with the Trudeau sisters-in-law, and

Elena Trudeau had just started telling us her son said Brother Gilbert was a creep."

"Yes. That's where we were." Mr. Strait turned to Sheriff Gabrielle. "I now have a new report, this one from the Superintendent of Schools of Iberia Parish. A student told his counselor about a game the assistant pastor of the Believers played last summer. Musical chairs with a twist. When the music stopped, the boy without a chair had to take off a piece of clothing. The first boy to be completely naked had to run to the assistant pastor's cabin. When three boys had gone to the cabin, the pastor followed. The student didn't know what happened after that, but he was freaked out." Mr. Strait took a deep breath. "So we have corroboration. We must get to the bottom of this immediately."

He paused. I waited for the assignment.

"You know, the school system is extremely reluctant to breach a student's confidence, and what's more, they usually hate to claim ownership of anything that might reflect badly on one of the schools. Surprisingly, in this case, the parents, the student, and the boy's counselor all agree the matter should not be swept under the rug. They've asked us not to reveal the name of the student. I've spoken to the counselor, and she believes questioning him at this stage of his treatment would be harmful. Maybe later, if absolutely necessary. Please not now, she said. I didn't make any promises, but I came close."

Crap. Mr. Strait wanted me for sex offense duty, which I hate. I reached for one of the bottles of water set out on the table, with a glance to the Sheriff asking for her permission. She nodded her head OK. Mr. Strait continued.

"I've been talking this matter over with Sheriff Gabrielle. She has approved my asking you to help."

Why not an Iberia detective—Deuce for instance? He knows as much as I do about the Believers. Mr. Strait answered the question I hadn't said aloud.

"Any offenses that might have occurred would have taken place in St. Martin Parish."

Does the guy read minds?

The Sheriff and Mr. Strait waited for my response. I accepted my fate.

"How can I be of help, sir?"

With that question, Sheriff Gabrielle knew I was on board. She reached for a legal pad and placed it in front of me. A hint of a smile softened Mr. Strait's face. He began a briefing.

"I'm told the present pastor at the Church of the Believers, Brother Noah Norbert, came here only a little over six months ago, after the death of his predecessor, Brother Allen. The assistant pastor ran the camp during Brother Allen's regime, but at one point he was dismissed. That's where I think you should begin—learning all you can about the assistant pastor and his dismissal. Now he's disappeared. No one knows where he went."

Ah, yes. The activities of the mysterious Brother Gilbert.

Mr. Strait's tone hardened. "I want you to find him."

I considered the assignment for only a second. I couldn't refuse, even if I didn't exactly have a good record in the 'finding of missing persons' department. I asked for the help I might need while declining the assignment was theoretically still a possibility.

"Will I have a partner?" I asked Sheriff Gabrielle.

"Detective LaSalle, if you'd like."

"Very good."

Indeed, very good. Another assignment together would give me cover. I found I wanted to be with Lorraine any time, all the time. I could swear Mr. Strait had a knowing smile. Or was I just being paranoid? Most people have no interest in how other people pass their spare time.

"Do either of you have any special suggestions for where I should begin in my search to find Brother Gilbert?" I asked.

Mr. Strait had a suggestion. "When the subject of the Church of the Blessed Believers came up in the last two homicides, Chief Roland said he'd once heard something about a scandal out there. His thought: The church records may tell us where the assistant came from or where he went. Chief has found Brother Norbert to be a pretty straight shooter. He wouldn't repeat a rumor, but he might share facts and figures. Chief suggested you start with him."

I continued. "Do you have any objection to my asking Sonja Trudeau and her sister-in-law Elena to come with me to see Brother Norbert?"

"Good plan. They were willing to work with Deuce in the Cane case even though there was a possibility the investigation might hurt their church. In fact, they said their pastor had encouraged them to do so. And you will need to consult with Deuce. He may have picked up something. Mr. Strait stood up. "It's settled then. Feel free to call me anytime for help, to report, whatever."

A cut of *On the Road Again* played in my head.

I called Deuce as soon as I left Sheriff Gabrielle's office. He suggested I take only Sonja. She was the one with backbone, he said. He liked the idea of my partnering with Lorraine. He thought she'd make Sonja comfortable. After seeing Lo with Virtua's sister, I knew she would.

Lorraine, Sonja, and I made our plan. Right up front, I'd tell Brother Norbert why I had come. I wanted information about the assistant pastor. I'd claim I brought Sonja Trudeau along to vouch for my good intentions.

The following afternoon Brother Norbert welcomed the three of us into his office in the compound of the Blessed Believers. He looked even taller than he had at Kitty Ernest's service, but not threatening in any way. An open face, wide smile, courtly manner. Although I guessed he was in his forties, but grandfatherly, the way I pictured General Eisenhower.

"You're a wise man to bring Sister Sonja with you, Detective D'Aquin. She's a treasured member of our congregation. By the way, I believe I noticed you and Detective LaSalle with us at the service for Kitty Ernest."

"Did we stick out that much? We tried to be inconspicuous."

He laughed. We exchanged pleasantries, but I detected a touch of wariness on his part; he probably detected a bit of calculation on mine. But no more than what is to be expected from a couple of guys with a bit of experience in the world.

"We have a small congregation, Detective. We always look around to welcome visitors who might have an interest in our church. Something about your presence told me you were making a business visit. You know, we're still in shock over the proceedings involving Brother Thomas and Brother Robert. We pray for them daily. Is there something about them I can help you with?"

"We've come on an entirely different matter, Pastor. We're looking for a bit of information about the man who was an assistant pastor when Pastor Allen was here. Before your time, I know. I believe Brother Ben Gilbert was his name."

He hesitated just a moment before answering. "Yes, before my time. I've heard we once had an assistant pastor, but I never knew him. I was in training in Houston at that time."

"Do you happen to know what Brother Gilbert's duties were?"

"I'm told he handled the youth group and ran the summer program. I don't believe he preached very often. I do know he designed all our grounds, and he maintained them. He actually lived on the place. We've never had anyone to match him as a caretaker. I'm pulled in many directions. Sister Sonja here has been looking around for someone to help me out."

Sonja picked up on that. "I have a line on someone who has a seasonal job at the pepper plant, Brother Norbert. He needs a place to live. He might be able to help us when they're not packing peppers over there. I've been checking his references. If they look good, I'll bring him out here for you to interview."

"That would be very good. Which reminds me that I have yet to open the door of the cabin where Brother Gilbert stayed. I'll have to get to that. What is it you want to know about him, Detective?"

"We'd like to talk with him. Do you have any idea where he is now?"

"I don't know anything about him. I have no idea where

he could be."

"Do you have any church records that might help us locate him? If we knew where he came from or where he went we might be able to find him now."

"Why do you want to talk to him? What interests you about him?"

Suspicious. Pastor Norbert is no dummy.

"You've been straightforward with me, Brother Norbert. I'll be straightforward with you. We have information that some questionable activities occurred when he ran the summer camp. And... He may have information we need."

I wasn't *totally* straightforward. I didn't say Brother Gilbert was my target. I couldn't look at Sonja Trudeau. I hoped like hell she wouldn't blow my cover. She kept silent. Brother Norbert's narrowed eyes told me he hadn't been totally straightforward with me either. He knew more than he was telling.

After a few seconds, Brother Norbert turned his chair and reached to a filing cabinet behind him. He took a key out of his pocket and unlocked one drawer.

"Brother Allen died rather suddenly and he didn't leave us many files. All I found from my predecessor is in this drawer. I've been completely through it and don't remember any mention of Brother Gilbert except this." He pulled out a folder, withdrew a brochure for the summer camp, and handed it to me. I scanned the pages: front, back, front, back. Nothing that would help. I handed the brochure to Lorraine. She did the same and handed it back.

"I don't know where else I could look, Detective." Brother Norbert replaced the brochure. He closed the drawer, locked it, and returned the key to his pocket. "I'll let you know if I get any ideas."

He stood up. A dismissal. Dead end. We said our thanks and goodbyes.

Back in the car, Sonja told us she had the same impression I did. Brother Norbert knew more but honored the church taboo. "Usually so do I. The only reason you got more out of me is because Elena was upset about what went on."

"Do you think Elena might talk to us again?" Lorraine asked.

"She might. I'll ask her. She was quite impressed with what your office did about our dear Sister Virtua." She looked at Lorraine. "Especially how kind you were to Virtua's family."

Sonja Trudeau lived just the other side of the cemetery. We dropped her off and returned to the Sheriff's Office. We cranked up a standard manhunt for a Ben Gilbert. Just logging into the National Crime databases depressed me. I couldn't count the number of days I'd started every morning putting Eugénie's name on the wire. But for Eugénie, I had a world of information. I knew everything about her: driver's license, social security numbers, hobbies, the scar on her right knee from when she fell down on the playground in the first grade. The Acadiana Crime kept her DNA and cross-checked everything that came in for a possible match. All I knew about Brother Gilbert were the guesses Sonja had made about his height and weight. Medium.

We hadn't been working long when Sonja called.

"Elena says she'll talk to you now. It's pouring rain. Could you come to my house? Elena lives next door."

"We're on our way."

We talked to Elena for a half hour. She said the Believers' camp was a Godsend. She did secretarial work for an oilfield equipment shop and her husband worked seven-day shifts offshore. She couldn't afford day care. Summer before last her boy said he quit and wouldn't go back. She thought he'd had a falling out with his best buddy. No. That wasn't the reason. Nor anything else she could think of. And her son was weird about it. Afraid, maybe. She described the game and said other mothers told her that when three naked boys had gone to the cabin, Brother Gilbert joined them... Then she stopped. That taboo.

Lorraine gave it a shot, without success. Elena wouldn't repeat what she'd heard from other mothers.

We were done. I told the sisters we were returning to town and I'd drop them anywhere they might need to go.

Sonja said she wanted to go the pepper plant. "I need to talk to the man I told Pastor Norbert about, the one who might do some maintenance and gardening work at the Believers. He said he had a list of references he could give me." Then the kicker. "They call him 'Digger' because sometimes he takes care of the cemetery right there at the bridge."

I felt a vise close around my ribs. And tighten. "Digger Jeanbaptiste?"

"Yes. Do you know the man?"

"I believe so. I'd like to go to the plant with you?"

Sonja agreed but looked puzzled. "Do you know something about Digger? We need to check him out before he comes to the church."

"I may, but nothing that would bear on him working at the church."

We had to wait for the packing line at the pepper plant to close down for the day. Yes, he was the same Digger who'd been Eugénie's last probation visit. He remembered our conversation but repeated what he had said over a year ago. He didn't know where Miss Eugénie went after the visit. He did remember she'd pushed him to get full-time work and suggested he find something like his old extra job at the cemetery. "She said she'd check around the neighborhood for possibilities."

My God! Could Eugénie have checked in at the Church of the Blessed Believers? Could something have happened to her out there?

"Did anyone ever get back to you about finding work in the neighborhood?" I asked Digger.

"No. I never saw Miss Eugénie again. Probation assigned me a different officer. I had just a few months left on my probation, so the new guy let the full-time work requirement slide."

I put Digger under oath and handwrote his statement. My hand shook when I gave him the paper to sign. Sonja and a line foreman witnessed for me. While Sonja finished her business with Digger, I tried to be realistic about what I had.

Eugénie had spoken of looking around the neighborhood

for part-time work for her probationer. The Church of the Believers is in the neighborhood. The Church employed part-time gardening help. But I had no verification that she actually went there. Did I have enough probability for a search warrant? I tried to reach Mr. Byrne but he'd left for the day. I disturbed Chief Roland after hours and ran it by him. No way he could approve that on his own, he said, but he'd set up a meeting with Mr. Byrne in the morning.

Realistically, I knew there was little chance of good news about Eugénie after a year and a half. Did I even want to keep up the hunt? Yes. I needed certainty. And of course, I had to do everything I could for Mr. Strait's investigation. Brother Gilbert could have set himself up somewhere else to play games with little boys.

Lo came with me to pick up André from my mother's. The wounds made by those Dobermans were healing nicely, except for the one on her temple. She had already talked to a plastic surgeon. My mom asked us to stay for supper. Lo was perfectly comfortable being at her table, but I felt guilty enjoying having her around. Indeed, I needed certainty.

That night I got very little sleep. I ran through every possible fate that could have befallen Eugénie. And I considered what each scenario might mean for me—and for Lorraine and me together.

21

My "first thing in the morning" meeting with Chief Roland and Mr. Byrne got bumped. It was Arraignment Day, and both Robert Cane and Thomas Ernest were on the docket to be arraigned. That's how the system works. We deal with the most urgent problem at hand. I could hardly say time was of the essence for my investigation into the dismissal of Brother Gilbert, nor into Eugénie's disappearance either. Neither defendant would speak at his arraignment, but every court appearance is an opportunity to size up counsel. And you never know what might happen.

Chief Roland brought Thomas Ernest over from the jail first. The Clerk of Court read the true bills returned by the Grand Jury, two counts of first-degree murder. Unlike ninety-nine percent of our defendants, Thomas Ernest had money to hire a lawyer—actually two lawyers. Two are required to satisfy the standard for competent counsel in a capital case. Gordon Stone and Georges Dieudonné, well-known criminal defense lawyers from Lafayette, stood with him. Tall and straight, Thomas Ernest had a certain dignity, even in his jailhouse orange jumpsuit, shower shoes, and shackles.

On behalf of his client, Mr. Dieudonné entered a plea of Not Guilty to each charge. Ernest said nothing. They left the courtroom by the way they had come—out the back door.

Chief Roland brought over Robert Cane. The Clerk of Court read the true bills against him—also two counts of first-degree murder. To defend Robert Cane, Sarah Bernard had been joined by John Clark, the head of the three-parish Offices of the Public Defender and lead PD in St. Mary Parish. A formidable team. Brains and beauty both of them. In contrast to the other important defendant this morning,

Robert Cane slumped before the judge like a whipped dog.

Ms. Bernard also entered a plea of Not Guilty for her client. And she added a second plea—Not Guilty by Reason of Insanity. I hadn't expected that. I guess you have to come up with some kind of defense when your client has admitted he killed his pregnant wife. Tony Blendera looked stunned.

After the arraignments, Tony, Lorraine, and I followed Mr. Byrne into his office for a strategy session. Chief joined us a few minutes later.

Deuce Washington had delivered to Tony a clean investigation file on Robert Cane, and Tony believed he was ready. The insanity plea changed everything. What had been an open and shut prosecution, with good hard evidence and a confession, became something much more complicated. Preparation for presenting and defending Cane's mental capacity to assist counsel, an issue for the judge to determine, and preparation for the jury's consideration of Cane's mental state at the time of the crimes, would all take some time. Tony's face no longer looked like a cherub in an Italian painting. More like a character from Dante's *Inferno*.

The insanity plea changed my schedule also. If he couldn't get Robert Cane to the next jury term, I'd be on with Thomas Ernest. No one had yet said that aloud.

One topic was sure to be Cane's religious beliefs. Did fundamentalism itself, or the particular version practiced at the Church of the Blessed Believers, have an effect on his mental condition? I already had that damn place in the Ernest case, and on top of the two prosecutions, the Blessed Believers just might be the new 'last place Eugénie had been seen alive.' And Mr. Strait had his eye on the onetime assistant Pastor, Ben Gilbert, for something totally unrelated. Wow!

"Does anyone know which psychiatrist Sarah and Mr. Clark plan to have examine Robert Cane?" Mr. Byrne asked.

Chief answered. "My guess is Dr. Allen Hubbard in New Orleans. The Parish President is already moaning about the high cost of experts for capital cases, and Dr. Hubbard doesn't come cheap."

Mr. Byrne offered a sobering opinion. "Dr. Hubbard's good, and an examination closest to an event carries extra weight. I asked John Clark if they already had an appointment with a doc, and he said yes, next week. I notified the Feliciana Forensic Facility to be ready to take Robert Cane the week after. There couldn't be that much difference in the weight of an opinion, give or take a week.

"Are we stuck with the state public mental health facility, Feliciana Forensic, and Dr. Consuela Mavinata as our expert?" Tony asked.

"The Parish Government says yes."

Tony was not pleased. He said he could have done better dealing with the St. Mary Parish Government instead of St. Martin. Mr. Byrne defended the St. Martin policies.

"I know how you feel, Tony. The State hires a recent immigrant from the Philippines, a woman with Asian features and a heavy Spanish accent, and expects her to connect with our prison population that's poorly educated and ninety percent African-American. Dr. Mavinata doesn't have the credentials of Dr. Hubbard, and she has to contend with an incredibly huge public caseload. But she's well known for being skilled and conscientious. She has her staff administer an MMPI—the Minnesota Multiphasic Personality Test. That test approaches objectivity and juries understand it. The bonus: the psychologists who administer the MMPI are much better on the witness stand than she is."

Feliciana Forensic said they could accommodate Robert Cane in ten days. I bet it would be a month, but that would be OK.

With Robert Cane getting evaluated, and Thomas Ernest on ice while his attorneys prepared his defense, I did my routine work. In my spare time, I thought about Brother Ben Gilbert. He couldn't have come from nowhere and vanished into nowhere, without a trace. What could I do to shake information out of a Blessed Believer? I knew only one person in the church other than Sonja and Elena Trudeau— Thomas Ernest's busybody friend Mark Gander. I had nothing to lose giving him a try. One thing I thought I knew about him was he liked to think he was important. I called and told him I needed him for a very serious matter.

I didn't plan to mention Patrick Ernest. Gander probably had no idea we'd used his surmise about the location of the tapes to get a search warrant. We were saving that information for the trial.

I thought of a way to be ingratiating.

"Mr. Gander, I really appreciate how helpful you've tried to be—telling us that Patrick Ernest had a house in the country. That poor man, losing his father then having his house burn down. I really feel for him. Of course, I can't go telling him so. Maybe you could do that for me?"

"I don't see him often, but if I do, I'll sure tell him."

I bet he'd call Patrick as soon I left.

"I'm here asking for help on something entirely different. There used to be an assistant pastor at your church. Ben Gilbert, was his name. Do you remember him?"

"Oh, yes. I remember him. He was a wizard with our landscraping. (That's what Gander called it —landscraping.) He's not with us any longer."

"I know. Do you know where I could find him?"

"No, I don't. He left us under a cloud. There were rumors, of course, but in our church, we don't believe in spreading rumors."

"I know, and I admire you all for that. But I'm not looking for what happened. I have a friend who has a problem at his church. On the QT, he wants to look into a possible replacement. Someone young, just starting out. Does your church have schools or seminaries that supply your pastors?"

"Yes, we do. I was actually on the call committee for Brother Gilbert."

Wow. How lucky is that?

"You're fortunate you get a say about who comes to be your pastor. We Catholics take whoever the bishop sends. Tell me how you went about choosing Brother Gilbert."

"We—our call committee—drove over to Houston. We went to the school, they called it a college, named Crossroads

Cathedral. North Houston, close to the airport. We spent a day talking to young men. We brought three of them back here to meet Brother Allen. He made the decision to hire Brother Gilbert."

I whipped out my cell phone, clicked on Google, and found an address for Crossroads Cathedral. I thanked Gander and beat it out of there before I was tempted to tell any more little white lies.

A two-day trip to Houston with Lorraine to visit Crossroads Cathedral? Maybe three days? Now that had possibilities. Walking down the hall to my office I ran smack into Chief coming the other way. "Crap. Look where you're going."

"Sorry, Chief. I was—"

"'…Thinkin' about my partner, Lorraine.' Go ahead. Admit it."

He walked around me and kept going. I liked him better for that kindness. No. I needed to put Lo out of my mind. And anyway, my first priority was helping Mr. Byrne get ready to fast forward his preparation for State v. Thomas Ernest.

Wasn't this a very different ball game from my ill-fated experience with Nicole? Lorraine and I were the same age, she'd been married. There was no reasonable hope Eugénie could now be alive. I found myself wanting certainty above all else, and then guilt hit my gut like a bad oyster.

Before I could sort out what to do about Gander's information, Tony came to call. "What do you and Lorraine know about mental illness?" he asked.

Lorraine answered. "Not as much as we need to in preparation for Robert Cane. I know not everybody we think is crazy can punch that ticket to avoid criminal responsibility. Louisiana has the McNaughton Rule: Expert opinion has to establish the defendant has a mental illness that prevents him from knowing the difference between right and wrong. So, there are three parts: mental illness, not knowing right from wrong, and a causal connection. It's a jury question. That's about all I know. What's up?"

"Pretty good summary of the law, Lorraine. We've been given a copy of the report from Dr. Hubbard, dated one month after the murders."

"And?"

"He found Cane to be a hallucinating schizophrenic, in a 'fugue state', not competent to assist his counsel. And, more probably than not, suffering from mental illness at the time of the crime. But the doctors at Feliciana Forensic examined Robert over a period of time beginning two months later. They've submitted an entirely different diagnosis. They find Robert to be depressed and a substance abuser but not suffering from any mental illness. Competent now to assist counsel and competent at the time of the murders, therefore criminally responsible. To make matters more complicated, but better for our side, Dr. Hubbard just saw Cane again. Now he reports his previously diagnosed psychosis has resolved. But it's generally agreed that psychosis does not resolve without treatment, and Cane has not been treated. Dr. Mavinata says that proves he wasn't psychotic to start with. I say we're good to go."

"And Mr. Byrne? What does he think?"

"Mr. Byrne thinks we should have a consulting psychiatrist help us prepare. I don't want another two-month delay while we wait for an appointment with another shrink."

"So, it's between you and Mr. Byrne. What have we got to do with the decision?"

"Nothing, I guess. I just wanted to let off steam. My real problem is I'm pissed. With experts like those, I can't have Robert Cane ready for the next jury."

Who should come across the street to our offices at this point but Mr. Byrne. We played around with the possibilities until he was ready to announce his conclusion. "Present competence is an issue for judicial decision. I say we take the easy part first; submit the issue of present competence to the judge right now. I don't think Sarah will object. Live witnesses or just reports, if the judge is willing to take the evidence that way. There's not a lot of risk for us. The experts pretty much agree Cane is competent at this point. The advantage of putting the issue in play now is we get a window into how the defense experts, and Judge Johnson for that matter, are thinking about mental illness."

That's what we did, and it came out just as Mr. Byrne thought it would. The judge found Robert Cane competent to assist counsel. His next suggestion told me something I didn't know—Lorraine's sister is a forensic psychiatrist practicing in New Orleans. He suggested we ask her to consult.

"Is your sister coming home anytime soon?" Mr. Byrne asked Lorraine.

"She'll be here next month for the Crawfish Festival. She's a former Queen, you know. She wouldn't miss it. You should see the dress she has to wear. She'll look like a pink mermaid with feelers."

"I'd like to pick her brain about mental illness and see what she thinks about the effect of fundamentalist religion on the thinking of a guy with problems to start with. I don't want to ask the two experts we have to deal with before I know a bit more about what the answer might be."

"I'll see what she says."

The word came back through Lorraine. Her sister would talk to us but she wouldn't give an opinion without examining the defendant. And if she examined Cane, both sides would get her opinion, whatever that might be. Lo asked me, "Do you want to take a chance?"

Several chances. I hadn't asked Lorraine about taking a trip to Houston to talk to the school about their former student, Ben Gilbert, but I was thinking of taking a chance on that too.

No. Mr. Byrne said he really needed me to be on hand for the preparation of State v. Ernest.

"I can go, Ted. One day over, maybe another day to run down anything they might tell me, and one day back. I bet I could get home before they finish picking the jury."

"Give those wounds a bit more time to heal. The plastic surgeon said you'd be released in two weeks."

I couldn't put her off any longer. She made the trip and called before dark on the day she drove over. Crossroads

Cathedral found Ben Gilbert's record. He'd given his home as Houston. They hadn't heard from him since he went to St. Martinville, Louisiana.

Lorraine said she had a buddy in the Sheriff's Office in Harris County. She'd check into that before coming home the next day.

I missed her.

PART VI

22

Closing arguments in a capital trial always draw a crowd, but especially so when Special Assistant District Attorney Dennis Byrne is scheduled to make one of his legendary summations of the evidence for the jury. Judge Johnson kept everyone late to finish the last rebuttal witness in the guilt/innocence phase of the trial. She likes her juries to be fresh for the close.

For twelve straight days, Thomas Ernest sat immobile at the table for the defense, a statue between his two lawyers, Gerald Stone and Ronald Dieudonné. Every day he could have turned and looked over the bar to his supporters in the first few rows behind him: his daughter, her husband, his son, and a couple dozen members of the Church of the Blessed Believers. Occasionally Pastor Norbert joined the family. Thomas Ernest rarely turned his head in their direction.

Dennis Byrne and Mandy Aguillard sat at the table for the prosecution, closer to the jury box, of course. One of the prosecution perks. Occasionally, Mandy sat forward in her chair and reached around to knead her back. The twins she carried might come join her at the table if the trial lasted much longer. A dozen members of the car wash crowd, Jubilee's sister, his brother-in-law, his barber, and the man who owned the Chicken Quick-Serve on General Mouton in Ledoux Subdivision, scattered themselves farther back on the prosecution side of the room. Behind the supporters of the prosecution and the defense were the witnesses who had been confined to the sequestration room during the presentation of evidence save for the time they entered the courtroom to testify.

I spotted a number of lawyers from the three-parish district. They came to watch the master. Tony Blendera and

John Clark came from St. Mary Parish. Close to the rear exit, District Attorney Gerald Strait sat with Mandy's husband Tom—on hand in the event he and Mandy needed to make a fast trip to Women's and Children's Hospital in Lafayette.

The trial would be one of the last before the scheduled major courthouse renovation. State of the Art security and a sophisticated sound system would bring the building into the twenty-first century, mostly a good thing, but I'll miss the cypress paneling and the yellow glow from the creepy old wagon wheel light fixtures in the ceiling.

Mr. Byrne walked to the podium in front of the jury box. He appeared composed, but I detected a quiver teasing one pant leg of his dark pinstriped suit. He began by offering the mandatory words of appreciation to the jurors for their service, honoring each juror, one after the other, with a direct gaze and a courtly nod. He had said in his opening statement and repeated, as he began his close, that the jury and the prosecution function as society's instruments of justice. *We're together in this business.* Clever. I hadn't heard that technique to seduce the jurors into feeling a bond with the prosecution.

So much for the courtroom courtesies. Mr. Byrne took a deep breath and set sail.

"Up until one fateful afternoon less than a year ago, it appeared to all the world that Mr. and Mrs. Thomas Ernest had a happy and conventional marriage of thirty-one years. They lived in a fine home in a small subdivision about a mile out of town. Their back yard ran more than fifty feet down to a picturesque curve in the Bayou Teche.

"The Ernest children were grown now, living elsewhere in town. Mr. Ernest owned a cleaning shop on Main Street here in St. Martinville, just four blocks down from this courthouse." Mr. Byrne waved his left hand in that direction. "Mrs. Ernest, Kitten Ernest, known as Kitty, did not work outside her home. Most days she could be found in a studio workshop in what was once the dining room. There she kept the supplies for her painting and for the fabrication and adornment of little dolls. She loved dolls.

"On September 30th of last year, a Thursday afternoon, at

precisely eleven seconds before 3:26 p.m., the dispatch officer in the radio room of the office of the Sheriff of St. Martin Parish received a call forwarded from 911. *Two persons dead at 205 Evangeline Street.*" Mr. Byrne paused. "Ladies and gentlemen of the jury, Thomas Ernest murdered those two persons—his wife Kitty, and Charles Joe, called Jubilee Joe, a poor black man he had picked up in town on the pretense that he needed someone to rake leaves. Thomas Ernest murdered his wife because she was not faithful to him. He brought Jubilee Joe to his house for the express purpose of framing him for her murder. He murdered Jubilee Joe."

Thomas Ernest's lawyer. Ronald Dieudonné—God-given in French—had presented the defense evidence in this guilt/innocence phase of the trial. Should the jury unanimously find Ernest guilty of first-degree murder, co-counsel Gerald Stone would take over the lead in the penalty phase, presenting mitigating evidence by which he hoped to persuade the jury to spare his client's life.

"Ladies and gentlemen," Mr. Byrne continued, "when we began this trial I told you the evidence would come to you through the testimony of a number of witnesses and from items picked up and cataloged by the detectives who investigated the two homicides. I told you that when you had heard and seen the pieces of evidence, you would be able to fit them all together. The pieces of the jigsaw puzzle make one and only one picture, the picture on the cover of a puzzle box. Our puzzle pieces will make a picture of two first-degree murders."

I've heard the puzzle analogy a hundred times. I like it. Regrettably, someday soon the analogy would have to be retired. No one selected for jury service would be old enough to be familiar with a jigsaw puzzle.

"Of course, the witnesses presented to you did not see these crimes committed. They know only the circumstances right before and right after these two persons were killed. Circumstantial evidence. You, as the jury, will use your common sense to draw the picture *in between*."

I held my breath. Had Mr. Byrne successfully

242 — Anne L. Simon

maneuvered past the bear trap? Thomas Ernest would have been the only person now alive who had been present in between. He had not testified. Ordinary people believe it simple fairness to hear both sides of a story before coming to a decision, but the law does not allow the prosecutor to "comment" on a defendant's exercise of his constitutional right not to testify. Would Mr. Dieudonné rise to claim Mr. Byrne had left an impermissible impression that rose to a "comment on the evidence?"

Dieudonné lifted his rear six inches off his chair—and froze. He opted not to take the chance of an over-rule. The aborted objection conveyed weakness.

Mr. Byrne moved out from behind the podium. He had now reached the part of his closing statement the crowd had come to hear. Without a note in his hand, he summarized the testimony of each witness who testified: the detectives who investigated the crimes, the experts who examined the evidence and gave reports of their scientific conclusions, the ordinary citizens who had information to help the jury understand the circumstances. When he had completed this feat, he returned to stand behind the podium.

"Ladies and gentlemen of the jury, to decide this case, to put together the pieces of evidence you have heard in order to complete the picture on the cover of the puzzle box, you must ask yourselves two key questions. The first question is this: who killed Kitty Ernest?"

Mr. Byrne walked over to an easel and drew a clean floor plan of the house at 205 Evangeline Street.

"The best way to find the answer to this first question is to examine the scene in which the detectives found the body of Kitty Ernest, the scene you viewed on the videotape the detectives made the night of September 30, 2001, at 205 Evangeline Street."

Mr. Byrne repeated, in a short version, the testimony given by Richard Levy of the Acadiana Crime Lab concerning the bullet holes and the blood on the body of Kitty Ernest. He then reviewed the bullet holes and the blood on the body of Jubilee Joe. Visibly pained to hear of jerking bodies and spurting blood, several jurors closed their eyes. A woman on the front row dropped her chin to her chest. Who knew whether such a detailed description of gore would be a plus for the prosecution? Perhaps one juror would think the prosecutor had contrived to make him, or her, react emotionally rather than to examine facts. Aware of the risk, Mr. Byrne hastened to move to the hard evidence in his favor.

"You watched the video of the scene taken by the detectives who responded to the defendant's call to 911. Two things are important about what the detectives saw and what you were able to see in the video. First, they saw and you saw a paintbrush carefully propped on an open paint can sitting beside a little fence Kitty Ernest had been painting for a doll display. That paintbrush tells you something—Kitty Ernest had not been startled. She had carefully balanced the brush to give her attention to the person who had interrupted her work. Tell me, would Kitty Ernest, a conventional, middle-aged white woman born and raised in St. Martinville, have such composure when confronted by a black man she had never seen before standing in a back room of her house holding a rifle aimed at her chest?"

Mr. Byrne silently shook his head slowly from side to side.

"The second item of importance about the video the detectives made and you saw three days ago is the spread of newspapers on the floor in front of the body of Kitty Ernest. Mr. Levy told you that a scientific examination of the dust on the newspapers revealed one and only one visible shoe print, that of an EMT who removed her body. Why is that important? Because only on Kitty Ernest's right side, the direction of the bedroom, could someone have taken a position close enough to her for his gunshots to leave powder burns on her blouse *without walking on the spread of newspapers*. Someone who came from the hallway would have had to cross directly in front of her to reach her right side. Again, would she have watched a maneuver such as that with equanimity? Er-r-r... without reacting?"

Only with that correction did I realize how Mr. Byrne

244 — Anne L. Simon

had reviewed complex evidence in simple language. Next to me, I felt Lorraine eliminate the two inches that separated us from each other as we leaned against the wall.

"This is damn exciting stuff," she whispered.

"From these two facts—the balanced paintbrush and the absence of footprints on the newspapers—there is only one conclusion. Kitty Ernest's husband Thomas was her killer. He came from their bedroom. He spoke to her for a moment. She was not alarmed. Ladies and gentlemen of the jury, Thomas Ernest shot his wife in cold blood."

Mr. Byrne returned to the prosecution table, consulted his yellow legal pad, placed it back on the table, and returned to his position before the jury. I recognized the practiced choreography, designed to keep him calm and give the jury time to absorb his argument. He then addressed the hard evidence they had been shown. He reviewed my collection of guns and bullets and complimented my work. Next to me, Lorraine whispered an *attaboy*. Mr. Byrne reviewed the testimony and the exhibits admitted into evidence by Richard Levy, explaining the scenario of the killings from the trajectory of the bullets and the spattering of blood. Even with the use of the model as he drew his conclusions, I thought the jurors looked dazed—until Mr. Byrne pulled it together.

"Remember ladies and gentlemen, both Kitty Ernest and Jubilee Joe were shot with the .22 Rossi rifle. The coroner told you they were shot in exactly the same locations on their bodies, in exactly the same sequence. The left chest, the forehead, the throat. Consider this. What are the chances Thomas Ernest's written statement *is* correct, that two persons who never knew or saw each other before that day—Jubilee Joe and Thomas Ernest himself—would fire bullets that afternoon at exactly the same part of a body in exactly the same sequence? No chance.

"Furthermore, the Rossi rifle the detectives found on the floor next to Mr. Joe had one shot remaining. You had an opportunity to hold the weapon when I entered it into evidence. And as you observed, the rifle was damaged. It had suffered a blow on the magazine which Richard Levy opined —told you—came from a .380 pistol. On the floor, spattered with blood, lay pieces of a .380 pistol. The detectives later *found* a .380 pistol." Mr. Byrne smiled, partly lowering his right eyelid. "They found *the* .380 pistol, with identical missing parts, hidden in Mr. Ernest's garage."

Mr. Byrne raised his hands, signaling the climax of Act IV of his play. He pantomimed each action he described.

"Ladies and gentlemen of the jury, here is the picture on top of the puzzle box. Thomas Ernest shoots his wife four times—bam, bam, bam, bam." Mr. Byrne strikes himself twice on the left chest, once on the forehead and then once on the throat. "He places the rifle in his left hand and starts down the hall." Mr. Byrne walked to the end of the jury box. "At the opening to the dining room, on his right, he raises his right hand and takes his .380 pistol from the top of the cabinet." Mr. Byrne reached into the air and groped blindly on an imaginary high surface. "In the crime scene video, you saw the empty holster the officers found on the cabinet next to the entrance to that room." Mr. Byrne dropped his hand and squared himself before the jury box.

"During all this time, Jubilee Joe, the patient yardman, waits in the carport for leaf-raking instructions. Thomas Ernest goes to the back door and summons him inside. Jubilee takes a few steps inside, his last steps on earth they were to be. Thomas Ernest hands the rifle to him. Aha. Perhaps he tosses the rifle to him saying, *here, hold this for me boy.*"

I watched the faces of the jurors as they listened to Mr. Byrne's conjecture. The woman I'd been watching pinched her lips together, perhaps in disgust at the disparagement of the poor black man. Mr. Dieudonné's behind again rose a few inches off his chair. He came close to saying I *object*—but didn't. He couldn't be sure he would have his objection sustained. An overrule at this point could poison the jury's mind against his client.

Beside me, Lorraine put a warm hand on my arm. "My heart is racing, Ted." I covered her hand with my own. The hell with prying eyes.

"Jubilee Joe, the good servant, takes the rifle by the barrel, suspended like so." Mr. Byrne held the weapon out before him, shrinking from it like it was a snake. "A few feet away, Mr. Ernest raises his pistol and fires dead on. Bam!"

Mr. Byrne paused to milk the emotion of a cold-blooded murder. Then came a slight smile and a twinkle in those Irish eyes.

"To the utter surprise of both of them, both Thomas Ernest and Jubilee Joe, *nothing* happened! Thomas Ernest was stunned because he had plugged a man, and the man did not fall. Jubilee Joe was equally stunned, to be still upright after he'd been shot dead on.

"How could this be? I will tell you how. One chance in a hundred, a thousand maybe. The bullet from Thomas Ernest's pistol struck the magazine of the rifle. You held the rifle in your hands. You saw the damage on the magazine. Richard Levy testified that the damage tested positive for lead. A bullet."

Sitting below us, Chief Roland muttered, "Ernest baby, you're fucked."

I wish I'd been on the other side of the table to see Mr. Dieudonné's face. The prosecution is required to give the defense all of their evidence, but not their interpretation of it. Dieudonné had not put the picture together.

"Now Thomas Ernest thought there must have been something wrong with his pistol. He had to act quickly. He threw the weapon to the ground. The base plate fell off and the clip came out. He reached over to an utterly stunned Jubilee, grabbed the rifle from him, and finished him off—with the exact same pattern of shots he had delivered to his wife."

Lorraine's hand squeezed tight on my arm. "Do you think the jurors got it?" she whispered. "I had to have Mr. Byrne explain his theory to me three times before I saw how he figured it out."

I whispered back. "Me too, Lo. Maybe they'll just go with him because he's so certain. No matter what, we owe a debt to

Spike for working until he found that pistol. We'd have no case without it."

"Now, ladies and gentlemen of the jury, here is what I cannot comprehend. When poor Jubilee lay on the floor, Ernest shot him in the head—again, and again, and again."

I watched the jurors take each one of the shots themselves. That woman on the front row grimaced and squeezed her eyes shut. We had her on our side, but we had to have eleven more!

How could Mr. Byrne be so totally sure of the exact scenario? I would never have made such a certain statement. If a juror questioned any one detail of Mr. Byrne's story, he or she might well have a reasonable doubt, and the prosecution needed the vote of every last one of them for the result Mr. Byrne asked for. We had never found the shells and the bullet from the .380 pistol, and by God, we looked. Our case was not perfect. I would have hedged my bet.

Maybe for a capital crime prosecutor, you need a military officer trained to take command.

Then Mr. Byrne did a job on motive. He reminded the jury of the tape of Kitty and her paramour Reggie Throckmorton exchanging playful giggles as they planned their next rendezvous. The jurors were ready for a comedic breather. They swallowed giggles of their own.

"Mr. Byrne is playing them like a piano," I whispered to Lorraine.

"I suggest to you, ladies and gentlemen of the jury, the taped conversation between Reginald Throckmorton and Kitty Ernest was the last straw. Thomas Ernest had his suspicions; he heard proof of his suspicions. He made a plan. He put his plan into action. A plan for a double murder disguised as a heroic defense of his home and his honor.

"Ladies and gentlemen, Thomas Ernest is guilty of first-degree murder, two times. Thank you." Mr. Byrne returned to the prosecution's counsel table.

Judge Johnson announced a fifteen-minute break. Everyone needed time to decompress.

*   *   *

Mr. Dieudonné gathered a sheaf of papers and made his way to the podium. He wore a dark gray suit today—no brown. He had prepared well and spoke earnestly. He couldn't match Mr. Byrne's aplomb, but the hayseed manner with which he first addressed the jury had melted away. He no longer played the rube for their empathy. He told the jury Thomas Ernest appreciated their attention to the evidence.

If Ernest appreciated anything, it didn't show. He continued to stare straight ahead.

"You must not be fooled by the barrage of so-called evidence the prosecutor has brought you. I know you'll not be fooled because I've seen you paying close attention to all you have heard. Mr. Byrne has shown you pieces of a puzzle. I agree with him there, but I suggest to you that all you have now is just that—a pile of puzzle pieces. He has never made the picture he says is on the cover of the box. And that is his burden."

Mr. Dieudonné had probably heard Mr. Byrne's puzzle analogy a number of times. He'd had an opportunity to practice a response. Not bad.

"The story is preposterous. Every bit of evidence is consistent with another picture on the cover of the box—the true picture. Here it is."

Mr. Dieudonné then proceeded to recite the story Thomas Ernest had told on his very first interview and maintained for over a year. Thomas Ernest saw Jubilee Joe shoot his wife, he followed Jubilee down the hall, wrestled the rifle him, and shot in retaliation. Then Mr. Dieudonné pinpointed weak spots in our case. We had never found the .380 bullets or shells. Mrs. Ernest was shot from a distance of three to five feet—consistent with the length of the barrel of the rifle held out toward the victim over the newspapers. An open purse lay on the kitchen counter. A neighbor testified that someone of Jubilee Joe's description cased the neighborhood a week before and returned to burglarize Mr. Ernest's house. Mr. Dieudonné suggested everyone should have the courage to act as Mr. Ernest had—wrestling the rifle away from an intruder and killing the man who had just killed his wife. Mr. Ernest was to be commended, not punished, for this act, said Mr. Dieudonné.

Mr. Dieudonné played the usual defense lawyer card. "From the beginning of this case, we have had some pretty questionable police tactics. When Mr. Ernest gave his statement the night after the shootings, the police did not tell him he was being taped. They spied on him, that's what they did. And they got an arrest warrant based on a statement about a money motive when there was no such thing. Thomas Ernest was not angry with his wife; you heard Mark Gander tell you they each had substantial life insurance policies in favor of the other. Had Thomas Ernest been mad at his wife, he wouldn't have provided for her over his children. And as for those tapes, Detective D'Aquin got a warrant to search Patrick Ernest's house by lying about what Mr. Gander had told him. You should disregard evidence illegally obtained."

I could hear Lorraine breathing deeply beside me. I patted her arm and whispered, "Get used to it. We always get trashed."

"Ladies and gentlemen of the jury, this is not first-degree murder. It is self-defense, manslaughter, not guilty, something else. Jubilee Joe met a man defending his home. Mr. Ernest did what any man in these parts would have done in these circumstances."

Mr. Dieudonné closed with more thanks to the jury, adding a few tears to water the flowers of sympathy. Mr. Byrne returned with a brief response.

Lorraine held tight to my arm until she had taken several deep breaths.

23

Spectators fled the courtroom as Judge Johnson gathered her notes for the Charge to the Jury, her hour-long explanation of the law the jurors were supposed to apply to the trial evidence to reach their verdicts. Not even Judge Johnson could hold the crowd for the info dump. But no judge, not even the usually bold Judge Johnson, would risk Appeal Court reversal by rewriting the Charge in more entertaining prose. The words had been carefully crafted to distill a century of legal decisions. Better safe than sorry, as they say.

But we didn't have to sit through it. Lorraine and I joined the stampede to the double doors of the courtroom exit.

Lorraine turned around to me before we reached the door. "There goes Mandy, Ted. She doesn't look comfortable. Those twins could be on the way!"

"God, I hope so. Tom is on the run."

"Say a prayer."

Chief Deputy Roland wiggled his way upstream to reach us. Two urgent messages had come into the Sheriff's Office during the close. My mother-in-law implored me to come out to Catahoula as soon as possible. Lorraine's note asked her to return a call from Detective Kay Roberts in Harris County, Texas. We had to split up to tend to these separate requests.

Maman's message worried me. She'd broken a pattern. I usually dealt with Grampa for our comings and goings, and he always called on my cell phone. Had something happened to Grampa? No. He answered my return call and said he was fine, but he backed up Maman's request. Please come. Please come now, he said.

I swung by school and picked up André. We headed out to Catahoula. I hoped André could spend the night with his

252 — Anne L. Simon

grandparents. Maybe the whole weekend. I'd probably be tied up with the trial for another two or three days.

Maman came out of the house to meet us at the top of the porch steps. Strands of gray hair escaped from a scarf on her head. Her dark eyes darted left and right. Dammit! I knew the signs. She'd been treating again. Maman circled her hand in the air to signal Grampa to take André down to the lake so she could talk to me alone.

"I had a session with my friend Sylvia Bonin today. Do you remember Sylvia?" she asked.

Her words uncapped a bottle full of anger. Damn right, I remembered Sylvia. One of her cronies in the blasted treating business. I took a few deep breaths to get control of my annoyance and nodded yes.

"Ted, Sylvia and I reached the beyond." She looked at me square in the eye. "Eugénie has spoken to me."

For just a moment I accepted what she said. No, no, no. No one walking around on the earth had the ability to communicate with the beyond. We could have dreams, nightmares, hallucinations, whatever. But no real communication.

"Maman, I respect your right to do what you do, to believe what you believe, but—"

She interrupted, imploring my patience. "Listen to me, my son. This is important. Eugénie asked me to deliver a message to you."

"OK, Maman. What's the message?"

"Don't be like that. Please. Eugénie says you will find her very soon, but she isn't going to be able to come back to us. She says we need to be prepared."

For this nonsense, I drove all the way out here. With difficulty, I thanked Maman for giving me the message, and I stood up to get the hell out of there. I was already in my truck when I realized my presumption. I came back to the house to make certain Maman and Grampa could take André to school in the morning and keep him for the weekend. By Monday I should be able to be Dad again.

When I crossed into the city limits I called Lorraine.

"Is everything alright out there?" she asked.

"Perfectly normal, you could say. Grampa lives in his bateau and Maman is getting messages from the beyond. Just your ordinary grandfather and grandmother."

"What? I think you're showing a little sarcasm."

"Only to you."

"Do I need to know about these messages from the beyond?"

"She says Eugénie told her we're going to find her soon, but she won't be able to come back to us. I have an ache in my jaw from clenching my teeth. I was a good boy. I didn't say anything."

"Remember she's Eugénie's mother, Ted. It's got to be as hard on her as it is on you and André. Her 'messages' help her cope"

"Right, right. I'll try to be better. So, what about the call from your friend Detective Roberts?"

"I waited for you."

* * *

"Do you think the man you want could be the same person as John Benjamin Gilbert?" Harris County Detective Kay Roberts asked.

"Maybe so," Lorraine responded. "Who's he?"

"Orange County, Texas, has an outstanding arrest warrant for a John Benjamin Gilbert, white male, 31 years old, 5' 8", approximately 150 pounds. Rape of an eleven-year-old boy."

"Holy, shmoley! Could be. How did you ever run across that info?"

"I could tell you by brilliant deduction, but I'd be lying. Pure luck. People probably wonder what's wrong with someone who passes time looking at fugitive files, but I got in the habit when I was on the sex offense unit a year ago. When circumstances change, murderers stop murdering, burglars stop burglarizing, but the guys who are into this behavior never change. They just move around."

I left Lorraine making arrangements for Detective

Roberts to wire us what she had in the way of a description and for doors to be opened for us in the Criminal Investigations Division of Orange County, Texas. I headed to the office computer to search the state data sources for the one-time Assistant Pastor Brother Gilbert, but with John as his front name.

Ordinary civilians would shudder if they knew how many records of their behavior are out there in the cloud. I traveled down more data trails than passages in an ant farm. I'd done this work for Ben Gilbert, and scores of times for Eugénie. Concentration is required. I shut out all extraneous sound—until a few of my hearing receptors picked up Lorraine's half of her conversation with Detective Roberts.

My partner is sitting with this capital trial and can't leave for a few days, but I can get there... Orange is about half way to Houston. I can start first thing tomorrow morning and be there before noon. Can you arrange for the investigating officer to meet me? ... Great. Gather up whatever you have on the case and fax it. I'll print what you send and work the copy machine until it cries uncle... Thank you.

Lorraine read dismay on my face, but she got the reason wrong. I understood the wisdom of jumping on the new information. I knew I couldn't leave until the jury had been dismissed. I hated to miss a great investigative opportunity. But my distress concerned Lorraine. So, dammit, I told her.

"I hate you going over there by yourself."

"A drive to Orange, Texas? You think some bad guy is going to get me on I-10?"

"The price to be paid for caring about someone is worry. Please call often. I'll be very glad when I see you back here again."

I loved the soft look on her face. She took my hand and held the back of it to her cheek.

The crackling of the radio cut off my response. *Attention. The bailiff has sent word to the judge. The jury is ready to return a verdict.*

"Let's go, Ted. Mr. Strait will probably be in the courtroom for the return. We need to tell him about Orange,

Texas."

The crowd reassembled. Judge Johnson called for the jury and asked that they be polled. She then asked the question that always sends chills down my spine. "Ladies and gentlemen of the jury, have you reached a verdict?"

Mary Marshall, the woman on the front row who had grimaced when Mr. Byrne described the gratuitous shots delivered to Jubilee Joe, stood up. "Yes, we have, your honor."

"I think we got it, Lo," I whispered. "I've watched that juror react, and she's the foreperson."

The bailiff took the verdict sheets from the juror and handed them to Judge Johnson. Judge Johnson read the two sheets to herself. She held them for a few extra seconds before returning them to the bailiff. He handed them back to Ms. Marshall. When they were in Ms. Marshall's hands, the judge addressed her.

"Madam foreperson, will you please read your verdicts."

First one: "We, the jury, find the defendant Thomas Ernest Guilty of first-degree murder of Kitty Ernest." Then the second: "We, the jury, find the defendant Thomas Ernest Guilty of first-degree murder of Charles (Jubilee) Joe."

The jurors did not look at the defendant while Ms. Marshal read the verdicts. Some experts on reading juries would have an opinion of what that foretold for their inclination to vote for the death penalty in the next phase, but I couldn't read those tea leaves. Judge Johnson dismissed the jury for the night and set the penalty phase to begin the following morning at eight-thirty.

"Lorraine, let's go give Mr. Strait a report on the search for Benjamin Gilbert, now John Benjamin Gilbert."

24

The season passed from fall to winter while the trial of Thomas Ernest confined us inside. Dawn came later and dark came earlier. I hadn't seen midday sun since the bailiff called the courtroom to order two weeks ago. Today a cold rain fell on the town, slowing traffic and sinking spirits. Deep coughs skipped around the crowd.

The lawyers wore expressions appropriate for the task ahead—dealing with a matter of life or death. Tony Blendera had taken Mandy's place at the prosecution table. Only the defendant looked exactly as he had at the beginning of the trial: straight back, composed expression, crisp shirt. Washed and pressed at Ernest's Quality Cleaners, no doubt. He sat perfectly still. I thought again he must have some good meds. As at the guilt/innocence phase of the trial, there were few empty places in the courtroom.

Lorraine had a rainy day for her drive to Orange. Weather in Louisiana is never cold enough to make winter driving a problem, but rain and fog can drop visibility down to a few feet. Lo kept her part of our agreement, texting in when she had to stop for gas. I texted back. *Please take care on the wet roads. Let the trip take an extra half hour. Promise me you'll pull off if you run into a blinding downpour.*

I had a place to sit today, behind the prosecutors. Faithful Spike joined me but left an empty space for Lorraine. I signaled him to my side. "Come closer, Spike. Lorraine's away on another case. I wish Mr. Byrne had let you testify about finding the pistol. You deserve the credit."

Gerald Stone had taken over first chair at the table for the defense. Shorter, broader, framed round glasses. He leaned close to his co-counsel, whispering in his ear. The live mike picked up a mumble rising to a hiss. Arms tight against his sides, eyes squeezed shut, Ronald Dieudonné was not a happy man. Mr. Stone stood up and beckoned his co-counsel to follow him. Stone and Dieudonné disappeared into an anteroom behind the bench.

Fifteen minutes went by. Chief Deputy Roland came by to give us a report.

"Ernest's two lawyers are screaming at each other back there. Best I can figure, Stone just now told Dieudonné that Thomas Ernest would take the stand in his own defense, and —here's the kicker—admit he killed both his wife and Jubilee Joe. Apparently, Ernest came clean to Stone months ago, but Stone didn't tell Dieudonné until just now. Dieudonné is so pissed he's actually crying!

"Crying?"

"Sniffle, sniffle. *But I told the jury he didn't do it!*"

I got it. Mr. Dieudonné felt well used.

"I've been dealing with lawyers for a long time, but this is a first," said Chief. "Dieudonné is close to the edge. I'm afraid he's going to make some kind of scene and cause a mistrial when we are so-o close to the end. No one wants to put this trial on again. I stuck my nose into their argument."

"What? You got into it?"

"In a way. I found where the witnesses were waiting and asked the defense psychologist to go talk to Dieudonné. He did. Can you believe it? Counseling for the counsel?"

One way or another, the psychologist must have gotten Dieudonné under control. The lawyers reappeared. We lost an hour of court time with the drama.

Judge Johnson took her seat on the bench, not looking happy. The jury filed in, their faces as somber as those in an old Dutch painting. Every one of the jurors selected to serve had told the judge he or she could, under some circumstances, bring a verdict of death. Looking at their faces, I bet not one would answer the same way right now.

Mr. Dieudonné moved to the far end of the defense table. Mr. Stone's eyes nailed him to the spot. The defendant sat close to Mr. Stone.

Mr. Byrne stood before the jury box to give an opening statement for the penalty phase of the trial. Just a couple sentences. He said he would put on no further evidence. He asked the jurors to consider all he had presented to them during the first phase of the trial, take into account the aggravating and mitigating circumstances of the crimes, follow the instructions of the court, and make a just decision. He sat down.

Reassured that Dieudonné wasn't going to upset the trial with some kind of scene, Mr. Stone launched into his opening statement for the defense. Until this moment I had little impression of Stone's ability. I soon knew Mr. Byrne had a worthy opponent. Smooth, almost slick, he spoke precisely, appearing totally at ease.

"Ladies and gentlemen of the jury. Today, and perhaps tomorrow as well, I'm going to present to you evidence to help you make a very important decision—whether to spare a life." Mr. Stone reached out his left hand in a graceful gesture that importuned but did not threaten and caused not a rumple in his Italian tailored suit. "As you will be instructed by the judge, the law requires you to consider all the mitigating and aggravating circumstances of the events about which you have already heard. Right now, you do not know the defendant. Soon you will. I will bring to you people who know him well—his family and his friends. I will bring to you some experts who will help you understand what brought Mr. Ernest to this point in his life. You will then retire to consider whether he is an appropriate person to receive the ultimate penalty."

Mr. Dieudonné's chin dropped and his head fell forward.

Mr. Stone had not yet revealed that Thomas Ernest planned to testify. Dieudonné knew and we knew. The jury and the courtroom crowd did not.

During the next hour Mr. Stone brought to the stand a neighbor, a church friend, the aerobics instructor, and Mark Gander again, all of whom described Mr. Ernest's exemplary life. They assured the jury he would never, ever, plan to do anything criminal. Next came the family parade. His mother said as a boy and young man her son liked to plow the fields on the farm. His kids said they loved him. His sister said he was kind to animals. The usual stuff, but necessary. Competent defense requires counsel to show the jury a human being, one of God's creatures, just like themselves.

One response by Ernest's daughter hit me wrong. When asked if her father ever told her he didn't shoot her mother, she said she couldn't recall. Really? Isn't that something anyone would remember?

The experts came after a break. Dr. Edward Freeman, a clinical psychologist, described Mr. Ernest as a man seriously depressed and repressed. His expert opinion? Unexpressed anger caused Thomas Ernest's outbursts against his wife. If he were confined to prison for life, he would never commit another crime because he would never again be in a relationship with a woman. That was also the opinion of the social worker. Then a professor of criminal justice showed a movie of prison life. He believed the defendant would be a successful inmate and a force for good at the institution where the lifers go, the Louisiana State Prison at Angola, known as *The Farm*.

Next to me, Spike mumbled a few choice words about that testimony. "Now isn't that a nice bit of information to hear. There are openings at Angola for good farmers like Thomas Ernest. Shit, the jury is supposed to care about Ernest having a good life?"

Spike and I were still whispering when Mr. Stone called his next witness—the defendant Thomas Ernest himself. A rumble passed through the crowd. Judge Johnson sat forward. The side doors of the courtroom banged open as the hallway hangers-on scurried in to find seats. Mr. Strait slipped into a bench in the rear of the courtroom. A defendant testifying in a capital murder trial is rare. There's usually some part of a defendant's life he doesn't want to disclose. Once he takes the stand, there's not much limit to the topics he may be forced to discuss.

In his chair at the prosecutor's table, Mr. Byrne's back stretched two inches and his eyebrows rose. He was incredulous at this turn of fortune. Prosecutors live to have a defendant on the witness stand. The opportunity to probe the mind of a murderer is a rare treat.

"Do you solemnly swear to tell the truth, the whole truth, and nothing but the truth, so help you God?"

I'm not sure the Clerk of Court is supposed to add the God phrase.

"Oh yes, ma'am," Mr. Ernest responded to the clerk. He remained standing, at attention.

"You may sit now, Mr. Ernest," Judge Johnson directed.

"Oh, yes, sir. Er… ma'am." He squeezed his tall frame into the witness box. One leg didn't make it. The pointed toe of his right boot protruded, aiming straight toward the jurors. Ostrich boots strikingly similar to those worn by his son Patrick on the day we went to search his house. I wondered which one of them bought the boots for the other, maybe as a present for Fathers' Day?

Mr. Stone began with questions about Thomas Ernest's childhood. Ernest said he was born in Turkey Creek in March of 1944. Ah! That explains the drawl. Central Louisiana. He enjoyed outdoor work, especially caring for cattle. He began to list his daily chores, on and on, with more detail than Mr. Stone wanted. Mr. Stone interrupted when Ernest began to describe the path he took to walk to school for first grade.

"Mr. Ernest, can you tell the jury something about your father. Did you two get along?"

"Well, my father was a hard man. He wasn't the kinda fella you could get close to. He never drank or anythin', but…"

Was the jury going to spare Ernest's life because he had a less than perfect rapport with his father? That's an unfair criticism. Mr. Stone had to start somewhere.

We heard Ernest say he was 27 when he met Kitty; she was eighteen. "She was just the prettiest thing I'd ever seen. We went out for ice cream. I was pretty skittish about being with her because… Well…"

"Because it was the first time you had been out with a girl, right?"

"That's right. It was."

Mr. Stone had Ernest tell about how he worked offshore until he had an accident. He got drilling mud in his eyes and lost his sight.

"Rehab sent me to school to learn how to walk with a cane, read braille with my fingers, all that. We'd moved here by then. Kitty grew up in St. Martinville, you know. We had a nice little house…"

Mr. Stone prodded his client. "Did you come to have a miraculous cure of your eye problem?"

"I sure did."

"Tell us about that, if you please."

"One night Kitty and I went to a Revival in a big tent out at the end of Center Street, New Iberia. The preacher put his hands on me and prayed. My sight began to clear. In a few days, I could see pretty well. I even thought about goin' offshore again, but they weren't so sure I could do that. So, I set up a partnership to open a café."

"That was a partnership with your friend, Reginald Throckmorton, right?"

"Yes, sir."

"Is that when Mr. Throckmorton started to have a sexual relationship with your wife, Kitty?"

A little hiss passed through the crowd.

"Yes, it was."

"Did your friendship with Mr. Throckmorton end?"

"Yes."

"How did it end?"

"I told him if he ever did that again I'd kill him."

Mr. Stone walked back to the table for the defense, ostensibly to consult his co-counsel. I didn't imagine he'd get anything out of that effort; Dieudonné was an inanimate object. Probably Mr. Stone just wanted a break before launching into his next line of questioning.

At the prosecutor's table, Mr. Byrne sat erect. A fresh yellow pad lay on the surface before him; his right hand held a pen at the ready. His eyebrows were so high he had three deep indentations across his forehead. His blue eyes followed every move by his opposing counsel. On high alert. Mr. Stone returned to the podium before the witness box.

"Mr. Ernest, at some point recently did your relationship with your wife change, for better or worse."

"Yes, sir. About then it started deterioratin' a little more."

"In what way, may I ask you?"

"Kitty got kind of distant, and I didn't know why. I tried to do better around the house. I kept up the yard, did the washin' and ironin', gave her a hand with her crafts. She'd made a few comments about my weight so I went to exercise class. I went on a diet. But nothin' seemed to do any good.

"At some point did you begin to suspect your wife was again having an affair?"

"Yes, I did."

"And did you do anything about that?"

"I couldn't do anythin'. She wouldn't talk to me."

"Well, did you make some tapes of her telephone conversations to see if your suspicions were correct?"

A leading question, but everyone in the courtroom, including the lawyers and the judge, wanted to get to the end of this road.

"Oh, that. Yes, I did."

"How did you do that?"

Mr. Ernest warmed to this topic. He was proud of his skill at putting together the wiring under the bed. We heard a lot about which wire he attached to which other one.

"At this time, Mr. Ernest, were you having sex with your wife?"

Ernest looked down at his hands. "No, sir."

Judge Johnson caught a signal from the court reporter and asked Ernest to speak up.

Mr. Stone asked him about needing to get the yard ready for Kitty's doll friends—the same story he told in his statements to us.

"And did you find someone to help you get the yard ready?"

"Yes."

"And who was that?"

"The gentleman who is expired, Mr....er...uh..."

"Jubilee Joe?"

"Yes, sir."

My God! He didn't even remember the name of the man he drilled. *The gentleman who is expired!*

Mr. Byrne drew two lines across his legal pad, creating three areas. He labeled the areas I, II, and III. I've seen this method of organizing topics for cross-examination. Watching that, I missed a few questions. When I came to, Ernest was describing how he told the colored man to wait in the garage while he went inside to change into yard clothes. When he had changed clothes, he went into the bathroom. Ugh, that again. He came out of the bedroom and stopped in the den where his wife was painting a little white fence. They chatted for a bit.

"I figured it was a good time... er... well. Let me say this. I confronted her more or less with what I knew."

"What exactly did you say to her?"

"I said, 'Honey, I know what you've been doin.'"

"Did you speak that calmly?"

"Oh yes, sir. I was very calm. I never raise my voice. I'm not that kinda fella. I don't believe in fighting and fussin'. Our church says we shouldn't do that."

But you do believe in killing? Good grief!

"And how did your wife react to what you said?"

"Well, if she'd said, 'Honey, I'm sorry,' I'd have forgiven her in a minute. But she didn't." 'There's nothin' you can do about it,' she said. 'I'll do what I want.' I think that was it. I just snapped. I went to the bedroom and picked up the rifle and came right back to the den."

Mr. Byrne sat forward, boring his eyes into the witness. He was dying to hear how close he'd come to figuring out what happened.

"Were you angry," Mr. Stone asked, his little round eyes peering through his big round glasses.

Thomas Ernest answered carefully. "I wasn't maliciously angry. No, sir. Somethin' just came over me, worked on me right quick."

Ah, ha! There was the story he and his counsel wanted the jury to believe. Mr. Ernest was admitting he did the deed, but he would make the case for a killing in the heat of the moment. No premeditation; therefore, no ultimate penalty. In the jury box, a few brows wrinkled.

"Mr. Ernest, were you sorry for what you did?"

"Sorry? Oh, yes. The minute it happened I knew I'd lost the best thing in my life. I want you to know that I loved my wife to that very minute. I love the memory of her today."

I did a quick inventory of the jurors. Several of them sat back and lost the worry lines between their eyes. They had struggled for over seven hours to reach their verdicts in the guilt phase. Now they knew they'd made the correct decision.

Their reprise did not last long. I could see brows and lips tighten as they returned to the task ahead. A decision on life or death lay just around the corner.

"And what were your next thoughts, Thomas?" Mr. Stone finally remembered what they teach you in defense lawyer school—call your client by his first name to make him seem human.

"My next thoughts were—well, I didn't have any, really. I just panicked. I knew I'd done somethin' wrong and I tried to find a way to cover it up. I remembered that I had this guy out there ready to clean the yard. I went to the back door and asked him to come inside. I handed him my rifle. I had my pistol in my hand and I shot at him, but the pistol didn't work. The guy didn't fall down. So, there was this guy standing there with a rifle pointing at me. I dropped the pistol and grabbed the rifle from him. I turned the rifle point blank toward the guy. I shot him. Yes, I shot him."

"What did you do then, Thomas?"

"I went back to check on my wife, but it was too late for her."

Ernest paused and turned wide, melancholy eyes to the jury. "To this day I wish I'd been the one who died and not my wife. She was such a talented and perfect person. My wife was just beautiful."

His wife, his wife. Ernest didn't have a shred of concern

about Jubilee Joe. But wait. He may not have followed the script for a heat of the moment defense for the second killing. He didn't say he polished off Jubilee in a fit of passion.

Dammit! Maybe he and his lawyer thought he didn't need the sudden passion/heat of blood defense for killing Jubilee. Did they think the jury wouldn't impose a death penalty on a Caucasian for killing what he called a *colored* man? The thought made me angry.

Questioning by Mr. Stone continued. "And what did you do then?"

"I called the Sheriff's department. You have that call there."

"And what did you do with the pistol?"

"At the time, concerning the gun, my mind went completely blank. I do know I stepped on a couple pieces of something on the floor, so I picked them up and put them in the garbage."

That response caused Mr. Byrne to make a couple more notes on his pad, in the third box. Over at the defense table, Mr. Dieudonné fell all the way forward until his forehead rested flat on the table. So, this was what the argument between counsel was all about. Up until this moment, Mr. Dieudonné really thought the guy was innocent. His co-counsel Gerald Stone, with whom he'd driven back and forth to and from Lafayette for two weeks, knew otherwise and didn't tell him. No wonder Dieudonné was pissed.

But perhaps Mr. Dieudonné's ignorance of the true facts served his client. Wasn't Mr. Dieudonné more ardent, and thus more credible, as he defended his client believing in his innocence?

Maybe, but who appreciates being used.

Mr. Stone asked a few more questions and then sat down.

Mr. Byrne pushed back his chair and stood. His eyes sparkled. The three straight lines across his forehead had vanished. I've never seen a hungry dinner partner fall on a Kansas City steak with more relish.

"Mr. Ernest. A few questions, if you will."

"Oh, yes, sir. Yes, sir, Mr. Byrne." Ernest had just admitted to a double killing but still played the people pleaser.

Mr. Byrne walked forward to the podium. Armed with his legal pad rather than a rifle, the white hunter stalked his prey. Mr. Byrne first probed Ernest's original account of events, the one Ernest gave to us right after the night of the crime.

"Mr. Ernest, you say that Jubilee Joe pointed the rifle at you." Mr. Byrne pantomimed holding a rifle at the ready. "If the rifle was horizontal, how, pray tell, did the bullet from the pistol come to hit the magazine of the rifle? Would not the magazine of the rifle have been behind the barrel, protected by Jubilee's left arm?"

No response.

"On the night after the murders, you said you had not remembered using a .380 that night. Now you do. Were you lying then?"

"Lying? Oh. No. My mind just got unconnected. I was in such turmoil."

Mr. Byrne mumbled 'unconnected.' He looked down at the yellow legal pad on which he had taken notes during Ernest's new and improved version of events. He tore off the top three pages and took them to the prosecution table. He left them there. He rubbed his hands together and returned to the podium as if to say all that's water under the bridge. He turned to testing Ernest's contention that he acted in the heat of the moment.

"Mr. Ernest, I believe you said you put a wire on your phone over a month before these tragic events. Correct?"

"Yes, sir."

"That's when you started to tape your wife's conversations with Mr. Throckmorton, right?"

"Yes, sir."

"Didn't these conversations, so hot and heavy, make you angry?"

"No, sir. I wasn't angry with my wife. I don't believe in gettin' angry. I don't believe in fussin' and fightin', you know."

That again. He wouldn't fuss and fight but he would kill. This is one sick dick. My words, not Mr. Byrne's. He'd never

268 — *Anne L. Simon*

say anything like that.

"And didn't you start to make lethal plans at that time?"

"No, sir."

"When we searched your house, Mr. Ernest, the tape recorder under the bed had been disabled. When did you do that?"

"After I killed my wife."

"You didn't tell us that before."

"I didn't think of it, sir."

"Ah, yes. Your mind got disconnected." A pause. "Mr. Ernest, your wife was unfaithful to you. Did you ever think about getting a divorce?"

Mr. Ernest jerked his head back, incredulous that someone would think he might consider such a course. "Divorce, Mr. Byrne? That would be against my religion. Divorce is a sin."

Mr. Byrne had been totally composed, but at this statement, he jerked *his* head back. "Mr. Ernest, is it not against your religion to kill?"

"Oh, I have regretted that every moment since then, Mr. Byrne." He babbled. "She was the best thing that ever happened to me. She was so beautiful." He had not answered Mr. Byrne's question.

"Mr. Ernest, when you went down the hall and called Mr. Joe in from the garage, did Mr. Joe say anything to you?"

"No."

"You just hauled off and shot him—twice in the chest?"

"Yes."

"He fell. You shot him again, right? In the forehead?"

"Yes."

"And again. And again. You emptied your rifle into his head as he lay on the floor?"

"Yes."

The lady in the front row, who we now knew was Mary Marshall the foreman, almost imperceptibly moved her head from side to side.

"What were your feelings about Jubilee Joe at that time, Mr. Ernest."

"There was no feelin' there, except that I knew he was dead."

"No feelings. Maybe your mind got 'unconnected' there also."

Mr. Byrne returned to his table. No feelings, Ernest had said. Now that was one bit of truth from Thomas Ernest's mouth.

Mr. Byrne made a brief closing argument, repeating his request to the jury to consider the factors and return a fair verdict. In his close, Mr. Stone laid it on about how Ernest got mad when his wife didn't ask to be forgiven. Hot blood. He pleaded for his client's life. Again, he said nothing about *heat of the moment* in the shooting of Jubilee Joe.

The jury did not take seven hours for this decision. After an hour and a half—time to stretch their legs and have coffee —they returned to the courtroom and handed the verdict sheets to the bailiff. The bailiff gave them to Judge Johnson. She read the sheets, her eyebrows lifted, her freckles turned darker, her face redder.

"Madam foreperson. You have left one verdict sheet incomplete. Do you wish to have additional time to deliberate to reach a verdict on the second charge?"

"No, your honor. We are hopelessly deadlocked. Each of the four votes we have taken has been identical."

Judge Johnson asked the Clerk of Court to read the first verdict sheet.

"For the murder of Kitty Ernest, the jury unanimously determines that the defendant should be sentenced to life imprisonment without benefit of probation, parole, or suspension of sentence. This verdict is signed Mary Marshall, foreperson."

OK, I didn't agree but I understood. Mrs. Ernest had been a bitch.

The Clerk held the second paper. "Your honor, the other verdict sheet has not been completed."

The clerk handed the second verdict sheet back to the judge. Judge Johnson again asked the foreperson, Ms. Marshall, if the jury wished to have additional time to deliberate to reach a verdict on the second charge. Ms. Marshal again said they did not. With a deep sigh, Judge Johnson dismissed the jury—which dismissed me as well.

Mr. Byrne received everyone's congratulations. He had one regret. "If we have a death penalty at all, Thomas Ernest should have gotten it, if only for the murder of Jubilee Joe." He deflected praise to me—generous of him but unwarranted. He's the one who made sense out of the evidence I gathered.

I felt profound relief. The case for which I had been lead investigator had concluded with two guilty verdicts in the guilt phase. Thomas Ernest would spend the rest of his life at Angola— farming, I supposed. State v. Robert Cane lay down the road. I would be interested in how that prosecution turned out, but I was not the lead investigator. I could watch from afar.

Later, much later, I learned that the seven women on the Thomas Ernest jury voted for death on both charges. Five of the six men voted for life in prison for the killing of Mrs. Ernest and refused to vote at all on the killing of Jubilee Joe. For the men, at least, the life of one white man was worth more than that of an unfaithful wife and a black man put together.

I called Lorraine. The detectives in Orange had traced John Benjamin Gilbert to his last known employment— Shangri-La Botanical Gardens and Nature Center. He disappeared at the end of the summer. Lorraine had an appointment with the manager of the Gardens at ten in the morning.

"I'll be there. Give me some directions?"

"You can't miss it. In Orange, all signs and all roads lead to Shangri-La."

25

The town of Orange lies just over the Texas border. I'll always connect Orange with a midwinter getaway Eugénie and I took one weekend six weeks before André was born. Eugénie needed a distraction from dragging around her heavy body. I was exhausted from a week on loan to a narcotics task force in North Louisiana. For narcs, the workday begins at nine at night and ends at dawn.

Eugénie loved camellias. She'd been trying her hand at creating new varieties with little success. The grafts wouldn't hold. A gardening website pumped a free workshop on camellias at the Lutcher Stark Gardens in Orange, Texas. Let's go, I said. We drove over early on a Saturday. I'd planned to kill time in town while she had her class, have a good dinner together, spend the night, and come home Sunday in time for the last Mass.

From the parking lot, I walked with Eugénie between ten-foot-high walls of camellias in bloom—and got hooked. The bushes wore jewels from scarlet to white, and from the size of a quarter to a bread and butter plate. Lutcher Stark gave winter lodging to artists from the north who set up easels around the three hundred acre gardens to paint his prize specimens. I ended up joining Eugénie in the horticulture class and brought home a student artist's watercolor still hanging in my bedroom. The birth of André torpedoed Eugénie's career as a camellia grower, but we'd both treasured the memory.

What would it be like to be there with Lorraine? A litmus test for my intentions.

While babysitting the Ernest case, Lorraine learned from the local detectives that John Benjamin Gilbert last worked at

Lutcher Stark's gardens, now expanded and improved into a showplace called Shangri-La Botanical Gardens and Nature Center. At first light, I drove west on I-10 to join her for a ten o'clock appointment with the manager.

I brought news for Lorraine. "Mandy and Tom are the parents of twin boys, Lo. Three weeks early. They barely made it to the hospital."

"Is everybody OK?"

"Yes, indeed. Except for Tony Blendera. The trial of Robert Cane is set to go in a couple weeks. He's lost his second chair. Maybe Tom will come over."

"You're kidding, Ted. Mandy has a supportive family, but twins? She's going to need Tom at home, at least to start."

"I bet Mr. Byrne steps up to the plate. Capital murder is a piece of cake for him.

Rudy Corbett, the manager of the Gardens, met us at the entrance, precluding any public expression between Lorraine and me of our feelings about the prospect of a couple days alone and away together. Unnecessary anyway. Her touch on my arm told me we had the same program in mind. We didn't need to talk about it.

Rudy, Lorraine and I took a winding gravel path to his office. He showed us to modern chairs set in front of an expanse of glass looking out onto a serene pond. Splashes of pink, red, and violet camellias bloomed along the shore. A bird rookery on the far side of the pond appeared placed on a canvas by an artist. Rudy could tell we admired the view.

"That's our beaver pond out there," he said. "I can't call up a beaver to prove it. You'll just have to imagine the wildlife at this time of year."

"I came here ten years ago. You've obviously done a lot since then."

"Oh, yes. And we haven't stopped making improvements. Attractions like this begin as someone's passion—the bottom line is irrelevant—but the next generation wants to turn a profit. Or at least break even. We're just getting in the black now. We make a little on visitors and supplying flowers to flower shops, but our profits come mostly from sales of camellia plants."

Lorraine interrupted, "Look at that Roseate Spoonbill! Banking and turning, carried into port by the wind in his pink sails."

"Do you see the twig in his beak?" Rudy asked. "The spoonbills are just now beginning to build nests in the stand of cypress on the far shore. The population has increased a hundredfold since we first opened. Maybe you'll have time to see more of the nature center after we talk."

We settled in the chairs. Loraine took charge of the interview. I hadn't been in on yesterday's meeting with the local detectives so I kept quiet.

"I think you know we're here about your former employee, John Benjamin Gilbert." Rudy nodded yes. "And you know, I'm sure, that he's wanted for a serious sex offense."

"Which totally shocks us. We couldn't believe it."

"Innocent until proven guilty, of course, but the detectives tell us they have no doubt about what the victim says. They videotaped the boy's first report and other boys provided corroboration."

"We had no idea..."

"I'm sure. Can you tell us what work Gilbert did for you?"

"Sure. J.B., that's what we called him, began as a walk-on hand. He came in the fall as we started to prepare for the holidays. That was a year and a half ago. He potted camellias into decorative containers, tied about a hundred red, silver and gold ribbons, and generally prepared the plants for gift sales. One day he gave one of our horticulturalists a hand trimming plants in the nursery, and we learned J.B. had talent. He shot to the head of the class, so to speak. We moved him to major plant care. He was with us just a little over a year."

"He kept that plant care duty until he left?"

"Not quite. In the spring, he had an idea for increasing our appeal—a summer educational program for school children. He didn't just suggest someone else put together the program, he took on the task of setting it up himself. We jumped on the idea. We needed just a few additional child-friendly pieces of equipment—paddleboats on the Lake, was one thing—but under his direction, the kids enjoyed all aspects of this place as much as adults. He had them drawing the flowers, building a rock garden, identifying birds, really engaged in the nature center projects. He really had a way with children."

Lorraine rolled her eyes.

"We got very good press for the program. And then—Rudy stopped dead."

"Did something happen?

"No. Nothing happened. He just disappeared. He didn't come to work and left no forwarding address. We haven't seen him since."

"And all the time he worked here, you never heard of any inappropriate conduct?"

"We never had a single complaint. You do know that whatever they say didn't happen here. He'd already quit us when he allegedly picked up the boys to play some 'games.'"

"Yes. We know that. We're really hoping we can get some idea where he might have gone. How about your employment records? Do they have any information that might help? Like where he came from?"

"We've looked back at our records. All we had on J.B. was a glowing recommendation from the landscape service he'd been with for a few months. When we heard about the charges against him, we immediately changed our employment policy. Now we do a complete background check on anyone who comes to work here, even if all they do is dig a hole or hold a hose on a camellia bush."

I bet the insurer for the Gardens helped draft the new employment policy.

"Did you spend much time with J.B.? Maybe see him after work? Or perhaps work with him?"

"No. I'm mostly in the office now. But I know someone who did spend time with him—his work partner Willy. Willy's a black guy who's been with us a long time. I don't know that they saw each other in town after work, but when

J.B. first moved out of the gift shop they worked in the nursery together. They moved to the next level at the same time. J.B. probably taught Willy better than we did."

"We'd like to talk to Willy. Is he here today?"

"I think so. I'll check."

Rudy left us and returned a few minutes later carrying a walkie-talkie. "He's working down by the east sculpture gardens. I hate to ask him to come up here, but I don't mind if you go down there and talk to him a bit. I can get word to him that you're coming. I think you'll enjoy the walk."

"We'd appreciate that very much."

Rudy gave us a colorful map of the Gardens and showed us to the head of the gravel path. I took Lorraine's hand as soon as he turned to go back to the office. Other than saying we missed each other, we hadn't talked much, and we didn't now. I savored being with her in this lovely garden.

"Look at the cobalt blue sky behind the cypress trees just turning green. I feel as if we're walking in a fairy tale," Lorraine said.

We found Willy. He put down the edger he was using and pulled off his garden gloves to shake our hands. I took the lead and told him why we'd come. He had the same impression of J.B. that we'd heard from Rudy.

"When they told me about the charge, I said no way."

"Unfortunately the evidence is pretty clear."

"I owe J.B. a lot. He helped me. I'd still be hauling around heavy loads if he hadn't taught me about the plants—how to prune them inside, how to pinch off one of two buds to produce larger flowers."

"You worked with him a lot then. Did you see him after work?"

"No. Well, once we went to a diner together when my family was out of town, but usually, after work, I go straight home. I have kids."

"Did he have a car?"

"No. He came to work with a couple of Mexican guys. They lived in the same apartments he did. I think it's called Starks Village. Everything is Starks around here, you know."

Lorraine had her notebook out to write down the name of the apartments. "I think I passed the place on the way in," she said.

"Do you have any idea where J.B. might have gone? Like to family or friends somewhere?"

"No. He told me he doesn't have family. He never knew his father and was not at all close to his Mom. He never mentioned any friends."

"How about his past? Did he talk about that?"

"He did tell me he worked a while in Louisiana. He really liked his job there. Taking care of the grounds of a church, I think he said."

"Did he ever talk about going back there?"

"Yes. He said he wished he *could* go back. He had some unfinished business he really needed to tend to at the church, but he didn't feel he could go back quite yet. Maybe someday. He didn't explain."

We talked some more but didn't pick up anything else. We thanked him, gave him our contact information, and told him we'd love to hear anything else he might remember.

As soon as we were out of earshot, Lorraine and I spoke at the same time. "J.B. wanted to go back—" We both laughed. "Your turn first," I said.

"He had unfinished business at the church in Louisiana. What could it be that he wanted to go back to? I would think he'd want to stay as far away from the place where he'd been a bad actor."

"Return to the scene of the crime? Who knows. No one could ever persuade me criminals have good sense."

I saw a bench by the side of the path and gestured to Lorraine to sit with me.

"We could jump in our cars and go home right now, but I don't want to," I said.

"I don't either. And anyway, I think while we're here we should find the Mexicans he lived and rode with. Let's go back to the office and ask Rudy if they're at work today."

"Definitely."

When we questioned Rudy about J.B.'s Mexican pals, he

laughed. "On any day we have a half dozen Mexicans working in the Gardens. We pick them up in front of Lowe's in the morning and pay them by the day. I couldn't even tell you their names. I shouldn't admit this but we call them all Pedro."

"Willy says J.B.'s buddies, two, in particular, lived at Starks Village and had a car. He rode to work with them."

"Oh, they'd be a bit different. Maybe even legal. You could maybe find them through the manager of Starks Village."

"That's just what we'll do. We have all afternoon to go there," I said, and shot a quick smile in Lorraine's direction. Rudy directed us to a shopping center a couple miles closer to the highway. Restaurants and a nice Hampton Inn, he said.

"We're staying there." Lorraine shot a quick smile in my direction.

We had lunch, dropped off one car, and went to the desk to check on accommodations for the night. I stopped just inside the lobby to ask Lorraine a question.

"One room or two, Lorraine?"

"What? You ask now? We've been hanging off the edge of the Grand Canyon for weeks. Right now, I'm holding onto a skinny branch growing out of a crack in the rocks. Are you trying to drive me mad?"

I love Lorraine's directness. I had trouble getting out the statement I was determined to make. "You know, Lorraine, in the eyes of the world I'm a married man."

"And I don't give a rat's ass." Lorraine touched the Glock on her hip. "You get two rooms and I'll be using 'persuasion' to get you to come to mine."

We found Starks Village but had to wait an hour for the manager. He located a record of J.B.'s occupation of Apartment 11 for the period we had already figured he'd lived there, but many Mexicans lived at Starks Village during that time. The manager had no idea who was friendly enough with J.B. to be taking him back and forth to work. There were some guys out in the courtyard right now we could ask if we wanted, but he said what usually happens is they say they don't speak English.

He was right. We talked to a few Mexican men. If they ever heard of J.B. Gilbert, they weren't going to tell us. The code of the underground economy—don't talk. The manager suggested we post a notice on the bulletin board asking for information, include our contact numbers, and say we would give a reward. We did just that.

Lorraine had a suggestion for killing the rest of the day.

"Let's find the detectives I talked to yesterday. I'd like to tell them what we've done, and see if they have any suggestions." I approved the plan, with one addition.

"We need to report in to Mr. Strait, but not until we're pretty sure he won't ask us to drive back today."

"Do you suppose we have enough probable cause for a search warrant for the Church of the Blessed Believers? That unfinished business in Louisiana?"

"We'll have to ask Mr. Strait. Either way, I'd like to talk with Pastor Norbert."

We waited until just before five to place the call. When I suggested to Mr. Strait we make an appointment with Pastor Norbert for the next afternoon, he snapped at me.

"No. Hell no, Ted. We go over all our options carefully before we talk to anyone. Check in as soon as you get back."

Ouch. Of course, I didn't bring up the subject of a search warrant.

The restaurant next to the Hampton Inn served a pretty fair steak and a good Cabernet, but we didn't give it a fair test. We had our minds on what would follow. Lorraine began unbuttoning my shirt in the elevator. Once in the room, we stripped, opting for the efficiency of each taking off our own clothes. We quit holding on to the cliff. We plunged over the edge—much too fast.

"Let's just rest here a while and go again," Lorraine mumbled against my chest. We didn't climb back to solid ground until the morning. Good thing for the safety of drivers on I-10 East we were in separate cars for the ride home.

26

We dropped off one car in St. Martinville, picked up a sandwich, and headed to Mr. Strait's office in New Iberia. We found him sitting at a clean desk. Not a single piece of paper lay on the surface. I got the message; the search for J.B. Gilbert had his total attention and it better be ours as well. He put down the number two pencil he had in his right hand only long enough to shake ours.

I fleshed out the report we'd made on the phone from Orange. Mr. Strait interrupted a few times to ask a question, but mostly he took in information without giving any out. I wish I could be as disciplined. To think clearly, you have to listen. When I finished, and he had no more questions about what we did, he reached to the table behind him and picked up a yellow legal pad and a pen.

"OK. Let's review our options. First question is this: do we act now or sit back and wait for the corrected name—John Benjamin Gilbert—to produce results? You two are the experts on investigations. What's your opinion?"

Lorraine and I looked at each other. She dipped her head to me, signaling I should answer.

"Sir, I say we act. J.B. Gilbert told his buddy at work he had unfinished business in Louisiana. He left Orange in a hurry. Perhaps he has a person he needs to see here, but my money is on a place. We need to go over the whole Believers compound with a fine-tooth comb. Especially the so-called cottage where J.B. lived."

"Lorraine?" Mr. Strait asked.

"I agree. The matter is urgent, sir. Sonja Trudeau is scouting around for some maintenance help for Pastor Norbert. The one candidate we know she has is Digger

Jeanbaptist, and he would need a place to live. The cottage is what the Believers have to offer. If we wait, and somehow, he gets wind of our interest, he could compromise any evidence there might be in there."

"I agree with both of you. I can't think of any downside to trying to get in there as soon as possible. But how? Search warrant? Do we have probable cause to believe a crime has been committed?"

Lorraine spoke up. "Sir, now we're into your field of expertise."

Mr. Strait smiled and leaned back in his chair. "You both know we'd have no problem getting a judge to sign a search warrant. Our difficulty would be down the road. We haven't a clue what we're searching for. If we did find something, a good defense attorney—read Sarah Bernard—would probably succeed in throwing whatever it is out as the product of a mere fishing expedition."

"So we're f…, sunk?" I asked.

A long pause before Mr. Strait answered. "Plan B. More times than not, public figures who have nothing to hide agree to a search. They feel they have an obligation to be good citizens. Pastor Norbert may balk at opening the door to something that reflects badly on his church, but I say it's worth a try. I have a good feeling about him. I think the three of us could go out to the Believers, plain clothes, no hardware, and talk. Are you game?"

Lorraine and I nodded our agreement.

"You could take the lead, Ted. Start with what you learned from Lorraine's contact in the Harris County Sheriff's Office—the existence of a fugitive warrant from Orange County for one John Benjamin Gilbert for a sex offense. Then go on to tell about your visit to Orange County— what the detectives had to say and your visit to the place of Gilbert's last employment that we know of. I'll come in at this point and outline what we have for a search warrant—a statement from his co-worker that he wants to go back to Louisiana where he has *unfinished business*. If we imply that all we're looking for is clues to where Gilbert might be hanging out, and in our remarks, assume the Pastor would want to "do the right thing," I think we have a fair chance of wooing him into giving permission."

Mr. Strait had a more positive impression of Pastor Norbert than I did. I doubted he'd give us consent. When Sonja Trudeau took us to visit, Norbert opened the file drawer of the former pastor's records, but he kept all the material in his sight only.

"Just in case we do not succeed in getting permission, Mr. Strait, I think we should be careful not mention the cottage at all. I don't mean to be attributing to Norbert any ulterior motive, but merely hearing of our interest in the cottage is going to remind him he hasn't gotten around to getting in there. He might hasten to do so."

"Very good, Ted. I agree. No mention of the cottage."

Mr. Strait outlined how we should proceed. "Before we ask Pastor Norbert for an appointment, have everybody we need for the search on board and available on a few hours' notice. If we're successful in getting permission, the crew needs to get out there immediately. Try to make an appointment with Norbert for tomorrow morning, Ted. No, that's unrealistic. Wednesday morning."

Lorraine had a suggestion. "We could have one less person on the team if I could be the photographer."

"Very good. Ted, line up the Crime Lab and Martin and his search dog Hans. No, both dogs. We'd better have Plug also."

"Really? We're not expecting there's a cadaver out there, are we?"

"We've nothing to lose by having Plug sitting in the K-9 van."

All day Tuesday Lorraine and I worked on putting together the moving parts for the search. Every once in a while, we looked at each other and smiled. Memories. But for now, we stuck to business.

Detective Martin Castille and his dogs were the easiest part of the search team to line up. Martin cleared his schedule for Tuesday and Wednesday. Hans and Plug are always ready. They need no more than a single command at any time, day or night.

The first stick in the spokes came with my call to the Acadiana Crime Lab. I located Richard Levy in Baton Rouge teaching at a training at the State Police Headquarters. He wouldn't be back until next week. I didn't like the idea of having the second team because I didn't know the testing equipment well enough to be sure they got all bases covered. I persuaded Richard to line up a substitute prof who could replace him with a guest lecture on short notice.

"You owe me big time, Ted," he said.

With the team all ready to go, I called Pastor Norbert and oh so casually asked if I could bring Mr. Strait out to meet him. Then came the second stick in the spokes. Pastor Norbert said he'd be out of town the next few days, be back for the services Sunday, but of course, he had no spare time on the Lord's day. I told him we were in no hurry. Monday morning would be just fine. At your convenience, sir. We rescheduled everything for the next week. If Pastor Norbert went out of town, he wouldn't be going into the cottage.

Which gave us more time to rehearse our little play.

Our meeting with Pastor Norbert on Monday morning went off like clockwork. We timed the call for mid-morning so there wouldn't be much time for him to check out the cottage before we could get there after lunch. Pastor Norbert played his part just as if he'd rehearsed it with us. Mr. Strait was right; Pastor Norbert agreed to let us bring out a team to conduct a search.

We had only one tricky moment. Pastor Norbert bristled when I pulled out the Permission to Search and pointed out the place for him to sign.

"You don't need anything in writing," he said. "You have my word."

Mr. Strait came to my rescue. "Oh, that's just a technicality. We need to keep a record every time we go into someone's private building. Just government regulations. You know how that is."

Before the ink was dry on the Permission, I slipped into

the hall to call Spike to set the planned search in motion. When I returned to the Pastor's office, I heard him inviting us to have lunch with him at St. John Plantation. Mr. Strait declined, saying he had to get back, and Lorraine and I were his wheels.

*   *   *

Pastor Norbert unlocked the door to the cottage for us. I had one primary function during the search—minding Pastor Norbert. We needed his cooperation and didn't want him spooked. Lorraine handled the camera, multi-tasking to downplay the seriousness of our efforts. I introduced the Pastor to Richard Levy, the science guy. As Richard unloaded his suitcase of equipment, I pulled on a pair of surgical gloves and offered a pair to the Pastor.

"I assume you want to have a look around yourself. We don't want to add our fingerprints to any that may be in there. While Richard gets set up, let me introduce you to Martin Castille and his dogs. They'll be walking the grounds."

Lorraine went into the cottage with Richard. I steered the Pastor toward Martin and the K-9 unit. He brought Plug out first. After introductions, Martin and Plug took off. I withdrew a notebook from my pocket.

"I'm going to have to inventory anything in your office that might belong to Brother Gilbert. Let's go back there for a minute."

"As I told you, all Pastor Allen left behind was the desk, the chairs, and the file cabinet. His family came for his personal belongings, certificates on the walls, things like that. You saw the one drawer of files that predate me. And nothing in there *belongs* to Brother Gilbert."

"Yes, but just show me the drawer again so I can describe it accurately for the Return. I think I told you the Return is the receipt we have to file in the record after a search."

For a moment, he looked hesitant, but he fell into line. I killed about fifteen minutes with the diversion, enough time for Richard and Lorraine to make a preliminary inspection and to photograph, swipe, and record a boxful of evidence.

We joined Lorraine and Richard in the cottage,

"What have you found guys?" I asked.

Lorraine pulled out seven plastic bags and held them up one by one. "We found a shirt and a pair of pants on the closet floor, a plate, a glass and can opener on the corner shelf that serves as a kitchen, and a comb on the lavatory bowl in the bathroom. We also found a couple of dozen dead roaches! We'll not be giving you a receipt for them."

Norbert smiled. "Thank you."

I realized he hadn't smiled until that moment. He hadn't been hostile, just wary. He had taken the procedure seriously.

"How about the outside shed?" Pastor Norbert asked. "That's where we keep our tools. Did you look in there?"

"Yes. I was getting to that. We need to receipt you for a small sledgehammer that was on the floor. I'll let you know if we find any reason to have to keep it. If not, I'll return it in a few days. I'm sure you need your tools."

"I do hope to have someone get onto our maintenance before too long."

Pastor Norbert stood in the middle of the floor and looked around. "Did you take the bedding? Not that I want it. Just curious. I don't think he slept on a bare mattress."

"That's just the way we found the bed, Pastor Norbert. And there's nothing in that bureau over on the side. The drawers are all empty."

"So that's it?" I asked.

"Not quite." Lorraine pulled out an eighth evidence bag. "We found one sheet of paper behind the toilet fixture. It appears to be something printed off the internet." She passed the sheet to Pastor Norbert. I looked over his shoulder. A grown man walking on a beach with a naked, prepubescent Asian boy, holding his penis.

Pastor Norbert shut his eyes tight and let out a huge sigh.

"I'll receipt for one piece of computer paper that appears to be a printout from the internet," Lorraine said.

With that, we had verification of one conclusion. Brother Gilbert was a pervert. But we hadn't found any breadcrumb trail to his present whereabouts.

"So are you all finished in here?" I asked Richard.

"That's all I can do now. I have testing ahead of me."

"OK. Let's check on Martin and the dogs outside."

"Just a minute." Pastor Norbert walked into the bathroom. He flushed the toilet and turned on and off the shower and the lavatory faucet. In the bed/living room, he checked the closet and the bureau. He turned on the hot plate that sat on a shelf in the corner. He licked his finger and touched the surface to see that it started to warm. "Looks as if I'll need to give the place a thorough cleaning and maybe put in a few supplies. Other than that, it should be ready and waiting for a new custodian. Let's hope I can find one. I've put it off too long already.

Martin waited for us outside. He'd put the dogs back in the K-9 unit. "I've crisscrossed the entire clearing. The dogs found only one area that interested them. Let me show you." Martin went to the unit and came back with Plug on a loose lead. He and Plug walked slowly around the climbing wall toward the basketball pavilion. Plug's tail stiffened; he pulled on the lead. Martin loosened the lead even more and let Plug go where he wanted. The dog lowered his quivering snout and kept moving. Before reaching the pavilion, he stopped at a patch of dirt. He circled this way and that, sniffed the ground, and whimpered.

"What's that, Martin?" Lorraine asked.

"I'd know if I had a shovel. Pastor Norbert, could I use the shovel that's in the outside shed?"

"Oh, yes. Of course."

Martin asked me to do the digging while he held Plug. It took me about ten minutes to come to a wad of cloth.

"Looks like the bedding. I guess we need to take it," Richard said. He stuffed the material into a large evidence bag and sealed and signed the outside. He made out an additional receipt. He gave Brother Norbert a carbon copy of all receipts and kept the originals to file. I thanked him for his superb cooperation, but not enough for him to suspect that giving permission to search was not our usual experience.

"I'm happy I could be of help, although I don't think you

found what you wanted. We still don't know what Brother Gilbert wanted to come back for, why or where he might be now. Is it OK if I have the cottage cleaned up? I have a line on someone to be a replacement for Brother Gilbert and he probably needs housing."

Richard answered. "I'm pretty sure that'll be OK, but out of an abundance of caution, I'd rather you wait a few days. Let's say a week. I took a bunch of swabs in there. My squints might have a question or two. "

"Fine. I've put off going in there for six months, so I guess I can wait a bit longer."

Thanks all around and we headed back. I called Mr. Strait on the way to give him a report. We had probably discovered no clues to where Gilbert might have gone.

"I think we're entitled to some comp time, Lorraine. How about I pick up André and we go to Breaux Bridge to see if we can find some crawfish at a reasonable price."

"I say we look for some at any price."

"You know, dealing with that sicko makes me want to have André close to me all the time."

"Ditto for me, and he's not my child."

PART VII

27

Waiting for lab results, Lorraine and I returned to our regular routines. We reviewed incident reports and made run-of-the-mill investigatory calls and follow-up interviews in the field. I checked with Tony to ask if he needed any help with prep for the trial of Robert Cane. Yes, he said and asked me to go over the list of everyone called for jury service—four hundred residents of St. Martin Parish. In between these tasks, I reactivated every avenue I could think of for finding John Benjamin Gilbert. For good measure, I added Eugénie's name to my inquiries.

The following Monday, Richard Levy of the Crime Lab called. He, Mr. Byrne, and Mr. Strait wanted to come to my office to talk. I offered to go over there but he insisted. "Mr. Strait wants you on your turf," he said.

"What's on your minds?"

"We'll tell you when we get there. About twenty minutes."

I was sure he had a line on where Brother Gilbert might be. I walked across the hall to tell Lorraine.

"Thank God," she said.

"They didn't ask me to invite you to the meeting, but I want you. You're as much the detective on Gilbert's trail as I am."

"I'm junior to you, Ted."

The arch look on her face signaled the presence of what Eugénie used to call a feminist fit. I call it paranoia. I'd already picked up that Lorraine had a detective's keen instinct for noticing when 'the boys' would meet first and decide what role the female person might play. I wasn't going to be an enabler of that attitude. If Mr. Strait and Richard had a problem with having Lorraine on the inside, they'd have to come right out and say so.

"What they think is not relevant to me, Lorraine. I want you here. I'll buzz you when they show."

"I've asked Lorraine to come over," I said when the three walked in. "OK with you, I hope."

"Definitely," said Mr. Strait. "I should have asked Richard to include Lorraine when he called."

"Oh, yes, yes." Richard chimed in.

They fell over each other getting Lorraine into the chair next to me. So much for borrowed resentments. Mr. Strait gave a signal to Richard for him to close my office door. Odd behavior. What did they have on their minds?

Mr. Strait passed the ball. "Richard has some results from the tests he made at the Cottage."

Richard opened his briefcase and withdrew a sheet of paper covered with graphs and numbers. He handed it to me. I recognized the patterns.

"A DNA report?" I asked.

"Yes, it is. No point beating around the bush, Ted. Brace yourself. I tested the traces of blood on the lavatory bowl at the Believers' Cottage. I came up with a match for the DNA of your wife Eugénie."

I hadn't braced well enough. I felt dizzy. I couldn't find a place in my head for what Richard had just told me. I sputtered out questions.

"What? Eugénie's DNA? How could that be? Does that mean she was in the Cottage?"

"Not necessarily."

"Do you think he did something to her? Did you find her DNA anywhere else around there?"

"Last question first. No, I didn't find a match to Eugénie's DNA on anything else I tested, and I can tell you I worked like hell on the deteriorated bedding. I ran tests on twenty-five samples and found no trace of blood. Lots of semen. I'm pretty sure the semen will turn out to be Gilbert's because I'm pulling up the same DNA readout as what I'm getting from hairs in the comb. My conclusion? Brother Gilbert played with himself in bed."

"With a little help from the pornography he kept behind his toilet," said Mr. Byrne. "Yuk!"

"So, that's it? Nothing else in there?" I asked Richard.

"We haven't finished processing the samples, but so far I have one other finding to report to you. The tools I found in the outside shed carry the usual accumulation of residue you'd expect in such a collection, with one exception. The little sledge-hammer I picked up on the floor had the physical marks of use, but except for a light dust, the head and the handle are totally clean. I believe the sledgehammer had been scrubbed."

My mind jumped to a dreadful scenario—Gilbert hitting Eugénie with the sledge-hammer, cleaning up the weapon, and washing up in the lavatory sink. I felt sick.

"Does that mean—"

Mr. Strait cut me off. "We don't know what any of this means, Ted."

"What do I do now? Do I tell Eugénie's parents? Do I tell André?"

"I can't advise you on how to handle the information with Eugénie's family, Ted, but my preference would be for us to restrict the distribution of these findings to the four of us in this room, plus our two sheriffs and their chief deputies. We need to think through what, if anything, we do next before this becomes general information."

"If I talked to André or Eugénie's parents right now they'd just have a lot of questions I couldn't answer. I'd probably say the wrong thing."

I looked over at Lorraine and read pain on her face—pain she was feeling for me. No one uttered condolences, but I felt empathy from all three of them.

"You know what's crazy?" I asked. "You may know Eugénie's mother is a *traiteur*. I don't put any stock in that stuff, but last week she called me out of court to tell me she'd 'reached Eugénie in the beyond.' Eugénie had a message for me. Eugénie said we would find her soon but she couldn't, wouldn't—I can't remember the exact word—come back to us. At the time, I was furious with Maman, but now…"

Mr. Strait was silent, letting me work through my thoughts. "Now I'm trying to tie these findings in to what Brother Gilbert said to his work buddy Willy—that he had 'unfinished business' in Louisiana. Could any of this relate to his 'unfinished business'? I don't get it."

"I'm not an investigator, but I can't see a connection either," Richard said. "Gilbert wouldn't have expected us to be doing a DNA test in there. You couldn't even see the blood without the blue light."

"What do we do now?" I asked.

Mr. Strait counseled patience. "I won't stop working through the situation, I assure you, but I can't think of anything we can do right now except continue to wait for results from the general search for Gilbert, with the correct name of course."

"Just wait? God, that's a tough assignment for me."

"I understand. I'll be making the guy a top priority in both Iberia and St. Martin, and I have assurances from the DA in Orange County, Texas, that he's doing the same. They tell me they've put finding Gilbert into the most urgent category. I promise to let you know of any report we get."

"And in the meanwhile?"

"In the meanwhile, it's important that no one talks. It would not be helpful for anyone connected to the church to change the usual routines out there."

Lorraine found Mr. Strait's last sentence troublesome. "Mr. Strait, you are thinking that the 'unfinished business' is connected to the Believers Church."

"It's a possibility."

"If so, we're using the Believers as bait."

Mr. Strait sat up and looked Lorraine square in the eye. "In a way, maybe so. If Gilbert does plan to come back there, we don't want to scare him away. We want to get a collar on him so he can't prey on young boys anywhere else. "

"He may be dangerous."

"That's a risk I'm willing to take. And I'll take the rap for my decision if I prove to be wrong. After what happened, I'm sure Pastor Norbert now keeps very close track of the youth in his flock."

And I'm going to keep very close track of André.

When Mr. Strait, Mr. Byrne, and Richard were ready to leave, the handshakes were strong. "Keep an eye on Ted for us, Lorraine. Call us for any reason."

Lorraine came to me as soon as the three were out in the hall.

I held her close. She tipped her head back to caress me with her eyes. "I think both of those guys have a pretty good idea what's going on with us. Now I have reason to keep you in my sight. Mr. Strait has ordered me to do so."

I hoped our new sheriff didn't have another one of her ivory tower procedures that said two people who love each other can't work as partners.

28

I threw myself into investigating the four hundred names of prospective jurors called for the trial of Robert Cane. Chief Deputy Roland helped with the prospective jurors a generation older than I am. In St. Martin Parish, we aren't limited to knowing name, age, and occupation. Families have been here for generations. We know all the secrets, or to use the local expression, we know where the bodies are buried.

Rather than write a report of my findings and recommendations for acceptances and strikes of prospective jurors, I offered to sit with Tony during jury selection—the most critical part of trying one of these capital cases. We worked well together, even though in slow places I had to jerk my mind back from worrying about the location and future plans of John Benjamin Gilbert. And waves of heavy dread came over me from time to time. I couldn't keep from thinking Eugénie might have interrupted something dreadful and…

Every time I sit through jury selection, I get aggravated at the people who say they believe in capital punishment, but under questioning, we find out they aren't sure they could, would, or want to vote to impose it. Dammit! Be honest and say you don't believe in the death penalty. Until there is some change in the law, you'd be disqualified from jury. Jury selection would take half the time.

It took eight days to seat twelve jurors and three alternates, all willing to impose death under some circumstances but only particularly heinous ones and all able to tolerate being sequestered for a week to ten days of trial. Not everybody is willing to be cut off from family, friends, and outside news for that length of time. As is her usual practice, Judge Johnson told the jury panel that serving on a jury is a public service. I agree.

Once the trial began, the testimony of the State's witnesses went quickly and according to our plan. With Robert Cane's confession and the testimony, we had from the manager of the hardware store where Cane acquired rat poison, five yards of rope, and a burlap bag, there was little reason to doubt Robert killed his wife. Public Defender Sarah Bernard found some inconsistencies between the initial statements and the present testimony of some witnesses, and she implied their testimony was therefore suspect, but she scored few significant points. The real issue in the trial proved to be whether Cane had the requisite mental capacity at the time he cooked up the fatal supper.

I thought the guy must have a screw loose, but I reminded myself Louisiana follows the McNaughton Rule. To avoid criminal responsibility, the jury must decide if the defendant had a mental illness that caused him not to know the difference between right and wrong. The only help the jury got for the tough decision they had committed to make was that of the psychiatrists, and they disagreed.

All three experts, Lorraine's sister, the psychologist at Feliciana Forensic who administered the MMPI, and Dr. Allan Hubbard for the defense, agreed that Robert Cane did not have a mental illness at the time of trial. Dr. Hubbard, however, said it was his opinion that Cane was psychotic at the time of the crime. Impossible, said Lorraine's sister. Psychosis does not cure itself. Cane had never been treated. If he were psychotic at the time of the crime and had never received treatment, he would be psychotic today. And we agree he isn't. OK, jurors. Pick the expert you believe.

Pastor Norbert claimed his priest/penitent privilege and did not take the stand. Robert claimed his privilege not to incriminate himself and didn't testify either.

An interesting wrinkle for me was what part the beliefs of the Church of the Blessed Believers, or rather how Cane interpreted those beliefs, played in Robert Cane's motivation. The experts all seemed to say someone of Cane's mindset would be particularly vulnerable to religious suggestion. Robert Cane told the experts who examined him that Virtua yearned to go to her heavenly place. The world might think his actions wrong, but he believed he was right. He was doing her will and God's will also, by sending her off to heaven right away. Does the religious motivation give Robert a pass on responsibility? Not according to the McNaughton Rule. Nothing short of mental illness depriving him of knowing right from wrong as the world saw it would give him a pass.

Even if the jury voted unanimously for guilt, and in the penalty phase to follow voted for death, the fatal needle would not stick into him anytime soon. Mr. Strait predicted the post-conviction process in this case would go on forever. In addition to the usual issues in post-conviction relief in both state and federal appeal courts, the whole country might weigh in. The second 'person' he killed had not yet been born. We were in the throes of the culture wars.

While Lorraine's sister, the former Crawfish queen, was in town, Lorraine and I had the distraction of going to Crawfish Festival events. What a whacko way to get through the month of March—thinking about mental illness in the day and going zydeco dancing at *La Poussierre* at night!

At the end of the day, as Mr. Strait predicted, Tony won the Cane case all the way. The jury found Robert Guilty of first-degree murder, and they voted unanimously for the penalty of death. Mr. Strait didn't show up for either phase of the trial, not even for Tony's closing arguments. By contrast, Tony's wife came to court every day. I guess Tony saved his marriage. I doubted he saved his job.

* * *

One week, two weeks passed without any news from the search for John Benjamin Gilbert. Sometimes I forgot about him for a few hours at a time, but that's all. I'd toss and turn all night considering dreadful possibilities. Then came a break.

Sheriff Gabrielle came to my office to tell me they'd picked up news on the wire of a man matching the

298 — Anne L. Simon

description of John Benjamin Gilbert at a Texaco station outside of Shreveport. The man in question came inside to the counter and put down a twenty-dollar bill for gas. When the attendant looked out to see which island to put his credit on, she saw the rear of a dilapidated brown truck with no license plate. She commented to the man about the lack of a plate; he said the plate fell off, but he'd applied for another. The attendant let it go.

That night, when the attendant was recounting the events of her day to her husband, she mentioned the truck with no plate. Her husband happened to be a state trooper.

"Could the truck have been white but old and dirty enough to just look brown?" he asked.

She said yes.

The trooper filed a report, and the next day followed up with an interview of the attendant. The All-Points-Bulletin was amended. The truck J. B. Gilbert was driving might be white, dirty, and have a missing license plate.

I thanked Sheriff Gabrielle for the report. But what was I thanking her for? By then the man had slipped away. For keeping up with the search, I guess.

Another week passed. Slowly. I had a visit from Mr. Strait and Mr. Byrne. After six months and the two capital trials, Mr. Byrne still stayed with us as the top ADA in St. Martin Parish. I think he'd come to like it here.

"Dennis has an idea. Go ahead, Dennis."

"J. B. Gilbert seems to have come into Louisiana through Shreveport. He grew up in the northwest part of the state. He may be returning to where he has connections to help him. After all, he needs to eat and doesn't seem to favor the go-to occupations of the desperate—theft and selling drugs. What can he do to survive? I can think of one skill he has. He's a top-notch gardener."

Once again Mr. Byrne thought circles around the rest of us.

"Have you ever been to Hodges Gardens?" Mr. Byrne asked.

Mr. Strait and I both said we hadn't been there.

"You should go sometime. Lovely. Informal gardens, more like a well-tended woods minus the poison ivy and plus wild azaleas. You have to watch for ticks, however. The place must be beautiful right now with the azaleas in bloom. As azaleas fade, there's a need for trimming and fertilizing. I'd hire J. B. myself if I could. Maybe he could please my wife. I'm kidding. Anyway, on a whim, I called the Hodges Gardens, identified myself, and asked if they'd run across anyone meeting Gilbert's description in the last few months. If not, they might know of other possible openings for a gardener."

"And?" I was impatient.

"Yes. A month or so ago they'd taken on someone who met our very limited physical description. They watched the man work and he seemed quite knowledgeable about plants. He stayed four weeks, got two paychecks, and vanished."

I counted on my fingers. "So the last they saw the man about a week ago?" I asked.

"Yes."

I called Lorraine over to my office so she could be part of the discussion. We tossed around possibilities. All four of us thought more likely than not Gilbert was working his way down to St. Martin Parish, but we still couldn't figure out what might be his 'unfinished business'. Opinion split on whether to go public with the latest sighting.

Lorraine and I favored some limited spreading of the fact that someone who used to work at the Believers, and was now wanted to answer for a crime in Texas, might be headed our way. We tend to get a lot of leads from the public. Someone might spot him or his vehicle. And people should know to be wary of an overly friendly young man with a green thumb. Mr. Byrne came down on the other side of the argument. If Gilbert should find out we were looking for him, he might move on and set up elsewhere to be a menace in some other community. That's what had happened before.

At the end of two hours, we had made some decisions. The elder statesmen won the day on disclosure; we would keep the scientific evidence under wraps. But he said we had an obligation to let Pastor Norbert know Brother Gilbert might be making his way back here, and Lorraine was the person to deliver the message. She agreed to let me come along.

We found Norbert in high excitement about news he had for us. The Parish of St. Martin would begin road construction work on Oak and Pine Alley in the morning. The cane field across the alley had been bought by a developer who would share the cost of access with the parish. The interim plan was to put down an oil field board road outside the oaks and pines during road construction, but for a few days the church would not be accessible from the Catahoula Highway. The only route in would be the levee road behind. Pastor Norbert seemed more interested in his access road situation than in Brother Gilbert. A good thing. But we had to get our report across to him.

We did, by the hardest. We told him a man meeting Brother Gilbert's description had been seen in the Shreveport area buying gas. He might be the same person who had worked for a month as a groundskeeper at Hodges Gardens. He had left north Louisiana suddenly and might be headed this way. Pastor Norbert heard us but was not engaged in our report.

"I will certainly let you know if I see him or hear anything about him. But he's not dangerous, right?"

"We don't really know," answered Lorraine.

"What? I wouldn't think so. Except, of course, for his compulsion to befriend vulnerable little boys. We don't have children hanging around out here now. They're in school. We'll monitor our weekend activities very carefully, and we should be fine if that's what you're worried about."

"Please take precautions."

We called all the local nurseries and public gardens. No news of anyone meeting Gilbert's description had applied for work. Maybe he decided to go back to Texas.

We'd done what should be done. Again, we waited. Waited for a break.

29

The rain and chill of wintertime slipped away, but not the strong winds. Eugénie used to say sailors could take their boats down to the Gulf as soon as the azaleas bloomed. Blasts strong enough to fill the sails—and strip the branches of their flowers—would be no more than a few days away. She threatened to replace the azalea bushes across the front of our house with plants delivering a longer return, but every year the fuchsia explosion earned them another reprieve. Maybe this year the spring breezes would remember her and be gentle.

On school afternoons and on Saturdays, André prepared for the baseball season. He threw balls with his buddies or pitched into the backstop I'd constructed in the backyard. On Sundays, Lorraine, André, and I went to Mass in the morning and then drove out to Catahoula. Chicken every Sunday on Maman's table. André often brought a friend to spend the rest of the day out there—to fish with Grampa or poke around the lake in the pirogue, whichever they chose. Tonnère also had a choice to make. Should he follow André or Grampa? He usually jumped into the pirogue with the boys, even though he loved to feel the wind on his face when Grampa turned up the speed in his bateau and zipped full throttle across Catahoula Lake.

Going and coming from Grampa's, we passed the road construction on Oak and Pine Alley. The oilfield board road on the edge of the neighboring cane field looked smoother than the old alley of potholes, but the Believers would have a service of thanksgiving when the mess came to an end. The heavy equipment dragged more mud onto the roads than the sugarcane trucks did during a rainy grinding. A new caution

302 — Anne L. Simon

sign warned drivers to reduce speed where the highway curved toward Catahoula. If you hit a patch of mud on the highway, you could slide right off into a ditch.

One Sunday at the end of March a call from André interrupted our afternoon pleasure. Lorraine handed me my cell.

"There's a truck in the woods at the outlet end of Catahoula Lake, Dad. Bud and I didn't even see it until Tonnère jumped out of the pirogue and swam in that direction. We called him back and paddled home as fast as we could. Grampa wants to know if you want him to check it out."

"Absolutely not. Are you back in the house now?"

"Yeah. We're here."

"Stay there."

Lorraine and I dressed quickly, pulling on heavy clothes and boots. We went by the office to tell the duty patrol where we were going and to switch my truck for a heavy ATV. We headed to Catahoula.

The road around the lake is close to the shore on three sides, but at the end farthest from Grampa's house, the road veers away and becomes a raised bridge over the swampy outlet from the lake. Then the road leads to the levee.

We followed the shoreline until the turn, then left the blacktop and pulled about thirty feet into the underbrush. No truck in sight. I thought I could see broken branches and beat down grass in the swamp, but I couldn't be certain. Dusk comes quickly under the heavy cover of cypress and oak. No place to fool around in the dark. We opted to search the swamp in the morning. We pulled back onto the road and continued, crossing the lake outlet and climbing the levee to the shell road on top. We saw no vehicles in either direction nor any trucks at the camps on the far side. We returned to Grampa's.

"You didn't see the truck at all?" I asked Grampa on our return.

"Sure didn't, but then I didn't go looking. As soon as the boys got back here we called you."

"You did exactly right. Stay inside for now. I'll check with you in the morning."

We hustled the boys into the ATV and headed to town. I told the boys Catahoula Lake and Grampa's house were off limits until further notice.

I called Chief Roland, Mr. Strait, and Mr. Byrne. They took André's sighting seriously. Mr. Strait said he'd meet us at the Sheriff's Office in twenty minutes. Ditto Chief. Mr. Byrne wanted thirty-five minutes to come from New Iberia; he would never speed.

When we had assembled, Mr. Strait assumed he would be the chairman of the meeting; that's how it is when he's involved.

"Whatever action we take, or even if we take no action, we need to keep Pastor Norbert informed," Mr. Strait said. "The website says they have a Sunday night service, but I don't know if the schedule holds during the road construction."

"I think they're keeping their Sunday schedule," Chief Roland said. "Wednesday nights also. The Parish Government drove a hard bargain with the developer. He has to provide temporary lighting on the board road for the entire term of the contract."

"OK, guys. Let's consider next steps. Your thoughts, Ted?"

"I try not to be paranoid, but I can't help thinking John Benjamin Gilbert, aka J. B. Gilbert and Brother Gilbert, has come back to carry out his 'unfinished business' in Louisiana, not that I have any idea what the fuck his business is."

Dammit. I slipped again. With Lorraine around, I'd been trying to clean up my language. I noticed she'd been doing the same. I continued.

"If Gilbert saw the pirogue and its occupants, he'd be miles away by now. But the area where he had his truck is a jungle. There's a good chance he didn't see them and doesn't know they saw him."

"And your recommendation?" Mr. Strait asked.

"Contain and search. Try to isolate the area where he's

likely to be and look at every inch of it."

Mr. Strait, Mr. Byrne, and Lorraine nodded their heads in agreement.

"Chief Roland, what are the chances of being able to do that, of sealing off the area of the lake and searching tomorrow when it's light?" Mr. Strait asked.

"Surprisingly good. I'm thinking that through right now. We could put a unit on the highway from the St. Martinville Bridge to the town of Catahoula, another on the road from Catahoula east to the levee road, a third on the levee road to the turnoff to Oak and Pine Alley, and a fourth on the board road back to the Catahoula Highway. Four checkpoints would close off the entire area around Catahoula Lake. Of course, Gilbert may have made it over the levee. If so, he could slip away or hole up in one of the camps on the other side and slip away later."

"Can we set up the checkpoints tonight?"

"Yes, we can, if we limit ourselves to containment. It's pretty tough to do any searching in the dark.

"OK. Now we need to consider any possible downside of that plan of action. Is there any argument for doing nothing? For watchful waiting?"

Mr. Byrne still had the floor. "Once we activate containment, we blow our cover. Right now, more probably than not, Gilbert doesn't know we're aware he's in the area, that he's wanted, anything about him at all, let alone that he is —according to our best guess—tending to 'unfinished business.' When we put officers out there, he knows. He could go back underground."

"What is that 'unfinished business' anyway?" I asked. "Does anybody have any idea?"

No one answered my question. I looked from one person to another. Four sets of eyes—Mr. Byrne's, Mr. Strait's, Chief Roland's, and Lorraine's—stared back. I took a deep breath. "OK, guys. I'll say what you don't want to say. Ever since Richard made the DNA match on the blood in the lavatory sink in the Cottage, I've been haunted by the thought the 'unfinished business' might have a connection to what happened to Eugénie. And that what happened to Eugénie was not good."

Mr. Byrne slowly nodded his head.

"The elephant in the room," he said. "I'm glad you realize the possibility."

"I've had the same thought," said Mr. Strait. "Which is why, Ted, we're probably ultimately leaving the decision of what course to take up to you. If you want us to do nothing, that's OK. If you want us to stake the lake out tonight and search tomorrow, we do that. I want you to know I'm willing to look at every vehicle, every structure, and every inch of ground between the Catahoula Highway and the levee, all around the Lake, and every camp on either side of the levee from I-10 in the north to Morgan City down below. The offense Gilbert is wanted for in Texas is serious enough for us to command help from every force in the area."

"Thank you."

We knocked around alternatives for fifteen minutes, until Mr. Strait was certain everyone agreed on 'contain and search.'

"We have only one action we can take tonight, guys. The checkpoints. We can set them up in an hour. If at daybreak we've heard nothing more from Gilbert, we begin the search."

We set our next meet-up for seven in the morning, unless, of course, Gilbert crossed one of the checkpoints during the night. That would change everything.

Mr. Strait didn't forget Pastor Norbert. "I don't think we need to notify Pastor Norbert about four units on the road, but if in the morning we plan to blanket the area with searchers, I'll take on letting him know. Time for dinner."

Overnight the weather changed. A front came through around midnight, not ushered in by the gentle spring rain usual in the rest of the country but by a tropical deluge. The forecast called for wind and thunderstorms for the next twelve hours—a reminder that in Louisiana we humans are not in control. We may plan all we want, but Mother Nature calls the shots.

During the night, the four units at the checkpoints saw

no sign of a dirty white truck. Chief sent out replacement deputies and assigned eight additional deputies to make four teams of two each to search house to house and camp to camp in the town of Catahoula, the surrounding area, and the camps over the levee. Penetrating the swamp at the far end of the lake had to be delayed. The rains had created a quagmire. Lorraine and I took our assigned places in the checkpoint rotation. I could sense that she and every deputy kept eyes on me, ready to cover my duty should anything develop.

Nothing developed.

Tuesday morning, thirty-six hours after André and his friend Bud had seen a dirty white truck at the end of the lake, I noticed new uniforms hanging around. State troopers and city police had joined our force. Once more I drove the ATV down the road to the far end of the lake to check on access. The quagmire had drained some but still held too much water for an effective search. Maybe tomorrow. Chief knew I wanted to be present.

After consulting the weather service, Chief made the call. "We go in tomorrow morning. Other than the deputies assigned to the checkpoints, I suggest everyone go home and get a good night's sleep. I have some equipment coming from Lafayette to give us a hand."

"What kind of equipment?" I asked.

"Chief Roland knows somebody who can supply us with a vehicle the exploration companies use in the Atchafalaya Basin. They call it a Swamp Buggy."

"What about dogs?"

"Of course. I've called for Detective Castille and his pals."

I'm staying at Grampa's tonight," I told Lorraine. "André is with my Mom until further notice. You're welcome to a cot on Grampa's porch, or you could go on home. Your choice."

"I'm with you, Ted. Not just you. I've already smelled the gumbo simmering in Maman's kitchen. She's cooking for everyone." The next time I saw Lorraine she had an apron over her camo uniform. She and Maman were peeling shrimp.

When the house quieted down, I set up a cot for Lorraine close to mine. We talked. I thanked her for helping Maman cook, for serving the deputies, and for cleaning up.

"Maman is amazing, Ted. She knows we're out there looking for some clue about what happened to her daughter, but she isn't afraid of what we might find. She says she talks to Eugénie. Seriously, Ted. And she thinks Eugénie talks back."

"Yup. She thinks she has an open line with 'the beyond.' I get irritated with her about that, but I shouldn't. It gives her comfort. Right now, Lo, I'm falling asleep. I didn't go to bed at all last night."

"I forgot. Sorry. I'll see you in the morning."

*   *   *

When I awoke, Lorraine's cot was empty. The sun was up. I heard voices outside and the hum of a diesel engine. I shook the cobwebs out of my brain.

I found Lorraine in the kitchen. Manna from heaven couldn't have smelled better than bacon, biscuits, and French drip coffee. Grampa and Chief Deputy Roland sat at the kitchen table. When Chief saw me, he looked at his watch and stood up. "We'll be set to go in three-quarters of an hour, Ted."

"I assume no sign of Brother Gilbert during the night."

"None. We'll probably have to accept that he got away."

"But we're going ahead with the search?"

"You bet. We have a monster Swamp Buggy being revved up out there right now. Bigger than a tank. You probably want to ride on it."

We were going to discover what Brother Gilbert had been doing in the swamp. This time neither one of us mentioned the elephant in the room.

30

Chief got us the equipment we needed, all right. The Swamp Buggy led the parade down the lake road, followed by an industrial-sized tow truck and a flatbed stacked six feet high with composition matting. Thank goodness, each vehicle came to us with a football tackle in the driver's seat. Imagining any of us, including herself, driving one of those pieces of equipment made Lorraine's eyes sparkle. Yes, we could joke a bit on what we feared would be a grim mission. Action raced our motors.

The Swamp Buggy towered over the rest of the assembled vehicles: taller than I am, at least twenty feet long, and able to travel on the road, in the mud, or float on water. I climbed a ladder to reach the platform set high above the tractor wheels and gave Martin a hand hoisting up Plug's cage, with the dog inside. The Sheriff's Department fleet of five ATVs accompanying us looked like foothills around a mountain.

The armada pulled slowly out of Grampa's yard and took the road along the south side of Catahoula Lake. The procession halted where the road turns away from the lake. Martin, Plug, and I jumped down from the Swamp Buggy. The operator of the tow truck attached his hook to the hitch at the rear of the Swamp Buggy. Our operator drove the Swamp Buggy off the road onto saturated land, but thankfully not standing water. The flatbed stayed on the blacktop. Three men offloaded rolls of mats, carrying them on their shoulders. They created a mat floor next to the road. Mr. Byrne came out of one of the ATVs and watched operations.

Now I got the picture. The tow truck and the flatbed would remain on solid ground. The Swamp Buggy, tethered to the tow truck by a cable, would make a way into the wooded swamp. If the Swamp Buggy got mired in the muck or stuck in the wooded thicket, the operator of the tow truck could grind the cable and pull it free. The crew on the flatbed would lay down mats to create a floor from which we could launch a search. Good. I had major anxiety about being stuck in the muck or lifted high in the air over a sucking swamp.

Chief Roland briefed us on the execution of the search. He divided the area into four arcs fanning out from end of the lake. Martin and Plug were to traverse each arc first. If Plug did not alert, we'd move forward to search on foot. If Plug did alert, I was to summon Lorraine with her camera and, guess who, trusty Spike with a shovel, a bucket, and evidence bags. Two other deputies would join Lorraine and me for a visual and probing examination of any suspicious area. When an area had been thoroughly searched, the guys from the third truck, the flatbed, were to lay matting, where needed, to stage the next search area. As Mr. Byrne continued to observe, at least three furrows crossed his brow.

We first searched an arc between twenty-five and forty feet off the edge of the lake, that being our estimate of where the truck had been when seen by the boys. The ground was reasonably firm, but our boots took a lot of mud. Plug had mud up to his belly. He loved to wallow! Tree trunks served as our canes, steadying our steps. Neither the dog's nose, our eyes, nor our probes found anything unusual. Plug alerted on many a dead animal, mostly *rodentia*, but nothing that could connect to human activity. When the first arc had been thoroughly searched, we took a break for a drink of water. The matting crew picked up the mats they had laid, and we moved farther out to the forty to fifty-foot strip from the lake. No mats needed here, just a sharp machete. Nothing interesting.

Then we moved forward to examine an arc between ten to twenty-five feet from the shore. The ground was spongier and the search more difficult. Still nothing. We'd been working for over four hours, exhausting our patience and Plug's. We took a break for water and a snack. I was discouraged, but we had one more promising strip to cover—the shoreline itself. I asked for matting along the edge of the prior strip from which we could stage our final assault. The Swamp Buggy couldn't maneuver in here. Both humans and Plug would have to work through a Maginot line of cypress knees, greater variation in footing, alligators on their nests, and cottonmouths swimming by. Dead marine life fed the false alarm totals for Plug. The mosquitoes were fierce.

With only a few more yards to complete the last arc, I caught sight of a stake at the water's edge. I called for Plug. A surveyor's marker perhaps? Why here? A piece of rotted rope circled the stake; one frayed end hung into the water. On a loose lead from Martin's hand, Plug wiggled his way up to the stake. He started a dig. I called for Lorraine and her camera, and for Spike to bring the shovel, the bucket, and evidence bags.

Martin had a time pulling Plug away from the stake. He whipped his muzzle from side to side, fighting to keep the prize he held in his teeth. Martin commanded Plug to drop it —a bone almost two feet long. Spike picked up the bone, called for an evidence bag, and stuffed the bone inside. Spike wielded his shovel and uncovered three smaller bones. Martin kept Plug in the area to see if he could locate anything else of interest. No. Lorraine came and stood by me. I wasn't tired anymore, but I was very cold.

"The big bone could be a deer," She said.

It took over two hours to close down our operation—to pick up all the mats, get the Swamp Buggy back onto the road, and to line up the three vehicles for the trip back. When Lorraine and I had done all we could physically do, we pulled out our notebooks and wrote a narrative of the operation with sketches of the discovery site. Richard did the same.

I asked Richard if he could get DNA from buried bones.

"Not in my lab in New Iberia. We're going to have to send the specimens away, probably to Century Biologics in Boston."

"How long is that going to take?" I asked.

"It all depends on the state of degradation. Buried bones

are more difficult than fresh, but long bones are more promising than small ones. I think we have a good long bone —a femur. That's the thigh bone. I would have told you five years ago we couldn't do it at all, but a lot of progress has been made. There are at least three methods in use now." He interrupted himself. "I could go into them but you don't need to know all that."

"Right, I probably couldn't understand, anyway. But are you talking weeks, months, years?"

"At least a month. That's all I can say."

The exhilaration I felt on the search had vanished. More waiting. And for what?

* * *

It took a month. During that month, a very sad conclusion sat in the back of my mind, waiting for me to let it out. Eugénie probably went to the Church of the Blessed Believers the afternoon she disappeared. DNA in blood on the lavatory in Brother Gilbert's cabin matched hers. Brother Gilbert, a known deviant, fled under a cloud. He returned to Louisiana to tend to 'unfinished business,' most likely to clean up traces of what he had done. If and when we got the word we were waiting for, it would probably not be good. That's the way I thought when I was being rational.

Occasionally, Lorraine and I dragged the issue to our conversation and talked it through. We agreed that without proof, we could not be certain of my grim assessment. Only a couple times I sank into imagining what Gilbert might have done to Eugénie. More often I beat myself up about wanting certainty so I could get on with my life.

Determined to enjoy every moment of our deepening feelings for each other, Lorraine and I reburied the subject. I welcomed routine, even an investigation into a public official suspected of embezzling public money to fund an affair and the ever-present work on burglaries. Lorraine handled several assignments to gather evidence for cases in the juvenile court. Together, we took André and his friend Bud hiking in Kisatchie National Forest and fishing in the Basin.

And we watched the boys play baseball—a lot.

Eugénie's Mom and Dad didn't need any confirmation of the death of their daughter. Maman said she knew already. Eugénie told her as much from 'the beyond.' Grampa was never one to show his emotions. I found he cherished his time with André even more than before, and he had a shadow behind his eyes.

I found a few occasions to talk to André about his mother. He was prepared for confirmation of his loss. As the expression goes, you can get used to anything but hanging.

When I got the call from Mr. Strait asking if he, Mr. Byrne, Richard Levy of the Acadiana Crime Lab, and Sheriff Gabrielle could come over to meet with Lorraine and me. I knew what they would have to say. I called it. The DNA extracted from the femur we had uncovered matched that of Eugénie. Mr. Byrne would be preparing the prosecution of John Benjamin Gilbert for second-degree murder.

"Now for the good news." Mr. Strait pulled a rabbit out of a hat, or rather a brown paper bag out of his briefcase. Inside the paper bag, a bottle of champagne. "The Sheriff of Webster Parish, that's way up there near Arkansas, has booked into his jail a certain fugitive from Orange County Texas wanted for rape of an eleven-year-old boy. This time, the car Gilbert drove into a gas station had a license plate, but it had expired. The Sheriff says he thinks the sheriffs should deputize all the gas station employees in the parish."

"Who gets first crack at him?" Lorraine asked. "Our jurisdiction or Orange, Texas?"

"Ah-h. What a nice problem to have. There are a lot of considerations. Homicide usually trumps rape, but the DA in Orange has two kids to put on the stand—the victim and the witness. He may need to get them to court while their families still have fire in their bellies. Most of the witnesses for our case are experienced with the judicial system; they won't waffle. And there's another issue. Which state will incarcerate him first? He may not survive prison in either state to get to the other one. Fellow prisoners are damn hard on molesters. Mysterious deaths behind bars. One way or another, I think we can be certain Gilbert will never be a free man. So, we are all sorry about your loss, Ted. We thank you for the job you and Lorraine did, and wish you the best from here on."

Lorraine came over to hold my hand. "I need to talk to you, Mr. Byrne. As my lawyer. I want you to see to it I'm not getting hooked up with a married man."

ACKNOWLEDGEMENTS

The author acknowledges the counsel of Ann Dobie, Diane Moore, Vickie Sullivan, Stephanie Judice, her more than daughter-in-law Margaret Simon, and Bette Kolodney, accomplished writers all, who patiently guided the development of the writing abilities of someone from another field. Without their encouragement, this work would never have been completed.

ABOUT THE AUTHOR

Anne L. Simon was born in the East, educated at Wellesley, Yale and Louisiana State University Law Schools, and moved to south Louisiana fifty years ago. She practiced law with her husband, raised a family, and became the first female judge in the area. Now retired, she travels, enjoys family near and far, takes long walks with her dog Petey, and writes stories based on experiences in her adopted home.

Made in the USA
Columbia, SC
13 May 2017